I0674114

Vampire rEvolution

Fangs & Halos Book 3

Charlayne Elizabeth Denney

Heavenly Fangs
17003 Blackhawk Blvd
Friendswood, Tx 77546

Copyright © 2015 by Charlayne Elizabeth Denney
Print Edition
eBook ISBN: 978-0-9897685-4-2
Print ISBN: 978-0-9897685-5-9

Heavenly Fangs and the halo/fangs symbol are trademarks of
Heavenly Fangs Books

Layout by Paul & New, BB eBooks
Chapter Charms © Dreamstime.com: Russel Shively, Zts, Kuzzie, Risto
Villaten, Dagadu

Cover Pictures
Photo 60665552 © Fotoatelie – Dreamstime.com
Photo 131148078 © Anna Krivitskaia – Dreamstime.com
Photo 66334091 © Viorel Sima – Dreamstime.com
Photo 107764812 © Edward Zhuravetc – Dreamstime.com
Photo 34881372 © R. Gino Santa Maria / Shutterfree, Llc – Dream-
stime.com

Dedication

This one's for my mom, Jeanne Louise Coan Brown. You were so proud of me and when the first book was published, you gushed to all your friends. I hope that you're up there in Heaven, telling all the angels how I'm disclosing all their secrets down here. You and Alice have fun, and save me a seat.

I love you.

Chapter One

THE WANING FULL moon painted silver highlights onto the tangled and gnarled forest trees. The shadowed figure of a slender man, his jaw set in wrathful thought, sat tall in the saddle of the black horse that wended its way up the narrow path.

It wasn't the nearly 13 hour overseas flight alone. It wasn't the drive to Amsteg or the less than five star hotel he stayed in waiting for the next sunset. It wasn't even the drive up the mountain switchbacks to Niderchäseren or this hour-long horseback ride through the trees to the Schloss Feufeldunkheit.

It was the very fact that Marcus had been imperiously summoned to make this tedious trip at all that made him angry. He should be back in the states, taking care of his business and his family instead of wasting his valuable time on this command performance. He had no use for the Council and especially the leader, or Anführerüberlegen, Lian Xun. The whole thing with the language and naming was ridiculous. The name of the stupid castle was Castle Dark Demon in

English. The communications involving Der Vampirkammer, the vampires, was always done in German, a hard, guttural and brutish language. No other language was good enough and Marcus have to admit it did fit the harsh and inhuman mystique the Vampire Council had sought to convey. It was absurdly pretentious when the heads of each founding house composed the rules and regulations governing the Council, they signed their assent and fealty in their own blood. The tradition of blood oath remained to this day, each new member of the Council had to sign in blood upon ascending to their Sitzplaz Fursten-haus.

"This is so damned ridiculous. I am NOT going to play their little game by speaking in German," he thought angrily. "It's the Vampire Council, not vampirkammer. It is Supreme leader, not anführ-eruber whatever. I have not taken the blood oath because Lian Xun wants to keep me off the Family Seat, sitzplaz that!"

His tirade did not dissipate his anger, only fueling it, stoking the coals of an already smolder-ing contemp. It also annoyed the horse, who kept throwing his head around. It just kicked off a new round of talking to himself and listening for the horse to agree that it was all bovine guano. Hell, he didn't even get regular cell phone reception out here, just the satellite and that could be sporadic at best due to the mountains.

The castle loomed over him, like a vulture, a wraith waiting for him to die. He chuckled at that, he was already dead, the vultures missed their chance. He knew he needed to get all of the anger out of his system before he reached the gates. Going into the Council Chambers angry was the most unwise thing he could think of and he wasn't sure he would be able to purge his anger without hitting something, or someone.

There was someone riding fast down the trail leading from the castle. Marcus stopped and waited for the rider to get near him.

"Identify yourself" came the challenge from the approaching rider.

Marcus knew that the castle had its own security force and while everything else was old-fashioned and antiquated, the system was very modern with cameras, motion detectors, and a force that was better trained than most special operations soldiers. He should know, he helped the contractor design and implement it. He was still pissed off that Xun had not allowed him to be the one with the contract.

He looked up and into the eyes of the rider, "I'm Marcus Lancaster, I have business with the council."

"Deutsch sprechen!" The rider ordered.

"No. I will speak my own language, deal with it." Might as well start offending now, he thought.

In German, the rider, a member of the elite security force, ordered Marcus to dismount and submit to a search.

Marcus complied, letting the man pat him down and then search his saddle bags on the horse. He wasn't going to do something as stupid as bring a weapon, which was just asking for being kept in a cold, dark, nasty cell in the catacombs below. He had heard of vampires on the wrong side of the council being starved for centuries before being staked out for the sun to finish off and he wasn't entirely sure it was a boogie man story.

"Mount up," the rider ordered in guttural German as he pulled himself up to his own saddle. He leaned over to take the reins of Marcus's horse. Marcus jerked them out of reach, startling the already nervous horse.

"I will do it myself," he said indignantly.

The rider leveled a cold gaze at him. "Silence! You will allow me to lead you in or you will not be admitted."

Marcus threw his hands up and let the guard lead the horse into the castle compound. If this was an example of how things were going to go, it was going to be a long visit. None of this was usual, when he had come to council before, he got the challenge and the search but he was allowed to ride his horse without interference. Something was up.

Once he dismounted and grabbed his saddle bags, he headed toward the main doors but two guards came out of the shadows and took either side of him. He rolled his bright blue eyes at this new stupidity and allowed them to escort him into the entryway.

Waiting for him was a woman in a dark purple dress that flowed to the floor. Her black hair and pale complexion combined to make her blue eyes very prominent.

"Hello Calina. You are looking beautiful as always." He poured on the charm he was used to using on mortal women.

Her eyes swept over him, he was dirty, his dark hair was falling into his eyes, and he was dressed in jeans and a plaid shirt, not the usual choice for the usually fashionable man.

"Save it, Lancaster. I'm doing my job, not flirting. Liam Xun has set the beginning meeting of the council for midnight. You have about three and a half hours to get cleaned up, rest, or whatever you do with yourself alone. These gentlemen will take you to your room and will stay outside your door until time to take you to the Council chambers. Be ready when it is time." Calina gestured to a lower level hallway.

"That's not the direction to the Drachenfeur suite, I am the eldest and I..."

"No. The council has said that you are not the holder of the Drachenfeur sitzplaz, you will not assume the right to their suite. You are going to be given one of the guest quarters until or if you ever are named to that seat." She smiled a leering smile that told him that she was holding knowledge of what the Council was going to talk about and she was certain he would be in trouble. She turned to walk away.

Screw her. Or, better yet, he wouldn't touch her with anything, but he would love to hand her over to the soldiers for, well, even better, somehow make her turn someone without permission. The two marks on her hand showed him that she was one step away from being dragged to Hell, it would be a pleasure to watch that. He laughed, not bothering to cover it at all.

Calina whirled back to face him, "Laughter? How inappropriate. You obviously do not under-stand the gravity of what is and will be going on here. You are here for a reason and I would advise you to take it with all of the seriousness that it warrants." She looked at the guards and waved her hand toward the hallway again. "Take him out of here."

It was obvious, he was not a guest this time, he was being held prisoner, granted in a gilded cage, he saw when he entered the beautifully apportioned room in dark jewel tone colors, but a prisoner nonetheless. As the door shut behind him, the one of the Imperial Guards, or more like the Goon Squad locked the door from the outside.

He took a nice long bath in the big claw-foot tub in the bathroom, dried and laid out his robes that were to be worn in Council. He would have worn robes of black, red, and gold, the Drachenfeur colors, but since he was not seated, he had brought his personal crest, an actual registered crest that graced his shield at the Battle of Towton in his human youth. The medallion, with its prominent gold dragon blowing flames, under black bar outlined in red cutting the image in half with silver fleur-di-lis on either end and the red Lancaster rose in the middle hung on a black and red ribbon. He pulled the black robe over his naked body and then combed his hair and then lifted the medal. It was heavy, made of gold with colored precious stones of red, green and black forming most of the details. The black background only seemed to push the brightness further. He smiled as he watched himself in the mirror as he put it on. To complete his ceremonial attire, he donned a pair of soft, handmade Italian boots. An extravagance to be sure, but he deserved it.

Dressed, he wandered the suite, looking for something to read. He would rather have been online, checking his emails, the weather, the news, or anything else. Or checking with Izzy, Jesse, and Lilly back in the Alamo city. It occurred to him he didn't know what the status of the hurricane was and that was enough to worry him into premature gray hair, which he would never really get. But that wasn't going to happen so he contented himself with a copy of *The Picture of Dorian Gray*. His copy was better, signed personally from Wilde to him with "I think of you often, O." He had read it a few times, always thinking of his time with the author. He lost himself in the story until the sound of the lock being turned pulled his attention away. He rose as one of the Goons stepped in and told him, in German again, to follow him.

Marcus thought about playing at not understanding but given the situation, his plan of not speaking in anything but English melted. As angry as he was at the summons, he was bright enough to know when he had walked into the lion's den. It was a better plan, at the moment at least, to keep the lion placated rather than poke him.

He followed Goon Number One, like the dutiful puppy they wanted him to be, with Goon Number Two walking behind him. This was maddening because he had a policy of never letting someone walk in his blind spot, it was safer, but not this time.

They continued silently down the stairs had been carved into the bedrock under the castle. These led to a set of large, heavy doors. Goon Number One turned and wordlessly pointed his sword at Marcus's feet. He knew what was meant by the gesture. He obstinately removed the boots and tossed them to the side. Turning back to the door, the Goon used his sword hilt to bang on the wood, furthering the dent that had formed over thousands of knocks just like it. They waited for a signal to open the doors, it came with Goon Number Three opening the door from the inside. He strode in, his head held high and a defiant set to his jaw. He was not going to let the sanctimonious Liam Xun bully him with these amateur theatrics. He was followed in by the Goons.

The domed room of the Council chamber was lit by torches on the walls. Never mind the rest of the planet functioned on electricity and instant communication, even meetings via the internet, the vampires of the Der Vampirkammer were hidebound and clung to the past as a life jacket when they entered this room. The castle had electricity and modern conveniences stored behind fixtures looking like the 14th century. A large circular table filled the center of the room, surrounded by fourteen large, elaborately carved chairs. On the high back of each was engraved the name of each bloodline and the names of each man who had held that seat carved into the table from the middle out. Maybe they needed their names on everything to remember where they were to sit. He reminded himself again not to antagonize the lions. In the middle of the table was a hole. Twelve seats were filled, two were empty.

The last was the largest seat, more aptly identified as a throne, the Anfüherüberlegen Sitzplaz, the Supreme Leader's seat. In it sat Liam Xun, staring at Marcus as he reached out and pulled a lever in the table.

The table began to move, separating into fourteen different wedges. Once the movement stopped, another Goon walked to one of the lanes that had opened up. Without a word, he pointed at Marcus and then at the center of the table.

Once Marcus reached the blood circle that had been drawn into the floor, the level was thrown and the table reassembled and he was trapped. He turned to the one vacant chair in the circle of bloodlines. He scowled. That, by all rights, should be his seat.

"Marcus Lancaster, face the Leader, not that empty seat." The Goon standing behind Xun said, loud enough that the German words echoed. Marcus turned. At Xun's right hand sat the other empty chair, a very ornate chair with gold and silver cushions. The name Der Gottmutter was inscribed in bright blood red on the top of the chair and the name Tsatiki was carved into the table, alone.

No one had ever seen Tsatiki, anyone that was alive, anyway. The lore talked about her being the first vampire, born of a lesser princess from Egypt who was raped by a stranger named Nulial. Her pregnancy produced a child with a small set of retractable fangs. The princess died from blood loss, no one knew that a pregnancy between a fallen angel, or demon, would result in a vampiric child and cause the human mother to die of what was defined many years later as Hemophilia Birth Syndrome. Only those who gave birth to these babies were affected. In honor of their ancestors, the seat was left at the table in case she ever came back. No one expected to ever see Tsatiki seated there, no one even knew where she was, or if she still was alive.

His thoughts were interrupted by Xun using his commanding voice, in German. "Marcus Lancaster, you stand before the council to account for actions taken by your bloodline. As the Law requires, the oldest living male of the line is responsible for all others."

Marcus ground his teeth as the man spoke. How dare they bring up the duties of the lineage without allowing him the courtesy of holding the seat of that lineage? With his anger building every second, he had to find a way to calm down before he exploded. He dug his finger nails into the palm of his left hand, hoping the pain would soothe the raging anger.

"In particular, we have come into information that you have turned a vampire without notifying us and that vampire has made two more vampires without your informing us of the fact either. Please give us the information on these illegitimate progeny. The please was a formality, Marcus could tell Xun was finding the fact he was trapped in the room amusing. There was no getting out of this so he might as well cooperate as far as he could.

"Lilly Lenora Marchantel is the new vampire that I made. However, I did not make her recently, she was thought to have failed the turning and was buried in 1900. I only found out she had survived a few weeks ago. She turned a cat that she has named Baron Bast von Samedi and the other was supposedly an angel. I know where Baron is, he's with my family, as is Lilly. The angel has been dragged to Hell, according to my maker, Eadwina."

Why they wanted him to tell them all this when it was evident that they already knew pissed him off more. It would be one thing to bring this to the council willingly, quite another since he was not allowed to take the seat he rightfully should hold.

"So you say you thought this woman was dead when you left her and she managed to live without contacting any other vampire. When did you turn her?"

"As I already stated, I attempted the turn in 1900, in New Orleans. It wasn't meant to be a turning but I had taken too much of her blood during sex and she died. I tried to revive her by giving her my blood. The attempt was unsuccessful, or so I thought. I stayed in town until I saw them bury her in a crypt. I had Eadwina check and she never found her. But, according to both Eadwina and Lilly, she was living in the crypt, eating rats and other small animals. She turned Baron by mistake, she says, she did have a memory of what I had done and she tried it with the cat. He survived remained as her companion. He hunted for her and they stayed hidden until Katrina devastated New Orleans."

"You believe this tale? Are you sure you didn't hide her away and not tell us, to keep her from us and for yourself. And who ever heard of a cat, or any animal, being turned? There are no references to this being done in all of the Lore." Xun and Marcus were focused on each other's eyes, almost waiting for the other to blink.

"Surely this is something we should have heard about before now." Djutimos Sadiki pulled Marcus' attention away from Xun. Marcus turned.

"I can assure you that it is all truth. You can interview my ghouls, by telephone because I left them in Texas, they know what happened. They will corroborate all that I have told you. Jesse was there in 1900 and he was with me when we went to try to find her in New Orleans after Katrina. Isobel was the one who found her, as a refugee in the Astrodome, searching for me. All she knew was my first name, the brothel where she worked did not want last names used. I had visited Lilly for several years when I would go to the brothel and she only knew me as Marcus, that's it. She had no way to find me even if she hadn't been in the crypt with the cat for over a hundred years."

"Why didn't you tell us the angels had visited you? You bear the mark of a maker, someone who turned a person without permission." Peter Gray was sitting to his right as he faced Xun and had a good look at the mark he had. He hadn't even tried to hide it.

"Have I had a chance? No. It's been a whirlwind of two weeks, my business was in chaos due to the hurricane in New Orleans, I was looking for Lilly. Then I was trying to get her acclimated to life in the 21st century and now there's another bloody hurricane heading toward my city and I have a lot of things going on. That's why I wanted to do this later, I have a business to tend to and property to protect. I've not had much time to think about combing my hair, much less contacting you with all the information you are seeking. It wasn't due to lack of willingness, it has been a lack of time."

A self-righteous smirk crept across Xun's haughty face. "I see, you're too busy for your obligations to the Council. It seems that I made a correct judgment when I said that the Drachenfeur seat would not be going to you. You're way too busy."

Talk about painting yourself into a corner, Marcus wasn't sure whether wanting to choke the undead life out of Xun or screaming in frustration was going to win out. He explained and now he was being accused of being too busy. He was beginning to see this was going to be a no-win situation.

"Oh give the vampire a break, Xun. You know he's been busy, we've talked about it in this very room. I'm told by my lineage that the world outside of this place is going constantly and no one really has rest time now." Vladamir Trawkin spoke up, pausing from buffing his nails. "I think it would have been reported, after he got a moment to do it."

"Vlad, you are the only one who wants to go lenient with him, are you sure you are not wanting to pull him into your bed?" Xun knew that entire sentence would infuriate the Romanian head of Furstenhaus Amwichtensten. Vladamir managed to contain the angry retort that crossed his mind. He was no fan of Lian Xun as Supreme Leader but he also knew that he needed support of the Council with business objectives outside of it. Of course, he had wanted to get Marcus into his bed for at least a century, the man was easy on the eyes and, he had heard, a tiger in bed.

"The lore books have nothing on turning angels. I would not believe that rumor until verified." Jesus Antuenez Diego Franco Benalcazar's voice had Marcus turn again. At this rate, he would be dizzy from keeping up with the conversation, obviously something whoever planned the Council table had in mind.

"You may be correct, if this was an average situation. However, I have confirmation from my maker and her ghoul that this man was an angel and, once his wings were taken, he was easy to make a vampire," Marcus said.

"Your maker? But he's been dead since your

turning. I know Cishipi died, I received his shield so I could record the death. It happened at the Battle of Towton." Tendaji and Cishipi, although from different lineage, were known to have been good friends and Tendaji had taken Cishipi's death hard.

"Yes and no. I am the progeny of Eadwina, progeny of Viktor Alexandru. I have confirmation of this by the angels themselves. 'Wina lied to me all these centuries, she drained me and gave me Cishipi's blood but then she gave some of her blood to me as well. She then gave Cishipi the final death and took me to train. Therefore, I have dual parentage, of sorts."

"I knew you weren't the person you said you were." The triumph in Xun's eyes sparkled in the torchlight. "This is why you have never ascended to the Drachenfeur Sitzplaz, you were never of that house."

Marcus smiled, "That is where you are misinformed, Xun."

"To you, in this place, I am Anfüherüberlegen Xun and you will address me with respect."

"Sorry, mein Furher, but I am of Drachenfeur Sitzplaz. Cishipi was an early ancestor of the line, Jesus can tell you the lore about his making. Eadwina is also of the line, which you well know because Viktor Alexandru was seated in that illustrious seat prior to his final marking and fall." Marcus pointed to the empty chair, calling to attention again that it was empty. "So, by that lineage, I am now the oldest living male of the line and I am the one who should be seated. Unless, of course, mein Ferher, you are still holding a grudge toward me for luring your top people to work for me."

There, it was out, again. Marcus reminded Xun of the fact that he not only lured the top executives of Shanghai Security to his company, he took the Chief of Operations, Gunnery Sargent Jorge Castro, which not only hurt Xun's company through loss of personnel, Marcus was able to leverage the operations and customer lists of S.S. and had been systematically dismantling the operations, bringing them into the Lancaster fold. The last time the subject came up, there was a huge shouting match that split the Council three ways, Xun's supporters, Marcus' supporters, and those who would just like the whole thing to go to hell and leave them alone. At that time, Xun's supporters on the Council won.

Marcus could not help but wonder what would happen with Xun this time.

To his credit, Xun did not explode in anger like before. While the temper was showing in his eyes, the rest of his demeanor was calm, eerily calm. The rest of the council whispered between themselves.

"You may think that helps your case, Lancaster, but it is water under the bridge." His smirk sent a shiver through Marcus. "It has come to our attention that the angels are suspicious of you and what you are doing. My sources have said they have found a way to get into your operations and determine just what it is you are planning, or have already put into motion."

Marcus suspected a trap, there was no indication that he had any actions with the angels. He passed it off as something Xun was saying to get a rise out of him. He wasn't going to take the bait, he stood silent.

The chamber seemed to freeze in that moment. No one was willing to speak up and Xun was allowing that information to settle into everyone's brain. Marcus shifted uncomfortably from foot to foot, impatient to hear the rest of the lies Xun was concocting.

"You are believing that I am being false, aren't you?" Xun broke the silence. When Marcus didn't reply, or even change his countenance, Xun smiled. "You just go right ahead and feel superior. You go ahead and do what you are doing. I will still be here when the angels drag your ass to Hell. I might even declare it a vampire holiday."

It took everything he could muster to not climb onto the table and push down to be able to break Xun's neck. It wouldn't kill him, of course, but it would put an end to the meeting and incapacitate for a while. There was, however, the little matter of the Goon Squad to stop him.

"We will see, Xun. I have, as you well know, the best operation on the planet with a very good reputation for taking care of business. I don't think the angels give me or my operation a second thought. They are out there to kill vampires. Mine is not a vampire operation, a vampire happens to be the C.E.O and sole owner but not staffed by vampires. I'm the least of their worries unless I make a bunch, make them without their permission, they don't care. Got another thing to try to throw on the wall and try to make stick? Because this one is pretty much liquid." Marcus finished the statement with crossing his arms across his chest and striking a pose of 'I don't care."

"Believe what you will, Lancaster. I've provided you with information about your operation being under suspicion and that's all I am going to do. But, and hear me out on this, if you antagonize the angels, if you try to give them payback for whatever slights you may harbor, or any other action, you will be held responsible by both them and us. We have a good relationship with the angels, it's been long in coming and I do not want to see that relationship sullied by an egotistical hot head with delusions of godhood. Mess with that and we will make sure you are where you cannot do it again."

"Threats. Of course I am not stupid enough to mess with the angels. They are, however, given to putting their noses where they don't belong and I will not be interfered with by them, or by you and this council. You do not own me, my family, my company, or any of my assets, thus, you have no say in how I manage any of them."

"We could own every one of them. The council could vote to buy you out, summon your ghouls and progeny here and keep them. We could turn over certain sensitive information to the human authorities and get you more involved with them than you are with everything you own. Do not push this, Lancaster. I will bury you." Xun slammed the lever forward and the table separated. "Get the hell out of my sight and be gone from here at dusk, but remember my promise. I will bury you."

Marcus' dismissal was punctuated by Xun turning and walking from the chambers himself. The Goon Squad went with him so Marcus was on his own. Some of the other council members left the room without speaking but one or two came up to shake his hand and give him their regards. Once they left, Marcus was in the chamber alone. He walked around the table to the Drachenfeur seat. He ran his hand along the top of the chair and looked at the lineage carved into the table. He had a schoolboy's mischievous thought to just step up and sit in the chair just once, but with the surveillance, he would probably get spotted and Xun might take that as an invitation.

He took a last longing look at the seat, turned, and left the room. He retrieved his discarded boots and his assigned escorts dropped into step behind him.

Chapter Two

THE LATEST MEETING between the archangels and Mikhail, the chief archangel, had come to an end and the archangels on duty in the various departments glided back to their stations.

The Headquarters: Host Assignment Division, or H.H.A.D., was always a busy place. It was in this room that the angels got their assignments to Earth. Each archangel was a department head and Mikhail was the head of not only H.H.A.D., but all of the angelic host.

As Ranguel, the gray-winged archangel in charge of the Enforcers, the unit that dealt with vampires and other paranormal beings, glided toward his station, he noticed that someone else was handling the operation. He had left Kozmeil in charge during the meeting but the angel was nowhere to be seen.

"Negiel, where is Kozeil?" As he waited for an answer, Ranguel checked the assignment board floating in the air.

The angel turned to see the gray-eyes of the Archangel staring at him. "I am not sure, sir. He called me over and told me he needed to run an errand. I was to keep the board until he got back." The blue eyed angel with gray wings of the Enforcers was nervous, he had no idea where the missing assistant was.

"When did he leave?" Ranguel was obviously not happy. His face didn't change but Negiel could feel the aura energy around the archangel change to more stressed.

"One hour and twenty-six minutes, sir."

Ranguel stood silently, not speaking further. He wondered just what was going on with his assistant. "Negiel, please remain here, doing what you are doing until I return." He glided back up to see Mikhail.

As he approached, the mist that curtained the office pulled back and the door opened. As he glided in, he saw Mikhail sitting at his desk, writing. Ranguel stood silently still until Mikhail acknowledged him.

"Yes, Ranguel?" Mikhail stood up, his blood red wings stretching and then coming back to their resting position. He ran a hand through his dark, curly hair once again.

"I had assigned Kozeil to handle the boards while I was in the meeting. I came back and he has been gone for one hour and..."

"Twenty-six minutes. Yes, I am aware."

Ranguel wasn't surprised the chief archangel knew about it, this was pretty standard operating procedure when it came to dealing with Mikhail. "Is this your assignment?"

"No. I have no assignments for Kozeil." The only indication that Mikhail was concerned was his clasped hands, his thumb ran a circle around the other palm, like rubbing a worry stone.

"This is not the first time I have come back and found him gone from his post. And there have been days when he has not come in, or came in late. I'm not sure what he is doing. I've had him paged and he doesn't answer. I'm beginning to get suspicious about what he is doing."

"As well you should. I have noticed his energy signal is evolving. Whatever he is doing, it is having an effect on him. I suspect he is not the angel we thought he was."

This revelation did astonish Ranguel because he didn't remember when he had ever heard Mikhail voice any doubt about his perceptions about anything or anyone. Mikhail was uncannily and constantly amazed the archangels with his knowledge of things that had seemingly never been discussed with him.

"Do you know what he is up to?" Ranguel queried.

Mikhail actually snickered. "No, but I have my suspicions. I believe you want permission to ask Uriel to assign a Shadow angel to him, to find out just what is happening, am I correct?"

He nodded. "That is what I had decided to ask, yes. I don't know what he is doing but there are a lot of questions I want, I need answered."

At that moment, Uriel glided into the office, "Yes sir?" His brown wings fluttered as he stopped next to Ranguel.

"I need four of your best Shadows for an assignment. They need to be very adept at shadowing unseen because the target is one of our own, Ranguel's, who has been suspiciously absent from his job on several occasions." Mikhail put the information out in its entirety.

"Let me guess. This is about Kozeil?" Uriel first looking at Mikhail and then Ranguel, who obviously had been surprised by the statement.

"Yes, it is.: Mikhail replied, unfazed. "What do you know about the actions of this angel?"

Uriel moved to where he could see both Ranguel and his boss. "I know he is the talk of the break room right now. His comings and goings have been noticed by several of the angels around H.H.A.D. and a few have openly asked if this was becoming the official policy." Uriel smirked, "Of course, I and others have dissuaded them from that notion."

"How is it that you have been kept unaware of the gossip, Ranguel?" Mikhail asked.

Ranguel's brain whirled as he tried to figure out an answer to that question but it was Uriel who spoke up, "Most of us just assumed he knew where Koziel was and what he was doing. Since it is not our department, we didn't see any reason to talk with him about it. The angels in the break room are not in charge and they should have been minding their own business, not trying to deduce what assignments the angel in question was doing and for whom."

Mikhail nodded. "I was aware of the chatter among the hosts. You are correct, it should not be any concern of theirs, no matter how curious the situation is. I am glad you handled the, gossip, when you heard it, as you are now aware Koziel has been suspiciously absent from his job on several occasions."

"I had no idea that this situation had become a major topic of conversation in the break room." Ranguel had to admit.

"It is not like you have had nothing on your plate of late." Uriel defended his fellow archangel. "You have had your hands full with trying to keep up with the vampires as they moved back into New Orleans. From what I hear, there have been vampires made by the displaced vampires that needed finding and tuning. I also heard that India was full of ghosts and Jinn from the recent earthquake there. Sounds like the Enforcers have had their work cut out for them."

Ranguel was somewhat disconcerted that Uriel had some information on missions that had just arisen. "Yes, we have been quite busy of late. But I should have paid more attention to what my angels are doing. The missions should not take precedence over them."

"I'm not holding you responsible on this, Ranguel. Uriel is correct, you have been extremely busy. Kozeil has taken advantage of that to do what he is doing." The chief looked to Uriel, "I need you to get those Shadows out immediately and track down that angel. Make rotations where he is never without a watcher, even here. Listen to any conversations he has. I want to know who he is seeing, what they are doing, and any other information you can find."

Uriel acknowledged the mission order. "I will

get them out immediately. Anything else, sir?"

Mikhail chewed his lip, a habit the archangels had noticed he did when he was deep in thought. He shook his head and waved his hand, a dismissal for Uriel.

Once the Shadow Chief was gone, Ranguel spoke up, "I have to admit, I missed this one. I thought he had only done it recently. I had no idea. I apologize..."

Mikhail held his hand up, "No apologies. Kozeil has been very circumspect with his activities and has only recently mis-stepped in them. I will keep you apprised as to what we find. Meantime, you might give the job of your assistant to Negiel. He is able to handle the job well. If Kozeil asks, tell him that I have asked for you to set up a rotation within the Enforcers so they can get a rest. Any objections should be referred to me to handle."

"Yes, sir." Ranguel nodded. Mikhail waved his hand and the mist parted, a signal that the meeting was over. Ranguel glided out to inform Negiel of his promotion.

As the mist closed back around the office, Mikhail said to himself, "Lucy, what are you planning this time?"

Chapter Three

LILLY AND ISOBEL came into the hotel suite, followed by one of the bodyguards who carried shopping bags.

"Jesse?" Isobel called. There was no answer from her fellow ghoul. "Looks like we have the place to ourselves tonight." Her bodyguard, Edward Garcia, placed the bags on the bar just as his counterpart, Payton Naismith, Lilly's bodyguard, walked in with Lancelot on a leash. He bent down to release the leash and the energetic sable Sheltie jumped on him and started licking him in the face. He was not behaving like the disciplined award winner.

"Lancelot! You know better. Stop." Isobel commanded.

"It's okay, Ms. Kincade, Lance and I have an agreement. I don't mind his kisses." Payton said, laughing as he ran a dark hand through the dog's fur.

"Yes, but he gets out of line and it makes Marcus nuts. He wants the dog to be the perfect dog. We can't indulge Lance every time we want, he would break training eventually and embarrass

Mr. Lancaster.

"Yes, ma'am. I will stop the behavior." It was clear by the guard's face, he wasn't happy that he and the dog couldn't be more relaxed.

"Who's on the door tonight?" Isobel inquired as Lilly walked into the bedroom and shut the door.

"Carter Hughes" Garcia answered.

"Could you check on Jesse and his guard? It's not like him not to call us at least once a night, even if he picked up a friend to spend the night with. Maybe Mr. Kennedy will have heard from the guard, at least."

"Yes ma'am." Garcia lifted the radio from his pocket and keyed it, walking to the windows so he wouldn't disturb.

Isobel knocked on the bedroom door, "Lilly? You okay?" Her friend had not been looking well since before the trip started and Izzy was worried. She dismissed Garcia and turned back to the bedroom. When there was no answer, she opened the door and entered, gently closing it behind her. "Lilly?"

That was when she heard a retching sound coming from the bathroom. The vampire was getting sick again.

Isobel raced to her side and gently held her dark hair back. "Oh sweetie, you are not doing well at all, are you?"

Lilly was unable to answer, she continued to be sick. "I wonder if I need to take you to the hospital, I'm worried about you."

The spasms stopped just long enough to let

Lilly shake her head and then the next one hit. It was a few more minutes until she sat back on the floor and shook. As Isobel handed her a damp washrag, she looked up, her chocolate eyes almost pleading for help. "I don't understand this but I seem to be unable to hold anything down."

"I still think we need to have a doctor check you out. If something happens to you, Marcus will kill me." She put out a hand and helped Lilly to her feet.

"No, no doctors. I'll be alright. I just need to rest now."

Holding onto her friend's arm, Lilly fought dizziness. She was terrified of what was going on but she couldn't allow Isobel to take her to a human doctor, that would cause a commotion that would call attention to the entire vampire world. Isobel helped her change into her nightgown and she settled on the turned down bed, shaking. Isobel pulled up the covers.

"Thank you, Isobel. I don't know I would do without you." She tried to smile but it was lost in the pallor of her face.

"You probably need blood, you've tossed quite a bit tonight. I can go get a couple of bags from. . . ."

"Oh, no, please, bagged blood sounds awful." She held her hand on her still queasy stomach."

Isobel rubbed gentle circles on her friend's back, trying to comfort her. "I've got it!" She leapt to her feet and rushed out the door. Seconds later, she returned with a towel wrapped around her just-washed arm. "Remember, I feed Marcus from time to time. It's been awhile so I don't see a problem letting you feed from me."

"But that's not right, I shouldn't be feeding from humans, I did fine for over a century, existing on rats and other animals that Baron would bring to me."

"You did what you had to do back then. But this is a whole different time and situation. We have the bagged blood and the entire definition of a ghoul as someone who feeds a vampire in exchange for the blood that extends our existence is obsolete. I feed Marcus and he allows me to feed from him. It's a reciprocal, mutually equitable relationship."

"Oh Izzy. I'm so sorry. You never told me about yourself and I never even bothered to ask. That was so selfish of me." She burst into bloody tears.

"Hey, Stop that! You can't afford to lose any more blood." She used the towel to daub Lilly's eyes.

"I was only thinking of myself. Please, forgive me." Tears continued to leak from her eyes and accented the distraught expression on her face. "What was your life like before Marcus?"

Isobel smiled. "I'll tell you IF you stop crying." Lilly stifled a sob and nodded.

"I was born in England, in a little town in Worcestershire in February 1958. I liked living there with my Mum and Da. I had two younger sisters and a brother. One night as I was ending my Sixth Form." Isobel noticed the confused expression on Lilly's pale face. "That's like college prep education." Lilly nodded. "I was out at the pub, hanging around with friends when this dark-haired man came in. I swear, it was like instant attraction. He locked eyes with me and I found myself unable to stay away from his table. I joined him and we talked for a couple of hours, then he wanted to take a walk and I went with him. Once we were out of the pub, he started telling me that he wanted to get to know me better. We ended up talking about him and his family and we went back to his hotel. I didn't know why we went there but he was a great lover, right up until he grew fangs and bit me. He acted like it tasted great, I freaked out."

"Seriously? You didn't know he was a vampire until then?" Lilly smiled, "Of course not, he never tells anyone he is, he just goes ahead and bites, like he gives himself permission."

"I agree. Once he calmed me down, using glamoury, I was told he liked me and wanted to turn me into a vampire as well. There was no way I was going to do that."

"But he made you a ghoul and you stayed with him. Why?"

"Because he was cute and well-off. There were not a lot of prospects in the West Midlands, my parents couldn't send me to college, so I was stuck. If I was lucky, I would marry a farmer and raise a dozen kids." She smiled wistfully, remembering the charm of the ordinary. "But Marcus offered a new and exciting life. One I had never considered. A grand adventure, at least that was what I started out thinking. But he grew on me.

Yes, he's aggravating, self-centered, and a large asshole, but he's also smart and he does appreciate what I do for him." Izzy stopped talking and stared out the window.

"You aren't going to remain with him forever, are you? What happens when you meet the right man? Do you think he will let you go to live your own life?"

"I don't know. I've not found the right guy yet, I guess. It's never been discussed." Izzy looked back at her. "You look very pale, even for a vampire. We need to revisit that intention to feed."

Lilly sighed and closed her eyes. The thought of a bag of blood made her queasy.

"*I could bring one of the big, fat rats I'm finding out here. They are great. I like this city.*" Baron said through their link.

"No, that sounds horrible." Lilly said.

"You really need to eat something, even if it sounds horrible. You are weak." Isobel thought that Lilly's answer to Baron was to her.

"Oh, you are probably right, I am feeling weak. But my stomach is still unsettled." Lilly still didn't want her friend to know that she was talking with Baron in her mind.

"*Well, if you say it that way, just never mind.*" Lilly could imagine Baron flipping his bottle-brushed tail indignantly in a display of pronounced Catitude. "*It leaves more for me. And that little gold tabby that lives down here. I'm telling you, she's a great lay.*"

"Baron! You know what that causes, right? You want to be saddled with kittens? You keep it in your...your...fur!" Lilly actually said it out loud.

"No, I've had plenty of ladies, after all, I am a handsome cat and the kit-tetas can't get enough of me. But none of them have had kittens from me. I guess being a vampire keeps me from getting them pregnant, which is fabulous because I like making the ladies..."

"Baron! Enough. Go do what you are going to do and leave out the narration." Lilly cut off the link and looked at Izzy.

Her friend was staring at her, mouth agape. It dawned on Lilly that she had spoken her side of the conversation and Isobel had heard it.

"I'm sorry. I bet that sounded strange."

Isobel continued to stare but managed to say, "That's not the half of it. You are talking to Baron and he's not here. You can communicate with that feline with your mind, can't you?" She had heard of telepathy between masters and their progeny but Marcus never acted like he did so.

"Yes, I can. We had always been able to think in pictures at each other but, once we got to Houston, he started talking in words in my head. I know that's weird but it keeps us close. I'm never alone that way, he's always here with me." Lilly gave up the secret.

"You told her I was talking?" Baron barged in, *"I thought that was our secret, I've never told anyone that we can do it."*

"Excuse me, Isobel." Lilly switched communication targets, "It was, it is. I trust her..."

"But I don't. She's friends with that vampiric fiend who hurts you." Baron snarled.

"You don't get to pick my friends, I don't get to pick your...paramours. And who would you tell? None of the 'ladies' know how to talk to humans so it wouldn't matter."

That's when the bomb got dropped into her world. *"I have been talking to that angel of yours, Sullivan."*

"He's not MY angel, Baron..." she thought back at him, not willing to let that bit of information out to Isobel.

"Well, he's not as bad as Marcus and, at least, he cares about you. He's very sorry he hurt you and almost went to Hell for it. He knows how close he came." The cat went silent for a moment. *"And I believe we can trust him, at least a bit. He says the angels are watching you and protecting you."*

Lilly sat there, mouth agape, unblinking brown eyes staring straight ahead in disbelief and not saying anything. She had no idea that Baron had a link to Sullivan, but if vampires could talk with their progeny this way, maybe progeny can talk together as well.

"Lilly. Are you ok?" Isobel shook her, bringing out of her shock.

"Yes. Baron just told me something I didn't know he was doing. It surprised me."

"He sounds like an interesting guy, even for a cat. No wonder you fight for him and wouldn't let him stay behind when we came here. I kind of envy you that relationship."

Lilly nodded, tried to smile, and then collapsed unconscious, scaring Isobel.

"Lilly!" She shook the vampire, "Lilly, wake

up." She begged.

Nothing. No movement, no speech. She looked dead.

"Of course you look dead, you're a vampire. What the hell do I do now?" This was something that never happened to Marcus. She had no point of reference for a vampire who passed out.

"Damn it, come on Lilly. Wake up! I don't know what to do for you. I wish Baron was here or could hear me, he might know what to do." She kept shaking Lilly, trying to revive her.

First a picture of Lilly sucking on an arm came to mind, then she heard, "*Can you hear me, woman? She needs blood, now. I can't drag enough rats up there to help her before she goes into final death. You need to feed her, from your arm.*"

Baron had pushed past the barrier and was talking to her. "Okay, I need to get a knife..."

"*Can't you just bite your own wrist and draw blood?*"

"I'm a ghoul, not a vampire. I could bite but it would take too long." As she talked to the cat, she started toward the door leading into the hallway to look for one of the guards. As she crossed toward the door, Lancelot ran up next to her and headed her off.

"Lance! No! Go away! Go lay down." She scolded the dog, who looked at her with the sad brown eyes he used for treats.

"No!" She repeated as she jerked open the door and put the privacy lock out to keep the door open. She wasn't sure that she had a key card and didn't want to be delayed.

She looked over the railing and spotted Carter Hughes sitting in a chair, reading a book. "Carter! I need a knife."

Carter put aside the book and stood, "Something wrong?"

"I need to open...something. Do you have one?" Isobel didn't have time for the inquisition.

"Yeah, I'll bring it up..." He started toward the elevators.

"NO!" She shouted loudly. Carter stopped. "Can't wait! Toss it! Now!"

"What is..." Carter started to say.

"Damn it, Carter!" Isobel was getting frantic. She was away from Lilly and this guy was trying to stall.

Carter walked closer and tossed the pocket knife up to her. She caught it and ran back into the suite, slamming the door behind her neglecting to throw the privacy lock in her hurry. She sprinted into the bedroom, unfolding the knife and launched herself onto the bed beside the unconscious Lilly. Sliding the blade across her wrist, wincing, she grabbed Lilly, pulling her close and pressing her lips to the open wound. Lancelot jumped on the bed and laid down on Lilly's other side, laying his head on her leg.

"Lilly, drink. Come on sweetie, drink." She pried lips apart and allowed the blood to trickle into her open mouth. Lilly didn't stir. She reached out, "Baron, it's not working!"

At the cat's name, Lance pulled his head up and looked around like he expected the cat to pounce.

"*Calm down, your heart rate will mess up the blood. Put your other hand on the front of her neck and rub downward, this might help. Also, give her the command 'drink and live.' That's what she says when she's turning someone. It has always worked.*"

Then the pounding on the door started. "Isobel, Lilly? Open the door." Lancelot jumped off the bed and started barking at the door.

"Lancelot! Shut up!" Isobel commanded. The dog stopped for a split second and then continued to bark as the pounding resumed.

Great, it was Brian Kennedy, the head of the bodyguard detail. He was the last person she wanted in the room. Marcus didn't tell any of the guards that Lilly was a vampire and Izzy was certain that he wouldn't want that particular fact known.

"Woman, open this door before I knock it down. I need to check on you both." Brian didn't back off.

"NO!" Izzy shouted. "We are okay, I just had to cut a cord that I got wrapped around my wrist by accident." Damn, that lie didn't even sound plausible.

"Then let me in to check it."

"We are fine, Brian. Just leave us alone, we're headed to bed."

"Ok, I'm kicking the door in. One, two..."

"STOP. Brian, I'm in the middle of something, Lilly's not well. If you are going to get in, you need to go get a key card and use it. I don't think the hotel, or Marcus, would want to pay for a door."

Brian hit the door but not hard enough to cave it in. "I will get the key, then I'm coming in there." He ranted so loud on the way to the elevator that she heard him. Lance left the door and ran back to jump on the bed to try to help.

Isobel put her hand on the unconscious vampire and rubbed her throat. "Lilly! Please. Drink and live!"

Maybe it had taken too long. What if she really died? Marcus was going to have...

There was a sudden pull of suction on her wrist. Lilly was pulling the blood into her. Isobel ran her fingers through Lilly's hair, "That's it, sister, keep pulling. You need this blood."

Isobel pulled away from Lilly's mouth when she began to feel dizzy. In her present state, Lilly didn't know when to let go. She grabbed the belt of the robe on the bed and wrapped it tight over the cut to stop the bleeding. Hopefully Brian wouldn't be able to...

"Okay, what's going on in here?" Brian stood at the door of the bedroom. "What's happened to Lilly?"

"She's been ill since before we left. I've been taking care of her. She went to sleep and scared me, she was so pale."

"And the knife? What did you need a knife for?" the head bodyguard walked over to the bed, an action that was met with growling by the Sheltie that guarded Lilly.

"I had a cord wrapped around my wrist, it knotted and I had to cut it off. I slipped with the knife and gouged my wrist." She held up the arm with the belt over the cut.

"Why am I not believing one word you are saying? All of this is way too strange and I need to be told the truth before I give Mr. Lancaster the report."

"Will you please stop shouting? My head is hurting." Lilly moaned, holding her head.

"Lilly, sweetie, you're back. Sorry about the noise." Isobel turned and ignored Brian as she took the revived vampire's hand. "Are you okay?"

"Head hurts...stomach hurts...need sleep." She turned on her side. "So tired."

"Isobel, what is going on here? Do we need to take her to hospital?" Brian Kennedy was from Ireland and used the word 'hospital' without the definitive. It was comforting to Isobel to have someone who understood the language nuances.

"No, sir. I am fine," Lilly said weakly. "Too much rich food, too much beer. I'm sick but I'll be okay." She struggled to sit up, Isobel helping her.

"*Lilly, listen to me. You need to glamour that guy and get him to leave your room. He's close to finding out our secret.*" Baron urged her quietly.

The vampire nodded, then looked at the body-guard's face, focusing on his eyes. "Thank you, Mr. Kennedy, I'll be fine. I'm just tired from the night's activities. You might want to go put in your report that we got a bit excited over the cut on Isobel's arm. But that all is well, it isn't deep and will heal up quickly. Now I'm tired, please remove yourself from our room, and shut the door on the way out." Lilly yawned and rubbed her closed eyes.

The head bodyguard blinked for a moment and then said, "If you two are finished making a big scene, I'm going to go now." He turned, but turned back and grabbed the pocket knife off the bedside table. He saw the blood but didn't mention it. "I will take this back to Carter Hughes. You both settle down and try to get some sleep." He turned and walked to the door, Lancelot walking in back, escorting the man out.

Isobel followed him and checked the door. "Good dog! You were protecting us, weren't you, Lance? Well good riddance. I did not need that guy butting in this situation." She turned back to Lilly, Lance on her heels. "I think you need to sleep now, get your strength back." Lance jumped on the bed and snuggled close to Lilly's side, facing the bedroom door.

Lilly tried a smile. "I do. I'm still hungry but nothing but fresh blood sounds good, which is strange. We may have to go hunting tomorrow night."

"*You can come down here to the river, I can bring rats.*" Baron. The cat was a one-track eating machine. Lilly and Izzy laughed at the same time.

"No, I don't think rats will do it this time, sweet kitty. I need human blood right now, I think."

"*Well, pass up a good rat, see if I care. You need to get some sleep, we can talk about this again tomorrow. Isobel, you will watch over her for me, correct?*"

Lilly looked up at Isobel, "You can hear him

too?"

"I didn't think so but while you were out, he helped me figure out what to do for you. I guess his need was so great he just forced his way in." She walked over to the bed. "And to answer your question, Baron, yes, I will watch out after her while she's asleep."

"*Good. Make sure that stupid mutt doesn't try to take over my place, he won't like my reaction. And with that, I say good night. I'm going to find that little tabby and...*"

"Baron!" Lilly and Izzy said simultaneously, the cat laughed and cut the links.

Isobel helped her friend settle in the bed, pulling up the blankets and fluffing the pillows. "You get some sleep. I'll be here in the evening when you wake up. If you need me sooner, just call out. I'm not going anywhere."

"Thank-you, Isobel. I'm glad you are my friend." Lilly closed her eyes and drifted off to sleep.

As she turned off the light, she whispered, "This will give me a chance to try to figure out what's wrong with you." She went to the desk and set up her laptop and started typing.

Chapter Four

THE GOON SQUAD escorted him back to his room, opened the door for him, and after he walked in, closed the door and locked it from the outside again. As they were locking it, Marcus said loudly, "I don't think you guys could talk above the grunt of your gorilla family. Ook Ook ya Mooks!"

The key was pulled out and the sound of jack boots retreated back toward the stairs. Marcus went to the table and picked up the copy of Wilder's book and started leafing through it, then put it aside. He was still angry at Xun for trying to dictate to him about his business. The stupid-Führer was probably pushing his buttons, it wasn't bloody likely that there could be an angel in the organization but in the even there was such a security breach, Marcus was absolutely sure he would recognize him/her immediately and there would be one dead angel for heaven to cry over. But it was none of Xun's business what was going on in Lancaster Industries and Marcus planned on getting with Castro when he returned and have him go through the entire HR files and pull anyone who looks even a little suspicious. Marcus would interview each of them under glamour and make sure they were genuine humans, unless he detected that angel smell first, angels reeked.

To get his mind off of Xun and the others, he changed out of his robe and back into his jeans and t-shirt. It wasn't his favorite look but horses were smelly and dirty and he didn't want his good clothing messed up. He would change on the plane back home.

He picked up his cell phone and pushed the button to turn it on. Maybe he could start the ball rolling on... "Damn it! No bars!" He threw the phone in anger. He now had no way to contact his people.

"Stupid move, Lancaster, very stupid move." He berated himself.

He was stressed. Usually that meant sex but not here. He couldn't even go looking for a maid or one of the male servants to seduce, trapped as he was by the Goon Squad. Looking out the window wasn't going to happen either, the shutters on this room were in place, and he would have to break the window to get to them. He made himself sit down and pick up Wilder's book again but he couldn't concentrate. He tried for a while and then decided to lay on the bed and stare at the ceiling for a while. His first thought was Jesse. Damn he missed that ghoul. He could be such a queen at times and he always was ambitious. He loved Marcus, through everything they had been through, Jesse was always his and the ghoul always loved Marcus. It was a century-old, comfortable relationship.

He thought of Lilly, how she looked, how she smelled and how much he had to still do to get her to stay with him. He knew she wanted to leave but he wasn't going to let her do that. He knew her scent, he could feel her hands on him. Her voice echoed in his head. He hated to say it aloud but he was becoming obsessed with a woman, that woman.

And there it was, his cock hard and straining against his jeans. Right on cue, think of Jesse or Lilly and he was ready to fuck immediately. He was worse than a 12-year old hitting puberty. He released the snap and carefully unzipped the jeans, not wanting to catch his skin in it. He closed his eyes and started jerking off.

A pounding on the door brought him out of his masturbation fantasy, not allowing him the relief that he was seeking. The pounding continued until he pulled up his jeans, fastened them, and then went to the door and pounded back, shouting, "What the hell do you want? I can't answer the door, you troglodytes locked it from that side."

Once his voice faded, he heard the key turn the lock and the door opened inward so fast he had to jump back to keep from getting hit with it. The Goon Squad was back.

"Come." Goon Number One growled in German, indicating down the hall toward the entry.

"Let me get my things…"

"No, not leaving, summoned." The big guard looked him up and down, frowning at the protocol violation of not wearing the ceremonial robes while in Schloss Feufeldunkheit.

"Okay, who is summoning me?" Marcus ran his fingers through his hair to straighten it.

"Change. Then follow." Goon Number One crossed his huge muscled arms across his chest and tapped his foot in annoyance.

"Nope. First of all, I would not change with you and the other Goons standing there with the door wide open. Call me body shy. Second, I'm comfortable in this." He lied on that second point, he wasn't comfortable in the jeans, much preferring slacks or a suit.

"You will obey..." Goon Number One, he had to give these guys names, started to order.

"No, I go like this or I don't go. Your choice." Marcus loved baiting guys like these. He stared into Goon Number One's eyes, pushing to glamour.

The Goon, Marcus found the perfect name, Booger, laughed at him. "Doesn't work, vampire." Behind him, Huey, Dewey, and Loony all laughed. "Coming? Or carrying?"

Marcus acted like he had to think about it, then grinned evilly, "Carry me. I'm tired of walking."

Booger stepped aside and Loony advanced. He grabbed Marcus and hefted him over his left shoulder like a sack of potatoes.

"Put me the fuck down, NOW. I will walk." He started pounding on Loony's back.

"Made your choice." Booger said, leading the pack down the hall. "Oh, and we are quite fluent in many languages. Gorilla included," Booker taunted him over the earlier gorilla comment.

Marcus ground his teeth, being carried, especially in such an undignified way, was humiliating. That thought was front and center as a flash was aimed toward him. Blinking from the sudden, blinding light, he sought out the source.

Calina. He should have known.

"Looking awkward there, Marcus. I had to add this to my collection of stupid pictures on Facebook. It will probably be my profile picture, that will make sure it gets seen all over the world.

He started to say something and then shut his mouth. Slapping the Goon on the back, he said, "Fine. You do that. Loony, let's get moving." Peals of laughter echoed in his ears as they carried him into the council suites hallway. They stopped in front of Xun's door and knocked. A scantily clad ghoul answered, after looking up at Loony and Marcus's ass she invited them in.

It was only then that Loony put him down. Straightening his shirt, retucking it into his jeans, Marcus strode into the living area of the Suite, trying hard to ignore the Goons as Xun told them to wait in the hall.

"So, you decided to break the rules even more? No robes, refusing to come here without being forced..."

"I'm here. They offered to carry me and since I'm tired, I took them up on the offer, they just didn't let me decide how I would be carried." Marcus walked around the room, touching several things he was sure were worth more than his entire business empire. "Besides, I am more comfortable in jeans and the ladies love them, gives them a hint of what is to cum, or rather come." He chuckled at his own joke.

"This is going into the..." Xun tried to say.

"I know, I know, it's going into my personal record, and I might not get accepted to vampire college if I don't behave. Heard the lecture before." Marcus knew he was baiting Xun and considered stopping, however it was in character that the council knew and, more importantly, he was having too much fun at Xun's expense to stop.

"Sit down, Lancaster. I want to talk to you about your place in your bloodline." Xun threw the one thing out he knew would make Marcus sit and listen. As he sat, Marcus glared at Xun.

"First, I'm tired of seeing the Drachenfeur Sitzplaz vacant. Your behavior still gives me cause to not appoint you."

"Well, your choices aren't very good, now are they? It's either me or, if you want to begin to give women the chance for council, Eadwina." Marcus knew the answer to that, no women was the rule and the Council was hidebound when it came to rules, almost as bad as the angels.

"No, no women. I am speaking of your male progeny, Guseppi, Yosefu, or Jean. Each are still active and are not causing the trouble you seem to gleefully cause at every turn." Xun paused.

"I'm the oldest, the rule is the oldest active vampire sits in the Council. Are you proposing to change centuries old vampire law just to spite me?" Marcus wondered what the leader had planned, he knew something had going on.

"Who says you will be remaining active? I can foresee you getting your last two marks and going to Hell. Or, retiring from active life and disappearing. Both of those outcomes are in play..."

"Never!" Marcus yelled, "You would have to force me and I don't plan on being a sitting target for you." He stood up, "I will be leaving just as soon as night falls tonight and I would advise you to not come at me with any intention of harming or killing not only me but anyone in my bloodline. I will not be merciful." He was shaking he was so angry.

"Marcus, my man, you are positively shaking and radiating anger. Calm down. No one is threatening anything." Xun smiled, he had managed to get under the younger vampire's skin, as usual. It was getting to be so routine, it was almost boring to do. But not yet, he was still enjoying baiting.

"Bullshit, Xun. I can read between the lines, you're transparent. There is an underlying threat and I will be on my guard now." Marcus had started pacing the room to calm down before he did something that would trigger any of the variety of punishments that could be handed down by the Council.

"Well, don't worry, the Drachenfeur Sitzplaz will remain empty for centuries longer because I have no intention of allowing you to be seated."

"You may say that but we shall see." Marcus dared Xun to try anything, he had imagined every scenario of how to kill the leader and was looking forward to trying many of them.

"Believe what you want, it doesn't matter to me. This was not what I wanted to speak to you about. You are a guest in the Schloss Feufeldunkheit. I have been remiss in providing properly for your comfort and feeding. I intend to remedy that."

Marcus let out a laugh. "Really? That's what is so important, giving me food? Okay, I like to have a corned beef sandwich and a beer, make that a couple of beers. And chips, salt and vinegar."

"You know damned good and well that the rules of the Council state that human repast is forbidden here. I will be sending you a ghoul for your feeding, and whatever other activity you would like. The only question I have is what gender of ghoul would you want?" Xun wasn't surprised at the push he was getting from the vampire in front of him. It was completely within character. Lancaster was a hot-head who thought his jokes were amusing.

"Which gender? Female. No, wait, male. No, female. I can't choose, go ahead and send one of each." Marcus wasn't sure that this offer was valid or if Xun was trying to get to him again. And, if it was legitimate, he would have a pleasant orgy to pass the day.

"I've already given the word. I'm sending Lia Rees to your room. She's young, very tasty, and very willing. You should have fun with her."

Xun's personal ghoul. Marcus was willing to bet his plane that Lia Rees was being sent in as a spy, but he was willing to take that chance for a quick shag and a bit of blood. "Okay, sounds good. I'll take a raincheck on the male, though. You are well aware I swing both ways."

The entire vampire world knew that particular fact. Lancaster had taken his male ghoul to council meetings before, Xun was surprised that the ghoul wasn't stapled to his side on this trip. Marcus had been blatant with his preference, practically fucking the man in the council room. Like everything else, it was purposely done to aggravate Xun. Somehow Lancaster had found out that Xun was part of the anti-homosexual government in the Tang Dynasty and had started using his actions with the ghoul to taunt Xun. Every time he brought the ghoul, Xun wanted to kill the man and lock Marcus into a coffin forever.

"Go to your room and I will send Lia readily." Xun turned his back on his nemesis.

"Ah, I can't stay and play with my good friend Xunie?" Marcus couldn't resist.

Never turning around, Xun barked, "Out!"

The door opened and the Goon Squad circled Marcus and walked him back to his room. Once he got inside, the door was locked once again. He turned and a small woman with strawberry blond hair, dressed in something that would get her arrested if she were on the streets, sat in the wingback chair by the fire.

"Hello Lia." He wasn't going to refuse a meal, especially since Xun had probably sent his personal ghoul to spy on him as she fed him.

"Hello Mr. Lancaster." The smile on her face was pretty, nice teeth. Her hair was pulled back to accentuate her neck. Marcus had barely heard the greeting in his assessment.

"It's Marcus. What did Xun tell you would be going on in this room while you are here?"

Her hazel eyes looked him up and down. "I was told by one of the other ghouls that I would be providing you blood and any other services you might require."

Marcus mulled that over, the 'other services' sounded interesting. He walked over and ran his finger up and down her neck, over the artery. As he did, he looked around the room. His suitcase was turned sideways, the curtains had been moved, the covers on the bed were rumpled and he was sure his shaving kit had been searched. He also knew that the Goons had not been in the room, there was no trace of their rather stinky scent. But the woman had been in long enough for her scent, and her perfume, were very prevalent in the room, more than just the faint smell from someone who just entered the room.

He put his hand in her hair, taking hold of a big hank of it and twisted to keep her from pulling away. "Did you find what you were looking for, Lia?" He felt her begin to shake.

"Sir?" She answered the question with a question.

"I asked, did you find what you were looking for in my things. I know how I placed them and things are moved. What were you seeking?"

"I don't know what you are talking about, I only just arrived. If things are moved, maybe the maids did it, they have a key to almost all of the rooms."

Marcus smiled, one of the smiles that puts the fear in many of his own people, then he pulled her head around so he could look into her eyes. "I know a lie when I hear it, I also know how long you have been here. Look at my eyes, Lia."

She knew what he was going to try to do. She also knew it wouldn't work because Xun had given her strong enough mental keys to keep any other vampire from glamouring her. She stared at him, thinking she might be able to fake it.

"You will tell me everything and the truth."

"Yes, sir." Lia said.

"Were you searching my room before I entered?"

"No sir, I have only been here a few minutes." She pushed back at him just a bit, the hand in her hair was beginning to hurt her scalp.

"Really?" He knew she was lying. He pulled her to standing and dragged her to the window. "Curtains? Why would I hide things in one of the more evident locations?"

She whimpered as he dragged her to the dresser, "You see this? I had placed it in a particular position because I wanted to tell if anyone decided to check it for something or another. Your scent is on the leather, I know you have tampered with it."

"I didn't sir, I promise." She had started to cry.

He dragged her into the bathroom. "This, your scent is also on this. I know you have handled it. What would I have that would be so important I would hide it with my toiletries?" He dumped the small case into the sink, "There's nothing in there that would concern you unless you wanted to shave your legs before I came in."

Finally, he dragged her to the bed, "And you were here too. I bet you looked under the pillows, between the mattresses, and under the bed, trying hard to find something that would incriminate me in some way or another. Here's a news flash, I don't have anything with me that would be of any interest to Xun or the other council members."

He pulled his hand loose from her hair, lifted her, and dropped her on the bed, "Since you are so interested in me and my actions, I think I will take advantage of your..." He ripped the barely there clothing off of her in one movement, "nicely shaped body."

Lia reached up to touch his face, hoping that he would be willing to be gentle. The movement and the doe eyes made Marcus stop and rethink his intentions. It would be much more profitable to lure her into talking about Xun's plans. He could always give the leader a message just before sundown as he was leaving.

He laid down beside her and stroked her arm, eventually calming her and drying her tears. "I guess it's not fair to rage at you for what Xun does. He's my issue, not yours, and whatever you did was at his behest. So my fight will be with him. Can we start over again?"

"First you are evil, then you're nice. I've got whiplash." She said, quietly.

"I did react, I am suspicious of everything Xun does, he's a very treacherous man, I would be a fool not to be suspicious." Marcus knew of at least a dozen deaths that notched Xun's belt, the Chinaman was no delicate flower nor was he innocent as he tried to portray. And there was the business aspects, Xun was ruthless and Marcus had been blatant in his attacks on Xun's Shanghai businesses, it was a wonder that there weren't more bodies outside the ones which were left by both sides for beware signs. "So, we start again. What should we do now?" He managed to turn on the charm.

Lia smiled and moved where he could reach her neck. "I was sent to give you sustenance. Shouldn't we feed you first? So you can have stamina for whatever else will be happening today?" She ran her hand down his still covered chest, "I think you need to take off a few of the clothes, you must be hot."

"Seduction? I'm still not sure that I will give you that kind of treat, after all, you did go through my things. You have free will, as most ghouls do, and you could have not done so and then talked to me. I would have shown you everything you needed to see."

"We were starting over?" She pulled back, not sure how to handle this schizophrenic man, one minute kind, the next vicious.

"Yes we are, I'm sorry for bringing it up. Feeding sounds wonderful, I'm positively parched." Marcus ran his hand down, brushed her hair out of the way, and cut her neck slightly with his fingernail to get a taste. "Good, Xun has not poisoned my dinner." He smiled, pulled her close, and sunk his fangs into the artery. She melted into him and he took the chance to arouse her to the level his feeding was arousing him. He pulled his fangs and then sank them again, pulling more blood and leaving gaping holes where his fangs were. There was no way he was going to close those holes, he wanted Xun to know just what he had done. He maintained contact with her neck as he pulled the button on his jeans and pushed them down. He nudged her legs apart and ran his cock up and down on her nether lips, eliciting a moan.

He spent most of the day fucking her, he wouldn't call it making love, having no feelings for her at all. He would screw, climax, then feed again, then go at her again. He was only aware of the sun setting by the pull of the darkness.

He struck one last time, in the femoral artery, and drank deeply. She was no longer conscious and he knew she wasn't far from death. By the time they figured out she wasn't just sleeping, he would be on his way out of Switzerland and to San Antonio to see Jesse and Lilly. As he pulled out his fangs, and sealed the holes to only allow a small trickle of blood to come out. He stood up and pulled on his jeans and stashed his toiletries in his bag. As he started for the door, he smiled, the kind of smile an alligator might get when finding prey. He walked back over and gently put his hand on her face. She didn't stir. He lifted his hand, then used his fingernail to carve a deep M into her cheek, then he covered her as if she was sleeping it off, and went to the door.

When he knocked, Goon Number Three, Dewey opened the door. He looked over the top of Marcus's head toward the bed.

"Shhh, she's sleeping it off. I gave her a long and hearty shagging today. Wore her totally out."

"We heard." Dewey said, rolling his eyes.

"As well you should, she was making enough noise to wake Spain. Just do me a favor and let her sleep, she needs the rest." Marcus did not want the Goon going into the room and finding Xun's surprise before he was well away from the castle.

"You leaving?" Dewey asked.

"Absolutely. You can follow me out to the stables if you must, but I can find my way out." Marcus lifted his bag and started through the door.

"I have to go with you. Orders." Dewey said, following Marcus down the hall and out of the castle's door. He followed only until they were in sight of the stables and then left the observation to the outside Goons and returned to the castle.

Marcus was aware of still being watched. There was very little that escaped the Goon Squad and their illustrious boss, Xun. As he walked into the stable, he was met by a groom carrying a saddle. He trailed behind as the horse was saddled and his bag secured. Then the groom handed him the reins and there was a paper wrapped around them. The two men looked at each other, unsaid assurances passing between them. Marcus thanked the man for the horse, mounted, and left the compound of Schloss Feufeldunkheit, headed back to human civilization.

Chapter Five

W ITH MARCUS GONE and the girls being the bitches he knew them to be, Jesse was glad he was able to go out alone.

He had asked the hunky concierge where a good gay bar was. The recommendation was the Bonham Exchange, just a couple of blocks north of the hotel. He would rather take his chance with a random pickup than go shopping and the other shit the girls were doing.

The only bad part? Marcus' insistence in having a bodyguard following him 100% of the time. Marcus had told him about the threats to assassinate him that had been made by a human owner of a rival mercenary company. So each of them got assigned a bodyguard. Marcus had Castro pull together an entire team to go with them to San Antonio. The word was that Marcus had wanted 24 hour guard walking next to them. Jesse had already argued that point with Marcus, he didn't need a guard sitting next to him when he was trying to pick up a casual date.

Jesse still wondered why Marcus didn't just nuke the asshole human and his company.

Kennedy, the leader of this particular team, had assigned Duncan Morrison to guard him. Jesse was certain that the old man had done it to annoy both of them, he had no love for the upstart 27 year old former Marine and the feeling was mutual. While he had to let the guard follow him around, he didn't have to like the guy.

So, as he had walked down Bonham Street toward the bar, he could feel the bodyguard behind him, looking around to keep him safe like he was a 5-year old kid who needed a nanny. Jesse got into the bar easily, flash an ID and smile at the bouncer and he was inside. Jesse wasn't sure how Morrison had managed to follow him but there he was sitting at a table in the corner drinking a beer and watching the room.

Jesse finished the latest beer and tequila piggy back, motioning to the bartender for another. Running his hand through his blond hair to make sure it was perfect, he scanned the room. Among the interesting people was a very good looking muscular distraction at the end of the bar. He had caught the man sneaking long looks at him but the stranger would turn away as he noticed Jesse looking his way.

The bartender placed the next two glasses in front of him and Jesse smiled, "Put it on my tab."

"No sir, I've been told your money isn't any good here. This is compliments of the hot hunk at the end of the bar." The bartender pointed at the guy Jesse had noticed earlier.

Damn, the guy was right, the man was six foot of streaked red and blond hair, abs from heaven straining his tight t-shirt, and judging from the bulge in his sprayed on jeans, he was hung as well as gorgeous. Jesse licked his lips as he lifted the glass of Shiner in salute to the other man's generosity.

Gorgeous Toy stood up and sauntered over to the vacant stool next to Jesse, looking him up and down, then smiled. "Who left you all alone, blue eyes?"

As pick-up lines went, that was a grade-A fail but his voice was sexy enough to go with the rest of the package. Jesse liked what the man was selling so he answered, "I'm on my own this week. My regular lover is in Europe so. . ." He let his words drift off, hoping the intent was obvious.

"Well, his loss appears to be my gain, now doesn't it? My name is Nicholas."

The billion-dollar smile made Jesse even hotter. "I'm Jesse." He picked up the tequila and threw it into the back of his throat, drinking Shiner after it.

Nicholas was watching him, sipping on a red wine. "Do you want to go get better acquainted?"

No kidding? No long talks to scope out his background or pry into his life. Hi there, let's go get busy was it. Jesse could handle that. "Yeah I think that would be great." He slid off the bar stool and started back to the men's room.

"Not a good idea." Nicholas spoke up. "While the bar encourages people to get drunk and dance, the two-backed beast is off limits, they have cameras so they can keep an eye on everything."

Cameras? In a men's room? Unusual but it sounded like Nicholas was aware of another place to go.

"The back end of 3rd is really an alley. I know of a place that is hidden by trees that we could go discuss our impending relationship."

Jesse thought it over a moment, knowing that Marcus would be okay with the liaison but he also had Duncan Morrison in tow and a third wheel was going to make the situation tense in the wrong ways. "Hang on a sec, I'll be right back."

The ghoul walked straight back to the big guard dog, "I've got an invitation for a little recreational stress relief. I'm going outside for a few minutes."

The big man scowled, "No dice, Chamberlain, the boss told me to stick with you like a cheap suit and I'm going to do just that. I've already made concessions to you by sitting back here, don't make me have to follow you outside."

"Look," Jesse's tone of voice reflected his rising anger, "If you want to come along, fine and dandy. We will try to give you a great peep show because I'm planning on getting sex from that good looking guy and I do know you don't swing that way. But hey, it's your call." Jesse turned and walked toward Nicholas and with a couple of whispered words, the two men went out the front door.

Duncan Morrison sat still, trying to decide whether to stay back or follow. Chamberlain had been right, he did not want to have to watch over his charge while the man was getting a blow job, or worse. But, at the same time, Brian Kennedy, the leader of this particular guard team would probably throw him in the river tied in chains with weights if he didn't stay with his charge. He rose, talked with the bartender, paid both his and Jesse's tab and walked toward the door.

JESSE AND NICHOLAS talked as they went around the north corner of the building and into the alley. It was open, with dumpsters along one side. Jesse had some experience in back-alley sex but it wasn't his favorite thing, he much preferred a bed and a door that locked.

Nicholas walked toward a small group of crepe myrtle trees in back of a building. There was a corner of that building that provided enough privacy with the trees as a curtain. As they walked up to it, Nicholas made a small bow, "After you."

It wasn't bad, it was darker than he thought it would be, which was good because, as he reminded himself again, he hated having sex in back alleys. The only reason he wasn't going back to the hotel was the girls, having drawn the bed, he wasn't going to fuck on the fucking couch or a fucking rollaway.

Nicholas stepped through the tree branches and pushed Jesse up to the wall, locking his lips on the ghoul. His tongue pushed its way between Jesse's lips and he moaned. Hands were every-where at once, pulling at his shirt, unbuckling his jeans, holding his head, the world seemed to spin as the passion rose. Never one to wear underwear, once the zipper was moved, his cock leapt out of its enclosure and jutted out. Nicholas took hold of it and began to work it, never breaking the kiss.

"Well lookie here, looks like a porno show, boys." The words drifted into the corner and broke the kiss. Jesse bent to pull up his jeans as Nicholas stepped away.

"Leave those pants right there, I kinda like the way you look." Between the darkness and the trees, Jesse couldn't see who was talking. "You want to step out here, Mr. Chamberlain?"

The use of his name was unnerving. What the hell? "I am fine back here, who are you and what do you want."

"Who I am will become crystal clear in a few minutes, as for what I want, I want you." The voice wasn't recognizable as anyone Jesse could remember.

"Me? But I've not. . ."

Two beefy men stepped into the corner and grabbed him by the arms, dragging him out into the alley, his jeans sliding further down to his ankles leaving him totally exposed. He could see the man who had been talking, big, very heavy, dressed in khaki pants and a Hawaiian shirt like a very porky Magnum P.I. The guy smiled.

"Yes sir, I think I want you just like that. You are the little gay prick that Marcus Lancaster keeps as a pet, right?"

How the hell did he know that? Jesse's mind raced, trying to figure out what was going on and alternately wishing that he hadn't told Duncan to stay behind. He could see Nicholas standing behind Fat Magnum and that confused him further. Nicholas spit to the side and then wiped his mouth like it tasted nasty. He was part of whatever this was.

"Cat got your tongue, fag? I asked you a question, you are Marcus Lancaster's pet."

He managed to squeak out a "Yes" before another man stepped up beside Fat Magnum. This guy was double the size of Duncan with huge hands. Jesse had no idea what was going to happen but he opened his mouth to scream bloody murder.

And that action got Hamfist to grab his cock and balls and twist, the pain shutting down the scream before it exited his mouth. He could barely breathe.

"I see you want to do this the hard way, pussy. So Ralph here will handle things for me. And don't think you will get out of this alley or find someone to help," the boss indicated both ends of the alley, Jesse could see two more big men loitering there. "Karlos and Frank will help you stay upright as I have a message fashioned for your lover."

With the last word, Ralph dropped his hold on Jesse's cock as he changed positions and hit Jesse in the diaphragm, shutting down the ability to speak, scream, or even breathe. The ghoul tried to double over but the other two guys had a firm hold on him. Jesse looked up in pain at Nicholas.

"I'm not into guys, asshole, I just wanted to

bring you out to see my friends."

Betrayed by his own cock. Damn.

Then he saw red. Ralph had aimed his fist into his limp cock and balls, knocking them almost through his body. Tears began to stream down his face.

"Awwww, poor little pansy is crying for his mommy." Fat Magnum said as Ralph continued his beating. The big hammy fist hit him in the mouth and Jesse tasted blood, then spit some hard things out.

Teeth, how many?

Jesse knew he was going to die in an alley in San Antonio with his pants down around his ankles. He tried to pass out.

"Oh no, you are NOT going to go to sleep on me." Ralph had a voice. And a large container of ice water, which he poured over Jesse's head, pulling him back to the present, and the pain. "Now, where were we?"

A shout came from the direction of Bonham Street, it was Duncan, calling his name. Jesse was turned so he could watch as Duncan started to run into the alley to the rescue. The goon who was guarding that end of the alley stepped in behind him and raised a pistol.

"Dun..." Jesse tried to yell a warning but Ralph hit him in the jaw. As he spit yet more teeth out, he could barely see as Duncan was shot in the head and torso from behind. He took one more step and fell dead in the dirt.

At that point Jesse knew his own fate. Ralph continued beating him on the head, face, torso, where ever there was a place he hadn't hit much. Jesse couldn't stand any longer, slumping without being able to think.

And got the ice water bath again, dragging him back to the reality of the pain.

"I need your ass awake for this next part." With both eyes punched into his head, he couldn't see Fat Magnum any longer.

"I want you to give that bastard lover of yours a message. Stay the fuck out of my business." Jesse tried hard to remember who he was talking about.

Then he felt it.

White hot pain over rode the throbbing and blinding pain everywhere else. It started just above his belly button and ran straight to his balls and cock. As he floated on the pain, he had a chance to take inventory of his body. Right arm broken in two places, fingers of the left broken. Both eyes swelled shut, nose broken, lips swelled. Both knees were broken from being kicked backward, left shoulder probably broken. Now the knife cut in his lower abdomen. Everything was beyond hurting. He had been able to divorce his mind from his body and just float.

A hand grabbed his hair and jerked his head up. Another white hot pain pulled him into his body. This time it was in his face, from his forehead to his chin and he finally managed to scream.

"Awww, the poor little nancy boy's face. It's such a mess, you know. No one will be able to think of you as pretty again. Too bad."

He could feel someone pulling his jeans up far enough to reach into the pockets. Robbery was the least of his problems he thought as he was let go, falling face forward into the dirty pavement.

"You be sure to tell Lancaster my message, it's the last one he's going to get." The statement was accompanied by a hard kick to his ribs.

His last thought was of Marcus. "I love you." He thought as he gave himself over to the blackness.

Chapter Six

I N THE LATE afternoon Isobel rubbed her eyes. She had slept with Lilly, as planned, and that let her keep an eye on her friend. Thankfully, after the blood, Lilly had gone to sleep and never stirred. Izzy had stayed up late into the morning trying to figure out what was wrong with the vampire. She knew she could not just Google "throwing up vampire" and get a list of symptoms. WebMD didn't have vampire listings. There were websites of authors of vampire fiction that touched on the physiology but she knew that those were probably fiction unless the author was acquainted with a vampire and ghostwriting the novels based on the real story.

She finally found what she was searching for in human physiology. After checking the symptoms Lilly was showing, Izzy had a pretty good idea what may be going on with Lilly.

She was pregnant.

It all fit, the nausea, the need for sleep, and the mood swings. Lilly tended to cry at the least little thing and Izzy knew that she was stronger willed than she was showing, she wouldn't have survived the crypt if she hadn't been. The website wasn't much help on what to do for the full-blown vomiting, just saying that each woman reacted differently to smells, tastes, and such. Great, now it was down to trial and error to help her.

Isobel silently got out of bed and closed the door to the room behind her as she walked into the main area. She picked up the phone and called the front desk, asking for Gregory Freeman. He was the doorman who had escorted them to the King Suite when they first checked in and Marcus had tipped him very well to be on call for them if needed. Well, she figured she needed him.

She explained to the desk clerk that her room mate was sleeping and she didn't want to wake her so she wanted to speak to him on the phone. Once Gregory was on the line, Isobel asks him to go find some saltine crackers, ginger tea, and a pregnancy test. She instructed him to get a key card from the desk clerk so he could just come in without knocking. She wanted Lilly to sleep as long as she could.

After she hung up the phone, Isobel began to worry about how Lilly would take the news. Whose baby was it? She had never heard of a vampire getting someone pregnant and never heard of a pregnant vampire. From what she had learned, it was something impossible since the vampire's system wasn't the same as a regular humans. Could Marcus have gotten her pregnant? Or, maybe it was the other guy, the turned angel, Sullivan. Isobel suspected that neither choice would be a good one.

Maybe Lilly would be better off getting an abortion? One of Izzy's internet searches had been to find Storyville, the brothel area of New Orleans where Lilly had died and turned in 1900. She discovered Mahogany Hall and the history of the brothels. She also had found some of the personal things that went on in that area, including babies being born to the prostitutes and the fact that some of the girls found people to perform the procedure to get rid of the unwanted condition. She wondered if Lilly had known girls who became parents or if she knew where the abortions were done. There were no clinics back then, no Planned Parenthood to go find help. She didn't know her friend's beliefs on the subject, but if her religious beliefs were any indication, Lilly would probably refuse the abortion and have the baby.

And what would the baby be? Human? Or Vampire? She wasn't sure if the Angels could reproduce, but maybe they could, maybe making the cherubs she had seen in pictures and books.

What a mess. This was a complication that wasn't needed right now, that was for sure.

GREGORY WAS ENTHUSIASTIC about the request to help the people in the suite 2052, the historical King Suite, originally occupied by the cattle baron who owned the King Ranch, Richard King. He was happy to be of service until the word pregnancy was said. He had to go buy a pregnancy test? He couldn't even go down the girl aisle in the stores because it was embarrassing. How would he be able to pick up a pregnancy test without becoming mortified? He could ask a girlfriend, if he had one. The last one dumped him after he wouldn't do drugs with her. He could ask his grandmother, no, not a good idea, she might think it was for a girl he may have gotten pregnant and the lecture she would give him was the last thing he wanted to listen to.

He would have to suck it up and just buy the test. But he wouldn't be buying it in his neighborhood, his grandmother seemed to know everyone in Denver Heights and there wasn't much he could get away with over there, if he did anything unusual, someone always reported it to her. He would go west from the hotel and find a store to pick the items up. He grabbed the card and the keys and went out to find a place to get the requested items.

As he drove, he thought of his grandmother. She had raised him after his father went to prison for killing someone and his mom died of an overdose with a needle in her arm. The little house on Fedonia Street wasn't large, or fancy, but it was home. His grandmother was one of the elders of the community, always sitting outside, talking to neighbors and watching for trouble. Word was, you did not want to cross Georgia Freeman, she wasn't one to hold back on what she thought. And he knew that all too well. She had kept him going to school, sometimes fighting with the teachers and administration to keep him in class. Back then, he was angry at the world and would fight at the slightest look. But his grandmother kept him busy with altar boy duties at church, choir, homework, and baseball. As he got better at all of them, she began to give him the will to be more than many of his friends were, parents, drug pushers, or burglars. With the power she had inside, from her fight for not only her kids but also her civil rights as a black woman, she instilled in him the work ethic he had now.

He found an all-night Walgreens way up northwest near the University Hospital. They didn't have ginger tea but they had regular tea bags and some Altoids ginger drops. He was looking for the pregnancy tests and he could feel the rent-a-cop watching him with his hand on his gun. Even in his uniform from the hotel, he knew a black man in this part of town was always suspected of something. He smiled and nodded at the guy a couple of times in his rotation of the store and the last time, the guy walked up to him as he passed into the front of the store.

"You lose something in here?" The guy asked.

Gregory looked at his name tag. "No sir, Officer Stafford. I am buying some things for guests at Menger Hotel, where I work."

"You're a long way from Menger. Where did you get that uniform?"

"I work for the Menger, I was issued this uniform." Gregory had pegged the guy, he disliked and distrusted black people and was enjoying hassling him.

"Well, I think I better call the SAPD and see if you're who you are saying you are. You just sit down on the floor, scoot those things in your hand away from you and put your hands on your head. We'll get a squad out here and test that information."

Gregory wanted to punch the guard in the mouth, he was delaying him doing what he needed to do for Mr. Lancaster's people back in the hotel, but even more, the guy had an attitude that probably came with the sheets hanging in his closet. If he got into trouble, his grandmother would have his head.

It took a few minutes but from his vantage point on the floor, Gregory could see the flashing lights of the police car as it drove up. Great, he thought, the guard decided to tell them who knows what to get them here with the flashers going. This might get rough.

A small woman officer came in, looking around. The nine millimeter on her hip was almost the same size she was. She spotted the guard and walked over.

"What is going on, Officer Stafford?" She smiled.

He must have took that as a come-on, his demeanor changed to what Gregory always thought of as "slimy stalker".

"Oh, Officer Fox, nice to see you again. I trust you're having a safe night?" Gregory cringed as the words, dripping in pure sugar, were said.

Officer Fox wasn't buying it. "What has this young man done?"

"I caught him casing the place. He picked up a couple of items but was wandering the store, checking where everything was. I thought it wise to stop him and ask questions. He says he's got a job at a hotel, but I don't believe him."

"He is wearing the uniform of the Menger, it says so on the name tag he's wearing." Officer Fox stepped around the guard, making sure not to brush up against him. As she was standing in front of him, the asshole had the guts to grab his crotch and thrust once. The officer didn't see him but Gregory had about all the floor show he could stand.

"Gregory Freeman, that's your name, right?" At least the woman officer had better manners. "Do you have any ID on you?"

"Yes ma'am." Gregory turned to balance on one hip as he tried to dislodge his wallet from his pocket.

"Get up." She shot another look at the guard, "There is no reason for you to have been placed on the floor like that." She took the offered driver's license and examined it, then handed it back. Gregory moved very slowly to his feet, not wanting to startle anyone, especially the guard, who had kept his hand on the gun at his belt.

"Thank you, Mr. Freeman. Can you explain what you were doing here?" She smiled at him, which was very appreciated, given how the night was going.

"Yes ma'am. I work for the Menger Hotel. I'm on retention for a group of big guests there. One of them asked me if I could buy some ginger tea, saltine crackers, and a..." his voice trailed off. He didn't want to say the last item to the woman. He blushed.

"And?" Officer Fox prompted, retaining the smile.

He looked down at his shoes and mumbled. "Pregnancy test. They need a pregnancy test."

"Oh bullshit!" Officer Stafford roared, "You got your girlfriend knocked up and are trying to see if she's got a baby."

Officer Vivian Fox whirled on the man, "You have no right to say that to this young man, or anyone else. Even if that is the truth, the rude way you keep talking with him is uncalled for."

"The kid is a criminal, don't let the uniform fool you. He's smarter than most but I guarantee you, if you check, he's probably got a record a mile long."

"Again, you don't know that and you need to shut your mouth and move away from this area, back to the door, and let me do my job. If you don't, if you say anything else in reference to this situation, I will arrest you for interfering with a police investigation. Got it?"

"Come on, sugar, you know I'm right." Stafford was not about to back down from a woman, no matter what the threat. Especially a beautiful and tough female, she was just the kind he liked to dominate, once he got them into his bed, of course.

"And that is the wrong anything else." She pulled up the microphone attached to her shoulder, "Central, 2214, send backup to my location."

The answer came over the ear piece in her ear and she acknowledged it before letting go of the mic and addressing the now angry security in front of her. "Turn around and place your hands behind you, please." The command had no warmth to it at all.

"Now honey, you don't have to be that way." He stood his ground.

Behind her, Gregory shook his head. This guy wasn't smart at all, obviously, or he thought he was so charming the police officer would just cave to his crap. He didn't want to get the guy arrested, even if he was a racist bastard but he also didn't want to get Officer Fox angry enough to include him in the bracelet ceremony about to happen either.

Another set of police lights came into view and a big Hispanic police officer walked into the store, hand on the butt of one of the biggest semi-automatic pistols Gregory had ever seen.

"You called for back-up Officer Fox?" The man walked past the security guard and looked over the female officer's head into Gregory's face, it was obvious who he thought was the problem.

"Yes, I did, Officer Robles. I am in the midst of an investigation here and Officer Stafford has seen fit to interrupt me. I warned him to back off and shut up and he refused to do it..."

"I didn't refuse, Fox!" Stafford interrupted. Officer Robles shot the man a look that silenced him.

"As I said, he wouldn't do as asked and I have

not finished finding out what Mr. Freeman is trying to find..."

Stafford chimed in, "He's looking for a pregnancy test for his knocked up girlfriend." Then he snickered.

Fox stared at him, let him finish, and then said to Robles, "See what I mean about not following orders?" She pulled out her handcuffs, "Stafford, turn around and put your hands behind your back, you are being arrested for interference with a police investigation."

"You have got to be kidding. I'm a licensed security guard and this is my place to guard. You can't arrest me instead of him." Stafford stabbed a finger at Gregory, who was studiously staying quiet with both hands where the officers could see them. He had grown up around police arrests, he saw the results of messing with cops and he was going to mind his manners.

At that point, Officer Robles started to put his hand on Stafford's arm and turn him so they could cuff him. He ended up blocking a swing aimed right at his head from the guard who had obviously decided that he was going to fight his way out of the trouble instead of cooperate. Gregory took three steps back, set the items he was going to buy on a nearby shelf and placed his hands on his head. Robles and Fox weren't watching him, they were too busy with the scuffle. Stafford shifted his weight, swinging around to try to throw the big officer off. He managed to get Robles into the end cap and bottles of hand lotion cascaded to the floor and some broke. Now the floor was slick with the leaking lotion and both of the men had trouble regaining their footing, sliding into other shelving and dislodging the contents. Officer Fox had requested further backup and was trying to help Robles get Stafford on the floor and stopped so they could cuff him but the guard pushed her into shelving and she fell, clutching her right arm.

Gregory was watching what was happening but staying out of the way until Fox had gone down. When she rolled off her arm, she was clutching it and moaning. Then he spotted the reason why, her elbow was at an odd angle and there was another angle a bit further down, bleeding. He could see bone poking through the skin. As the big men continued the fight, they were in great danger of falling on her, hurting her more. He lowered his arms, stepped over to where she was, and lifted her under the arms, pulling her out of the way and into the other side of the aisle. He eased her down to the floor to sit, trying not to jar her any more than he had to.

"It looks like your arm is broken. What can I do to help you?" Gregory knew there were things to help but in the chaos and emotion of the situation and he was having trouble thinking of them.

Vivian Fox looked up at the young man, "Can you help Raul stop that maniac? Just until the backup shows up. I'm out."

Gregory nodded, "Tell Robles I'm going to try to disarm Stafford, that I'm helping, not jumping to the other guy's aid." He knew well that sometimes the police just acted first and sorted out later and he didn't want to be the object acted on.

As Fox was shouting the information, Robles almost had the guard down, holding his right wrist to keep him away from the gun. Stafford was now screaming and cussing, mentioning lawsuits as he tried to punch the police officer and kicking to stay off his stomach. Gregory inched around between the now twisted shelving and the fight, reached out and grabbed the gun. It was attached by the strap and Gregory had to make another grab to pull it open before removing the weapon. Once he got a hold on it, he turned and slid it through the greasy mess right up to Fox. She managed a small smile and nod and Gregory returned his attention to the fight. Robles had the man on his side on the floor, trying to hold and maneuver him to his stomach. Gregory stepped up carefully and grabbed the leg on top and shoved it toward the floor. When he got it to move, he moved up, one knee on the struggling guards leg. He was getting kicked with the free leg so he moved to straddle the man's calves and held him down while Robles struggled to get his arms behind him.

Suddenly there was a rush of men, guns drawn, running into the store. Gregory's first thought was to stand, move back, and keep his hands up. But the way the guard was bucking, trying to throw off both he and Robles, he stayed where he was. Once the cavalry had come, Stafford had stopped fighting. He knew he was going to jail so he pulled his arms from below him and allowed Robles to cuff him. Both men stood and stepped away as fresh reinforcements took control and custody of the prisoner and hustled him out to a waiting patrol car.

The media had also flooded the area, remote trucks parked in the parking lot. Reporters gathered near the door, taking film and photos through the doors as the EMTs checked Officer Fox's broken arm. She refused to let them put her on a gurney, insisting on walking to the ambulance. After they helped her to her feet, she motioned to Gregory, who came up next to her.

"Thank you for your assistance with this matter. I don't know if I could have gotten out of it without much more damage. Come over here with me for a minute." She smiled at him and turned to walk away from the paramedics. They objected and she gave them the smile as well, "I'll be right back, I just need to do something for my hero, then I'll be ready to go."

They continued around the store. The manager came out of the back room where she had taken her staff to get away from the fight, in case it got to the shoot-out stage. Fox walked up to her and they talked in hushed tones. Gregory hung back to give her some privacy. The women shook hands and the manager walked away.

"Okay, I think I need to get back, my chariot awaits. But I have to make sure you realize what a hero you are You stayed calm in the face of that angry bastard, you kept your head when things got violent. You are my hero, if nothing else. Remember that." She walked up to the paramedics and allowed them to escort her through the throng of reporters and police, as she climbed into the ambulance, she gave him a little wave as the doors shut.

Gregory gave his story to the police at least twice. He dreaded facing the press but he knew he wouldn't get away without giving them what they wanted. He was a mess, his clean uniform was ripped, coated in lotion, and the pants were probably unsalvageable, they were coated in stuff he hated to try to think of. He would have to go back to the hotel with the items before cleaning up.

The items. In all the chaos, he had lost track of the tea and ginger Altoids. And he would have to pick up the dreaded pregnancy test before heading out to the awaiting press. He hoped the sack would hide what he had in it. He turned to track down the items again.

"Mr. Freeman?" The manager called as he circled the store. He followed her voice to the corner of the store where the pharmacy was. She was holding a sack. "I want to thank you for helping the police stop that man. He had been harassing my female clerks and me and I was afraid of him. I had reported him but he was left in place as the guard."

"You are welcome, ma'am." He didn't know what else to say to her.

She reached out, the sack in her hand, "This is what you were looking for. It is all there, the saltine crackers, the tea and ginger, and the pregnancy test. I wrapped it in paper before putting it in the bag so you won't have to look at it."

"Oh, do you have the bill, I can get my card

from my..." His hands searched his pockets for his wallet. It was gone. "I can't pay you, I have no idea where my wallet is. Can you hang onto that until I get my wallet back?"

"I'm sorry, I cannot. It's already been paid for. You will need to take it with you." She smiled. "Don't worry, it's true, And nothing will happen to you taking it with you."

He had a good idea who had paid for it and he made a mental note to talk to his bosses to see if he could send her a paid vacation weekend in thanks as he walked to the front of the store. Officer Robles saw him and excused himself, walking over to him.

"Mr. Freeman, thank you for your assistance back there. You were a great help in subduing the suspect."

"You're welcome, sir." He shook the man's offered hand.

"By the way, Freeman, I found this. I figure you want it." Raul Robles put out his hand and opened it. His wallet, a little worse for wear with lotion having stained it appeared.

"Thank you for finding it." He slipped it back into his pocket. "See you around."

"I'll go with you. You're going to be swallowed by the press, if there's a cop with you, they won't try to hold you too long, I'll get you to your car."

"Ok, thanks." Gregory hadn't thought of that. He found his keys in a front pocket and the two men, still coated in the spilled lotion, walked out the doors and into the glare of media lights.

Chapter Seven

LILLY WOKE UP feeling like someone kicked her in the stomach, everything hurt. She stretched and carefully sat up, casting a thought at Baron, wondering where the cat was.

"*I'm here. Just sleeping. I've got to save my stamina, there are three hot kitties expecting me tonight. One's a tabby, one's a tuxedo, and the other is one hot Siamese. By the time I'm done, I'll be well-fed and well...*"

"Save me the details, Baron. I'm just checking on you." She sighed, still too weary to think about leaving the room.

"*Are you feeling any better?*" Baron knew her and knew she was not acting right.

"It depends on your definition of 'better.' I've stopped vomiting, which is helpful, but I pulled some muscles while it was going on and everything hurts, but at least I'm not sick." She ran her fingers through her hair, it had been a couple of days since she showered and she should probably take one but she didn't want to move.

"*Well, if you need me to come back, I will. I hope that asshole Jesse isn't around, I get the feeling I may have to flay him if he keeps harassing you.*" Lilly could hear his purring through the link and it sounded like he was bathing himself.

"Actually, he's been gone for a day or so. I don't know if he checked in but he's not here and I don't have to listen to his constant complaints."

"*True. If you want, I can catch a couple of the rats down here and bring them up for your breakfast. I'm going to get mine as well, I'm hungry.*" Baron and his rats, he thought they were a delicacy but even the thought of rat blood made Lilly's stomach clinch.

"You have them, I've got blood up here. Go have a good time and don't get into trouble. If the dog catcher gets you, I may not be able to bail you out."

She heard a chuckle, "*Dog catcher, who cares? I've outrun faster animals than the humans can run, and have you ever seen a human climb as fast as I can? They usually stand at the bottom of the tree and mumble about how to get me down. If they jump out of the tree like I can, they would fall flat on their face, humans can't land on their feet like cats do. All-in-all, cats are the superior animal.*" Baron finished the statement with a yowl, as if he was agreeing with himself.

"Okay. Check in with me later." Lilly cut the link and eased herself out of the bed. Funny, she didn't have to go to the bathroom, there was no urge at all. She grabbed a robe that was hanging behind the door and pulled it around her as she walked out of the bedroom to the living area.

Isobel turned in her chair by the desk. "Well,

good evening Sleeping Beauty! Feeling better?" She shut the computer, she had been looking for vampire stories and pregnancy details, she didn't want Lilly to see the search results.

"Yes, much better, thank you. I'm a bit peckish but the thought of bagged blood, even warmed, ugh." She shuddered at the thought, made a squishy face and struck out her tongue. Sighing in resignation, she said "I know I need to eat, I wonder what would stay down."

"I've read that ginger tea and saltine crackers can help a sick stomach. I've sent Gregory out to pick some up for you. While we're waiting, maybe you need to feed so your system can calm down "

"Oh Izzy. I hate this." Her pouty face showed genuine remorse.

"Hey, I had liver and spinach for dinner so I'm raring to go." She wiggled in her chair, winked, and smiled playfully. She rolled up her sleeve and followed with, "I had them hold the onions. Besides, what's a little blood between friends?"

Both women laughed.

"I guess, short of going out and grabbing a stranger, this is the best option."

"Ok." Isobel stretched out her hand and took Lilly's. "It's ok, really. Go ahead and take what you need."

Lilly put the proffered wrist over to her mouth and struck quickly, knowing that slow bites hurt much worse than just getting it over with. As the thick, sweet substance pooled into her mouth, she let out a groan. This was so good, much better than any other type of blood she had taken.

She wondered as she kept feeding if it was due to Isobel being a ghoul, that somehow changed her blood chemistry so that it was sweeter and more...alive, that was the word for it. She focused on taking as little as possible and after the ten pulls she would take from a human, she pulled her fangs out and licked her lips.

"You didn't take enough. You need to go back." Isobel scolded but smiled.

"I don't want to cause you trouble and if I take too much, there's a chance you could die. I think you would have already become a vampire by Marcus if you had wanted that."

"True. But you also need to feed more to help, to keep yourself healthy. I'm the only one that can donate right now with Jesse gone." Isobel wasn't going to take Lilly's excuses, she needed to feed and that was it.

Lilly sat, glancing to her friend's wrist, then her neck, back to her eyes, and over again. The truth was, Lilly was having trouble keeping the feeding to just what she needed. She was so close to draining her friend to stop the nausea and pain that had been going on since before they left Houston.

"I have to go." Lilly stood up and fled, running very fast into the bedroom, shutting the door, and locking it.

Isobel watched the vampire leave and looks up at the ceiling, "Oh great." She stood up and went to knock on the door.

"Lilly, you need to open up the door. You need to feed more. I know you don't want to and I can stop you if I start feeling bad, but you have to come out and drink."

Inside, Lilly stood, leaning her back on the door. She wasn't sure what she was going to do but the one thing she was not going to do was feed. She had barely pulled off before the overwhelming urge came on her.

"I can't. I just can't." She said, choking back tears. The last thing she needed was to cry out the blood she had just taken.

"Sweetie, you need to open the door and let me show you how to do it." Isobel wasn't sure that Marcus had taught Lilly everything he had taught her. "I promise, it will be okay."

Lilly closed her eyes. "Isobel, you don't understand. I can take the blood, but right now I don't know that I can control the taking and not just drain you. Your blood tastes good, so rich and sweet, I had trouble pulling off. I don't want to take a chance of hurting you...or worse." The unwanted tears started to flow.

"You won't kill me. I can stop you before you get that far. I know how to do it. And besides, if you killed me, with the amount of vampire blood I have in my system, I would probably turn without intervention."

"I know what blood-lust is. I saw..." she stopped to take a breath, "I saw Sullivan drain someone after I told him to only take 10 sips. The taste of the blood pulled on him and he lost the ability to stop. And after he drained the man, he acted crazy, acting like some of the men who put cocaine in their noses back in Storyville. That's when he attacked me. I didn't believe him before but with the craving I am having for blood, I can see how hard it is to stop feeding to save the donor's life." She tried to wipe the bloody tears, smearing them across her cheeks, "I'm so close to having blood lust, I don't want to lose control."

Isobel didn't know what that was like, losing control of the ability to make decisions. "Look, I promise, I will be able to handle you. You don't think Marcus ever gets cravings? He's done it a few times over the years and I've been able to stop him. Come on out, we can do this. If you want me armed, I'll try to find a frying pan or rolling pin in the small kitchen."

Lilly laughed in spite of her fears. The thought of Isobel standing over her with a bent frying pan, like those in the Looney Tunes cartoons she loved, a dent the shape of her head on the pan was too funny. In the back of her mind, she was still afraid of losing control but she had to trust someone and that was going to be her friend, Isobel.

"*What am I? A fillet of fish bones?*" Baron piped up, making her smile. "*Hang on, kitten, I need to handle this,*" he obviously told to a date for tonight. "*You need to feed, you almost died last night and you're not doing so well today. Do I need to come up there and keep an eye on you while you feed? I will, if you need me or if you refuse to feed any longer. It's either that woman's blood or I bring a brace of rats. Your choice.*"

The mention of rat blood didn't do anything good for her nausea. "Okay, I'll go feed from her.

Keep the rats to share for your dates."

"*If she doesn't feed, or doesn't feed enough, please call me and I'll be up with some incentive.*" He must have said this where Isobel could hear, Lilly heard the giggle through the door.

"Ok, Baron. I will let you know. Have fun." Isobel still wasn't used to the cat speaking but it was good that he cared so much for Lilly. "You heard him, Lilly, he will bring rats if you don't feed from me and I can bet you big bucks that the management will not be pleased about that! Come out and let's get you to feeling better."

Lilly closed her eyes and sighed. She had lost that argument and hoped that the consequences weren't dire. She turned and opened the door.

"Good! Let's go back to the couch, I have some things to show you, alternate feeding sites." Lilly followed her to the couch and began to listen.

GREGORY FREEMAN WAS going to have to go straight up to the King suite. He had been gone much longer than he wanted to be, he wondered if the woman would be angry. As he walked through the front doors, Pete Swartz laughed, "What the heck happened to you and why do you reek like my granny's old lotion?"

"Shut up, Swartz. I had a little trouble getting the things for 2052. I managed to fall into a big puddle of lotion that was knocked down by..." He wasn't going to tell anyone about the altercation, he didn't want the boss to fire him for it. "Well, anyway, I'm going to deliver the stuff and then change uniforms."

"Have fun, Mr. Mrs. Doubtfire" Pete was still laughing at him when the elevator doors closed. Gregory looked down at himself. He was a mess and Pete had been right, he reeked of 'old woman.' "This is really nasty." He said to no one in the elevator. He walked down the hallway to the suite, hoping the smell wasn't too bad. Of course he looked worse than he smelled, the uniform now stained with the lotion and torn from the fight with the guard. He couldn't go home in this, that was for sure, his grandmother would snatch him bald if she found out he was fighting with cops. He entered the alcove to the room and stopped. Fishing out the key card from his front pocket, Gregory had to wipe it off on the one place not covered in ick, the top of his shoulder. Getting the slime off the magnetic strip, he used it to unlock the door. The woman had said come on in when she gave him instructions. He pushed the door open and walked in.

As he entered, he saw one woman sitting on the couch, her arm extended. Another woman had her mouth on the wrist. Then the second woman looked up and at him, blood on her lips and chin, dry blood smearing her cheeks. The woman the wrist belonged to had two big puncture wounds that were bleeding.

"Wait!" Isobel cried in surprised as she clamped her hand over the wounds.

He froze, even though his immediate instinct

was to run like hell. The bloody woman stood and started to take a step toward him. Slowly, carefully, he inched backwards toward the door.

"Lilly, honey. No," Izzy said in a very soothing tone. "You can continue once he's gone. Please sit back down." Having Lilly attack the bellman was not on her agenda for the evening.

Lilly sat back down, took the wrist and ran her tongue over the holes, sealing them.

"Wha…" he croaked.

"Lilly's a vampire, I'm a ghoul." Isobel explained in the same calming tone she had used with Lilly. She was counting on Lilly being able to wipe his memory once she got the kid to calm down, he was shaking.

All of the stories he had read, all the movies he had watched, were all leading in the same direction in his mind. "Does she sleep in a coffin?" Good grief. This was the first asinine question that fell out of his mouth? How embarrassing!

Isobel snickered, unable to suppress it. He would probably be asking all the usual questions.

"No, she doesn't sleep in a coffin. We are both more like the humans we came from." Why did every human see vampires as Dracula clones rising up out of the tomb?

"That's true, I guess. It makes sense anyway," Gregory said thoughtfully. "So, what's it like being a ghoul? You don't look like a zombie, you don't smell like a corpse and pieces of you aren't falling off when you move. Do you eat brains?" He rambled almost incoherently, while still considering making a mad dash to the exit.

Isobel had to stifle a giggle so she focused on tapping Lilly on the shoulder and trying to get her to finish feeding. The vampire didn't have to be tapped twice, she took the proffered wrist and bit. Gregory watched fascinated, yet repelled at the same time. He had never seen anything like this before.

"Ghouls are the personal assistants to our vampire. I'm Marcus Lancaster's ghoul, as is the man who was here that first night, Jesse." She wondered for a moment where he was, it wasn't like him to stay out this long without checking in. "I do daytime things he can't, I feed him if necessary. Keep things running and even clean up after him if necessary," she explained as she ran her fingers through Lilly's hair.

"That doesn't sound like much of a personal life," he said relaxing a bit. "Always being on call for someone else." Gregory put the sacks on a side table and sat in the chair facing the women.

"No, it's actually not bad. I can travel, my days are my own, and a lot of the nights as well. Right now, with Marcus gone, I'm taking care of Lilly until she can find her own ghoul."

"Is she a new vampire? Is that why she is...uh," He didn't know quite how to ask without sounding stupid or offensive. He just nodded in Lilly's direction.

"No, she's been ill for a few days and needs blood more than she needs food." At the word food, Lilly disengaged and licked the wounds. Isobel rubbed the wrist and tried to smile at her friend. Lilly was still way too pale and her eyes were dull. "I'm sorry, are you ok?"

Lilly managed a weak smile at both. "It's okay, I'm doing well enough."

Isobel took the sack he had placed on the table and walked to the small kitchen/bar. She had made hot water in the coffee maker, hoping that he would be able to find the tea. She took the items out of the bag and gave a puzzled look at Gregory.

"I know, it's not exactly ginger tea but I couldn't find any. My grandmother sometimes uses the tea and when she doesn't have anything else, she uses regular tea and puts the ginger Altoids in the steeping cup. She swears it helps her stomach." He had made the tea for his grandmother many times, especially when she was fighting the effects of the radiation for the breast cancer that was, mercifully, found soon enough to allow for the lumpectomy.

"Oh, that's a new way of doing it, thank you for thinking of it!" Gregory was making a very useful addition to the group, Isobel thought.

"I can stay, you know, and become a ghoul for Lilly." The words fell out of his mouth before he could stop them.

Isobel turned away from the cup of water she was pouring and looked at him, "What?" She was so distracted she didn't realize until it hit her skin that she had poured the cup full and now was pouring the scalding water over her hand. She screamed, grabbing her hand, knocking over the cup in her attempt to get to the water faucet for cool water, smashing it in the sink.

Gregory was at her side immediately, Lilly coming up behind. "Isobel, are you ok?" Lilly was very concerned, the burn was already blistering across the top of her left hand.

"I'm...owww." Isobel was holding her hand, the pain making her stop moving.

"Here, Ms. Isobel." Gregory had the water on and gently guided her to the small stream of water he had started in the sink. The scream she let out as the water hit the burn showed him all he needed to know. "This is bad. We need to get you to the hospital, they need to treat this." He shot a look at Lilly, "Can you stay with her until I get the car?"

Just as he finished the question, a heavy knock on the door followed by the sounds of the key card and door opening told the women that the cavalry had arrived. Isobel had hoped to get Gregory to back down on the hospital trip but with Brian Kennedy storming the room, the chances were very slim that she would escape transport.

"Who screamed and why?" he demanded.

Isobel looked to Gregory and then Lilly, hoping the pain wasn't registering on her face. "I did. I was making a cup of tea for Lilly and I spilled it....broke the cup...got startled...screamed." She shrugged. That sounded lame and she didn't think she could get him to believe it.

"Sir, I'll just clean this right up." Gregory noticed she was holding her hands behind her and that told him all he needed to know. "No harm done. I'll fix everything." He said in a very efficacious tone.

Kennedy wasn't buying it, the scream was more than just startled. But the three people in the room when whatever it was happened weren't going to tell him anything but the cup breaking. "Okay, you do that, bellman. I will send Garcia around in a bit to check on you again." He turned to go and then turned back, "I don't suppose you've heard from Jesse Chamberlain or Duncan Morris."

"No, we haven't, they've not been back here since they left, a day or so back." Lilly answered.

"She's right, but you know that it's not unusual for Jesse to leave and stay gone, sometimes for weeks." Isobel added.

"True, but it's not like Duncan Morris to not check in on his regular schedule on duty. I've tried calling his cell and it goes to voice mail. The texts just go out and he doesn't answer. I'm getting concerned." He said almost to himself. Then he looked up to see the concerned expression on Izzy's face. "About Morris, uh…his battery must be dead. I'm sure it's nothing to worry about." A sharp intake of breath and his hand grabbed at his midsection. "Oh, excuse me. I need to go take something for this indigestion." He turned, mumbling "Dang Mexican food."

Isobel and Lilly exchanged glances, they knew it wasn't Mexican food. Kennedy was worried and that didn't bode well for anyone. Was Jesse in trouble or did he just find a good lay and not wanting to talk to them? Kennedy was right, it wasn't like any guard who worked for Lancaster to not check in. The outfit was run as tight as the military. As if she was reading Isobel's thoughts, Lilly raised an eyebrow.

"If they come back or contact either of us, we will let you know, Mr. Kennedy." Isobel reassured him. Kennedy nodded. They needed time to figure out what was happening, find Jesse and his guard and get them back here before the man called Castro, who would tell Marcus, and Marcus would probably jump back here on a rocket ship, loaded for bear.

"You do that. No more screaming, okay?" He said brusquely, returning to his usual timbre. "We don't want to get thrown out of here for noise." Kennedy turned and walked to the door.

As the door closed, Isobel started to sink to the floor. During the interruption, the burn had done more damage, the blister had grown. Gregory caught her and he walked her, with Lilly, to the couch.

"We need to get you to a doctor, Isobel. That burn…"

"No. There's another way." She turned to Lilly. "Lilly, I need to feed from you. Can you manage that for me? I know you've just gotten a little better but…"

"Of course I will. What's a little blood between friends, huh?" Both women smiled at each other, they knew theirs was becoming more than just a blood bond. "Neck or wrist?" She smiled at her friend.

"Vampire blood heals you?" Gregory tried to wrap his mind around that.

"Yes, I'm a ghoul and I've been exchanging blood with Marcus for years now. My body knows how to deal with it and it heals me." As she was talking, she tapped on Lilly's left wrist to bring the vein to the surface.

Gregory watched the vampire bite herself and hold it out to Isobel, who pulled it to her mouth and began to suck in the blood. As she did, he could see the burn retreating slowly from the back of her hand. He wondered why the vampires hadn't gone into medical practice, the healing that could be done with their blood could help so many.

There was a scratch and a muffled meow at the door. "Gregory, could you let the cat in?" Lilly said, "I'm a bit busy right now." As he opened the door, the tortoise shell cat walked in, two rats held in his mouth.

"You're helping her, I'm helping you. Who's the guy in the stinky suit?" Baron had heard the commotion and grabbed the dinner he was going to share with a cute little gold tabby, and came running back to the hotel to help.

"Baron Bast von Samedi, meet Gregory Freeman. He works here at the hotel and has been helping me take care of Isobel," Lilly replied. The cat looked up at the man and then to Isobel.

"Why is he here, now?"

"Because he's been told what is going on and he was kind enough to go get items to make me feel better, Isobel was worried. I am glad he was here so that I had help when Isobel was hurt."

Gregory was really confused, she was talking

to the cat like he was understanding everything she was saying. And he wondered what was up with the "because" statement, like she was answering him. Then he felt a hot feeling in his brain, there one minute and gone the next.

"*I just tapped him, if you are thinking you're going to be able to glamour him into not remembering, it's not going to work. He's much too strong for it to work.*" Lilly was surprised at the brazen action, it wasn't nice to intrude on other people's thoughts without permission. "*I didn't need permission either, he is open and not shielding at all.*"

Isobel raised her head, licking the blood from her lips. "I think that's enough. You will need to feed again very soon." Lilly lifted her wrist to her mouth and licked the holes, closing them.

"*Which is why I brought dinner. Would you kindly take these things out of my mouth and put them somewhere that they won't scurry away, it was a bitch trying to catch them.*"

Both women laughed. Gregory wanted to know what was going on but he wasn't going to ask what the joke was, just in case he was imagining things. A talking cat doing the talking clairvoyantly might just be in his own head.

"*You might want to get him up to speed on me, He's standing there wondering if he's crazy.*" Baron swished his tail as Lilly walked into the bedroom, retrieved a small box with a lid, and took the offered rats from him, carefully placing them in and shutting the top. The scratching inside the box indicated that Baron had dropped the glamoury on them once she got them in the box.

"Gregory, Baron is a vampire himself, as far as we know he's the only vampire animal in the world. He's been with Lilly for a long time, almost a hundred years now. He can talk to her mind-to-mind and he's just started doing it with me a few days ago. You're not crazy, we are talking with him, he asked us to explain him to you." Isobel explained while looking at her hand. It had healed from being very burned to just a slight redness, nothing oozing or blistered.

"Your hand looks much better." He turned to Baron, "I'm pleased to meet you, Baron. I can't talk with you but I do want you to know that being with me will not endanger either of these fine ladies. I know how to keep quiet about what I hear and see."

Baron let out a short meow. "*I also want to know what the heck he is bathed in, he smells like a New Orleans whorehouse.*"

"Baron!" Lilly cried out as Isobel dissolved into giggles. "You shouldn't talk like that with him right here in the room."

"*It's truth, I knew the Storyville women before I met you. Many of them bathed in lotions and perfumes and it was just horridly smelly. He smells like one of them.*"

Gregory kept staring at the cat and Isobel caught her breath and translated, "Gregory, Baron just said that you smell like a New Orleans whorehouse in that uniform."

"Oh, I'm so sorry," an embarrassed Gregory

began. "I really should have changed but I did not want to delay my delivery any more. I got into a slight altercation at the drugstore and got rolled in the lotion you smell on me."

As he spoke, Isobel's gaze panned over to the television, it was 10 pm and the local news was on. The lead story was about a possible hate crime that happened outside of Bonham Exchange, a stabbing that left one man dead and another in critical condition in a local hospital ICU. Both men were unidentified.

A cold prickle began to creep up the back of her neck. Something told her that this was not a stranger and she started to breathe faster. Before she could find the remote and back up to see the story again, Gregory's face came into view, his clothing disheveled and drenched in lotion, along with a police officer coated the same way. She found the remote and punched the volume up.

"...and when the security guard was placed under arrest, he fought back. Never a wise thing to do when dealing with our PD," smirked the female reporter. "The gentleman behind me," she indicated Gregory. The camera panned to catch his escaping image and quickly panned back, "is the one that the security guard was detaining for the officers, he actually turned the tables on him and helped the officers subdue the guard. The guard is now under arrest, he will be charged with assault on a police officer, destruction of property, unlawful confinement, and I'm sure they will come up with a few more charges." The video showed Gregory shaking hands with the officers and nodding. Isobel hit pause.

Gregory's cell phone started ringing and chiming with text messages all at the same time. There was no chance this story had not been seen by his boss, his friends, and worse, his grandmother. "May I take these in another room to answer them?"

Isobel pointed to the bedroom and the bellman retreated, shutting the door. The story about Gregory was good but the one she was concerned with was the previous story about the shooting.

"Lilly, I have a bad feeling about this." She said after they had re-watched the story. "Baron have you heard anything about this or know where Jesse is?"

"*I don't keep up with that man but I can go check the location, see what I can find out.*" He answered.

Gregory came out of the bedroom. "I have to report in with my boss. Then I have to explain things to my grandmother." Isobel and Lilly looked a bit alarmed. Gregory held his palm in front of him, "No, no. Don't worry. Not about you, about the whole drugstore thing. Neither of them are very patiently but Granny is just scary." He wrinkled his nose, "Phew, Baron is right, I do stink." Both ladies relaxed in relief.

"Of course, you need to take care of your own life right now. Please give our regards to both and, if your boss gives you any trouble, tell him that I want to talk to him, I will make sure he knows you were helping us." Isobel took his hand. "Be safe."

He walked to the door and opened it, Baron streaked out past his legs and down the corridor. *"Gonna check on things, I'll report back, then I'm going back to my hot date."*

Lilly called out and Gregory turned. She was holding the box with the rats in it. "Would you be so kind as to take these outside and set them free?"

He took the box gingerly and nodded. He walked down the hallway and took the staircase, he thought about her "I wonder if she turns into a bat?"

Chapter Eight

MARCUS WAS VERY aware that the paper he was fingering in his pocket was something someone needed to get to him from inside the castle but he didn't dare look at it before he reached the bottom of the mountain, Xun's reach was far.

He arrived at the stable, and exchanged the horse for his keys to the rental car.

"Mr. Lancaster, a moment please?" the older man waved Marcus into the kitchen of the residence. "I have been visited by someone from the Schloss and he asked me to switch you to another rental car and he returned the one you were driving."

Marcus didn't show any of the anger, frustration he felt at that turn of events. He suspected Xun may have had the replacement car tampered with so that an 'accident' on the treacherous snowy switchback road would not be questioned. That might take care of the Drachenfeur Sitzplaz problem, if not permanently, it would be an emphatic warning. Then the man handed Marcus another note with the keys to the car. He thanked the man, slipped him another few Swiss francs and walked out to the car, a bright red Masserati Quattroporte Sedan. He opened the door and slid behind the wheel of the vehicle. He was used to the handling of other European models, this particular make and model had a bad reputation for being a richer copy of a F.O.R.D, found on the road—dead. It figured that Xun would try to put him in a car like this. Someday he would pay the vampire back for all of the things he had pulled over the years. For being so old, he certainly was a childish, petulant, arrogant, prick. Marcus took limited pleasure in heaping insults on the bastard even when he was not around to hear. He smiled, and thought about the 'message' he had left for him on the bed.

He started the car and then pulled the first note out of his pocket and opened it.

Mr Lancaster,

I am intrigued by some of the things brought up in chambers. I think I have another business venture for you. There are dinner reservations at Stern un Post in Amsteg under the name Raul. David and I will meet you at the restaurant at 8 pm. I assure you that this is a lucrative endeavor for both of us. Raul.

Marcus was intrigued. He had no idea who Raul or David were but he had to spend the night in Amsteg anyway so it wouldn't hurt to meet them in a very public, well populated restaurant. As was his habit with any meeting, especially with mysterious ones, he always positioned himself where he could observe the entire while they talked. Then he opened the second letter.

Mr. Lancaster,

Raul again. I had reason to believe that your automobile was tampered with so I took the liberty of bringing you the Masserati and returning the Ferrari. As I drove down the mountain, I discovered that the brakes and the clutch had both been tampered with. The car is now sitting at the bottom of the mountain, in the river. The local constabulary was called and the report made of the 'accident'. I know the replacement car is correct, untampered with, and I've been keeping it under surveillance since dropping it off with Lars Geist. Please meet with me and David when you reach the Stern un Post and I will explain further. Travel safe, Raul.

Great. The Ferrari had fallen off the mountain with no brakes and with a different driver than was on the rental agreement. He wasn't going to pay for the rental or the accident, that was Raul's accident, let him pay for it. Marcus put the car into gear and drove down the hill very slowly, making sure to keep to the left and not ride the brakes too much.

To his surprise, he made it down and to the inn and restaurant in one piece in time to hopefully get a corner table. As he walked in, the place was busy but not crowded. He scanned the room to try to pick out the Raul and David he had been asked to find. When no one stepped up, Marcus walked to the back corner of the room and sat down behind the table. He had a perfect line of sight to the door. The waitress was a cute blond with curves in all the right places accented by the tight shirt and short skirt she was almost wearing. She smiled at him and he ordered a Bloody Mary and a dish of Papet Vaudois, the red sausage and potato dish that so many Swiss loved. He wasn't hungry but he wasn't sure who he was meeting with so he wanted to appear as human as possible.

He was well into the second Bloody Mary when two men strolled in and looked around, heading for the table that Marcus occupied.

"Hello gentlemen." Marcus said coldly. "So, which one is Raul and which one is David?"

The Hispanic man grinned, "I'm David, and this guy," he gestured at the thin Frenchman at his side, "Is Raul."

"So, Miguel de la Cruz and Phillipe Lecuyer, why the unimaginatively false names, which, by the way, neither of you are pulling off well." Marcus indicated they should sit down in front of him, their backs to the door.

"What we're doing here is not exactly sanctioned by the Council." Phillipe said, omitting the word 'vampire' because if someone was listening in, they would think him crazy.

"Really? So this is something you could not have come to me at the Schloss and explained?"

"You were guarded 100% of the time. There

was no way that Führer Xun would have ever let you speak to us, he already suspects our mast..uh,..bosses of hiding information from him." Miguel looked around to check if anyone else had heard his slip of the tongue.

"But yet you were allowed to come down the mountain to Amsteg and he doesn't suspect you of meeting me here?" With the plot to assassinate him back in the U.S, Marcus was going to be suspicious of anyone, anything that didn't meet the smell test.

"Oh, they suspect someone of coming to see you but we were able to plant a couple of peasants with stories of our wild day and evening rendezvous with the daughters of a land owner a town away. Right now they're trying to unravel who, looking for ghosts. However, that little surprise you left in your bed is going to cause the manure to hit the osculation device once it's discovered." Miguel reported.

"They have found her already?" Marcus sent another glance around the room, if they had found her, it would not be long before the Goon Squad made it back to Amsteg to look for him.

"Someone has, but we have it covered, for the moment anyway. Hansel is on our side of the plan and once he got you to the stables, he went back and checked on her. It's just a good thing you didn't kill her, Hansel's buddy, Adolph, is in love with her." Phillipe said cautiously.

Marcus looked from one man to the other. "Hansel? Hansel? Dewey is a Hansel?" He laughed, "It's a good thing I didn't know that when I was there, I don't think he would have stood for the ribbing he would have received. Why hadn't I met the Goon Squad before this trip?"

"Xun just brought them on board within the last six months. He's growing more and more paranoid and is beefing up his security detail to hopefully thwart the impending attack."

Who does he suspect of coming for him?"

"You, who else?" Phillipe glanced around just to make sure that no one was within hearing distance. "You're a vampire, you know how to kill vampires, you have a proven record of killing opponents, you have a standing army, and," Phillipe paused for effect, "You are the one person in the world who goes after him and is not afraid of him. Plus, the empty council seat is at stake."

Marcus mulled this over for a moment, then smiled, "I'm glad I get that far under his skin. It will make him much easier to beat when I do go after him. Who is Adolph?"

"Remember the one you've named Booger?"

Marcus smiled. "Booger's real name is Adolph? That's rich."

"We thought you would laugh at that. Of course, if Adolph sees your little present before it is cleaned up by our boss, you can be guaranteed that you will be hunted down." Miguel explained.

"Okay, this could get interesting pretty soon. So give me the short version, what are we discussing other than the previous stuff? I know this isn't a social visit and we're not just gossiping about the hired help."

Miguel and Phillipe looked around the room to

make sure someone wasn't lurking too close or acting strange. Neither of them gave a second look to a man in the corner of the room, sitting alone.

"If you're worried about being heard, you can take me outside to talk or I'll glamour anyone who is needing it. What is going on?" Marcus was begin to lose patience with the ghouls. He wanted to be back in Zurich and on his plane headed back to Jesse and Lilly.

"Our bosses want to give you an idea. They are intrigued by how the various vampires of the Drachenfeur line are able to do things that other mere vampires cannot. They are aware that you are not a friend of the Enforcer angels and that you would like to get them off the backs of the vampires. With your progeny's successful turning of an angel, they now have reason to believe that they can persuade, by force, angels to switch sides by turning them."

Marcus pondered that possibility. An army of fallen angels, at his beck and call. Of course, he would be the one to lead them, there was no one with his background in tactics, both ancient and modern. He had a feeling that this might work, if the right people were involved.

But who was involved so far?

"Other than Frederick and Jesus, which other schloss-furhers are aware of this proposal?"

Phillipe answered, "A total of six of the Council are in favor of exploring this possibility. If they, and you, find that it is an idea that has sufficient possibilities of success, we will be able to disclose their names.

"I have to trust you that this plan has backers who won't sell me out to Xun, or the angels?" This was not a good bargain on his side.

"That's right. Our bosses don't want to be left out to dry if you decide not to do this. You will have the other's assurances once you have a plan solidified. And the only way they will reveal themselves will be with a suitable sacrifice for a guarantee that you won't sell them to the angels."

Philippe looked Marcus in the eye, allowing the vampire into just the part of his mind where the proposal was. Frederick had laid the traps in other parts of Phillipe's memory so that if Marcus tried to push further into the subconscious, which he did do, he would not be able to move past the one memory. Not trusting Marcus, the ghoul's master also did not tell Phillipe the names of the other Council members.

As Marcus was working to find the way to discover the other conspirators, Miguel reached for the vampire to pull him away from the mind of the other ghoul. He never reached Marcus's shoulder. Without breaking eye contact with Philippe, Marcus seized the other ghoul's hand and broke it.

"Do not touch me without permission, got that?" The vampire then shifted his eyes from the first ghoul to the one trying not to make noise with the pain. "I will go along with this, for the moment."

"Good..." Phillipe started, but Marcus cut him off.

"Provided you tell me what guarantee the others want from me."

The ghouls exchanged glances, then Miguel said "The guarantee is knowledge of where all members of your line, retired or not, are and a blood sample from each of them. If you endanger the council, they will find your line and end it, killing every member."

Marcus laughed long and hard. "You are going to end the Drachenfeur line, everyone, including Vlad Dracul, one of the strongest of all the vampires?"

"Our bosses are prepared to kill him, he is old and not capable of working with others, he's taken to his coffin." Miguel continued.

Marcus wasn't sure that the ghouls weren't messing with him. There were legends about being able to find a vampire by using the vampire's blood as a homing beacon. As far as he knew, this didn't work. He began to object, "I won't do the blood part. It's not..."

Miguel talked over him, "It is required. Without it, our bosses will not reveal the others involved and disavow all knowledge of what you are planning. There is no negotiation."

"Then, gentlemen," Marcus stood up, "This discussion is over. I will not acquiesce to that demand.

"Sit down Lancaster," Phillipe said, "We can start with the list of names and locations."

"But no blood. That is not going to happen, ever." Marcus returned to his seat. "And, as for names and locations, I will provide the list, with locations, however, this information will not just be laid into your bosses hands. I will provide it, but it will be put in a Swiss safety deposit box.

The key will be sent to Frederick, and if they need to access it, the banker will have the other key and they will be required to sign in. This is the only way it will be done. If you don't agree, our negotiation is over. The decision needs to be made now, I will need to get the box arraigned and the information to the bank."

The ghouls put their heads together and whispered. As he listened in to their conversation, he looked over their shoulders and noticed the strange man in the corner was watching them intently.

"Okay, Mr. Lancaster, we will deal with the arrangement. The list needs to be in place before you begin the project. Our bosses will require that. Please advise us of the completion of the deposit." As he finished, Miguel stood and held out his hand.

Marcus declined to shake it. "I will let you know when things are ready. Good night."

The ghouls left through the kitchen which seems odd when they had entered through the front door.

He was thinking over everything while sipping the scotch the waitress had set before him after his visitors left.

Then the man in the corner stood up and walked over to him and sat down in one of the vacated chairs.

"Hello, Mr. Lancaster. I couldn't help but overhear your conversation. My name is Gery and I think I may have some assistance you can use."

Chapter Nine

THE NIGHT HAD been rough. Lilly was doing better than she had been, but Isobel had worried about Gregory. The reaction to the story of his actions didn't seem to be taken as heroism. He had been gone all night and Isobel continued to worry about him.

Of course, all the talk about the ghouls and the television coverage of Gregory's adventure only postponed the inevitable, Lilly would have to use the pregnancy test and, if she was right, there would be a whole new set of problems to deal with.

Isobel took a deep breath as she opened the soda she had pulled out of the refrigerator. No time like the present.

"Hey, Lilly. I have an idea about what is wrong with you."

Lilly looked over from the book she was reading. "It's just food poisoning, I've had it before, it will pass."

"Sweetie, I don't know that is what is going on." The feeling of dread continued to haunt her. "I have a way to check for what I think it is."

"Oh?" Lilly closed the book and laid it aside, "What do you suspect?"

Isobel didn't reply, she reached into the plastic sack and handed a box to the vampire.

"Clear Blue Easy Digital—2 Pregnancy Tests" She read aloud. "Tells you if you are pregnant four times faster than the high priced brands." She looked up. "Pregnant? Can vampires get pregnant? I wouldn't think we could because we died before we became a vampire."

"I thought that was true as well but everything you are experiencing points to pregnancy. It's worth checking out, anyway."

"You are giving me a box to use to tell if I'm pregnant?"

"The item is in the box." Isobel had spent time on the computer while her friend had slept, reading about pregnancy and birth in the 1800s to 1900. "We can now find out at home, very early in the pregnancy, without a doctor or midwife.

The look on Lilly's face spoke volumes. She was doubting the test but, more importantly, she was doubting the whole idea of a pregnancy. She opened the box and slid out a paper with pictures and a long packet wrapped in shiny paper. "What do I do with it?" She was dubious of the 'test', a doctor or midwife always took care of finding out if the girls at Mahogany Hall were pregnant. Most took the herbs Miss Annie gave them to get rid of the problem. Some wanted to keep the baby and ended up leaving the house because Miss Lulu did not, as she said, "Run a nursery."

Isobel took the paper and read through the

instructions. Then she told Lilly, "Take the foil off and sit down on the toilet. Hold the stick like this with one hand, and pull off the blue cap. Then start peeing and put the other end in the stream and count to 5, then stop and put it on the counter."

"I have to pee on it? How does that tell me if I'm pregnant" It sounded strange and not just a little unsanitary.

"Yes, you have to pee on it. Once you do, the urine mixes with chemicals on the stick and the words 'pregnant' or 'not pregnant' comes into the window. Then we will know."

Lilly got quiet, trying to figure out what would happen if she was. The baby would be Marcus's and she would have to deal with it. How?

"Lilly? Sweetie, are you okay?" The quiet was enormous.

The vampire stood up. "I won't be able to make a decision until there is something to decide." Taking the package, she walked into the bathroom and shut the door.

Isobel followed her but the act of shutting the door told her that Lilly wanted to do this alone so she backed away and sat down on the edge of the bed to wait.

Her mind a whirl of questions and emotions, Lilly didn't know a lot of things. Would the test work? What happened if it didn't? What would she do if it did work and she was pregnant?

The wave of nausea at the thought of having Marcus's child must have alerted Baron. She could feel the push into her mind link but she cut it off. She didn't want him to know about this until it was clear what was happening.

She removed the wrapper and prepared to find out.

D*AMN IT, WOMAN, what is going on there?"* Isobel heard Baron's voice in her head.

"We're trying to figure out why Lilly is sick. She's doing something that might tell us." Isobel spoke out loud, knowing Baron could hear the thoughts behind the spoken words.

Baron chuffed. *"Why does she shut me out of it?"*

"You are not the only one, Baron. I'm sitting on the bed instead of being in the bathroom to help her."

"The bathroom? Oh the human litter box that growls is in there with the nasty water bucket." Baron had been bathed once in the one back at Marcus's building and that was an experience he would not be repeating. It took weeks to get his fur to stop reeking of flowers. He heard a short laugh. At least Isobel seemed to be concerned about Lilly. *"You suspect something if you're trying something. What is it?"*

"I'm not going to be the one to tell you, that's Lilly's place. But I am hoping I'm wrong about it." Izzy knew that if it was what she thought, the trouble would just be starting.

"Kittens??? You're thinking she's going to have

a litter of kittens?" Baron almost shouted.

Oops, she had been a bit too specific while letting her mind wander. She had to figure out how to throw him off, this should be Lilly's place to tell or not tell.

"Too damned late, woman. You don't shield very well. I already know what you think." Baron's statement was punctuated with a growl.

"Don't let on that you know until we are sure. And it's not kittens in the humans, it's a baby and we don't have litters, we have one at a time, most of the time."

"There are women who have two, or three at a time, that's a litter." Baron knew better. *"So you think she's going to have a baby or three."*

"She has all the signs."

"She didn't go into heat. I would have known, women howl when in heat, she's has howled once but that was when that evil man, hurt her."

Baron's words struck Isobel. How would Lilly react to being pregnant with Marcus's child?

More important, what would Marcus do with the news? Isobel had never spoken about the possibility of getting pregnant and she used the pill to insure that if he could get her pregnant, he wouldn't. He didn't always have sex when he fed but Izzy knew that if he did have the sperm to reproduce, she would possibly get that way. She didn't know Marcus's stand on having children.

"He will be good to her if she's pregnant or I will make sure he regrets it. I would rather us go home to New Orleans and leave him forever."

"That will be up to Lilly, Baron. No one has the

right to make those decisions but her."

She heard the toilet flush and then the door opened.

Lilly stood in the doorway, blood tears flowing down her face.

"I'm pregnant."

Chapter Ten

M ARCUS HANDED THE card back to the stranger who had sat down in a chair where the ghouls had been just moments before. "I have my own procurement staff."

"Not like my procurement you don't. I have special skills you need to perform the activities you just agreed to." The man never moved.

Marcus had been watching this guy since he had sat down to wait on his ghoul contacts. The procurement guy had sat in the opposite corner and had been quietly observing the room, especially Marcus's table, all evening, drinking beer.

"I am not interested..." Marcus began.

At that moment, two mountains with feet pushed open the door and as they stepped into the room, the stranger waved his hand.

Everything stopped. The waitress turning with a tray of hot food, a man kissing the hand of a woman, another table with people in various poses of standing up from the table. Everything was frozen in time except the stranger and himself.

"What the hell?" Marcus turned his gaze back to the man sitting before him. "Well, you are partially correct anyway." The man grinned and a shiver crawled down Marcus's spine but he managed to remind silent. "You obviously recognize the two bulls who just came in. I believe you call them Huey and Booger. I think they are coming to talk to you about that message you left at the Schloss."

"How the hell did you know that? Who are you, really?"

"You have my card and you have already figured out where I'm from. Let's not waste more time. You will need help with this project and I've been sent by my boss to extend that help to you."

Marcus still had no idea what he was talking about. "This is a good parlor trick but I'm afraid you have the wrong man."

Your name is Marcus Lancaster, you were born in Tregaron, Wales on August 1, 1430 to Edmund Lancaster and Katherine Tabor. You died in the War of the Roses during the Battle of Towton, 1460. You..."

"Okay, that's all public record, if you know where to look. You don't know anything about what I was talking with my two colleges about."

"The ghouls were suggesting the vampires, which you are one, turn a bunch of angels into vampires and go to war with heaven. Right so far?"

Marcus couldn't get a good read on this guy's mind so he certainly wasn't going to discuss the plans with him. Something strong was keeping him from being able to glamour the guy and get him to leave.

"Ok, you won't answer me. Let me explain further. I'm Gery, personal procurement of Tartero, which you know as Hell. I work for the Queen of Hell, Lucifer.

"Anyway, as I was saying, you're planning a little rebellion and Lucy offers you assistance."

"I think I've got this, no need to sell my soul to the devil."

Gery laughed so hard his eyes glistened with tears. "Silly boy, you have no soul to want. The agreement between Lucy and her brother, the Archangel Mikhail was that the demon-spawn known as vampires would have their souls harvested when they were turned, either going to Tartero or Heaven, where they would be kept abeyant. Of course, that worked up until that progeny of yours screwed up the delicate but uneasy balance of the world with the turning of that angel. Do you know that angels, supposedly God's perfect creatures, don't have souls either? God evidently decided they didn't need them. One of the reasons why Lucy vied with Mikhail for the rule of Heaven. She wanted to convince God, by whatever means necessary get him to give angels souls like the mere mortals have. But the war didn't end like Lucy and her angels wanted. Mikhail gave her the choice of being imprisoned in Heaven or find another dimension. Of course, she chose leaving and Mikhail opened up the portal between Heaven and a distant dimension so she could take her rebellious angels and go away.

That bastard, Mikhail, made it out to sound like a wonderful choice, all fresh and green..."

"Is this going somewhere? If not, I have several things to accomplish..." Marcus didn't like to waste time and this delusional idiot with mad magician skills was wasting his. He moved to stand but an invisible pull forced him back down.

"Just sit still there, vampire. You need to know this stuff, it will be important later."

Marcus was already tired of this and his anger was beginning to rise. He didn't think this lesson was going to anything. Unable to bend this upstart to his will, Marcus thought he would try negotiation.

"Look, let's just cut to the chase, what do you want? Money? A Job? What?"

Gery sat still. Not moving, not talking, just staring at Marcus, who let the silence go on for a full half-minute, then stood up. The world around them was still in suspended animation.

"Have a good day. I've got things to do."

"Sit...down...and listen. You arrogant little prig. You need to know this IF you have any hope of survival." It wasn't a request. "I did not stutter, sit down. You are going to hear me out. Lucy sent me here to tell you things and I will not go back to her and report that I failed. So," he paused and pleasantly continued, "Now sit down and let's get this accomplished so I can go back to my work and you can to yours."

Gery waved his hand around the room. "First of all, do you recognize anyone in here?"

"Other than the Goon Squad, no..."

Gery's hand shot out toward the waitress, still standing with the tray, the food probably getting cold. Suddenly, bright brown wings appeared, the tips of which touched the floor. "Yep, it is exactly what it looks like, Alice is a Shadow Angel. She has been listening to you since you sat down. All that talk about turning angels, the army, all of it. Guess where she is sending that information after I let her go?"

Marcus knew exactly what it meant; Mikhail and the angels would know everything. "We have to get rid of her memories."

"Oh, you are a genius," He said sarcastically. "Have you ever tried to glamour an angel? I can tell you have no experience dealing with my good-two shoes brothers." Gery was heading some-where, Marcus just didn't know where, but he was now willing to hear more.

"Okay, if you are so smart, what is your sug-gestion?"

Gery smiled and a slight shiver passed through Marcus. "We could use her as our first test subject, clip her wings and you turn her."

Marcus gave the suggestion all the thought it needed, immediately dismissing it by holding up his right hand, the marked back held toward the demon. "There is no way I am forcibly turning someone."

"You are that afraid of the angels, you would give up a chance to start your vampire army of angels?"

"Cautious, not afraid." Being called a coward annoyed Marcus.

"No, afraid. I think we chose the wrong vam-pire to handle this plan. If you will excuse me, I will be going. We need to find another vampire, this time with the balls enough to handle the details of this project." Gery stood up, "No problem, I will take my..."

"Sit down, demon, this isn't over." Marcus growled, his fangs dropping. "I will not be turning her, I will, however, take her wings and her ring and you can package her for delivery to me in Houston. If I'm going to have a target on me, so will you and the other demons.

Gery smiled a smug smile and sat down. "Okay, that will be acceptable. Put the dentures away."

As Marcus pulled the fangs up, he had a short flash of insight. "You have been whispering to the Council. Frederick and Jesus didn't come up with this plan alone."

"Took you long enough to figure that out. The demons have the plan, we know what has to happen to make the angels into vampires and we can help you gain the angels themselves."

"You think you have everything to do this so why involve the vampires?"

The grin Gery allowed to spread across his face reminded Marcus of the enigmatic Cheshire Cat. "The demons cannot send enough personnel out of Hell to do this without being noticed. Those of us who can come and go unchallenged have many different things to do, we can't be getting this war started and stock the army while doing all the other things we have to do. You are the one of the only vampires we trust with this, given your past and capabilities."

"So, exactly what will the demons be doing in this endeavor?"

"We are going to help by supplying the bait. The only other enticement an angel will respond to, other than vampires who go rogue, is a demon. I am thinking of setting up a partnership. You build the operational vampire groups and I will supply the demons. You get your vampires into place and we can lure them to you for turning. We also can assist with plucking the bastards."

"And I suppose your boss is on board with this plan?" Marcus was beginning to think the demon might have a point, a fact that was more than a little disconcerting.

"I have the backing of the ultimate authority back home. I could not offer this without it. So, do we have a plan?"

The smile that went with that statement was the smile of confidence that Marcus had seen on many faces of the countless mercenaries and corrupt businessmen. "Yes, we have a deal." Marcus extended his hand for Gery to shake and seal the deal, looking the demon directly the eyes.

"The demon took the vampire's hand and met the stare. "Remember, vampire, demons are not susceptible to your glamoury. Save your energy, you'll need it." He released Marcus's hand, then indicated the disguised angel, "You need to tend to her before you go. While I can freeze actions of humans and ghouls, I cannot shield vampires and angels from hearing what other angels and vampires, or demons, are saying. If you leave her unaltered, she will immediately report to Heaven and repeat every word, verbatim, that we have said here. She won't even wait until the end of her shift."

Marcus stepped up to the woman while the

demon was talking. He slipped her ring off and deposited in one of his pockets. The angel didn't move but her eyes followed him into the kitchen. He went through the collection the chef had. The knife he started to choose was a sturdy boning knife, then he caught sight of the one in the sous chef's hand, a big, heavy cleaver. He wasn't sure how hard it would be to fillet an angel so he removed the cleaver, replacing it with the boning knife.

Once he was back at the angel, he took her tray of now cold food and set it on the counter.

"You might need a hand," Gery stepped up and seized her wrists, nodding at Marcus.

The angel's eyes went wide in fear, then in pain as the vampire seized her left wing and deftly cut it off. As he worked, she grew pale and began to shake.

"You might want to step it up there, Drac, we're losing her and I don't know if I can hold her up and keep the rest of the building in suspension. This isn't brain surgery, you know."

Marcus's growl shut the demon up as he set to task removing the second wing. The smell of the very sweet blood made his fangs lower again. His mouth watered and if he had less control on his thirst, he would have her neck in his mouth, draining her dry.

As each wing was severed, Marcus threw them on the floor. "Can you take care of this mess, right?"

Gery grinned again, "Just wait a moment, you will see."

As Marcus wiped his bloody hands on a table cloth, he popped two fingers in his mouth and moaned at the taste. "That is...wow."

"You don't have time to eat, we need to get out of here, I feel my energy flagging."

"Okay, let's get out of here. I have to drop the rental in Zurich and..."

"Nope, not driving. I've taken the liberty of filing a flight plan, leaving this morning."

"Won't work. It is too close to dawn for me to make it to Zurich, turn in the car, and still get to the plane on time. I will have to wait until dark."

Gery shook his head as he lowered the unconscious angel to the floor. He huffed as if having to explain the simplest concept to an obstinate toddler. "You don't have to drive, I'll deal with you and I'll send the angel ahead to Houston. Stand still." The demon closed his eyes, raised his arms and palms out, he whispered a word Marcus could not hear.

Marcus felt a sharp blow to his stomach and he doubled over. He opened his eyes and straightened himself. Pivoting around, he realized he was in his own plane. In Zurich. The pilot was standing in the cockpit door, checking his clipboard. He glanced up, surprised to see his boss. His eyes traveled to the closed door. "It's okay, Pete. Let's go. I trust we are ready, you've already done the refuel and walk-around?"

"Yes, Mr. Lancaster, right away sir. I'll clear us for take-off." The man started to turn into the cockpit.

"Pete, are the cell phones restocked?"

"I'll check?"

"No, you get this crate off the ground and I will check." Marcus stepped to the cabinets on the side of the hull and searched a couple of drawers.

He located two cell phones, uncharged, of course. A satellite phone. He punched in the number. First he had to warn Houston that Gery would be arriving with the package, then check on family in San Antonio. Cracking and static was the only response. "Damn it! What the hell is wrong with this thing?" he shouted at no one in particular, staring down at the seemingly useless instrument.

"Solar flares," Pete stuck his head out of the cockpit. "Communications are screwy all over. That's why it too me so long to get clearance. We're okay for take-off now, sir."

Marcus took his seat and strapped in, still glaring at the offending phone. While he now had a phone, he couldn't use it until they landed due to safety concerns. He could have the pilot get the tower to patch him over but with the solar activity, it was probably going to be a mess, much less the various country restrictions of that sort of activity, some countries would allow it and some wouldn't. And he wasn't in any mood to deal with that sort of red-tape crap. It would just piss him off even further.

He had no way to check in with Houston to let them know to expect Gery and his package. Or, more important, call San Antonio to check on family and the safety staff.

He needed patience and that was the one characteristic he was low on, if he ever had it to begin with. He was already making solid plans against the angels as the plane lifted into the air and toward home.

Chapter Eleven

G REGORY DROVE TOWARD the Menger in the pre-dawn light. The meeting with the night manager had not gone as well. Michael Johnson had seen the newscast and called him in. It wasn't his actions Mr. Johnson had the problem with, the fighting the security officer or getting the uniform messed up, it was the fact that he was very far out of the area when he did it. Unless there was compelling reason to go that far, the rules were to stay within a half-mile when running errands for guests. Mr. Johnson had even told him that wearing the uniform and name tag on camera was good advertising.

His words after that were etched into Gregory's memory. "Rules are rules, Mr. Freeman, and they are there for a reason. You violated the rules when you left the area to drive halfway to Kerrville, you were not available to our other guest for over an hour and a half. We cover this in orientation. So I have no choice but to let you go."

No choice. He had choices but had not opted to use them. Gregory had argued the points of the matter, trying to get Mr. Johnson to see what he had done to no avail. Mr. Johnson had taken his badge, the key cards and then discussed returning the uniforms when he picked up his final paycheck. Still in shock, he left and drove home to face the music with his grandmother. This was one thing he did not look forward to.

Georgia Mae Freeman had been mother, father, and grandmother to Gregory since he could remember. She had told him that his parents were in heaven, it was only later he found his mom had died in a crack house in Dallas and his father was in prison for life. She gave him a home and schooling, always involved with what he was doing. He had promised to take care of her and never let her want for anything. Now he had to go home and tell her that their only outside source of income, other than her Social Security checks, was gone. He would have to search for a new job somewhere else. How long it would take would depend on whether the general manager of the Menger backed up the firing, allowed him to have a decent letter of reference, and how many jobs were available that he could do. He had wanted to go to college but taking care of his grandmother had been his main focus, he could go to school some other time. Then there was the problem of all the refugees from Hurricane Katrina in town. Those who weren't going back to Louisiana would be taking jobs in the city, competing with him for the scant, mostly unskilled jobs there were in San Antonio.

He pulled into the driveway of their house, the lights were all off except the porch light, and his grandmother always left it on so he could see to come in. He carefully unlocked the door and pushed it open, trying hard not to wake his grandmother. He took off his shoes and tried to carefully tip-toe into his room along the aged wood floor that could wake the dead when they creaked. He thought he had managed to slip in when the little barking menace, Hitchcock, his grandmother's Chihuahua went into doggie alarm mode. As he tried to shush the dog, his grandmother opened her door, her baseball bat in her hand. Thankfully, she noticed who it was before she swung for the back fence like he had taught her.

She made coffee as he explained about the whole incident and why it ended up on television. She smiled at him and told him she was proud of him for handling the situation like he did.

Proud of him. That didn't cushion the blow when he let her know that he had lost his job over it. She had not lost her temper with him, but was walking around the small kitchen in her gown and house slippers, ranting about incompetent people who were out to stop her grandson from learning a trade so they fired him without cause. It was so loud, Percy Whitcomb, in the house next door, came over and knocked on the door to check on her and see if there was trouble. The action warmed Gregory's heart. Percy was interested in his grandmother, he had worked to help her keep the place up and teaching Gregory to do the work as well. He also kept asking his grandmother to let him move in, or come live with him, or get married. As he was leaving, he tried again with the offer. Georgia had replied to it with the same line she always used, "I don't need a man, I already had one and the only good come from it was Gregory." She waved her hand toward the entrance to the small frame house, "Now go on home Percy, I will see you on the porch at a decent hour when I'm dressed for company." Percy mumbled something as he headed out the door, once again rebuffed.

After trying to make him feel better, Georgia had sent him to take his uniforms back to the hotel and to thank the nice guest who had advanced him the money to take care of them, refunding what was left of the money with an assurance he would repay the rest as soon as possible.

He almost tried to park in the employee's parking lot but the arm blocking the entrance needed the company key card he had surren-dered. He drove to a pay lot nearby and pushed a five dollar bill into the slot with the number of the space he parked in. Walking along the almost deserted streets of downtown San Antonio, he worried about talking to the people in room 2052. He had been proud when asked if he would take care of the people in that room, a special honor for a valet to be singled out like that.

And with the firing, he wouldn't be able to explore the information about being a vampire or a ghoul further.

He rapped on the front door to the lobby and Chris Seward came to open it. "You're putting on there, Greg. You're supposed to use the back entrance like all the hired help, remember?" Chris always kidded him about being hired help even though Chris himself was as well.

"Nah, hasn't the rumor mill caught up to you yet? I got fired tonight." It was all he could do to keep from ducking his head in shame.

"No shit?" the guy shouted, the desk clerk looking up at both of them. Quietly he asked, "What happened? You were one of Sam Keplar's favorite valets."

"It wasn't Kepler who let me go, it was Johnson. He said that I went out of the approved area to get something one of the guests, the ones in 2052, needed. That's when I almost got arrested and was put in front of the camera as some kind of hero. Worst night ever." Gregory wasn't up for small talk but he was willing to slow down to talk to his friend.

"I missed a lot then, I had no idea. Anything I can do for you?" Chris was a good guy.

"Actually, yeah. Go get a key made for 2052 for me, I'm supposed to go back and give them something. They wanted me to just come in, not just knock, one of the people up there is sick." Gregory didn't tell him about the fangs and blood.

"Ok, give me a few. You go back to housekeeping and turn in the uniforms, see Mr. Johnson, and I will try to have the key for you when you're done." Chris smiled at his friend, clapping him on the shoulder.

Gregory was able to get the check but no bank would be open early enough to cash it before he had to head home. He walked back to the lobby and Becca Tinsley, the night auditor called him over.

"Hey Greg. Chris wants to get a key for you to 2052. You're not the registered guest and you don't work her any longer so I can't do that."

"Come on, Becca, I need to go see those folks, I need to explain something to them. They wanted me to have a key card for the room, I was given one by the man myself. I had to give it to Mr. Johnson when I got fired."

"Sorry babe, no can do." She turned away to enter a code to the computer.

"Okay, try this. Call up there and ask for Isobel. She's the assistant of the guy who rented the suite. Tell her that I'm down here and ask if I am supposed to get a key card to their room." He hoped he wasn't going to get a no on that, the night would be complete if he did.

"It's 5:45 in the morning. I will not call up and wake those people on a hunch you might be telling the truth. I would lose my own job if they complained to Mr. Kepler or Mr. Johnson."

"You're killing me here, Becca." Greg looked around. "Okay, I have another idea. See that guy in the chair in the atrium? He's one of the security detail for the people in 2052. If I ask him, would you take his word for it?"

"Security detail, who do we have up there that requires private security?" Becca checked the computer. "Oh! Mr. Marcus Lancaster of Lancaster Industries is up there? He has more money than the U.S. Mint and he's better looking too. He wants you to just come in and talk?"

"Yes, he does, although he's not up there, he left his entourage here and said he would be back soon. He paid me in advance to help them out while he was gone."

"I don't know…" Becca was still unsure of the whole thing. She didn't want to lose her job to a former employee wanting to do something against the rules.

Gregory didn't wait for her to make up her mind. He walked down the lobby and up to a large man reading a romance novel. He had to stifle a laugh at the sight by clearing his throat. The man looked up, folding the page corner down.

"What can I do for you, sir?" The man stood. "Wait, I recognize you, almost didn't since you're not in your uniform. You are the valet Mr. Lancaster hired to help our folks while here, right, Gregory Freeman."

"Yes sir, I am. I no longer work for the hotel, long story, but I need to go up and speak with Miss Kincade. Is there any way you can get me in up there. I had a key card but it had to be surrendered when I got fired."

"They fired you? On what grounds?"

"The incident when I went to purchase supplies for Mr. Lancaster's people. I wasn't supposed to be that far away from the hotel when on shift. I got caught when the television covered it.' It seemed everyone knew what happened, the security guard in front of him didn't ask why the television covered him.

"They canned you for that? What the hell is

wrong with these people? You did something heroic and they fire you for it? Let me call up to Miss Isobel and see if she minds you getting a card and going up." The guard pulled out a cell phone and punched a button. As he talked, Gregory tried not to eavesdrop but the sounds coming out of the phone were not happy and his heart sank. Not only had he screwed up the job, he had ruined the chance to get to work for one of the richest men in the world.

"WHAT??" The guard held the phone away from his ear. Gregory heard a door open and then slam shut.

"Tell Gregory to wait right there, I'm coming down."

"Yes Ma'am." He disconnected the call. The big burly guard suddenly looked a lot smaller and not a little frightened. He swallowed hard, "Oh boy, she's got a whole load of mad on, I'm glad it's not me she's set her sights on." He smiled weakly at the confused and rather apprehensive young man. "Mr. Lancaster keeps her around as his female bulldog, if one of the guys can't get through to someone, he sends her in and things get handled." He shook his head.

The elevator opened and the energy resonating from the woman exiting was positively electric. She walked over to the guard, nodded to him, "Thank you for calling, Stanley." Then she turned to Gregory. "What happened? They fired you for going on an errand for us? What the hell is that?" He wilted under the anger emanating from her. She noticed it and reached out to touch his arm.

"Gregory, sweetie, what happened?" Her kind smile reminded him of his grandmother's.

"I got fired for going out of the area to get it. I wasn't supposed to be up there to buy it. I should have purchased it down here within a couple of miles. Mr. Johnson said that the television coverage was great advertising but he had to fire me for going out of bounds."

Isobel frowned. "Why did you go up there if that is the rule?" Gregory didn't strike her as a regular rules scoff.

He looked down at his shoes, the blush starting at his shoulders and going north fast. He cleared his throat and then mumbled, "I was embarrassed to be seen getting one of the items and so I went where I thought no one would know me. I know it's a stupid excuse but..."

"That's it? They fired you over a preg...a woman's item? Oh good grief, where is this special person?" She looked around and then started to walk to the desk.

"Wait, Miss Isobel, I want to talk to you privately before you go to the desk. Would that be possible?" He looked between her and the guard. She nodded and Stanley Moore walked off toward the elevator.

Once he was out of ear shot, Gregory looked back at her. "I don't want to go back to work for Menger. I don't think there is a future for me here. I mean advancement. People with more education have been promoted and I'm the same as I was when I started. I've spent some time tonight thinking about what you and Miss Lilly were telling me. I want to apply for the job of ghoul for Miss Lilly. She seems to need someone to help her and I wouldn't mind the work."

"Uh, okay. Not what I expected. You realize that you will be on call all the time and even while you will feel the pull to a more intimate relationship, the vampire, in this case Lilly, has the control. If she doesn't want intimacy, you won't be going there. You are going to be on nights with her and trying to sleep during the day between handling errands and any other requirements she has."

"I understand that. I know what you've said and I watched how you work with her. I am a night person anyway and I know how to behave, this job notwithstanding. I will be a good hand and work hard. I really want to be a ghoul." His smile was almost electric and his expression was of such eager to please innocence. If he had been a puppy, his tail would have been a wagging blur and Isobel knew he was telling the truth. She still stared at him in total incredulity.

"I don't think you have any idea what you are asking. You would have to move away from San Antonio, are you willing to move away from your grandmother? If she falls, your commitment will be elsewhere so you won't be able to come back to help her. To visit, yes, but not permanently."

"I understand," he countered. "She has Mr. Whitcomb next door. He's been fluttering around here for years. But she won't show him no nevermind. With me gone, maybe he will have a chance."

Isobel continued, trying to discourage the obviously stubborn young man. "You will not be able to talk to anyone about this...no one? You will have to make yourself a new identity. You will not only spend a lot of time away from the family you love and you will have to, eventually, walk away because you will age much slower that the average human. And you will have to stay away until they die and you can visit the grave. This is not glamorous, it's not "fun" and once you are in it, that's it. No changing your mind. No undoing it. There's no getting fired, no quitting, you're in it until your vampire dies, you die, or your vampire gets another ghoul and relegates you to just the hired help. No matter what, you are always on call and you cannot tell anyone about why." She was trying to impress on him the finality of the drastic decision he was trying to make.

"If you are trying to dissuade me, it's not working. I know it's going to be work and I'm willing to do it. I also have no other family than my grandmother. I've lived with her to be able to help her. My mom died when I was young and she raised me. I've been paying her bills, the Social Security doesn't cover anything much. She doesn't live rich, she doesn't want to be rich, she likes our neighborhood, she was born and raised in the house she still lives in. I would need to have some pay so I can keep sending her money. I don't know how many more years she has but I want her to be taken care of and not have to worry." He was looking her in the eye now, trying to convince her that he would take care of his grandmother no matter what. "And of course, Mr. Whitcomb will be there to keep her company, mow the lawn, and do the honey-dos." He smiled at the thought of the two of them sitting on the porch, drinking lemonade, and watching the sunset.

He had thought about it a lot, in a very short time. Isobel's heart melted. She liked this kid in spite of herself. Lilly needed someone to give her blood on a regular basis, especially because she seemed to not be able to eat food with the pregnancy. It might be a good solution. To his credit, he didn't break into her thoughts, instead standing still, still smiling, and watching, imaginary tail wagging, she stifled a giggle at the image.

Marcus may not approve but, at the same time, Lilly, even as progeny, was her own woman and would fight for whatever she wanted.

So she made a decision.

"Ok, here's the plan, I will get you a key card and put you on the list for staying with us. Lilly needs a feeding. We go up, you help her and then she will decide on whether you can work for her. It's her decision, not mine. You also need to know that Marcus is very protective of Lilly and he could put a screeching halt to all of this and tell you you're not working for her. If that's the case, Marcus will glamour you and send you packing.

"But Baron said I couldn't be...glamoured?"

"I think he meant Lilly couldn't. But Marcus, he's a whole different story. If he can't glamour you, well, let's just say that the alternative would not be pleasant."

She let that sink in and then continued, "Also, I'm going to tell Brian Kennedy to run the background check on you again, this time as he would for any Lancaster Industries new hire, if something crops up in your background, you may not be working with Lilly. Any questions?"

Gregory knew it was a big chance of failure but he was willing to take it. "I appreciate the chance, Miss Isobel. I.."

"Please, I know you're being polite but it's just Isobel, or even Izzy. And it's just Lilly. I would err on the side of caution with Marcus, however. You are definitely going to be a surprise and since Marcus doesn't like surprises, be safe and respectful with the whole Mr. Lancaster and sir and stuff. Let him tell you if you should use just his first name or the whole mister thing. Jesse, Marcus's ghoul, will just be Jesse, even if he says otherwise. He's an interesting guy, tends to think he's in charge so if he gives you trouble, let me know and I'll handle him." The more she talked, the more comfortable she became with this spunky young man.

"Yes ma'am. I am wondering if I will have time for a paying job on the side. I am supporting my grandmother and I need to continue to send her money no matter where I am."

That, in her mind, sealed the deal. He was hired as far as she was concerned.

"No outside job needed I can assure you, you will definitely not need to have one. You will have a salary over and above your living expenses, which are always paid by the vampire, along with the health and dental. Your grandmother will be added to the retiree's fund. We have other employees who have aging parents and they are paid a stipend as if they had retired from Lancaster Industries, it's company policy. We also set up the tax shelters to handle the stuff that the government will start trying to charge her about the funding we will be providing, keeping them from trying to take it all away from her. So you don't need to worry about her."

"Thank you, Mi...Isobel. Thank you for that." He had to forcibly keep himself from jumping and hugging her in relief.

"You're welcome, let's go get you that key."

Chapter Twelve

O H THE WAY toward the King Ranch suite, Isobel stopped a few doors down and knocked on the door, which opened into a room full of computers and equipment that Gregory had never seen before. A tall, red-headed man stood in front of them and he was scrutinizing Gregory to the point of making him feel like a bug on a microscope slide.

"Brian, this is..." Isobel started.

"Gregory Michael Freeman, age 21. Born in San Antonio on May 18, 1984, raised by his grandmother, Georgia Mae Freeman. Parents dead. Went to Brackenridge High School, graduated third in his class with a 4.04 average. One speeding ticket in 2000. Blood type B negative. Employed at the Menger part-time 2001. Upon graduation in 2002 full time until last evening."

The rundown of his live in such cryptic terms by this man was disconcerting, Gregory didn't know how he got the information. Suddenly he felt like he was standing there naked.

Isobel was amused at Gregory's startled expression. "Brian, that's enough. I know you did the background before we hired him as valet. Now I need you to do it again, the way Mr. Lancaster wants when he's hiring someone permanent. He's being considered for the assistance team as Lilly's personal assistant. As quickly as possible, please. We need the report before we head for home. Thanks." She smiled.

"Yes m'am. I will get right on it." Brian started to turn toward a computer, then spun back, "Mr. Freeman, since you will be working on the team, you need to be aware that we will require you to be accompanied by security whenever you leave the hotel. I will assign Carter Hughes to you."

"Thank-you Brian, I owe you on this one." Isobel smiled at him.

"No problem, Miss Isobel. It's my job."

Isobel shepherded Gregory into the hall and closed the door.

"Isobel? Am I needing to be followed around because you do not trust me?" It was a logical question to ask.

"No. There have been threats from one of the Industries competitors. Death threats. So Marcus isn't taking chances with anyone on the team, each of us has our own personal guard. You'll like Carter. He's a big man, a former Marine and tough as nails."

"Is that the guard from downstairs who is reading that bodice ripper novel?" It was hard to imagine a tough Marine reading that stuff.

"No, that's Stanley Moore. He wasn't a Marine, he was Navy S.E.A.L. And yes, he's almost famous for liking to read the romance novels. The guys tease him unmercifully at times and I thought Jesse was going to have a stroke when Stan folded down a corner in the book to mark his place, he started turning red and screeching 'book abuse' at the top of his lungs." They both laughed at the image, even though Gregory didn't know Jesse very well, only seeing him once when he escorted the group to the room the first time.

They entered the suite to the sound of retching. Lilly was sick again. Both raced toward the sound. She was kneeling on the floor, holding her hair back with one hand and clutching the porcelain bowl with the other. She glanced up looking so forlorn and immediately turned back to retch again.

"Oh sweetie, I thought we were past that " Isobel sounded tired.

"I was, but I got thirsty and I can't stand even the thought of bagged blood, warm or not. So I grabbed the orange juice and drank some....mistake."

"Ewwww, orange juice reruns, that is horrible." Isobel began to search the makeup bag for anything to help her stomach. She turned and saw that Gregory had left the room, probably has a twitchy stomach, she though.

Isobel was trying anything she could think of to help her friend, Gregory came in with a wet dish towel and a warm cup of tea that he set down on the vanity. He placed the towel on the back of her neck and rubbed her temples, saying soothing things softly.

It worked, soon she sat back and took the tea

that was offered. "That orange juice sure wasn't a good idea but Gregory, thank you for this."

"You're welcome. My grandmother always said that a cool cloth on the back of your neck and warm ginger tea for a sour tummy will calm things right down."

"A very wise lady." Lilly sipped the tea.

"That's truth. It cannot be comfortable on that floor, let me help you up and let you sit on the couch in the front parlor." He took the tea and handed it to Isobel, then offered both hands to Lilly and helped her up.

"You called it the parlor, that's a word I haven't heard since my days in New Orleans. How did you learn that name?" Lilly took the tea back and sat down on the sofa.

"My grandmother again. She called it the parlor, I picked it up from her. And I used to get laughed at for using it. But Grandmother Georgia was very formal with her speaking, she said it was a sign of good breeding." He found himself sitting next to Lilly, rubbing her hand.

"Well, she is correct." Lilly said, remembering the formality of Miss Lulu's parlor, Storyville was so far away, in both time and distance. She handed the empty cup to Isobel and her stomach churned and growled spectacularly. She grabbed at her waist, "Oh, I'm so sorry." She looked at Isobel and Gregory apologetically. "If I hadn't drunk that orange juice, I'd still be thirsty but at least I would have something in my stomach."

Isobel stepped forward, "No," Lilly said. "I've taken too much from you already." She smiled weakly at her friend. "But thanks." She looked at Gregory, "I guess I shouldn't have had you free the rats Baron brought me."

Isobel nodded to Gregory, who spoke up. "Lilly, I've talked to Isobel about you and what you need. I would like to, if you agree, to be your ghoul and assistant. I'm healthy, drug-free, and strong, I can do the job."

She looked from Gregory to Isobel, "Does he have any idea what he just said?"

"Yes, Lilly, he does. We've talked with him before, remember? He is willing to do it and you need a regular source of blood. We've got the background check going now, and Carter has been assigned as his guard. What do you think?"

"*Uh, Isobel, woman do you really trust this guy? I am far enough out that I'm not going to make it back tonight. I have a stash of rats, a sweet kitty to curl up with and I will be fine. But I will give all that up, try to get back through the light, if you need me to check this guy out.*" Baron had been listening.

Both girls laughed. "Baron, he's fine. We're going to be fine. You've met him, you know that this man is very nice and he's been kind to me. We are keeping him." Lilly clinched the young man's hand.

"*Well okay, if that's what you want to do. This group is getting too crowded. I miss our little crypt in the cemetery. Too many people.*" Baron chuffed his disgust.

"Baron, did you find Jesse and Duncan Morris? Brian is hasn't heard from them and he is angry and wondering where they are and I have to admit, I'm getting concerned too. Jesse is an inconsiderate jerk, at times, well, most of the time, but this is just not normal. Brian's people always check in on a regular basis, since Duncan hasn't, something is very wrong." Finally, Isobel voiced what she had been feeling and thinking for hours.

"*I found some blood that smells like him, another patch of blood that I don't recognize. It was in the alley next to the building you said he went to. I forgot to tell you, I was going to but this little Siamese kitty twitched her tail and I forgot to report that.*"

"When was this?"

"*Not sure. All the people were leaving the building. It was strange, I was out there looking for him and there were people rutting in the bushes. People don't rut outside, I thought.*"

"Baron! So it was just after two, then?"

"*Do I look like I wear a clock on my paw?*" Baron was anxious to get back to his pretty companion.

"Well, it was at least four hours ago, no sign of him?" Isobel's heart started pounding.

"*Just the blood. I know the obnoxious friend of your boss was there and bleeding. I don't know but maybe the other blood was his guard, maybe?*"

"Okay, go have your fun and be back here tomorrow night to check in. Everyone is going to be sticking close to the hotel until we find Jesse." Isobel turned and looked into Lilly's eyes, she had heard the discussion. Even if he was a 'jerk' as

Isobel had called him, Lilly still didn't like the thought of anyone being hurt or in pain, not even Jesse.

"*Can I bring a friend and dinner?*" Baron used that voice that he used when he was trying to get something he wanted.

"No friends and we've got dinner here for you, be here."

"*Let me think about it, I'll call when...*"

"Cat! You do what Isobel wants, I don't have time to deal with you and your attitude right now." Lilly sounded like she was angry, something she only rarely was.

"*Oh, all right. Good night!*" He cut the link petulantly.

Gregory had released Lilly's hand when she had scolded the cat. She had a temper and he didn't want to be in the way.

"Sweetie, I'm going to start calling the hospitals."

"And while she's doing that, you need to eat to calm your stomach." Gregory tried to soothe his new vampire and tempt her to eat.

"Look, I am not fragile, and even though my name is Lilly, I'm not a delicate flower. Please don't treat me like one."

"Yes m'am. But I am here to take care of you. Isobel..."

"Lilly," Isobel interrupted him, "He has offered to help. The ghoul issue can be decided later, but right now?" She pleaded, "Please?" Izzy was growing more concerned by Lilly's actions and mood swings. With no experience and nothing written to educate her on vampire pregnancy, everything would have to be dealt with as it came up.

"Oh all right." Lilly practically spit the words. She took Gregory's hand very gently. She studied his face for any sign of fear or discomfort. Seeing no apprehension, she said, "Sorry, this might hurt a bit."

"Don't worry, Miss Lilly. I'm tough," he said reassuringly.

"Just Lilly, please." She lifted his wrist to her moth, bit, and began to drink the sweet liquid life.

Gregory's head spun, the bite had hurt at first but then he started having the most intense desire he had ever had, wanting to take Lilly in his arms and make love to her. Or fuck her blind, whichever she wanted. He could not stop the moan that escaped from his lips. He let the emotion ease him into a dream state where he indulged in the sex fantasy, relaxing into the feelings.

He had no idea how long he had been gone but his arm was at his side, no holes to see. Lilly was over at the desk where Isobel sat crying, trying to soothe her. He got up and found he was woozy from the feeding but managed to stay on his feet. "What's wrong?"

"They've been found." Lilly said.

"Duncan was shot, he's dead. Jesse's in the hospital, in a coma. They don't know if he will survive. Whoever did this took their identification and just left them in an alley, that's why we couldn't find them. The police are on their way here." Lilly shook her head defeated. "You and Isobel are going to the hospital, I have to stay here because it's daylight and I can't go." A bloody tear escaped and made a red trail down her face.

Gregory wiped the tear and impulsively put the bloody finger in his mouth. He felt a small surge go through his body.

Isobel took a deep breath and calmed enough to speak. "Before the police arrive, Lilly, do you want Gregory to be your ghoul?"

Lilly and Gregory looked questioningly at one another. It occurred to them both at this sounded like a marriage.

Seeing their expressions, she went on to explain. "This is not a marriage, but it is a lifelong commitment. I want to make sure each of you enter into this association of your own free will." She had not been offered this choice and she wanted to make sure that the decision was theirs and entered into voluntarily. She restated the question, "Lilly, do you want Gregory as your ghoul?"

The vampire nodded and Isobel tried not to smile, "Gregory, do you want to be Lilly's ghoul and serve her?"

"Yes." He said, nodding.

"Lilly, you need to let Gregory feed from your wrist. Your blood is so much more powerful, even this soon after feeding, he will gain strength and health from it. Just a little blood, though," she cautioned. "Gregory, count to five while drinking and then pull away. It's going to be hard to do but you have to do it."

Lilly stiffly raised her arm and bit down, blood instantly welling on the holes. She held it out to Gregory, who put his mouth over the wound. As he counted to five, he also wondered if Lilly had the same sort of reaction when giving blood that he had. If so, this might just be a relationship, no matter what Isobel had said.

The authoritative rap on the door caused the dog to explode into a fit of furious barking. Lilly reacted, pulling her arm back and putting it in her mouth, cleaning and healing it. She looked at Isobel who nodded toward the sink. Lilly washed her face as Isobel walked to the door. She unlatched and opened the door to reveal a uniformed officer and a man in a gray pinstripe suit with a badge around his neck. Behind them was Brian Kennedy and Carter Hughes. None of the men looked particularly happy to be there.

Lancelot continued barking and spinning, excited to have visitors. Gregory tried to shush him and Isobel put herself between the yapping dog and the opening in case the dog made a break for the hallway. The two men looked at the animal, not taking a step.

"Heel, Lancelot!" Isobel said over the din. Lancelot dutifully stopped and trotted back to her, sitting down looking like he was unhappy with the command. He wiggled and began to whine, wanting to go play with the newcomers.

"Sorry, this trip has messed up his training."

The man in the suit didn't even wait for a greeting. "Isobel Kincade? You reported Jesse Chamberlain missing, then informed us he was in

University Hospital?"

"Yes, sir. We had missed him, oh, where are my manners, please come in."

As the four men filed inside, Isobel closed the door. She looked over at Gregory who was standing next to the bedroom door in an attempt to remain and observe.

After the police and security were seated, "I am Detective Major Dillon and this is Officer Matthew Oliver.

As interrogations went, this one was almost television scripted, who, what, when, where, the usual. At least the detective didn't say "Just the facts m'am". Isobel stopped her inner chatter and continued, her voice shaking from the emotion. "Jesse had gone out to party at a few bars and Duncan Morris went with him as his bodyguard. When they didn't returned or call in, we got concerned, especially after the local news report on the fight nearby. I called around and found Jesse. The officer at the hospital said that they had found a man badly beaten and barely alive in the alley of the Bonham Exchange. That is Jesse Chamberlain. The other man had been shot twice and was dead near the alley entrance. That was Duncan Morrison."

The uniformed officer was taking notes as the detective asked, "Why do you need bodyguards? Just what are you doing that you would need one?"

Brian took over, "The ladies and the two victims are employees of Lancaster Industries." Lilly shot him a puzzled look. "The company has had takeover threats as well as physical threats from Nelson Mishkoph, owner of Pricom, which is a rival security company. We were sent here with them to make sure that Mr. Mishkoph did not try to harm one or all of them during the chaos of the bug-out in front of Hurricane Rita. Mishkoph threatened anyone associated with Mr. Lancaster, at all levels of life."

"And who are you, exactly?"

"Brian Kennedy, head of the... this security detail. Duncan Morris is one of my guys."

"Lancaster Industries, the security, and some say mercenary company owned by Marcus Lancaster?"

"Yes, he owns the company." Brian had decided to be the spokesman for the group, a job Isobel would normally handle. But he saw she was in no shape to be patient for questions.

The uniformed officer tapped the detective and whispered, then indicated that Lilly and Gregory should follow him. He led them into the bedroom and began to shut the door, however Carter Hughes stopped it and then stepped it into the room around the officer. As the door closed, Carter noticed the detective hadn't missed a beat in the questioning in the main room.

"You think this Mishkoph guy was the one who had your guy beat?"

"It's possible, maybe even probable." Brian answered for Isobel, he could tell that she was very effected by the news that Jesse was in critical condition. She sat still, listening, but staring at her hands, then looking up at the door like she was hoping this was all a bad dream.

"Okay," he said, writing it down on a pad he had pulled from his pocket, "What are the roles of these people with the company?"

"Isobel Kincade." She looked up at her name was given by Brian and then looked down at her hands again. "She is Mr. Lancaster's administrative assistant. The other lady is Lilly Marchantel, a guest of Mr. Lancaster. The young man, who went into the other room with your guy, is Gregory Freeman, a new hire who is going to be working with Lilly as an assistant.

AS THE QUESTIONING continued in the other room, Officer Oliver began to question Lilly and Gregory.

"So, Mr. Freeman, you were the man who was in the altercation up near University hospital and at that time, you were working for this hotel, correct?"

"It was, however I no longer work for Menger Hotel, I have been hired by Lancaster Industries to be an assistant to Miss Lilly here."

"So why the sudden change?"

Gregory wasn't sure where this line of questioning was going but he was sure he wasn't going to like it. He had met cops like him in the neighborhood and they were all big egotistical pricks. He fought to keep his temper. "I got fired for my trouble, I was out of the approved area when that happened."

"Why were you out of the area?"

"I was getting items for Miss, uh, Isobel and, to be honest, I was not wanting to buy things here."

The officer looked directly into Gregory's eyes, "And why is that?"

It was obvious that the guy was trying to get into Gregory's head, "Quite frankly, that is none of your business. I already gave a statement to the police tonight and you should pull that paperwork if you want that information." He could tell the officer was more than a little annoyed with that answer.

"I can do that but I want to hear it from you."

Lilly looked up, fixing her gaze on the face of the officer," He was out buying a pregnancy test for me. There's no need to question any of us about Jesse's attack because we were all here at the hotel."

"And who are you?"

"I am Lilly Lenora Marchantel and Mr. Free-man is my assistant and driver."

"So, are you pregnant?" The officer was obviously trying to build a chance at being a detective, and Gregory thought he was trying a bit too hard.

Lilly came back at him without hesitation. "You are not entitled to ask me that and I will not answer. Now, my address and job title, and information such as that, I will comply. However, the intricacies of my personal life are not your concern, nor are they germane to this case." She was used to dealing with police in her former life, they no longer scared her. She could be respectful without seeming to be rude.

"You will answer my questions, here, or down at the station. You really do not want me to take you to the station, do you?" How dare the little slip of a girl dismiss him like this.

Catching his eyes, she stared into them and said slowly and deliberately, "You only need our name, address, and identification. You know that we are innocent of any wrong doing and you wish to get us to the hospital as quickly as possible."

Gregory stepped past Carter, opened the door, and ushered Lilly back into the living area.

Lilly stepped into the room looking for Isobel's attention. She was surprised to see that Isobel had shut down, staring into a corner beyond the detective's head. Instead of continuing to talk to the now docile officer, she walked over and put her hands on the ghoul's shoulders. It was a surprise that Isobel would react like this, she always seemed to be in charge and never flustered.

Lilly leaned down and whispered into her ear, "It's okay, we will get to the hospital." In response, Isobel looked over her shoulder into Lilly's reassuring face and laid her hand on Lilly's.

The detective had stopped talking and was watching the women.

"Sir, you may continue to speak with Mr. Kennedy, we are going to the hospital. Mr. Kennedy will provide you with any information that you require. Miss Isobel needs to be at Mr. Jesse's side, without any further delays." Lilly knew police would usually agree to a reasonable request if asked politely.

"I would appreciate your patience while I finish my questions." Detective Dillon motioned for Lilly to sit down.

"Sir, I am not feeling well and I am also allergic to the sun, a condition common in my family line. If I wait, I will be unable to accompany Isobel to the hospital and she needs me with her."

The detective began to stop her from leaving but changed his mind. "Okay, you can go but do not leave town while we sort this out. I will continue my interview with Mr. Kennedy and Mr. Freeman."

"Sir, I am Lilly's assistant. She has not been in Texas very long to know our Texas way of doing things. I will keep you informed of our whereabouts and anything we remember. Thank you for allowing us to check on Jesse, he and Isobel have worked together for a long time, they are more like siblings at times, including the bickering." Gregory offered the detective his hand.

The detective stood and shook Gregory's hand. "Thank you for your cooperation. I hope your coworker gets better soon."

Brian spoke up. "Gregory, I'm sending Carter here with you. I've sent a text to Payton Naismith and Edward Garcia, they will meet you in the lobby. No one is to go anywhere without a guard, even the bathroom. They will stand at the door until our women come out. Additional local security has been called and are already guarding Jesse."

"Now wait a minute, Mr. Kennedy, the San

Antonio Police Department will be handling the security at the hospital, we have an officer there now." Detective Dillon said.

"I understand that and usually would agree that is enough. But the person in that hospital bed isn't a regular patient who needs guarding, he is the partner to Marcus Lancaster, who has a major mercenary in town trying to intimidate him. If I did not assign a Lancaster team to him, I would be fired by dark. We won't be in your way but we have our orders and if someone tries something up there, it may be a race to see who can reach out and touch the guy first," Brian grinned, "And my people are very competitive."

From what he had heard, Lancaster's employees were top notch and he had no doubt they were competitive as Kennedy said. "Okay, just don't do anything I will regret later." He nodded to Gregory, who took Lilly and Isobel's hands and walked toward the door.

Isobel stopped and turned. "Brian, you will need to handle the care of Lancelot, feed him and taking him out. He gets the food on a ..."

"Izzy, I will take good care of him, promise. What about the cat?"

Lilly spoke up. "He is outside and a place I know he is safe. Don't worry about him, I can get him when I need to."

"Okay, just worry about the dog, got it." Brian changed the tone of his voice, "Carter, I am counting on your detail to keep everyone safe. I also expect you to check in hourly, not just if something happens. This may take some time so work out a schedule between yourselves."

"Yes sir, Mr. Kennedy." Carter Hughes turned and walked out of the door, shutting it behind him.

Chapter Thirteen

THE TRIP TO University Hospital was uneventful. The limousine that Marcus had hired had an armored second set of windows that were blackout around the passenger area, usually used for foreign dignitaries or celebrities who needed extra protection and anonymity. The driver of this particular stretch was the one and only Ace Abernathy, known to most of the better hotel concierge as a former Secret Service team member who gave it up to open the Abernathy Youth Centers. He had seen too many good kids from the poorer parts of town leave school, get into drugs, gangs, or sex and stop trying for a good life. He had managed to parlay his civil service pay into a tidy little sum through playing stocks. Along with a few well-heeled donors, he had managed to open and staff three youth centers in San Antonio, Austin, and Brownsville. Two more centers were in the works for Dallas and Houston and he had long-range plans for New Orleans, Amarillo, and El Paso.

Ace had tried the usual route of fund-raising but knocking on doors wasn't doing the trick, many doors got slammed in his face before he could start the pitch. He was complaining to an old government buddy who suggested something he had never thought about. Some limo companies had special cars for use when dignitaries came to the city. They preferred to hire former military people as added protection, they usually paid well, and it would provide access to the people who had the money he needed. He had all the requirements, from his stint in the U.S. Marine Corps to his time with the Secret Service, it made him able to land the limo driver/secondary protection position with Star Power Limousine and he had been on that job for the last fifteen years.

The employees liked him, he sometimes had to wait long hours for the client so he would tell stories of his time in the military or the life with the Secret Service and he would talk to them about the youth centers and how they needed volunteers to help with the kids. Several of them had signed on to volunteer and a few also went to work for Star Power as well.

Gregory had been one of those volunteers, tutoring some of the kids. He liked to help and he had gotten to know Ace. He was very relieved and encouraged to see that his friend was their driver. He knew he could relax because Ace was the best.

As everyone entered the car, Gregory whispered to Carter and then went to the front seat of the vehicle and sat down next to the driver's seat.

Once Ace had everyone inside and the doors locked, he got behind the steering wheel, not surprised at all that Gregory was going to ride shotgun, it would give them a chance to talk.

"I have to tell you, man, I'm glad to see you're our driver, Ace. We are headed to..."

"University Hospital. I was specifically requested, along with the shiny tank here. They said it was for Marcus Lancaster. Are we waiting for him?"

"No, he's not in town, this is for his employees. One of them was attacked and is at Uni. There is a chance that the perp may try an attack on us here."

"I'll keep my eyes open and my head down." The smile Abe flashed wasn't cocky, it was confidence that Gregory knew was born of vast experience.

"Good, just didn't want that sneaking up on you. We've got body guards, all former military."

"I thought you were working for Menger, you still there?"

"Nah, after my making my debut on the nightly news, they let me go because I went out of the area to pick up a pregnancy test for one of the ladies back there."

"Too shy to get seen in the hood, huh?" The grin got larger.

"Yeah, got over that quick enough when my mug got plastered all over the place."

"So now you work for Lancaster. That was a quick turnaround."

"Right place at the right time. I was paid a nice bonus to be on call for them, they just made it permanent. We get through this hospital thing and Mr. Lancaster gets back and I move to Houston."

That surprised Ace. "Really? How does your grandmother feel about this change, is she going with you?"

Gregory shook his head, "Things are happening so fast, I've not talked to her yet. She knew I was fired, I didn't get hired until just before we saw the news item about Mr. Lancaster's partner having been injured and called the police. I will get a hold of her as soon as I know what the time frame is and what I am going to be doing. I will ask if she wants to move with me to Houston but I know what she will say. She won't want to move from her house and the neighborhood. She will say the Lord still has work for her to do." He laughed, "She thinks she runs Denver Heights as it is. My salary will be enough to send money home and she will be comfortable."

Ace shook his head, "That's part of it, but you won't be there for her."

He had a point, but Gregory knew Percy Whitcomb wouldn't let that last long.

"I tell you what, I'll look in on her every week. Maybe I can talk her into coming to the center and helping out a couple of days a week."

"That's awesome of you, Ace. Thank you!"

The big limo pulled into the entrance to the South parking garage where the doctors and executives parked. The limo service had a key code to allow their cars to go into the garage to drop off patients who needed a bit more privacy than the regular patient garages. Ace pulled up to the area in front of the elevators. One of the guards got out first and was looking around, then Ace helped the ladies out of the back. He turned to where Gregory was waiting to accompany the group.

"I'm going to stay down here in the parking garage, in the corner of the first floor. If I'm there, it will be a good way to watch who is coming in and out. You got your phone on you? Let me give you my number so you can get me if you need."

Gregory was grateful for the foresight that Ace showed. "Here's my number. I'll keep you posted on what's going on." Then he Ace entered the number and handed the phone to Gregory, "Thanks, Ace." He turned and walked just behind the entourage toward the elevator.

If Ace hadn't known these were Marcus Lancaster's people, he wouldn't be able to tell by their looks, they were dressed down to look like any other hospital visitor. They casually paired off into couples. One of the guards held the hand of one of the women like it was a regular relationship. He wondered if it really was.

"Smart." He said to the air. He moved the car to the darker corner of the garage and settled in to wait for them to come out.

THERE WAS A Lancaster Security representative just inside the hospital door. He introduced himself to Carter and then escorted the group to the 9th floor of the tower where the Intensive Care Unit was located. There was already a police officer on one side of the door to the small room that held Jesse, and on the other side there was a uniformed Lancaster Security officer. Evidently the representative had spoken to the nurses, they didn't stop to talk with them as they arrived. The police officer stopped them and started to turn them back when the representative pulled him aside and whispered to him names, relationships, and other information. The entourage entered the room, Lilly and Isobel moved forward, the guards and Gregory taking up position on the wall.

Isobel took one look at Jesse and her knees buckled. Lilly tried to hold her up but she slid to the floor in tears, breaking. Gregory slid a chair forward. He carefully lifted the sobbing woman, hugged her and whispered to her, then sat her in the chair, pushing it up to the edge of the bed.

He was unrecognizable. The clear adhesive bandages held things together and distorted his appearance grotesquely. Bruises covered his face, swollen so large his closed eyes were almost invisible. Stitched strained to hold the two sides of his face together from something that looked like a cut that had carved it in half. Tubes in his nose and a tracheotomy held a larger tube. Several bags dripped clear solutions into the IV port, then into his right shoulder. Blood was being replenished via another IV located in the top of his right foot, an odd place for an IV but apparently there were few, if any, uninjured locations on his body. Beeping and flashing, telemetry machines and monitors kept the ever-vigilant ICU nurses apprised of Jesse's condition. Even the slightest change in any reading provoked immediate attention and skilled action.

As they looked him over, he seemed to become even more ashen and a slight blue cast crept into his busted and caked lips and an alarm sounded, showing that his lungs weren't functioning properly. A nurse appeared. Silently and deftly, she checked the placement of the oxygen mask on Jesse's face, reseating the strap under his head. She moved the level attached to the the oxygen on wall and checked the tube, then turned the level open again. She waited a moment, staring at the readout on the screen. She pulled the sheet back a bit to check the blood pressure sensor on the finger of his right hand. Satisfied, she nodded and said, in no one in particular, "That's better," then turned and glided out of the room. During all of it, he never opened his eyes and never moved as the room rang with the cries Isobel was letting go.

All attention focused on Jesse. Isobel smiled weakly through her tears, Jesse always wanted to be the center of attention. He had casts on both legs and right arm. His left hand was connected into a spidery metal device that held the swelled and bruised fingers in place. His upper torso was wrapped and a thick gauze bandage covered his lower abdomen. It was slightly tinged with reddish-brown. Isobel did not know if it was blood or medicine of some sort. He was wrapped on the upper torso and a bandage with a bit of red covered his lower abdomen. A tube protruded from his side, yellowish pale blood collected in a bag hung on the lower bed rail.

Lilly couldn't believe this was Jesse, the man who had seemed to go out of his way to make her life miserable since she arrived in Houston. He looked so small and frail. She felt her eyes well up with tears and fought them back in case someone came in and thought she was another patient.

"What's up? Who has you crying this time?" Baron pushed in with a growl, *"Do I have to go tear someone's flesh again?"*

"No, Baron. I'm okay." She didn't dare talk aloud, the guards didn't know about their abilities and she didn't know if they even knew she was a vampire and she was going to be careful not to let that slip out.

"You are not, don't lie to me, I can feel you."

"We found Jesse. He's almost dead, someone beat him up."

"Good maybe he will find some mann..."

"Not now, Baron. He's not just bruised, he's broken and cut up, it's horrible. Someone did this on purpose. He may be one of the meanest people I have ever met but he didn't deserve this."

"Isobel seems upset, hey Isobel, don't cry, he's not dead yet."

"Baron, not now. She's very, very upset. Your antics aren't appreciated right now, this is serious." Lilly patted and squeezed Isobel's hand as she continued to cry. *"We probably will not be leaving San Antonio until he's better. I don't know if Marcus has been told but when he hears..."* She shuddered.

"*Then we can go! He will be distracted and we can go hide.*" Baron sounded grim.

"*No. I have to be here for Isobel. She's been very good to me, to us, and now she needs my support. Keep close to the hotel, we will be coming to get you when we are going home. Lancelot is with Mr. Kennedy at the hotel, you might wander in once in a while so he doesn't worry about you.*"

"*That dog doesn't worry about me, he's too busy acting like a dog, undignified.*" He snorted.

"*Not the dog, Mr. Kennedy. Just do what I say and let me get back to doing what needs done here. I will check with you as soon as I know something.*"

She didn't even bother with the goodbye. She ran her fingers through Isobel's hair, trying to soothe her.

One woman and two men in long white coats walked into the room.

"This is not allowed! All of you but the ones who are related to this man have to leave." The woman announced, folding her arms in front of her.

"M'am, we are here for him and we have to stay within sight of the men who guard us so they have to stay here with us." Lilly spoke up and Isobel just rested her head against her friend's arm, defeated.

"And who are you? Are you a relative?" The woman snapped.

"I am Lilly Marchantel, Jesse is a friend, more like a brother to me. This is Isobel, Jesse is her brother. That man," Lilly gestured at Gregory, "Is my brother, Gregory. The other men are our guards."

The woman looked around, "You, you, you, and you two are leaving, go wait in the waiting room, the only one allowed in here is the patient's sister. No argument or I will have you thrown out of the hospital and barred from ever returning." She had pointed out everyone, including Lilly.

"No. We will not be leaving, sorry. I need to be here with Isobel and this is where I shall be. Gregory stays and our guards stay." Lilly wasn't backing down and Gregory tried to signal her from behind the doctors, the last thing they needed was to be thrown out.

"Excuse me? You are defying me?" The woman dropped her hands, which balled into fists. She acted as if she had never been told no before.

"If you insist on us leaving, then yes," Lilly looked closer at the words on the white coat, "Dr. Logan."

The woman started turning bright red. "You will all leave this room now or I will have the policeman outside arrest you for trespassing. You no longer have privileges in my ICU unit. Get OUT!" While she wasn't raising her voice, she was very emphatic and the sound carried in the quiet unit. Three nurses came running in at the sound, adding to the crowded elevator feel of the room.

Lilly just stood and watched her, not saying a word, hands rubbing circles on Isobel's shoulders.

The nurses and the Internist were talking over each other, Dr. Logan continued ordering everyone out and calling for the police officer all at the same time and a crowd of personnel began to gather in the walkway next to the room, trying to get a look at the excitement.

After enduring the chaos for several minutes, Lilly spoke quietly, "That's entirely enough."

The commotion continued and Lilly repeated "That's entirely enough," this time a bit louder.

Everything stopped and everyone in the room turned to her. "Okay, Dr. Logan, may I speak to you alone, please."

"You're not family, I can't disclose any medical information to you."

"That's fine, I just need to give you private information so that you may treat him properly."

Gregory caught what she was meaning and spoke up, "With the restrictions due to the HIPAA laws, you can't tell the doctor in front of all of these people without the patient's or family's permission. Neither the patient nor the family member," he pointed at Isobel, "Can give you permission right now. I know how important this information is to Jesse's health, you should listen to what Lilly has to say."

Dr. Logan stood silently contemplating what Gregory had said. "Okay, I will take you to the family consultation room and we can talk. Once we are done, I want everyone out of this room." She walked through the crowd to the door.

"Isobel?" Lilly knelt down so she could see Isobel's eyes and face. It was apparent that she was devastated with the sight of the injuries that Jesse had suffered. "Isobel, I'll be just a moment. I need to leave the room to talk to Jesse's doctor.

Gregory and the guards will be staying. Jesse needs you, he needs you to be strong for him until Marcus gets here. Does that make sense?"

The shocked woman looked into Lilly's eyes and nodded, "Yes."

"You talk to Jesse, he needs you right now. I will handle the doctor and details for you, okay?"

Isobel turned back to Jesse and took his hand, kissing it.

"Okay, doctor." Lilly walked with the doctor with Payton Naismith following. Once they reached the room, Payton stepped around the doctor and checked the room and then stepped back out. "Clear."

Doctor Logan stalked into the room, definitely affronted by Lilly's abstinence. Lilly following calmly. The room was small.

The room was furnished with a long divan, a couple of low tables with lamps on them and a couple of other chairs. A couple of uninteresting paintings hung on two of the walls. A light in a box on the wall shining brightly. "How many times have I told those ass, uh, doctors to turn the off the light when they are finished reading x-rays. She reached over and switched off the light, instantly dimming the room.

Lilly wasn't sure what the x-ray was but it wasn't what she wanted to hear or talk about.

"Now, Ms..." The doctor turned back to Lilly.

"Marchantel, Lilly Marchantel."

"What do you want to say? I am very busy and I have patients to see." The doctor was still being bossy.

Lilly frowned, then managed to smile, trying to catch the doctor's gaze. "We don't mean to up-end everything in your department. Jesse is very special..."

"Everyone is special, Ms. Marchantel. Every family feels that way. Patients are here for one reason. It's called ICU because that's what they need...Intensive Care. It's my job to make sure they get that without the interference of too many family members or friends.

"I can respect that." Lilly tried to keep the woman's gaze but the doctor kept looking at her watch, glancing at the door, and generally giving Lilly the impression that she didn't want to talk any longer.

"But you don't respect it. You are not allowing me to do my job. You want the entire tribe to be allowed to take up space. I suppose you also want to be the consulting doctor as well. Tell me, where did a girl like you go to medical school?"

Lilly had been trying to be reasonable with the doctor, guiding her toward the conclusion that the family was necessary. But now, something in the way the doctor talked to her, words she used seemed like pejoratives. So Lilly spoke up. "Dr. Logan. Stop." As the doctor puffed up to start another tirade, Lilly caught and held her gaze. "You. Will. Not. Treat. Others. This. Way." The glamoury was working. "Treat your patients with kindness and compassion. You will treat families with respect and understanding. This is difficult for them, they do not have the learning, knowledge, and experience you possess. They look to you to use that ability to make their loved one better as soon as possible."

Dr. Logan's eyes seemed to glaze over as the vampire spoke.

"You will allow reasonable accommodations for families. For us, that means one personal guard will remain in the room at all times for the duration of our visit. A second personal guard and security guard will be stationed just outside the door. Family members will be allowed to come and go as they please. You will keep us informed of Jesse's condition and answer questions in language we can understand." Lilly hesitated for a moment. "You shall be extra kind and especially conciliatory to Isobel Kincaid, do you understand?"

Dr. Logan nodded her head. Suddenly all hell broke loose.

Alarms screamed from everywhere at once. Over the P.A., an urgent voice said, "Code Blue, Room 920 C. Dr. Logan to ICU, stat."

The doctor blinked, then she yelled, "Move, woman. Now!" She pushed Lilly aside and ran from the room.

Lilly followed and was shocked when she saw everyone but Carter Hughes in the hallway, a nurse attempted to push everyone toward the waiting room.

Isobel was sobbing, supported by Gregory with her bodyguard, Edward Garcia rubbing her back. The hired Lancaster guard, Heith Spenser, was standing toe to toe with the police officer, refusing to leave and resisting the expulsion of everyone else.

Dr. Logan pushed her way past them all and disappeared into the room, beginning to shout orders. A male voice from inside said, loud enough to be heard over the cacophony. "My patient, I've got this." Dr. Young, Lilly remembered.

Lilly stepped into the knot of people around the door. "That is entirely enough. You," she pointed at Spencer, "You and you" pointing to the San Antonio police officer whose name tag read 'Blackketter,' "Stay at the door. Gregory, bring Isobel, everyone else follow me. Let them do their jobs." She pointed to the department doors.

Gregory led the group through the door, Lilly next to him, holding Isobel's hand, to the room recently occupied by the doctor and Lilly.

Once everyone was inside, Gregory and Garcia sat on the couch with Isobel between them, Gregory's arm still around her.

"Okay, what is going on?" Lilly demanded. "And one at a time, please, I cannot understand if everyone talks at once." She looked around and then pointed at Garcia.

"We were waiting for you and the doctor to return. A nurse came in and took Mr. Chamberlain's vital signs, then she..."

"Wait, vital signs, what are those." Lilly didn't know the phrase.

"His vitals: heart rate, blood pressure, and temperature, ma'am."

"Oh, ok, I know those things. And it's just Lilly, please. Then what happened?"

"The nurse gave him a shot in his leg, the left one." Gregory was nodding his head in agreement. "Once she had left the room, about a minute later, every alarm hooked up to him went off, seemingly at once, and he coded."

The thought of needing a dictionary floated through her mind even as she said, "Coded?"

Gregory spoke up, "His heart stopped." Isobel buried her head in his chest, a small cry louder than the others she sobs ripping from her.

"He died?" Lilly felt her own heart sink. "Why all the excitement and arguing if he died?"

"The doctors who were in the room took over, asked us to leave, and someone brought in the crash cart. They are still working on him, trying to restart his heart, saving his life."

She wanted to ask about the crash cart but Gregory read the question on her face, "The equipment they use to start his heart again."

"They can do that?"

"Yes, sometimes it works. More often than not, actually." Gregory was making faces that Isobel couldn't see, trying to get Lilly to abandon that particular line of questioning.

She wasn't sure what all those faces were for, but Lilly could hear the repeated anguish in the crying Isobel was doing and changed the questioning. "So, this happened right after she gave him a shot?" Almost everyone nodded. "Hmmm, could she have given him something bad by accident, or..." Her eyes widened as the other possibility formed.

Peyton spoke up, "It very well could be. We

need blood tests to check for anything it might be. I can ask one of the nurses to check."

"While you are speaking to the nurse, would you ask her to call a church and ask a priest to come and give Jesse Last Rights?" Lilly asked.

Isobel looked up at her friend, "Last Rights? You believe he's going to be dead?"

"No, no, no, Isobel. But with the circumstances, I couldn't let him take the chance of not making it to heaven."

"But he's not Catholic! He's agnostic. I doubt that he will appreciate your efforts." Isobel started to stand but her legs gave way and she dropped back to the couch.

It hurt Lilly to watch her friend so destroyed and no matter how much Jesse went out of his way to come between Marcus and Lilly, she knew what would happen if she didn't take the step to insure his soul would go to heaven.

"Please, Mr. Naismith, could you ask for a priest? Isobel, if he doesn't believe, it won't hurt him, if he believes, it might actually help him."

Isobel just looked down at her hands, much too much worried to continue the argument, and Lilly meant well.

Gregory patted Isobel's hand and stood up, Garcia slipping his arm protectively around her. "I need to go check on Ace. If they got in here to Jesse with all of the security..."

"I'm with you," Payton stood up from the squat position he had taken up in a corner. "Garcia can handle the girls and you have the guards at Jesse's door."

"No dice, man. We stay with our charges, so that means you," Garcia pointing at Gregory with his free hand, "will have to call him, to check."

By the time he got off the word 'check' Gregory was out the door and pulling open the one to the stairwell. Peyton shouted for him to stop and the only reply was the sound of the door closing.

Gregory had a bad feeling about the whole thing, there was too much coincidence going on. As he raced down to the main floor so he could get the elevator to the garage, he was hoping he was wrong about everything.

He hit the bottom and tried to jerk the handle off the door as he didn't slow his run. He sprinted to the garage elevator that was about ten feet from the stairwell and punched the button several times. He fidgeted, almost jogging in place, waiting for the elevator.

"Come on!"

The bell rang and the doors appeared to open one centimeter at a time so Gregory gripped them both and pushed them open enough to slip into the elevator and barreled straight into a black headed woman who looked vaguely familiar. She left the car without a word and Gregory called out "Sorry!" as she disappeared behind the closed doors.

The elevator eventually got to the floor of the garage that Ace was in. Pushing the stubborn doors open once again, Gregory ran out and stopped, trying to figure out where the limo would be parked. He looked ahead, his eyes trying to adjust to the dimmer light and he caught sight of

Ace leaning on the hood of the car, reading a book.

Then he saw it and time shrunk down to a crawl for him, an inconspicuous silver car was driving slowly down the row of cars toward the limo. He tried to shout a warning as the dark windows came down. Three sharp sounds hit his ears as he watched Ace looked up and realized what was happening. Ace didn't have time to move, the sounds became visible as it hit the paperback, knocking it out of his hand, another one hit his shoulder almost simultaneously with the one who hit his head, opening it up and spraying the limo and other cars bright red.

Gregory's screamed Ace's name as everything was happening. The car turned the corner at the elevator and he could see a figure in it. He threw himself toward the closing elevator just as he felt a hot sting in his right shoulder. The doors closed behind him to the sound of tire squeals.

The elevator rose, opening back to the lobby. Gregory tried to push the button but he couldn't raise his right arm, having to raise his left to complete the task. The elevator closed on him just as a woman screamed and crawled back to the garage.

He left the elevator, trying to run to Ace. He knew the man was dead even before he reached him. Ace was laying on his stomach, a hand raised toward his head. Jesse could see Ace's eyes, open but lifeless. He started to reach for them to close them when a hand caught his shoulder.

"Owww." He managed to squeak as he looked up, half expecting the hand to belong to one of the men from the car, there to finish him off. Instead of that, he saw a woman in scrubs above him.

"Hey, sorry to hurt you. You need to sit down, you're losing a lot of blood. I've paged for a doc and help." The woman had red hair and she had a shine to her that seemed to light up the dim garage.

She helped him sit down and held her hand over the wound, trying to slow the blood until help came. As the adrenalin left with his blood around her fingers, she felt the young man begin to shake.

"You're going to be all right. I'm here. You have something you have to do and I will be right here with you." She smiled into his eyes.

"Who are you?" Gregory managed to say through the growing fog in his mind.

"I'm Reba, looks like I've become your guardian angel." He heard as the world darkened around him and he let himself go.

Chapter Fourteen

THE PLANE HAD been pointed to the west for way too long. Marcus fought the pull of sleep as the sun glinted off the skin of the aircraft. He had not slept much at the castle and with the discussion with Gery, then the instant arrival in Zurich inside his plane was made him feel oddly disoriented. He fought sleep, finally giving into the pull as the plane took off from Reykjvic after refueling. Even though he slept, he still could feel the sun beating down on the skin of the plane. The plane was reinforced with darker windows in the cabin and very tight covers. Somewhere over the Atlantic, his brain shut down and send him down into the oblivion of the vampire sleep.

Which was why he reacted by sitting straight up and landing a punch on the person who prodded him.

"Hey! Is that any way to greet an old friend that you invited into this little party? You still pack a good right hook."

Fighting into consciousness, he opened an eye.

Jean Lafitte. The old pirate stood next to his

bed, that stupid grin on his face that Marcus remembered from the old days when they lived at Campeche, the settlement Lafitte had made on Galveston Island so long ago.

"What day and time is it?" He managed to pry the other eye open and noticed his mouth tasted like the entire British army had marched through it.

"That good a party, huh?"

"No, between the damned council and some other antics, combined with getting propositioned by a demon, then zapped to my plane at dawn, I have lost all sense of time. So, can you fill me in?" Marcus had imbibed alcohol in his living years, even gotten drunk a few times with the soldiers he served with. He had never had the problems this trip was causing.

"It's Friday, September 23, 2005, about 10:45 a.m, here in LA. You didn't plan this one too well, you got me to pack and come out to the airport in the daylight. Thankfully your pilot arraigned for the hangar, had the doors close after my limo came inside. I'm all packed and ready to go."

"Shit, I've been in this damned plane, and in these clothes, for almost 14 hours, all of it in the sun. I need a shower and a change before I'll feel human again." Marcus rubbed his face and then his hair.

"You figured out how to feel human again? How does that happen?" The pirate was smirking.

"You know what I meant. Let me grab a shower and I'll tell you what's going on. Let the pilot know we are ready anytime he is. I'm eager to get to San Antonio."

Chapter Fifteen

THE SECURITY OPERATIONS Center and most of Lancaster headquarters were in a controlled chaos. All attention was directed toward finding Nelson Mishkoph and every corporation, sub-corporation, mercenary squad, bank account, business partner, and client the man had. As Castro had put it in the staff meeting, "I want to know what this meat-sack owns, who he works with, works for all the way down to where he shits. Once we get that information, we'll castrate the bastard, slowly and very painfully."

Essex knew this distraction was his only chance to get through the very tough, almost impenetrable firewalls of the Lancaster computer network. The angel, working undercover on Mikhail's orders, had spent what felt like weeks working to try to pinpoint where the private files were stored. The surface files were all anyone would find on a human's security company servers. He had found the profit and loss state-ments, tax returns, purchase orders, client lists, and the employee's files from Human Resources very quickly.

As he continued to scan for the hidden files, he muttered a mangled phrase from a movie, "These are not the files you are looking for, move along." The angel smiled with the memory of Sullivan and Seth going with him to sneak into a Dublin theater to watch the blockbuster, taking three seats way in the back of the sold-out show.

Damn he missed Sullivan and he had to stay away from Seth while this assignment was in effect. He would give anything to go find a nice pub to drink a pint or three. Of course, there would be the usual argument about where to go, Sullivan always wanted Ireland, Seth would insist on going to Scotland, "Where men are men, and sheep are scared," Sullivan would always say, so Seth would end up punching him in the arm. But Essex wanted a nice, out of the way pub in Wales. Both the others would complain about every word everywhere was made up of multiple consonants or a morass of vowels with a sprinkling of consonants. When they picked a place, using the human tried and true method of rock-paper-scissors, they would adopt the language of the area they were drinking in, and he could count on Sully getting plastered enough to sing songs out of tune or Seth starting an argument with the locals over which British team had the best football, usually resulting in a pub brawl and all of them put out in the street. Those were the best, he thought as he turned his attention back to the computer screen.

As the day shifted into night, he scoured the database of the proof he needed to discover what the vampires were planning.

Bingo. He found a hidden database that listed the various holdings of Lancaster's vampire clients. Some names were very familiar but a few were new. He wondered if H.H.A.D. knew about them, had they been tuned?

Essex pulled a USB drive from his pocket and slipped it into the slot, copying the first of the proprietary information. While it was download-ing, Essex went back to monitoring the interior security to make sure the drive wasn't being found.

He pulled a second drive, replacing the first USB with it. As far as he could tell, no one was aware he was in the system. He continued to monitor as the drives filled.

CASTRO WALKED THROUGH the S.O.C. on his regular rounds of headquarters. The Gunny had spent too many years in the Marines to be relegated to flying a desk. Marcus Lancaster had trusted him to run things on a day-to-day basis and Castro was a hands-on chief. He knew the names of all H.Q. employees and all the information, including the top secrets and where the bodies were buried.

Benamim Senai walked up to Castro and handed him a closed clip board box. Castro opened it and read. He began to flip the cigar in his mouth, a scowl the other indication of his temper.

"You've tracked this down to an internal source?"

"No sir. The download appears to be from three IPs across the Internet and the trackers are on it."

"Good, find out who owns those IPs, ASAP." Castro looked up to the side monitor running CNN Europe.

"Sir, look at this line." Ben pointed to a small line of code.

Castro looked where Benamim pointed. He knew he was looking at a MAC address that came up for five seconds and then disappeared from the list code. But what that meant, he had no idea. "And what would cause that particular line?"

"What I am looking at is an internal ping that instantly disappears. I don't think it is really from the next address in the outside."

Castro pulled the cigar out of his mouth, "You don't think? You came to me with a hypothesis instead of facts, boy? Bring me facts and we will then deal with whatever the threat is. But I have to have facts."

Ben stood still, trying to find the words to explain, however Castro stabbed the cigar back into his mouth. "Did I stutter, Mr. Senai? Get on it and bring me the info." He stepped away so Ben could leave the room.

Castro shook his head and in a gravel-sounding voice said, "Just the facts, ma'am, just the facts."

Chapter Sixteen

L ILLY SAT IN the emergency room waiting area,
her bodyguard, Payton, was leaning on a wall
where he could watch her and the doors. A doctor
was in the trauma room stitching up the gunshot
wound after pulling out the small bone fragments
of her new ghoul's shoulder. They had lightly
sedated Gregory and had been giving him anti-
infection drugs as well as blood to keep his
pressure up. He was already out when she came
into the emergency center. Nurses dodged her as
they worked and then a young woman pushed a
big machine into the room and told Lilly to please
leave. After the machine was removed, Lilly
returned to his side to wait for the doctor, Payton
trailing behind.

Lilly had wanted to stay and hold Gregory's
hand but the doctor said he didn't want to get her
sick from all the blood that his patient was, and
would be, losing.

"Like I'm afraid of blood." She mumbled to
herself.

So here she sat, the area full of families and
patients, and because it was now dawn, the

parade of night visitors to the rest of the hospital were being redirected to the main entrance. Some of the controlled chaos left with them.

Lilly could feel the dawn sliding into full daylight. She tried to figure out the last time she had slept. She felt a cramp, a reminder she hadn't eaten either.

She was now very aware of the smells in the E.R. Not only various blood types but other bodily smells. She started to gag and stood up, trying not to vomit in front of everyone as she ran into the restroom, having to explain the blood she was throwing up would be difficult. She retched, the stall's door firmly locked behind her.

"Ma'am. Are you okay?" A feminine voice called from the other side of the door.

She stopped just long enough to say, "I'm okay, just something I ate." Then the retching continued. Once she got control of her stomach, she grabbed some paper and wiped her mouth, then flushed all of the evidence. As she stepped out, the person who had spoken to her was still in the room, leaning on the sink.

"I was worried about you, it sounded awful. Is there anything I can get you? I can go for the triage nurse..."

"No, I'm fine, no need to bother the nurses, I'm waiting for a friend to be fixed up." She stepped a bit closer and stared into the woman's eyes, "There is something you can do, let's step over in front of the room door."

Lilly led the now glamoured woman to the door, pushed her against it, and struck, taking some blood from the woman's vein. It tasted so good, she was starving, and she had to force herself off the woman before she drained her. After sealing off the holes and cleaning the area up, she said, "I'm feeling so much better now, I think it's passed." She walked the woman back where she was before.

The woman was blinking and looking around, holding the edge of the sink, "I'm feeling wobbly, I wonder what's going around in here?"

"You are a little pale, let me help you out to the waiting room and if you need the nurse, I can summon her." She steadied the woman to her chair and then walked back toward the trauma room.

She hated to take blood from potentially unwilling victims but she was taking for the baby and that was something that she was certain she could get absolution for from Father Keller. She wished she was in Houston, she needed to go to confession and mass with so much going on.

As she was saying prayers again for Gregory, she felt a hand on her shoulder. She looked up into Payton's eyes.

"Lilly, while you were in the restroom, I got a call from Brian. We've been warned that Mr. Lancaster is on his way to the hospital. We've checked out of the hotel and will be leaving here just as soon as we can get the doctors to allow Mr. Chamberlain to travel. I am to stay here with you until Brian gets here, then we will go upstairs."

Lilly wasn't looking forward to Marcus's arrival, he was going to be angry when he found out about Jesse. "We can't go up until they release Gregory. I won't leave without him."

"I know, Lilly, we'll wait for him before we go up."

The other part of his report dawned on her, "Wait, we've checked out of the hotel? Did Mr. Kennedy get Baron before he left?" She began to panic, Baron had not wanted to be inside and by now, with the sun up, he would be curled up in a dark place, sleeping."

"*I'm here, in the car. The big man was going to leave me behind but take that insufferable mutt. I had to run very fast and jump in just as the door was shut. I'll be around the hospital once we get there. Again, the stupid human rule will keep me from your side, I hope that guard with you will take care of you.*" Baron sounded tired, she wondered what had gone on in the last day or so.

"*I had to kiss the ladies goodbye, go hunt, and get back to the hotel. Not enough sleep and it's time for bed now but I am not sure that I will get any sleep until we get back to the big building.*" Was that a yawn she heard? His sleepiness translated through the link to Lilly and she felt the sun tugging her toward sleep.

"*Just stay close, Baron. Get some rest.*" Lilly laid her head back to try to get a little sleep.

She had no idea how long she had slept when she was touched on the face. She opened her eyes to see Gregory standing in front of her. She smiled.

"Hey sleeping beauty. We probably need to get

back to the waiting room upstairs, you can sleep there." He stuck out his good hand to help her up, the other shoulder being wrapped in gauze and tape. He had no shirt on.

"Are you okay? Don't you need to be in bed to get better before we go walking around?" Lilly walked with him to the door to the corridor leading further into the building and the elevators.

"Nah, I'm fine. Hurts like hell but I'm going to be okay according to the doctor. I hear you got thrown out of the room while they worked on me. The nurse said something about you being sick?"

"I didn't get food in time and I ended up in the bathroom. Nothing bad. They were more worried about me getting sick from the sight of blood when they sent me out." She took his free hand as they walked.

"Sure, that's going to happen, right? Did you look like you would get sick?" He looked at her, she appeared to be just fine now.

"No, I didn't get sick until after I had been out of the room for a time. When I asked to see you again, the nurse said the doctor had a policy about family and friends, he doesn't want to get sued for something he has to do to the patient. So, they put me out and I had to wait out in the room."

They stepped into the elevator and pushed the button for the ICU floor. As the doors began to close, they heard someone call out, "Hold the elevator, please" as well as the sound of several feet walking very fast toward it. Gregory pushed the door open button and then put his hand on the door to keep it open.

In stepped Marcus Lancaster, followed by Brian Kennedy, and someone that Lilly had not met.

"Lilly! Good, I've found you." He hugged her and then noticed Gregory behind her. "Gregory Freeman. What happened to you?" The elevator rose as they talked.

"Someone shot Ace Abernathy in the garage. I was trying to get to him, try to save him, and got shot for it. I'm okay, just got it taken care of in emergency."

"I am grateful to you for your care of my people. Kennedy tells me you've become Lilly's assistant. Good choice, girl." He turned and motioned for the stranger to come up next to him. "This is a very old friend of mine"

"Hey, watch the old comments, mon ami. I'm not as ancient as you are." He took Lilly's hand and kissed it. "I'm John Shipman. You must be the Lilly that this lout has talked about incessantly since I joined him in Los Angeles."

Gregory had been trying to figure out who the guy reminded him of. "I recognize you, I think."

Jean raised an eyebrow with a wry smile. "And who do you think I am?"

"Well, I don't know if Shipman is your real name or a stage name. You look like that guy who played Agent Smith in The Matrix, and that guy, the head elf, in the Tolkien movies."

Jean laughed, "You've hit the nail on the head but there's more to it than a couple of new identities." He turned to Lilly, "Miss Marchantel, my original identity is Jean Lafitte, I've taken the name Shipman to avoid getting accosted by the fans who think I am really Mr. Weaving."

Gregory was staring, "You're telling us that you are the famous pirate of the Caribbean? The one in the War of 1812?"

"Oui, I'm that privateer."

The doors opened, Marcus striding out and down the hall without any further talk. He pushed the red button that controlled the doors into the ICU and strode in. Lilly could hear the nurses questioning him and what business he had. Evidently he disregarded their calls to stop and passed the guards and into Jesse's room. Lilly hurried to follow him and the other men.

"Sir, I need all of you to come out of this room. Right now we have a no-visitors policy with him." A nurse stood at the foot of Jesse's bed and glared at the intruders.

"I'm staying."

To say that Marcus was shocked to see the condition that Jesse was in was an understatement. His eyes flicked from bandage to bandage and then to the monitoring equipment, quickly assessing his current condition.

"I want the chart and I want his doctor in here, now." Marcus continued to examine his ghoul as he spat out the orders.

"Sir, you cannot..."

"Woman, I'm telling you that you will obey me." Marcus turned to look at her, noticing her name tag read 'Valna Asterman, R.N.' and the words 'Charge Nurse, ICU'. "I will be obeyed and if not, I have the resources to remove you from your job with one phone call to the hospital administration and board of directors." Marcus turned back and took Jesse's hand, ignoring the fuming woman at the door.

Lilly stepped toward her, "Ms. Asterman, Marcus has just arrived from out of the country. Jesse is his companion and he didn't know until the last hour or so that he was hurt." Lilly hoped the time estimation was correct, she had no idea when Marcus had been told and what he had been told. "I know he doesn't mean to be gruff and growl at you, it's the circumstance." She took a breath, "Please excuse him. Also, please ask Dr. Young to come in and bring Jesse's chart. Marcus has some medical training and he can understand what is written."

The woman obviously didn't like the request but she turned and went to comply. Lilly watched from the door as the nurse spoke on the telephone and then picked up a book, walking back. She thrust the book at Lilly, saying, "Dr. Young has been paged and will be coming momentarily."

"Thank you, Nurse Asterman, you are very kind." Lilly smiled, "We really appreciate it."

In spite of herself, the nurse returned the smile and said, "You're welcome." Then she walked away, going into a room on the other side of the desk.

Lilly handed the chart to Marcus. He took it silently and began flipping through the material, copies of tests, and other material. His face hardened into a frown as he digested what he was seeing. Everyone in the room could see Marcus's anger rise. Lilly walked to him and put a hand on his arm. He didn't move until he shrugged the hand off as Dr. Young came into the room.

"Out, I want everyone out of here except me and the doctor. I will meet with you after we've had a talk." Marcus's tone left no space for argument. Lilly allowed Jean to take her arm to walk out. She stopped long enough to whisper very softly to her maker, "Isobel is his sister." Marcus's eyes sparkled as he picked up the storyline as Jean led her from the room. The door shut and Lilly showed everyone to the family waiting room the entourage had taken over.

"Well, what is happening?" Gregory asked from his place sitting next to Isobel who had managed to calm down. Her eyes were still dull and sad but she wasn't sobbing any longer.

"Marcus is in with Dr. Young, finding out the details. I'm not entirely sure what he wants to do, or wants us to do after the meeting, he said he would come and talk to us." Garcia stood and offered the other spot next to Isobel to Lilly, who sat down and took the ghoul's hand as they waited for news.

MARCUS STOOD, WATCHING the others leave as he looked at Dr. Young. Taller than Marcus, he sported the same, slightly wavy hair and blue eyes that Marcus had and, for one moment, Marcus wondered if his brother, Henry, or little brother Jacob had children whose descendants might have been in this man. He took an instant like to him.

"You needed to see me, Mr. Lancaster?" The doctor shook his hand.

"I have read the chart. His injuries are extensive."

Dr. Young took the chart from Marcus's hand and flipped through it. "It's still early, yet. He came into E.R. unconscious, a total bloody mess. I was called to handle the surgery needs, extensive damage to his abdomen multiple broken bones and contusions. I can deal with those things, I called in Dr. Anjeet Sharma to handle the delicate work on closing the deep knife wound on the patient's face, he is the best in cosmetic reconstructive surgery and he sews much nicer than I do."

"I want to talk to Dr. Sharma, have him come in as well." Marcus watched Dr. Young pull his cell phone out and type something, then replace the device in the holder at his waist.

"He's on the way. Anyhow, Dr. Eve Logan was originally on the case for internal injuries, which were extensive. After some drama, Mr. Chamberlain's sister fired her. If you look in the back of the chart," he handed it back to Marcus, "there is a complete listing of all the injuries found when he came in through E.R. Whoever did the beating knew what they were doing and how to inflict extreme damage without immediate death."

There was a tap on the door and Dr. Sharma entered. After introductions, the doctor said, "Mr. Chamberlain was very lucky. None of the knife wounds were ragged and could be carefully sewn to repair them. The clear bandages I use is gas permeable and will keep the scaring to a minimum. He may or may not want some touch up work."

Dr. Young continued. "Mr. Chamberlain was on the table for a very long time. While Dr. Sharma worked on his face, I concentrated on the extreme abdominal knife wounds. The intestines were cut in several places.

"When you have that much damage, peritonitis is almost inevitable. We have him on the strongest antibiotic available. I was able to clean and close those wounds and clean out most of the fecal material that had leaked into the cavity. I worked on all of the damage to the inside, Dr. Sharma did the delicate finish work. Then we turned it over to the orthopedist to set the broken bones."

"He is extremely lucky, Mr. Lancaster. Someone was very determined to hurt this man. I have a question about his medical history. When I was reviewing the blood work," he reached out to take the chart from Marcus, "I found some strange results. There's something about the way the blood cells are shaped and how they flow around the other white and red cells that is very unusual. I've never seen it before and I handed a copy of the report to Dr. Lawrence Brown, a hematologist, for his take on the anomalies. He, too, has never observed a cell like these. He paused, as if a bit unsure how to approach the subject. Considering the extent and seriousness of his injuries, we have noted his extraordinarily rapid healing. Granted, he has not regained consciousness, but his recovery is most encouraging.

"It is quite possible the hematological abnormalities may have a contributing influence on his accelerated improvement. We would very much like to study Mr. Chamberlain and his blood to discover what this means and if it can be duplicated."

"No." Marcus glared at him. "Jesse isn't a lab rat. He's human, same as you. If there's something different about him, he's gay, that's it. You can study what you have of him, he's giving you nothing more." He turned away from the doctors and stepped back to take Jesse's hand. "What I want is for you both to clear him to travel so I can take him to Houston for private care. I have an airplane ready and refueled, I will take him straight to a private medical facility where I can be with him as I search for whoever the hell did this too him. I can't do that from here."

"No way, Mr. Lancaster. He's still in extremely critical condition..." Doctor Sharma couldn't believe this was being asked.

"Mr. Lancaster, are you aware of the fact that yesterday Mr. Chamberlain was killed by an assassin and the only reason why his heart is beating is because we were able to fight the poison in his system to bring him back? He died, Mr. Lancaster, and he's not ready at all to travel, even if it is to another facility." Dr. Young had stepped in front of Dr. Sharma to face Marcus, standing so close to the vampire, he was invading his personal space.

"I know, I read the chart. But I'm getting things ready and I'm taking him home. No discussion, no arguments, it will be done." Marcus looked into Dr. Young's eyes, pushing the connection for glamouring. The doctor didn't succumb to it. Then he looked at Dr. Sharma, "I don't need to speak with you further, please leave." The plastic surgeon was glamoured in a second and complied, leaving the room and closing the door behind him.

"I doubt seriously your plane is set up for transporting a critically ill patient. And, if it's unpressurized, he could get a blood clot and stroke, or have his heart stop again. He's staying here. You are not next of kin and you cannot make the decision."

"I am, from way back. However, since this backward century doesn't recognize relationships such as ours, I will have to call Isobel in and let her tell you what will happen. She is, after all, his sister." Marcus was impressed that Isobel thought of that ruse while being very upset over the situation.

"Sir, I really recommend against this action, if he goes, it will be against medical advice and any problems will be on your conscience."

"Just a moment," Marcus reached for his phone and punched a button.

"Mr. Lancaster, you can't use..." the doctor

started to say as Marcus waved him off.

"Castro, I need you to call the medical supply company we use in San Antonio, I will need the following things picked up within the hour and delivered to my airplane." Marcus rattled off a list of medical equipment, everything from the IV pole and monitor to a portable EKG, EEG, and even a portable x-ray machine. The list also included blood that matched Jesse's type and the medication he was receiving. "I don't care if.... No, I will not accept the answer that they don't have the equipment. Tell the owner, not the manager, the owner that I will pay double the retail costs for each item delivered. If it takes longer than an hour, all of the bonus will be gone. He's got to figure out where to get the things, I'm not going to tolerate any shit from him, no excuses."

Dr. Young listened to the man next to him. He was ordering everything he would need but he doubted that Lancaster had the medical training to deal with any emergency. As Marcus ended the call, the doctor said, "Ok, I get it, you mean business and you're going to go with or without my approval."

"I told you I would."

"Okay, realistically, when do you want to leave? You gave the supplier an hour, how long after that?"

"Just as soon as the delivered items are set up, wheels will roll. I want to get him home." Marcus studied the man's face, picking up on something he wasn't saying. "You're thinking about going with him, aren't you?" He ventured.

"Yes, if you'll oblige me. I have no surgeries scheduled for today and another surgeon is on call. I don't have much to hang around for and I can go with you to your hospital and make sure the patient survives the trip."

Marcus was surprised by the offer. This was one thing he wasn't expecting. But he might just come in handy. "Okay, you're on. I have things ordered, if there anything else you need, let me know and I'll get it." He turned back to the bed and sat down, taking the one hand Jesse had that wasn't tied up in tubes and wires.

Jack Young knew he was dismissed so he turned and walked to the door, thinking of all the things that needed to be done to prepare for a short run to Houston. He looked back at the patient and the man sitting with him. He was certain that Marcus Lancaster loved Jesse Chamberlain, it showed in the way he held Jesse's hand and stroked his wrist. Jack was just hoping he could pull this move off, Marcus Lancaster was the type that wouldn't deal with failure well. He walked out of the room, closing the door behind him.

Chapter Seventeen

T HE MEDICAL SUPPLIER had found everything Marcus had requested. Several technicians rushed about the plane readying the materials and equipment for the flight. The two Lancaster jobs kept a watchful eye, staying out of the way.

Brian Kennedy arrived early and immediately set to task, double and triple checking everything. He walked through the preflight with the pilots to assure himself that no one had tampered with the plane. Deeply etched concern clouded his face. It was his failure that Jesse was poisoned right in the hospital. Ace was murdered and Gregory got shot...all of it on his watch. Damn it! He mulled it over. He felt sick and even more determined to protect his charges from this unseen madman. Before he had left the hospital, he had briefed Marcus on all that had occurred in his absence. In addition, his sincere regret in his culpability in the many failures that had occurred.

In an unprecedented act of compassion and pragmatism, Marcus chose to look past his fatal laxity and concentrate on the immediate situation. First priority was to insure everyone's safe return to Houston, with particular concentration on the proper and secure medical transport for Jesse. Even now, full medical accommodation was being readied at Lancaster Tower, where the security was much tighter than at the San Antonio hospital.

There, the entire might of Marcus Lancaster, Lancaster Industries, and all of his considerable influence would be brought to bear on discovering who was behind the assault on Marcus's family and personnel. When the truth was revealed, the cold fury of Marcus Lancaster would then be unleashed, and there would be Hell to pay.

JACK YOUNG WAS in the ambulance with his patient. One of the San Antonio Lancaster Security men was riding shotgun with the driver in the front of the vehicle. As they drove toward the airport, Jack tried to remember what he knew of Lancaster. The gentleman believed he owned the world and everyone would be required to follow him into any situation he wanted. Sure, he was a philanthropist, but he still was a ruthless businessman. One of the many facets of Lancaster Industries, it was rumored, that the security division had a secret subdivision that trained mercenary personnel. No one had caught him on that one, yet. He could imagine that the man responsible for Chamberlain's assault would want to be somewhere far away, like the moon, because if he was on the Earth, Lancaster would find him and it wouldn't be for a picnic.

The stretched and armored limousine carried Lilly, Baron, Isobel, Gregory, Jean, and Marcus with Lancelot—holding the dog because after Lance spotted his master, he jumped up on him, refusing to get down, and three of the bodyguards. Even with one of the guards up front with the driver, the car was very crowded.

As they drew closer to the airport, Lilly fumed. Isobel had begged Marcus and the doctor to let her go in the ambulance that was to bring Jesse to the plane. She didn't want to leave him. Marcus was annoyed that the woman was inserting herself between him and Jesse, he had said as much to Lilly, who scolded him about being insensitive to Isobel's emotions. The scene in the family room which had been their sanctuary since finding Jesse was a heated one, Lilly standing up to Marcus...

"Why are you being so unkind to her? Can't you see she loves him and she is devastated about what has happened?" Lilly had to work to contain her temper.

"I will not be challenged in this. Stay in your place..."

"My...place!?" Lilly lost it, "And where is my place, Mr. Lancaster?" As Lilly's voice rose, the uncomfortable witnesses could not surreptitiously exit because Lilly and Marcus stood in front of the door. Some looked at the old magazines piled on the side table, others turned their backs so they didn't feel like they were part of it. "Is my place it up in the bedroom having sex, or maybe you want a scullery maid, cooking your food and emptying your chamber pot?" She stormed past him toward door, not wanting to continue the conversation.

Marcus grabbed her arm, dragging her away from the door. "I'm not through with you..."

Her eyes shot fire, the look intended to wither his resolve. "Yes suh, Mr. Lancaster," she dropped an affected subservient curtsy. "I needs to go fetch my apron, turban and knee pads. I gits right to the kitchen, yes suh, mas'a suh."

The look didn't effect him but her words did. He caught himself looking at her, his mouth agape, no words coming out. He tightened his grip on her arm to the point she winced, "Stop it, Lilly," he hissed. "Your sarcasm is not becoming. Just shut up and let me deal with Jesse as I have planned. We will speak of this, later."

It was Lilly's turn to drop her jaw. It took her a few seconds to process the command to 'shut up'. When she finally did get it, she shook him off and turned, walking out the door. She wanted to slam the door in his face but it opened from the inside and it would make too much noise in a place with sick people. She stomped her way to the door to Jesse's room, looked in, and Marcus pushed past her to enter...

Neither of them had spoken since. Marcus made small talk with Jean, Lilly held Isobel's hand and studied the buildings passing by as they made to the airport.

"*I'm going to scratch that man's eyes out.*" Baron finally said. "*I'm tired of his talking to you that way and he needs to be convinced that you are not going to stand for it."*

"Baron, leave it alone. I know what he is and I have to think this through. I need to figure out how to care about him while I'm pregnant with his child. I can't just walk out and leave him, the baby deserves better than I had."

"But he doesn't deserve anything. He's been evil since he killed you and didn't wait for you to come back. He skipped town with that twinky fag and..."

"Baron!"

"What? Don't worry, Isobel can't hear me..."

You can't just call him names. And what's a twinky fag? I understand faggot, it's wood, but how does that relate to..."

"He's *gay!* You know, the pretty boys who worked with the brothels like you did. Like Georgie, remember him? He was working in Mahogany Hall, having sex with men that liked that sort of thing. Or that back door area in Emma Johnson's place?"

"I know that, I don't know where you get these words."

"I heard on the guards say it."

"Well, you shouldn't talk about Jesse like that, he's almost dead, it's just not right."

Baron chuffed, "I can. He is the love of that evil bastard who left you in that crypt, never checked to see if you were alive. Marcus is the reason you have to drink blood, avoid the sun, and everything else."

"But Jesse isn't involved in it, he wasn't

there..."

"*He was there, just not in your bedroom. He's been with that damned vampire for over one hundred years. You were probably just a distraction for him, nothing more. But it's your life, if you want to be nice to him, and that mean-assed ghoul, go right ahead. But don't tell me you didn't know any of this.*" Baron bent down to clean himself and studiously ignored Lilly.

Once the limo pulled into the hangar, security tried to disembark first, as was protocol, but Marcus stepped out first, put Lance on the ground and led the dog up the stairs to the plane. The security rushed after him, scanning the hangar to make sure things were safe. There was no way to make Marcus Lancaster wait until the area was swept, he didn't care, he expected the staff to do their jobs. The security relaxed as Brian Kennedy gave them the high sign that things were safe.

The others followed, Baron running ahead of Lilly to avoid any further unpleasantness. Lilly and Gregory walked with Isobel between them, Gregory falling behind as the started up to the stairs. Jean brought up the rear, watching everyone as he ascended the stairs and entered the plane. The private ambulance entered the hangar.

The ramp crew quickly removed the stairs and replaced it with a scissor lift. The ambulance crew unloaded Jesse with all the tubes and monitors still attached and operating on emergency battery power. Dr. Young stepped out behind the stretcher, stepping onto the lift. Once Jesse was on the lift, the crewman fastened the safety chain and the lift started its smooth ascent to the plane door.

Marcus stood at the opening, watching his lover. Looking at the still darkening bruises and the bandages, he once again swore an oath that the person who did this would pay and pay in a painful way. He looked down at his hand, at the burn of the angels and wondered if saving the life of someone would come under the edict about changing someone without permission. He didn't care, he would take whatever those winged bastards would do, the only important thing was that Jesse lived.

The lift came to a stop and Marcus moved back to allow the attendants to lift the scoop stretcher off the other one and swing toward the door. They lowered the end with Jesse's feet down to the floor, tilting the head up and pivoting around the bulkhead and into the entryway.

"Careful, gentlemen. Treat him as if he was a crystal chandelier that you are terrified of dropping. Because, if you do, you'll become the shattered crystal." Marcus's tone of voice belied the smile he tried to show. He was worried that they would misstep and drop Jessie and that would finish the job done on him.

"Yes, sir. I promise he's in very good hands," assured the EMT as he stepped totally into the aircraft. Marcus walked ahead of them to the bedroom. The EMTs carefully moved Jesse onto the bed. Dr. Young stepped forward and replaced the portable monitors with the ones for emergency distance transport. Once everything was changed out, the EMTs exited and the door was shut. Maneuvering out of the hangar and to the taxiway, the plane hit the runway and then gathered the energy to make it into the air, circling San Antonio once before heading east toward Houston.

Jack Young had never seen a plane like this one. He had seen pictures of Air Force One, and the movie by the same name, neither of which really didn't measure up to what he was in. He had no idea that anyone could own something like this. From the wood and tile to the furnishings, the entire plane oozed money. And the money it must have taken to furnish this one room with all of the medical equipment must have cost him hundreds of thousands, if not more. Top of the line and brand new.

As the doctor worked, checking Jesse's vitals and the bandages, Marcus stood at the door, watching. He could hear talk coming from the cabin, most of it reassuring Isobel that Marcus and the doctor would keep Jesse alive. "At least she isn't crying anymore," Marcus thought to himself. Women crying, something he had never been able to deal with. It got on his nerves because it wasn't necessary. If it couldn't be dealt with in anger, rage, or comedy, he just didn't relate to it. Tears were a way that women manipulated weaker men into giving them something or doing something. He was just as happy to stay in the room with Jesse and the doctor.

His thoughts drifted to Lilly. He had no idea where the backbone she was showing was coming from. He had fallen for her because of her shy and compliant ways, but now she was almost a shrew. "Probably learned that from Isobel." Izzy had a tendency of chewing him out when she thought it was necessary and the only reason he put up with her is that he had needed a woman to go to society events with and she was also a damned good administrative assistant. He had been giving thought of late to letting her go, wiping her memory of him and everything else around it and just sending her away in favor of Lilly, but now he wasn't sure about that.

"Mr. Lancaster?" Jack called from the bed. "There is new blood from one of the abdominal wounds. It may be just seepage, but I doubt it." He shook his head in obvious distress. "It's because he was moved too soon. Something pulled loose. We need to go in and it cannot be done here. How long until we get to this hospital of yours?"

Marcus turned to face him, "How bad?"

"Bad enough. We need to get him back into surgery soonest, this is not a wait and see situation."

Marcus ran his left hand through his hair, his mind going into speed mode working on a solution. He had wanted to wait until they got Jesse back to Houston before doing what was going to be necessary but this changed things. He walked into the closet and pulled out an empty plastic wide-mouth gallon jug and then walked to the bed. "You need to leave the room, doctor." He pushed the glamour into the other man's brain. "You are not needed here." He pushed harder.

Failure.

"No dice, Lancaster. He's my patient and I am responsible for him."

Great, he was a very strong personality. Figured. "I am in charge here and you will do as I say." Marcus picked up Jesse's hand, it felt colder than he remembered.

"No sir. He was released into my medical care. Right now, his sister gave me medical charge of Jesse Chamberlain. You do not have Medical power of attorney, you are not married and Texas does not recognize same-sex marriage, anyway, you have no say in what happens and I'm telling you that you will…"

Marcus threw the jug down, bending it, and stalked over to the doctor. All he did was flash the fangs that had punched down in his anger. "I am in charge and you would do well to step back.

"What the hell?" the doctor exclaimed in disbelief.

"I won't be drinking his blood." He held up the jug.

"You are a vampire?"

"Damn it, man. Yes, I'm a vampire." He popped the fangs back up, then back down again as he placed the jug on the floor to the bed and began laying out towels and a brown leather pouch.

Jack stared. In his psych rotation he had dealt with all kinds of psychosis, but this this was the most acute he had ever seen. This guy, his patient's partner, was psychotic, delusional, and possibly schizophrenic. He was going to end up having sedate the guy or he would lose his patient to the mad man in front of him.

Marcus reached into the leather pouch and pulled out a scalpel.

"Mr. Lancaster, I am warning you, do not..."

"Silence! I will do what I will and you will sit over there as a witness." Marcus pointed to the chair on the other side of the bed.

Jack looked helplessly at his medical bag next to Marcus, no way to get it and shoot him with something to stop this madness. All he could do was glare at the...vampire.

Marcus ignored the look. He took Jesse's hand, caressing his face. "Jesse, it's me. Baby, I have to keep you with me, you hear? I do not want you to leave me just because this happened. I let medical science work but it's plain that you aren't going to make it without help. Jess, I know we talked about this and I know you didn't want it done because you were afraid. Please don't be afraid. I promise you will wake up and this will be okay. I know that without your express permission, I will probably get another brand, but babe, I will take that chance. I love you and I want you with me forever."

Jack was listening to this monologue, not believing that the guy obviously didn't have a foot in reality. Then he saw something, tears of blood started falling down the mighty Marcus Lancaster's cheeks. Tears. Of blood. What the fuck?

"Okay Jesse. I'm going to make a little cut. I wish, darling, that I could take all of you inside of me but the doctors have given you medications that won't...I can't. So, we have to do it this way." He continued his soliloquy, gently stroking the hand. "So I will do it this way. But soon, as you are beginning to float away from me, I will give you the gift that Eadwina gave me, all those decades ago. Then you will..." He stopped and kissed his beloved's forehead, "You will come back to me. Stay calm, it will be alright." Marcus turned the hand over and made a long slit up the arm into the vein. The blood flowed down the arm to the hand, which Marcus laid gently into the neck of the jug on the floor, fingers pointing down. As the blood drained, Marcus sang a song under his breath, something from back when he had met Jesse in that saloon during the Civil War. It was comforting for Jesse and Marcus was also hoping to make himself stronger.

Truth be told, he was terrified. He'd been able to turn the other progeny he had. Three successes before his failure with Lilly. He still didn't know what went wrong with her turning, why she didn't turn as quickly as others. And now...and now he was trying it again. If it screwed up...

Jack couldn't see the jug but the pallor of his patient deepened, his lips and fingertips on the other hand turning an ash gray as the blood kept flowing. The heart monitor dropped, it would try to rally and then fall further as his body fought to stay alive. As it neared 10 beats a minute and his patient began to reflex breathe, Jack couldn't bear this atrocity any longer. "Mr. Lancaster, you are killing him! This is not a mercy killing, it's murder." He knew he had probably sealed his own fate but his oath would not condone this.

The look in the eyes of the man crying blood shined with sorrow. "Stay there, doctor. This is almost done." Marcus pulled the hand up from the floor and began to lick the cut liberally, taking care to go over each inch until it closed. What was left behind was a thick line where the skin had knit together.

Marcus pulled the intubation tube and laid it on the bed. It was all Jack could do to not get up and throw the obviously deranged man across the room. His patient would not be able to breathe without that tube and hookup. But, as he started to rise, he saw Marcus bite his own wrist, dropping blood across the bed as he reached out to lay the open wound over Jesse's mouth. "Come on, Jess. Drink to live. Baby, drink the offered life and come back to me." Jack was sure that the man...vampire...whatever... was pleading for the now dead man to come back.

Time seemed to stand still. Marcus bit his wrist another three times, holding the bleeding mess over Jesse's open mouth, occasionally stroking the throat so he would swallow. It wasn't working. Just like Lilly, it wasn't working. A gut-wrenching howl of pure agony and grief came from the depths of his being. He had killed another lover and the only one who ever truly mattered. He was weak and desperate, pushing himself up and away from the bed, trailing the blood from his wrist. He opened the door.

Everyone stopped talking when the door opened. Isobel cried out and stood up as Marcus stumbled into the room, his arm still bleeding and blood tears streaking his face. Jean and Gregory stepped up and Jean took Marcus's bleeding arm, licking it gently to close it.

"You look like death, mon ami." Jean said between licks.

"Mr. Lancaster, what do we need to do? How's Mr. Chamberlain?" Gregory put himself under Marcus's opposite shoulder to give him the ability to stand a bit longer.

"Lilly, I need you in the room, you need to feed Jesse or we're going to lose him." Lilly stood up and started to walk to her maker but Isobel grabbed her hand and pulled her back.

"Marcus, Lilly's in no shape to help right now. Can Jean do it?" Isobel didn't want to say why it was a bad idea for Lilly but she did want Jesse helped.

"Of course, ma belle. Marcus, is that suitable?" Marcus nodded and Jean left his side to go to Jesse. Marcus started to walk back toward the bedroom, trying to shake Gregory off but the young man stayed under his arm, supporting him as they crossed the threshold. Jack stood and motioned for Gregory to place the weakened man in the chair, backing into the corner. Gregory gently lowered Marcus into the chair and then knelt down next to him.

Jean sat on the edge of the bed and pulled up his sleeve to open his wrist. "Jesse, it's Jean. I am helping Marcus. I'm going to give you my blood to finish the change. Marcus is here with you as well, you're safe. Just drink and let us take care of you." He bit into his wrist and, just as Marcus had, he laid the wound over Jesse's mouth.

About two seconds after the blood started flowing, Jesse moved, grabbing the arm and making long pulls on the blood offered. "That's right, Jesse, drink deep. You're going to be well."

Marcus started to stand but found he couldn't. Jean looked at the ghoul and then back to Marcus. "Gregory, please feed Mr. Lancaster..."

"I'm fine, Jean, I just need to hold Jesse." Marcus tried to stand again.

"Yes sir, I can feed him, Mr. Lancaster, how do you want to take it, sir?" Gregory knelt down in front of him. Marcus pulled him up and pushed his head over, stabbing his fangs into the offered artery. Gregory moaned as he gave into the feeling.

Jack just stared. The men seemed to all be under the same delusion. Bloodletting and sucking, it was all too much. This was so bizarre He tried to push himself into the corner, hoping he could wake up from this horrifying nightmare.

Then he saw it. The stitches on his patients began to let loose, scar tissue under them fading a bit. Bruises faded entirely. He was sure the bones were knitting as the heart monitor lifted into a steady normal beat.

"Doctor?" He heard someone call. "Doctor, I need you over here. Jesse needs some fresh human blood to complete this, please, monsieur." Jean motioned.

"Me?" Jack became worried, this guy wanted him to donate blood in this strange blood ritual. Normally he would say no, not even hesitating. However, this was anything but normal by any standards, this was his patient and he needed blood. Jack walked over to the bed and knelt down. "Do you need to cut my wrist?"

"No, monsieur, that's not necessary. Give the wrist to Jesse and he will do the puncture. I shall warn you, you will become entranced with the feeling but when I say enough, you must pull away or risk your own death, nes pas?"

Jack nodded, reaching across to take his patient's hand. The now conscious man grabbed his hand and pulled his wrist to his mouth and bit. Jack stifled a bit of a squeal as the fangs invaded his arm, but then it felt very sexual and soft, luring him into an easy restful drift. He didn't notice at first when Jean tried to pull him away, finally pulling hard and tearing the wrist free from the fangs Jesse had in it. That time, Jack wasn't bashful, he yelled out an "owww" and grabbed his wrist. Jean grabbed him and pulled the wrist to his own mouth and licked it until it closed.

"You need to go out and wait for us, get Isobel to get you some orange juice and food, you need to replenish your blood, just as if you had donated at a blood bank." Jean helped him up and pushed him from the room. He noticed that Marcus had let go of Gregory's neck and was laving it closed, watching Jesse. Jean helped Gregory up and pushed him from the room as well. Marcus and Jean then disconnected all of the medical equipment and helped Jesse sit up. Blinking a few times, Jesse looked around, fastening his gaze on Marcus.

"How could you." He growled.

Chapter Eighteen

MARCUS STOOD AT the end of the bed, looking at Jesse. He knew he had stepped over the line in changing him. They had talked about it over and over since they had met. Jesse was fine with being a ghoul, allowing Marcus to feed from him and taking enough from him to sustain his own life. Marcus had run though the scenario's and tried to show him that there were things out there that would take him away, but this was no hypothetical incident, he had almost lost Jesse and there was no way he was going to let that happen, promises or not.

And damn the angels to hell, he wasn't going to let their "rules" stop him from keeping his lover with him. Let them come, that was one mark he would take gladly.

"I said, how could you." Jesse stood up beside the bed, ripping the casts and pulling at the bandages as he looked around the room for his clothing. The hospital gown he was wearing wasn't quite fashionable. He spotted his suitcases next to the door and walked over to them, never taking his eyes off of Marcus. He bent to pick one up but Marcus reached down and picked it up.

"Let me, darling. I want you to take it easy for a while until we make sure everything is back to normal." He smiled at Jesse, hoping he would understand the intention.

"Back to normal! Are you seriously telling me that I'm normal, Marcus? Look what the fuck you did to me! You promised to never turn me, no matter what! How the hell is any of this normal?" Jesse shouted, advancing on his lover, fists balled.

"This appears to be my cue to exit, stage left" Jean walked to the door, opening it as he turned back to the two men, "I don't mind the yelling, but please, don't make me have to come in here and separate you. Jesse, Marcus did what he had to do, and there's still the petite matter of who did that to you in the first place. They are the ones you should be angry with. I know Marcus wants to get his hands on the person that ordered, then the thugs that carried it out, but he will have to beat me to it, if I find them first. After all, mon ami, you are now my brother and we always take care of family." Jean turned and walked out, quietly shutting the door behind him.

Isobel stopped her quiet discussion with the others and stood up. "Jean, what did Marcus do? Did he turn Jesse?"

"Ah ma belle, oui, he did. There was no other choice, we were going to lose him if he hadn't. When Marcus planned to take the boy out of the hospital, he was afraid it might come to this. We brought the doctor, hoping we wouldn't have to,

Marcus tried to respect Jesse's wishes his condition started to deteriorate and Marcus was forced to do it immediately. I know he would have wanted to do this at home, in friendly and familiar surroundings but..."

"I'm glad he did, I know Jesse won't like it but he will get used to it eventually. Did he say who hurt him?"

"Non, he didn't. Right now it's the last thing he wants to talk about, he's busy castigating Marcus for the sin of keeping him alive. I've seen that reaction prior to this, it's quite usual. I almost killed Marcus after he turned me. I thought he was going to keep his promise of not turning me but that vampire has a mind of a shyster lawyer, he asked another other vampire to turn me and when the man turned him down, Marcus shrugged and said, 'Not my fault, he wouldn't do it. So I had to." The resultant fight lasted a full 45 minutes and started with sabers and ended with fists. At the end, we were both too tired and too sore to keep going so we went to town, had some drinks, and found a few pretty girls to have supper with, as it were."

"Mmm." Dr. Young mumbled, swallowing the bite of ham sandwich that one of the security guys had brought him. "I am curious about this whole vampire thing. I'm still not sure that I understand the whole medical process involved in changing a dying human into one of the creatures."

"Well," Jean turned to him, "We're not creatures, we're human. We just have a different makeup once the blood exchange is finished."

"But what does that blood do to the body to turn it into a human who can subsist on only blood?"

Isobel spoke up, "They don't subsist only on blood, they can eat food as well. It's not as nourishing and it makes their bowels work like humans, but if they just live on blood, there is no bodily secretions. As for the rest of it, the fangs are the biggest change, they are totally retractable. They hear better than us, they are faster than us, and a lot stronger."

"But I am interested in the cellular level changes. What does it do and how are vampires compared to humans? Are there changes to other systems, bone, nervous system, brain function? I'm very interested in studying them." He thought about the consequences of all the questions about as long as it took to take a sip of the orange juice. It was just all too fascinating.

"I minored in sociology so I have a hobby interest in that as well, what do vampires do to live in society? Are they all as rich as Mr. Lancaster or are there various strata of society. Is there a vampire king or queen? Are there doctors, police, and bankers? If they are sick with a disease, does the change take that away as well? I know that Mr. Chamberlain has had a lot of healing to his own body happen but given the extent of the injuries, he's got to still have problems from the beating. How long will it take to...?"

Jean began to laugh. "Doctor, you are indeed a very curious fellow! A bit too curious for my taste. What is that old saying about curiosity killing the cat?"

Suddenly Jack Young realized how outrageously rude and insulting he had been. Immediately, he retreated into a more differential mode, "Please excuse my brashness and my impolite questions. I was overcome...It must be the researcher in me, I'm very sorry"

Jean interjected, "Your giddiness can be attributed to the euphoric results of your blood contribution."

He thought for a moment. "If you would please indulge me, I do have one last question, do vampires only bite to reproduce? Or since they,...you...were once human, can you have babies? Are there any vampire children?"

Isobel and Lilly looked at each other.

"I've never heard of a vampire getting pregnant." Jean said. "Or impregnating anyone. There must be something in the change that causes sterility."

"Darn. I would have loved to deliver a vampire baby and see the whole process. Oh well." Jack went back to munching on the sandwich, washing it down with the Dr. Pepper next to him.

Jean did catch the look between the girls. Was it the doctor's inappropriate questions or was it something more? He started to ask but something about the way Isobel was holding Lilly's hand gave him the feeling that the question would not be proper with others around. He filed it away to ask at a later time.

THE REST OF the short flight was punctuated with the muffled argument, sounds from the room getting quiet and then loud again. Once the airplane touched down back at Ellington Field, Jesse jerked the bedroom door open and walked straight to the hatch for the aircraft, impatiently waiting for the staff to open it. Marcus walked out after him, picked up Lance, and waited until everyone had disembarked before he silently followed. The limo was running and waiting for him, the usual configuration of a guard up front, the entourage in the main compartment and the security chase vehicle behind.

Seating arrangements were stressed, Marcus with the dog on one corner, Jesse in the cross-corner. Lilly was sitting next to Marcus and holding Baron.

"Do we have to sit next to the stupid canine? It's bad enough he's sitting on that bastard vampire but the dog is staring at me." Baron told Lilly while cleaning a paw nonchalantly.

"Yes, we do. Things are rough with everyone right now, especially Marcus. And it is, I'm afraid, going to only get worse once I tell him about the baby. I'm really not looking forward to that."

"Does this mean that, since you're having kittens for him, you will have to live with him and Stupid the Dog?"

"It's babies in humans, Baron. And yes, he will have responsibility for us both, and you, of course.

Lance and you will have to just find a way to talk and be nice."

Baron growled. *"I really don't care about the dog."*

"I don't care, you have to behave yourself and no antagonizing the dog. I must tell Marcus and I'm not sure how he's going to take it."

"Well, until we have that solved, I'm ignoring the dog. It's just asking too much to make us be friends."

"As you wish, Baron. Just don't cause trouble." Lilly rubbed her temples, a headache was coming on fast. She probably needed to feed again soon.

After the short ride to the building, not only did Marcus and Jesse exit from different doors, they took separate elevator rides to the penthouse, Marcus allowing Jesse to go first. Marcus walked into the room just as Jesse slammed the door to his part of the floor, throwing the lock loudly. Marcus put Lance down and pulled out his phone and called the security detail to come up and take Lance for a long walk. Before the guard pushed the button to leave, the elevator doors opened and Lilly stepped out. She smiled at the guard, pointing at Baron standing on the other side of the elevator so the guard would be waiting to let the cat back in. She bent and petted Lance's head, and then watched them disappear behind the elevator doors.

"Lilly, listen, I am not in the mood for anything. This whole trip has been awful and I just don't want to do anything more than drink enough scotch to try to sleep." Marcus said to her reflection in the window glass.

"Marcus, I wouldn't be here if it weren't important." She laid her purse on the couch. "This can't wait, I'm afraid."

Marcus's usually rigid shoulders sagged as he sighed, turning back to face her, his drink in his hand. He downed it and then poured himself another scotch, no ice, pouring it to the brim. Swilling half of it, he then looked at her. "What is so fucking important that can't wait?"

Lilly stiffened, working up her courage. No time like the present, she thought, "Marcus, I'm pregnant."

Marcus laughed so hard he almost dropped the scotch, but pulled it to his lips and downed the rest of the glass and poured another big one. Through his chuckles he wondered how stupid she thought he was. "Bullshit, Lilly. Vampires cannot get pregnant. What the hell are you trying to pull? Do you want money? You've got it, IF you go away for a while and leave me the fuck alone. How much money do you want, whatever it is? Just. Go. Away."

"No money, I'm not that type of girl."

Marcus broke into grand peals of laughter at the sheer absurdity of that statement and turned to her, his eyes alight with cruelty. "You are precisely that type of girl."

"Not anymore. I'm telling the truth, I peed on a little stick and it says I'm pregnant. I would not lie about something like this. I don't know how, either, but evidently vampires are not sterile and I am proof.

Draining the last drop in the glass, he slammed it down hard on the bar, shattering it. "God damn it Lilly, you cannot be pregnant. I've been a fucking vampire since 1460 and I have NEVER known a vampire to sire a child or get pregnant. It's not something that happens. You're my progeny, it's my responsibility to take care of you. You don't have to lie about being pregnant, why the fuck are you lying." He stormed, face turning red and eyes wild. "Well?"

Lilly snatched up her purse, starting toward the restroom in his bedroom. He stepped in front of her.

"What the hell are you doing? Leave now or I won't be responsible for what happens. I'm too damned pissed off to deal with your bullshit lie, Lilly."

She stopped and held up her purse. "I have a second stick to do the test again and I'm doing it here so you can see the evidence for yourself. I am not a liar!" She stepped around him to go toward the lavatory. He let her get around him but he walked close behind her, all the way into the bathroom.

"Do you mind, Marcus. Toilet things are private. You can wait outside," she said as she dug into the purse for the test strip.

"Oh no. I'm going to be right here when you piss on that stick, I want to make sure you're not trying something like a gold diggers little whore."

She shook, the rage beginning to climb at the same time the blood tears started to flow. "I am not a whore, not anymore, I'm not trying to do anything more than prove the truth to you. Have it your way." She threw her purse to the floor, pulled up her dress and lowered her bloomers, beginning to sit down to pee.

"Nope, do it standing up. I want to see that it is done properly. Let me look at the package and the stick."

"You don't have to worry..." She began.

"No. I do." He stepped up close enough to snatch the box out of her hand. He read everything on it, pulled out the instructions on it and read those, finally looking at the stick. He handed the stick to her and watched her remove the wrapper.

It wasn't easy to do but she managed to squat and get the stick wet with urine. She felt worse than she ever had as a prostitute. She had done things she wasn't proud of but it was to keep eating and a roof over her head. But she had never had to perform her toilet with a man watching, there were things that were private. Once it was done, she laid the stick on the sink, wiped herself, flushed, and then rearranged her clothing.

Marcus wasn't watching her after she put the stick on the sink, he was busy watching the window on it to see what it would indicate. The instructions told him it would be a plus or a minus sign and he wanted to see it first so he could tell her to leave. He knew it was preposterous to say she was pregnant. Every female he had been with over the centuries, even Eadwina, talked about pregnancy but none of them ever became pregnant. When science finally figured out what happened in the sex act that caused pregnancy, he had his sperm test to see if he could father someone. Rajesh Kumar had his laboratory perform the test and it came back with 0% chance of pregnancy, his fluid didn't have any sperm in it. There was no way to...

The damned window in the stick changed: there was a very blue plus sign showing.

She wasn't lying. Lilly was pregnant. As a vampire. Pregnant. With child.

He shot a look up at her face as he stood up from the bent position he had held since the stick was placed. "Okay. It says you are pregnant. Who did you sleep with that could have done it?"

Lilly stopped in her tracks. Thinking back, she could remember being with Sullivan but he was an angel and they didn't have children either. She knew that the papers said a pregnancy could be found within a few days before a menses was due, but she didn't have regular menses, only a few times after she was turned. She didn't want to say anything about Sullivan, Marcus was angry enough, bringing him up would just push him further into rage.

"You. I slept with you."

"But you also had sex with that damned angel you pine over. Why can't he be the father?" As he said it, he began to wonder why he was trying to give the credit to Lilly's former lover. If the vampire world found out that he had fathered a child on another vampire, he would be able to move up in the council, no one else had achieved that. Not even that ass-clown Xun had managed to do it.

"Look, I came here to tell you because I thought, in error, that you cared enough about me to take responsibility for the baby. Angels can't have children, so I'm not bothering Sullivan. The angels are not human, vampires are. Even with all the changes, we are still human. I guess I made a mistake in believing you would want to be a father. I can manage for myself." She picked up her bag and the items that had spilled from it, and walked past Marcus, heading for the elevator.

"Lilly. Wait a moment. You honestly believe that I am the father of that child you are carrying? Do you want me to be the father?"

She stopped, turned to face him. "I don't know, Marcus. Honestly, I do not know. The way you act toward me belies your words of caring about me. I don't know for positive you are the father, there's no way to tell that. I do know that I am the mother and it's ultimately my responsibility to take care of the baby before it is born and see to it that, if I cannot take care of it, that the baby finds a good home with people who will love it."

There it was. Out in the air. Lilly had managed to take all the anger and all the certainty out of his argument.

She was pregnant. And the baby was, by all indications, his. He had no idea that it could have happened, but the baby was there, by the testing.

And the baby would be a Lancaster. And by the lineage, that baby could be in line to take over

England if it were known, at least if he was not a...

"Will the baby be a vampire from birth?" He had to ask, the lineage would demand it. He took her hand gently and led her back to the couch, trying to make her more comfortable.

She shrugged her shoulders, "I don't know, Marcus. I had hoped you would know, you've been a vampire a lot longer than I have."

"I don't think there are any vampire obstetricians, I want you taken care of, given every chance for this pregnancy to work."

Marcus pulled out his cell phone and hit a button, "Isobel, I need you to go to the guest apartment we assigned to Dr. Young and bring him up here. Never mind why, I need to see him, now." He cut the call off, not allowing Isobel to ask any further questions.

"But the doctor is a surgeon, Marcus."

"Lilly, a doctor does rotations, or cross-trains, in other disciplines. I am quite sure that Dr. Young has had training in obstetrics. I am going to talk to him about taking care of you, and our baby, and make sure that things go smoothly. I don't want to lose the baby, and I certainly do not want to lose you, my love."

"Love? That's a word I've not heard used much at all. You love Jesse, that is certain. Me? I'm not certain you do. But I will do everything I can to keep the baby and give birth. Some of the women in Storyville got pregnant and unless they went to a mambo to get a tea, they were at the mercies of those who would do horrible things to kill the baby. I will not do either of those things. Children are sacred and I want to be able to die with my honor and beliefs intact."

The elevator opened and Dr. Young strode out, followed by Isobel, who went straight to Lilly, sat down, and held her hand, "You okay?" Lilly nodded her head as Marcus shook hands with the doctor.

"Dr. Young. I have a few questions for you and, based on those answers, I may have a proposition for you."

"Okay, I will try to answer them for you."

"Dr. Young, you are a licensed doctor in this state, correct?"

The doctor smiled, "First, sir, I would ask you to call me Jack, there's no reason to stand on formality. Second, yes, I'm licensed as a physician."

"Jack." Marcus acknowledged. "Your training isn't just in surgery, is it?"

"No, when we are training as interns, we do rotations in all the major disciplines to learn what is there and how to handle it. Why?"

"I need you to become an obstetrician. I have a situation here requiring one. Lilly is pregnant and there are no baby doctors in our community. I will order any equipment you need, I will get you credentials in any hospital you wish to work in, however I would rather you work for me, I can pay very well and even provide a large apartment for you. But I need you to do this for me," Marcus took Lilly's other hand, "I mean us, and take care of Lilly and the baby."

"Oh, okay. I'm rusty on pregnancy care and delivery but I will review things. I welcome becoming a part of your operation."

Lilly sighed. Marcus had accepted the pregnancy, she had a doctor to care for her and the baby, and all was right in the world.

But why did she have such a feeling of dread?

Chapter Nineteen

M ARCUS SENT DOWN to the infirmary and had a few items brought up for Jack to use. He had a stethoscope and a few other items for emergency medicine but nothing for examination of a pregnant woman.

"Okay, Lilly, you need to tell me how long you believe you've been pregnant. What form of birth control were you using, are you on the pill?" The doctor started in on the medical questions while they waited for the supplies.

"I've been here about three weeks, which means I probably have been pregnant for almost that whole time. And I'm not on birth control, no condoms. And I have no idea what 'the pill' is, which pill are you speaking of? I don't take pills much, I don't need to."

Jack looked at Marcus for explanation.

"She was turned in 1900. She didn't come out of her crypt until about six weeks ago. She has no knowledge between being laid in the tomb and leaving it, no current references. I'm constantly having to explain things to her that every other person knows."

"Well, Lilly. The pill is a small amount of female hormones that women take once a day to fool their body into thinking it is pregnant for three weeks out of the month. The fourth week she doesn't take a pill or she takes a placebo, or sugar pill with no hormones so that her body has the menses and then she starts all over again for the next month. A condom is..."

Lilly smiled, "I do know condoms. We had them in the brothel when I was alive."

Jack arched an eyebrow, "Brothel? You worked in a brothel?"

"Yes, doctor. I haven't done it since I died at Marcus's hand, or rather fangs, in 1900. I'm trying to be a normal lady in this time."

"Did you have doctors or ever see one?"

"There were doctors who came in sometimes when a girl was sick or got beaten by a client. Our house wasn't one that had attacks on the girls often, Miss Lulu made sure that Abe, our house-man, was walking the hallways and monitoring things."

"I know you probably have seen someone with venereal diseases, like syphilis. Were you ever told or treated for any disease?"

"No sir, I was always clean. I took care to make sure my clients were washed and that they didn't have any wounds. I was required to have all gentlemen wear a condom. Some of the other girls would ignore the rules but I never did."

"I will be checking you for diseases now. I don't know how a disease would work with a vampire but I ..."

Marcus spoke up, "Turning usually will wipe any disease or wound out as the process goes along."

"But the cuts on Jesse that I worked on. When you turned him, those two things didn't go away when the rest of his injuries did. Any idea why?"

"I have a few ideas but I want to confirm them I actually may need your help it." Marcus stood next to the window and looked out over the city, the lights still on in several of the buildings.

"Me? What do you need me to do?"

"Now's not the time to discuss this part of your job, we will discuss this later. Right now, I need you to confirm that Lilly is pregnant and if the child lives and when it will be born."

Jack looked to Lilly, then to Marcus. "Where can we go for some privacy?" Marcus pointed toward the bedroom. They walked in and Jack motioned for Lilly to lay down. Once she was settled, he smiled and said, "I'll try to make this as easy as possible, please pull your knees up and let them drop toward the bed. That's right, now take a deep breath."

THE CHECKUP WAS quick and thorough. Lilly was sore and not sure what the doctor had found. He led her back to the living room and sat her on the couch.

"It's been a long time since my obstetrics rotation. I will need a sonogram to confirm my suspicions."

"No problem," Marcus responded.

"Suspicions? Is there something wrong?" Lilly asked.

"No, it just seems that the fetus is a little further along than we suspected."

"How much further along?"

"Five to six weeks along, which would put your due date about mid-May." Jack turned to Marcus, "I'm going to need a sonogram machine to do the examination, do you have one?"

"No, but I'm giving you the clinic down on the second floor so give Isobel a list of what you need and we'll see to it you have everything on it."

Lilly's mind dropped out of the conversation. There was no way she was four weeks along. She wasn't out of the crypt until four weeks ago, she and Baron were still living by themselves and she had kept herself well-hidden, not speaking to another human since 1900. The night with Sullivan happened on September 1, at most she could only be two weeks pregnant if he was the father. Marcus was after that. Neither man could have been the father.

Marcus's bellow of fury and frustration snapped Lilly out of her thoughts. He started to call her a liar again, his anger radiating out of him as he walked to her and took her face in one of his hands. "So, you're lying to me about being the father! I should have known that once a whore, always a whore. Well, you've been found out, I want you gone. Now. Take that disgusting fleabag cat with you...or I'll end him!"

He could have hit her and she would not be as angry as she was at his allegations and threat against Baron. "I beg your pardon. I'm not a liar. I am not leaving for you. I'm leaving for me and Baron, and...my...baby. And you won't see me again." She pulled loose from his grip and stormed toward the door.

"Lilly, wait." Jack stepped in front of her. "Marcus, this is all new to me. You are both vampires and I have no idea what that does to the gestation time. That could speed it up or slow it down, I honestly don't know. If you are correct and there is no other history of a vampire giving birth, then we're going to have to guess about everything, document everything and get it published for other doctors."

"No!" both Lilly and Marcus said in unison, going back to yelling over each other, their argument getting louder and louder as they talked.

Jack's hand went up, "Please! Just a moment. Lilly, I beg you, don't go until you hear me."

"There's no way I'm staying so I can be accused of further crimes. I'm leaving and I'll deal with my baby my way!" Lilly's hands went to her hips.

"Nothing will be published in journals, that will be out of the question for the Vampire Council. The information can be written and I will take it to the Council's headquarters and it will be deposited in the library there. But that's just a statement because she's leaving and not lying to me any longer." Marcus stood his ground, glaring at her.

"Fine with me. I'm going." She turned once again and headed toward the elevator.

"Just make sure that if you carry it to the conclusion, you do not implicate me in the documents, I will not stand for being named the father." He took a step further toward her. "That is, unless you don't abort it, I wouldn't be surprised if you…"

SLAP. The sound echoed throughout the penthouse.

"How DARE you! I am a good Catholic and Christian, I would NEVER do that to a child, even when her 'father'," she spat the word like it left a bad taste in her mouth, "Is such pathetic, selfish, and vile coward who doesn't want her." The elevator opened and she walked in, pushing a button, keeping her back toward the closing doors.

She didn't begin to cry until the elevator started moving.

"You're dismissed, doctor." Marcus wanted to just be alone so he could destroy a room or two. Lancelot had taken up a spot in a chair close to his master, sensing the emotional upset.

"Marcus, there may be a very easy explanation for this. It is DNA."

"I said dismissed, doctor." He turned to see the doctor had not moved.

He spoke faster, trying to explain all to the obstinate vampire in one breath. He hadn't been so challenged, or inspired, in a very long time. "Look your DNA changed when you became a vampire. While the basic strands that made you are there, it has been changed by the new DNA that filled in the blood and organs, giving you life. Lilly's did the same. She probably holds a part of your DNA within her blood since you are her maker, but that's not what's going on with the child. There is some specialized biology at work and..."

"I said NO, damn it. Spare me your attempts to get me to accept that whelp. I want nothing to do with it. She was a whore when I met her, a whore when I bedded her, and she's continued to be a whore. She was pregnant three months ago, so much for that sob story about being in the crypt for a hundred years. Nothing more than a lying, conniving, devious whore!" Marcus turned to continue studying the horizon.

Jack watched as Lance jumped down and walked to his master, whining until his owner picked him up. Marcus hadn't commanded to leave, again, so he carefully continued. "You saw how Mr. Chamberlain changed, how fast he healed once you gave him your blood. Do all vampires heal that fast when they are turned? Do they heal that fast when hurt?" By asking questions that needed a response, his hopes were that the vampire would engage and it would assuage his anger.

"Yes, they do." Marcus answer, still petting the dog in his arms, not turning around.

"That's the answer. His changing indicates that the vampire blood is very potent and can change the DNA, the cellular regeneration is sped up and you see the immediate restorative result."

Marcus turned and studied the doctor, not saying a word for several minutes. "So, you think that whatever happened could have happened after she arrived in Houston, and your hypothesis is based on how fast Jesse healed from his injuries? What else do you think? Are you still telling me that it's mine?"

"Yes, I am. She is progressing in the pregnancy faster than a human due to the vampire DNA. The fetus is growing rapidly, just like Chamberlain healed rapidly. At this rate, full gestation could be reached sometime between mid-March to mid-May. Just don't know, just yet. I'm telling you, Marcus, you're the father here, there's no doubt in my mind."

Marcus chewed on that information. Maybe the doctor was right, the vampire DNA would make a difference. He sat down in the chair that Lance had taken up previously, putting the dog down. Lance didn't move but lay down on Marcus's shoes. "But, one more hang-up, I have been a vampire since 1460 and I have not been celibate. I've been with many women, both human and vampire and not one of them has gotten pregnant. If they did, they miscarried and didn't tell me. I've been given a sperm test in another circumstance and it came out shooting blanks, no sperm. The records in our council library show no children born of any vampire. This may be a new development in vampire evolution....may, if and when she does or does not miscarry.

"Let's not get ahead of ourselves here. Right

now we have to do some damage control. You must calm her down and convince her to stay. Her blood pressure is through the roof and that is not good for any pregnant woman, vampire or not. Then there's the matter of her diet, I don't believe the usual prenatal diet and vitamins will suffice here." He patted Marcus's shoulder.

"Don't touch me." Jack jerked his hand away like it was scalded.

"Sorry, do you have any idea what to feed her? I don't know if my regular diet training will be good here."

"We can eat or drink anything humans consume but we do have to eliminate. If we adhere to a blood-only diet, that is unnecessary. I'll check with Isobel and see if she has any ideas and we'll keep whatever she needs near at hand." Marcus explained.

"First, you need to find her, talk TO her, not at her. Be kind, calm her down, and convince her to stay. If she leaves, we don't know what sort of difficulties she will have. Since her blood will contain some of the same anomalies that Mr. Chamberlain's does, and if she goes to a human doctor, no telling what tests they will do."

The chirp of his cell phone alerted him that there was a message. He glanced down and saw it was from Castro. Clicking on the alert, the words came up, "Found our assassin. The deed was done for Nelson Mishkoph."

The growl from the vampire caused Dr. Young to take an involuntary step back. From the drop in the temperature in Marcus's anger, someone was going to be very sorry for that message. He was just hoping that it wouldn't be him.

Marcus stood. "I'll walk you down to your guest suite and then go see her. We will need to talk more later." Marcus paused and read the odd expression on Jack's face. "You think things are strange now?" The doctor nodded. "You just wait, things are about to get a lot more challenging. I hope you're up for it." He smiled a shrouded, mischievous grin. "But right now, you must get some sleep."

The two men left the penthouse, each lost in his own thoughts.

Chapter Twenty

LILLY LOCKED THE door to her bedroom and flopped down on the bed. To hell with the linens, she needed a good cry and peroxide would get the stains out.

How dare Marcus call her a liar! Not a single word of concern, no support. She wondered why that even mattered, since she arrived in Houston, he had only showed he cared for her only a couple of times. Hell, he seemed to be casual about his relationship with Jesse and Isobel who had been with him much longer.

No, Marcus Lancaster was a full-blown narcissist.

"*I told you so.*"

She sat up, looking around the room. "*No, I'm going outside, waiting on the humans to open the door for me so I can get out for dinner. I need to go fast so I can get back up there. We need to pack and find our way back home. This time he's over the line, he hurt you one time too many. He doesn't deserve you and he doesn't deserve the kitten.*"

Lilly let his consistent mistake alone. "We cannot go back. I cannot have the baby in the crypt," she said aloud. It was her room, she could talk to the air if she wanted.

Baron continued, *"It's not a mistake and yes you can, I've seen it done a lot of the time."*

Lilly wiped her cheeks, smearing the blood across her face. "No, Baron. We're gone from there and never will return. Marcus has ordered us out. He wants nothing to do with me, or the baby. I have to find some way to stay. Even a selfish, arrogant narcissist is better than no father at all."

"That, I'm not sure of." Baron huffed.

"Mothers can do some things but there are just some things that the father can do. I miss my own father, I cannot do that to her."

"So she learns to be a bastard, to hurt others to make herself feel good. That's exactly what she doesn't need," the sentence was punctuated with a growl.

"I'm not going to New Orleans. If I don't stay here, I will at least stay in Houston. We may not live with him but we will let her be with him so she knows him. And that, Baron, is final."

"Final? Have you given thought to this being Sullivan's kitten? You were with him at home. Why couldn't he be the father?"

Lilly sat up, searching her memory. "No, he's not. It's got to be Marcus."

"Why?"

Good question. Lilly hadn't really thought about it, just dismissed it outright. She was with Marcus and that had to be the father of the baby. What if..."

"Lilly?" The Irish lilt wasn't Baron.

"*Yes, I contacted him for you. You need to talk with him, it's only right. I'm going to go find dinner again.*" Baron cut the link.

SULLIVAN COULD HEAR Lilly's heartbeat through the link. "Lilly? Baron told me you have news. What's going on?" Sullivan rose from his bed, not that he was sleeping anyway. Even though it was day, he couldn't rest. Something was wrong, but he hadn't pinned it to Lilly until Baron talked with him. He ran his hand through the dark brown curls on his head.

He heard a sigh and then "*Sullivan, I'm sorry. Baron is trying to interfere with something. I'm sorry he woke you.*"

"I wasn't asleep. We can talk. What's happening?" Rubbing the gravel out of his brown eyes, Sullivan paced the floor of his cell.

Lilly stayed quiet for a couple of minutes. "*Sullivan. I have news, yes. Once I tell you what it is, it's over. You need to promise me now that you will respect my request on this, I need to focus on myself and...*"

"I'll be around, but I promise that I not bother you," He paused and heaved a great sigh. "Because you are my maker and I lo...uh...we will always be connected."

"*Sullivan, please. I will not be able to talk to you again, unless it's as your maker for vampire business. Marcus will certainly insist on it.*"

"Fuck that bastard, he cannot tell me what I can and cannot do when it comes to you." Sullivan noticed he had clenched a fist.

"*No. In this case, he has every right. Sullivan, please. I need you to cooperate with this and do as I say.*" Lilly sounded stressed to him.

What in the world could be so bad that she would cut off communications with him?

Of course, Marcus Lancaster.

"*Sully?.*"

"I will do what I can, Lilly. Do not ask me to give my word on more. I don't want to have to break it." Something was wrong.

"*Ok, I guess that's enough.*" Another heavy sigh. "*Sully, I am pregnant. They say it's about six weeks along, which cannot be because I was still in the crypt at that time but, according to the doctor, I am that far.*"

Sullivan pulled up his pillow and screamed into it, the mental energy striking Lilly, causing her to wince.

"*Sullivan. The baby is Marcus's, we have had sex, made love,*" she corrected herself, "*and he...*"

Sully pulled himself together, this was important. "He HURT you! That's not making love, that's rape. I should know, I'm guilty of doing it myself."

"*You've been forgiven for that. But I am telling you that, since I am pregnant with Marcus's baby, I need to cut our ties. I know you've wanted to come see me since you were taken...wherever you were taken. But now, with the baby, it can never be.*"

He racked his brain, trying to remember what he knew from his time in Heaven and what he had read in the old scrolls. He could remember nothing that would confirm what he thought he knew.

"*Sultivan?*"

"Lilly, vampires cannot get pregnant. They're re-animated beings, there is no live sexual material to make a child. You've been dead, uh, alive, uh, oh you know what I mean. You've been dead for over a hundred years. There's nothing left of your former life except the shell and your soul. Same with Marcus. There's no way to make a baby like that."

It was her turn to be quiet.

"*I don't know how, but I peed on a stick that told me I was pregnant, I've had a doctor check, and my eating needs have changed, I require living blood now, no food or drink. I have to be pregnant and the more I, and you, try to deny it but that's the reality of the situation.*"

"Then why can't I be the father. I had you first and you could have become pregnant then. It's about the same reasoning. Angels don't have children either, but now I'm a vampire and I was then, why can't I be the father?"

A red tear slipped from his eye and down his face. His heart wanted to be with her, despite everything that had happened, the ache was strong. Could she be feeling the same way? "*No, Marcus is the one that had the best chance of it and that's who I believe is the father.*"

Another tear.

"Sullivan, you must now leave me be. Trust that I'm fine and I'm going to be fine, so will the baby. Marcus will eventually come around to accepting the baby and we will..."

"Wait, what! You're saying that he doesn't acknowledge that he's the father? He's denying it?"

"For the moment, yes. But I'm quite sure he's going to come around to the reality of the situation. That means you must stay away and let him be a parent. I want this baby to have what I didn't have, a father who was there for me."

"Like he's going to be there for you and the kid." Sullivan snarled. "He's a mercenary, he's always got some plan or another working, many of them dealing with killing people and breaking things. Oh, he plays the socialite playboy but in reality...Hell, he can't become a father, it would cramp his style with all the women he fucks before feeding off of them. And, has he even bothered to ask you to marry him? Is he going to legally take responsibility for the kid by making an honest woman of you?"

"Honest woman? I AM honest, Sullivan, I, he..."

"Not what I meant, he should be worried about you, your reputation, and the legal aspects for you and your baby. Or is he going to just cast you away once he gets his heir, taking the baby for himself? Is he going to prostitute you, acting as your pimp so he can make more baby vampires?" Sullivan hit the outside wall, a chunk coming out and rattling the window. Blood gushed from the torn flesh of his knuckles and he pulled the hand up to his mouth.

"*That is quite enough. He's not going to do any of that. I will not marry him unless he makes some concessions to me, to my freedom. And he's going to have to convert to Catholicism. I will raise this child in the Church and if he wants to be a part of that, if he wants to help raise the baby, he will have to do as I ask.*"

Sullivan let out a laugh, "That's rich, you're going to dictate terms to the great Marcus Lancaster. He will probably smile at you for that, assuming you're just an uneducated wench like he's dealt with since he was old enough to smile. As for the Catholic conversion, he was originally a Catholic, the Protestant Reformation didn't start until 1517. Lancaster was killed in 1461 so he was already confirmed. Don't know if the current Pope or the Church would welcome his evil ways back into the fold."

"*Sullivan, I'm tiring of this tirade. I will not...*" her voice faltered, "*I will not see or communicate with you again after this. Sully, have a nice life. Find a nice woman and settle down.*" She began to close the link.

"Wait! One last question, have you seen Essex recently? I need to know he's safe."

"*Not in a while, we've been in San Antonio. I hope he's safe. I will not bring any harm to him by telling Marcus he's an angel, if that's what you're getting at. I'm not evil.*"

She snapped the link, leaving Sullivan in the deathly quiet of the cell. He could hear the activities of the monks upstairs but he couldn't go up until the sun set. He doubled both fists, the fury within him exploded into a white hot rage. He pounded the door, like a prize fighter going after an opponent. The sound echoed through the quiet of the building. Yelling curses not used in the building, he continued to hit, making dents in the old, thick wood. He pounded the door, pummeling Marcus Lancaster's face with every blow, hitting not to hurt, but to kill. In his imagination, he killed the hated vampire over and over again, always reviving him to kill him again. Finally, he made one killing blow and knocked the heavy door off the hinges into the hallway, splitting it in half.

The bed followed it, then the chair and desk, all splintering into small pieces as it hit the stone wall.

The reverberating roar could have awakened people at the South Pole as Sullivan grabbed the neckline of his robe he was wearing and tore it asunder, followed by the belt. Naked, with bloody tears flowing, he stormed out of his cell, leaving a trail of blood and destruction in his wake. In his blind rage, he struck out and demolished everything within reach. He stalked toward the scriptorium, intending to ruin the entire history of heaven and earth.

In the cross hall, Brother Ingvar stepped in front of the raging man, "Brother Sullivan, calm down and tell me what I can do to help."

The words were like knives into his very soul, if he could possibly still possess one. He reached out, unseeing, to the sound of the voice and pushed the monk aside, throwing him into the stone wall where he crumpled, unconscious.

Brother Nicholass ran into the corridor from the sacristy, having to step over Ingvar to reach Sullivan, "Sullivan Kilcoan, stop this. Calm and we can go…"

"You can go to HELL!" Sullivan pushed him back, where the monk fell over the prone body of his brother monk and unceremoniously landed on his ass.

The angry vampire turned toward the stairs leading up to the common areas. While he was watched, no one else dared to stand in his way. As he reached the dining hall, one man, a vampire, did step forward. Brother Waldemar stood silently in front of him, not moving or making any gesture.

"Get out of my way, Waldemar or die." The words were quiet but held the entire force of fury Sullivan possessed.

"No."

"I don't want to hurt you but I'm going outside. No one will stop me. You, Gudrun…even Mikhail." He rubbed his face, smearing the blood. "No! He is a sadist! She can't stay with him, I can't live like this, not going to watch him take her. He's a sadistic animal."

Waldemar raised one eyebrow, "Who are you talking about? Who is he and who is she?"

Sullivan stopped mere inches from the other vampire. He wanted to rip the man's head off of his body and throw it at the growing group of monks on either side of him.

"Lancaster has gotten my Lilly pregnant, she's cut ties with me."

"Vampires cannot get pregnant. Proven fact, everyone knows that. And?"

"My worst enemy and she's going with him." He looked up toward the ceiling, shaking his head. "I can't stop it but I also won't watch it. Get out of my way."

Father Gudrun walked up behind Waldemar, flanked by Brothers Havvard and Ragnvar, each serious and wary. "Thank-you Waldemar, I will handle it from here."

Waldemar stepped to the side.

"Out of my way, Gudrun. I don't want to hurt you but if you try to stop me, I will." Sullivan was just on the ragged edge of control, hands and face bloody, the blood streaking down his chest.

"No, my brother. Stop this madness and come talk with me. We will work this out..."

"NO! You have no idea, there's nothing that can be done now. The choice has been made and I've lost. I can't kill him and I can't change her mind. The world, my world, is in ashes and I want to be also.

Gudrun took a step forward, hand out with his palm up in an attempt to calm the despairing vampire. Sullivan roared, his anger resurging, and in a desperate act of total defiance he grabbed the offered hand and pulled the monk to him, effortlessly lifting him over his head, throwing him into the other two monks. As everyone scrambled to help them up, Sullivan stepped past them and flung open the massive front door, allowing bright light to flood into the room. He moved boldly to meet his fate when an arm came out of the blinding light and propelled the vampire back into the room. The intense mass of light followed and the door shut behind it.

The light slowly dissipated and with it, the intensity of the negative emotions that had filled the hall moments before. Sullivan still held his wrath as if rage was all he had left.

An angel with gray wings stood before them and placed his hand on Sullivan's torso, above his heart.

"Sullivan, stand down." The words were said quietly but muffled all the shouting of the monks

Sully stopped, staring at the new arrival. "Sethiel. Don't stop me, I have to finish this. Mikhail can fuck the fuck off."

The angel raised his wings, blocking the sight of the door, "It's finished, Sullivan. I've been sent to stop you from destroying yourself."

"Sent? By whom? Ranguel?" Even as he argued, he could feel his anger begin to drain into the floor. "No, not him. This is from…"

"Mikhail, yes. There is still a path for you. You need to listen to what I've to say but not in front of everyone."

Laughing maniacally, Sullivan answered "Yeah, a path, I know what's coming, the express elevator straight into Hell. Where are your backups, Helmut and Nida?"

"I am alone. What I have to say is straight from Mikhail, no other knows what is transpiring."

"Yeah, I bet the old boss would love to see the fallen angel fall even further. Why send you to insure my demise?"

"You are failing the test, Sully. You are in great danger of earning that last mark and if you do what you are planning, you will be removed to Hell."

"So, leaving me to do what I'm planning will, will…" he began to stumble over words, "Save you the trouble of having to send for Nida."

"You believe this to be your only way forward, to destroy yourself and all the potential Mikhail sees in you?"

Sullivan nodded, feeling a heavy weight of guilt on his shoulders. To do what he intended would seal his fate, any chance of redemption of any kind, and send him to Hell. Not to the portion that contained the vampires, but the lower levels, the domain of Lucifer and the demons, relics of the Fallen from the first war in Heaven.

"I…need. To. Go. I…cannot bear to stay and see that bastard take away everything that means anything to me. I would not be able to stop myself, I would be there, trying to get her back. I either fall now, or fall later. Either way, I fall. Stand away, Seth. Don't fight me on this one. If you've ever cared for me, for our friendship, you will let me go."

The two men, more than friends since time began, stood toe to toe, neither moving.

Then the angel pulled his wings in and stepped aside. "I see you are determined to destroy not only yourself but everyone who has ever cared for you, me, Essex, Ranguel, and even Lilly."

"Do not say her name."

"You care for no one but yourself and your supposed failure. Go ahead, walk out that door and into the sunlight, I'm sure the demons will welcome you with loving arms. They will have so much fun tormenting and torturing you, a former angel. You think they may go easy on you because they are former angels? Think again, Sully."

Sullivan slowly walked to the door while memories flashed through his mind, times of escape with Essex and Seth, touring the pubs of Great Britain, drinking, throwing darts both physical and verbal. It was the way they stayed sane, a way to unwind after dealing with evil paranormals. Glimpses of the Heaven he would never again see. Flashes of Lilly, smiling, happy and safe.

He reached toward the door knob, his hand shaking. Grasping the handle, he began to turn it, then stopped.

A wail of raw anguish and pain echoed through the monastery as the vampire fell to his knees, doubling over, sobbing as his heart broke.

Seth pulled in his wings further and knelt next to his brother, holding him as he cried.

THE DISORDERED SCENE inside the monastery provided the perfect chance to slip out. A monk went to the back door and quietly walked outside. Running down the path into a copse of trees, Brother Hemmings begins to hum.

From behind a large bolder, a man stepped out, smiling. "Well?"

Hemmings didn't return the smile, scowling instead. "You may not have to wait to get that angel in Hell. He's determined to commit suicide over some dame."

"Evidently not. As you were walking back here, another angel has shown up. The boss wants to know why this angel is so important. It seems like Mikhail is playing favorites. Any other vampire would be in Hell right now with what he's done."

"Oh, I know. Since he's been here, we've had more visitors to the Abbot than we had in all the years since I arrived. They usually come early in the day and meet just with Gudrun, then leave. I've not seen any sort of vehicle and most of the time the snow on the road is pristine. I can't tell you for sure but they have to be flying in."

"What's this new problem? Did you hear anything?"

Hemmings glanced around to make sure they were alone. "From what the angel was saying, the woman is pregnant and doesn't want to see him again. Evidently the man she's with is a real bastard and the angel would really love to just kill him."

The other man laughed, "A bastard fathered by a real bastard. Poetic. Who is this mystery father?"

"Lancaster somebody. The dame's name is

Lilly."

"Ah, yes. We have contact with Marcus Lancaster and we had heard he has a progeny, a woman named Lilly who was a prostitute in New Orleans back when. The boss doesn't like her, says she's very pious and favored. Evidently she's also watched over by Mikhail's minions. We have to corrupt her before she has that baby or there is going to be huge trouble." The man's eyes fixed on a position behind and over Hemming's head. Hemmings turned to try to see what he was looking at. There was nothing unusual there.

"Ok. I understand." The man said, returned his gaze into Hemming's eyes, "You are to continue to observe the angel and report anything out of the ordinary. If he takes a shit at a different time, report it. Eats something different, same thing. Watch for a way to turn him to our side, not that the boss thinks that will ever happen but, if we can do it, we can probably parlay that action into more favors from the boss. Got it?"

"Got it. I better get back in before I'm missed. I'll be in touch." Hemmings reached out to shake the man's hand. Before he could get the palm to the other hand, there was no hand. The man had disappeared.

"Damned demons." Hemmings swore as he hurried back toward the monastery.

SULLIVAN SHIFTED UNCOMFORTABLY in the chair.

Beside him, Seth was doing the same, trying to get comfortable with the wings and not having much luck. Father Gudrun sat across from them, waiting for them to settle.

"Why don't you just put those away? No one here is going to say anything about you not having wings and you would be more comfortable." Sullivan said slowly.

"I have to remain as an angel, there are forces here that need to know we are watching." Seth finally managed to get both wings over the back of the chair without shredding feathers.

"Forces?" Gudrun's said, "What forces?"

"Demons. At least humans working with demons. That was one thing I was coming to tell you. Mikhail has picked up on them and wants to warn you to be careful."

"Oh, I know that Hemmings and Rikhard are both consorting with the demons. I have had Havvard, Lukas, and even Ragnvar has come to me at different times with reports of the stench of demons on those two. We're keeping an eye on them, right now it's just waiting for them to make a mistake before we handle them."

"Ragnavar? He actually came out of his scrolls and prayers to talk to you?" Seth shook his head, would wonders never cease, Ragnavar was never away from those scrolls, except to eat. There was even a rumor that there was a cot hidden away in the scriptorium somewhere.

"Yes, even him. We are sure there is a plot going on and we want it to play out to the end so we know what is going to happen. I do report to

Mikhail daily."

Sullivan was picking at his fingernails, trying to not look at Seth or Father Gudrun. He wanted to be very, very small so that the punishment for the destruction of much of the abbey wouldn't be so great. He seemed to keep getting into trouble since his days as...

"Sullivan, how is your rage level now?" Gudrun asked.

"I'm okay. I still want to kill that bastard for touching my woman," Wait, what? Sullivan caught his mouth saying what his heard demanded and stumbled on trying to cover the mistake. "Lilly. She's naive and trusting, she won't do anything to drive the baby's father away from them."

While it wasn't spoken, the other two men caught the ownership pronoun in the sentence. And all three decided to ignore it.

"Sully, you need to stay calm. This check about you comes straight from Mikhail, as I said. You have a destiny and many things are hinging on you completing your retraining. It would be very bad if you allow yourself to fall before you've done so." Seth looked at his friend, the blood streaks still on Sullivan's face and on Seth's robes.

"What is it? What is so all-fucking-fire important that I need to stay on this side of living? Everything has been taken from me, Seth, everything! The last thing I had was a sweet woman who hasn't ever done anything to warrant having to live with that vampiric bastard Lancaster."

"He's her maker, Sully, and..."

"I KNOW she's his progeny, but we both know that being a maker doesn't make you a good person and the longer a person has been a vampire, the more of a chance that the marks will be given in advance of going to Hell. Even Lilly has that possibility and I can't even think of that without tears." He dabbed at his eyes with the sleeve of the robe someone had handed him before he walked into the abbot's office.

"I cannot divulge all of the reasons, I'm not privy to them. Mikhail has made it known that whatever is supposed to happen will involve you, Lilly, Lancaster, and his employees. You can stop the world from going where its heading but you have to trust me Mikhail does know what he's doing. All will come out as planned."

Sullivan just sat quietly and looked at his hand, tracing the circle and symbols with his finger. He was trying to find the way to believe what was being said. It wasn't working.

"There's a plan? It involves Lilly, it involves Lancaster and his people? How will it come out? I need to know more if I'm going to do whatever it is that the universe supposedly dictating that I do."

It was the abbot that spoke, "Sullivan, you don't know the details, you can't know them. That's not how the world works. We have free choice here. You need to just keep going, working on the scrolls, working on finding yourself until something begins to happen. None of us, even former angels, are given their life journey in advance."

"But Lilly..."

Seth spoke up, "Lilly's in capable hands. We have angels following Lilly and the others. They will be keeping them safe so she can fulfill her own destiny. But right now you need to work through this and keep working on the scrolls."

Sully frowned, "That's the second time you have mentioned the scrolls. What is it that I'm seeking?"

"We're not sure. Mikhail himself wants that work done because there is something he's searching for, something that will turn the tide once things get started.

Sullivan sighed in frustration, his anger rising again, for a totally different reason. "How the hell am I supposed to know if I find what I'm looking for if I don't know what I'm looking for in the first place? All this ambiguity is driving me all around the twist." He stared back and forth at Seth and the abbot in rising frustration and total incredulity.

Seth continued, "We are not guaranteed that what the vampires and demons are planning is going to be easy to fix, but there is something being planned, Mikhail knows." Seth put his hand on the top of Sullivan's scarred hand.

Sullivan jerked his hand back and spit sarcastically. "Well, I'm terribly glad someone knows what's going on."

"Look," Seth said in his best mollifying tone, "I will tell you when I know what's going on. Meantime, please Sully, keep yourself safe. Not just for me, or for Mikhail, but for yourself and for Lilly. It's going to work out, but it could take decades, you know how slow the machinations of Heaven and Hell work. Give it time."

The calm being released by the big angel filled the room. Sullivan wanted to believe that everything would work out, that he would be able to be with Lilly again. He had to trust Mikhail, Seth, and Father Gudrun that everything would work out.

He just hoped he had that much trust left.

Seth smiled as he stood up. He pulled Sullivan to his feet and then hugged him. "Be good, Sully. I'll come when I can and give you whatever news I can."

"Thank-you, Sethiel. I will try."

As they pulled away from each other, the angel shook the hand of the abbot and then disappeared in a flash of light.

Gudrun smile, "Now, let's go tend to those knuckles."

Chapter Twenty-One

MARCUS WAS WATCHING the screens in his office. The Gulf Coast was still hurting. Hurricane Katrina had been over a month ago and even those who had taken refuge either inland or hunkered down were still hurting, their homes either damaged or destroyed. The news agencies were still chronicling the reactions of residents as they returned home to a mess and all of the work being done to start recovery. Lancaster Industries still had presence in New Orleans. Other departments had been sent to Central America, to the corporation's assets in Guatemala and southern Mexico because, once again, a hurricane had hit that area. This one was named Stan. Hurricane Tammy had hit some of his Florida holdings and now there was another hurricane heading toward the Gulf, this one named Wilma.

He shook his head, what the hell was going on? Marcus couldn't remember this much hurricane activity in his long life. Of course, world-wide communications was not as effective as it was now. There has to be a cure for hurricanes. "I would be rich if I could come up with an answer to stop or reduce them," he said to the empty apartment.

"You're already one of the richest men on earth, why do you insist on making more? You could live the next two centuries and not spend it all." Jesse said as he walked into the room.

"I don't trust that it will last, given the various government whims that have cost me dearly over the past centuries. I have learned that lesson. I can't completely trust anyone or anything to continue my comfortable life."

Jesse stared at him. "Talk about not relying on trust, we still need to make some plans for rebuilding the trust between us. We also need to discuss how we're going to continue our relationship given your new family situation."

Marcus turned back toward the monitors to avoid letting Jesse roll his eyes. The insecure ghoul, he corrected himself, vampire, seemed to need constant reassurance that he was loved.

"There's no change, Jesse," he turned back, "We ..."

"There is no we here, Marcus. You now have another family to deal with. I need to know how we are going to deal with the transition. Do I need to move out of the penthouse, back into my apartment, or should I find another place outside of this building?"

"Jess, you don't have to..." Marcus started, knowing there was no way of avoiding an argument.

"Yes, I do. I'm not going to be the 'other person' in this relationship. I'm not a third wheel. So, we need to make decisions about this so I can figure out the rest of MY new life, the one you forced on me." He sat down in a chair, crossing his leg over his knee and crossing his arms across his chest.

"Talk about a brick wall, Jesse. This is going to be your way or the highway, isn't it. Why, then, are we going to have this conversation?"

"Because I want to hear you rationalize having a family and a lover at the same time, living in the same place, maybe even in the same apartment. I need to hear you try to explain the unexplainable and try to get me to stay in this relationship."

"We are already a family, Jess, nothing has changed that. Just because she's pregnant doesn't mean I'm going to play house with her. And nothing says she will remain here if I decide she's causing more trouble than she's worth. I can take the child to protect and raise and send her on her way."

Jesse laughed, "That's rich. You think you will take her child away from her. That's the last thing she will let you do. No, she's going to insist on me leaving and making a little picture perfect family together. Hell, I can see the little picket fence around this building now."

"Jesse, stop it. None of that will happen. I have promises with you and I mean to keep them. A baby won't change that."

As Jesse started to speak, a bright flash lit the entire room, the monitors going to black and when Marcus's eyes adjusted again, three angels stood next to the window. "What the fuck?"

He recognized two of them, the bitch who marks the vampires and her goon with the big flaming sword. The other he didn't recognize. Taller than the goon, curly black hair and the disapproving eyes that so many of the angels wore around vampires.

His first thought was to order them out but that would work about as well as emptying the gulf with a teaspoon.

"Kneel, Vampire." Helmut said, pointing the sword at Marcus's chest. Marcus sunk to his knees, his body betraying him.

"Marcus Lancaster. After our last meeting, I had hoped you had learned your lesson. I warned you to obey the rules but it seems you have ignored my advice. You created another vampire without his permission."

Marcus couldn't speak, his voice held by the angel.

"No ma'am, Marcus didn't change me just to make another vampire. He did it to save my life, I died and he loved me and wanted me to stay."

Marcus turned his eyes from the sword to try to catch the look on Jesse's face. He had been berating him one minute, the next he was defending him.

"Love isn't a remedy for improper application of the rules set down to keep you vampires in line. You may not know the rules but I can assure you Lancaster knows them, right?"

Marcus didn't want to answer but he found himself nodding his head.

The bitch was manipulating him, moving his head.

"So, Lancaster, are you ready to go to Hell? You have more than run up enough activity to mark both hands."

He was back to not moving but he shot the diminutive angel a smoldering look of anger. If he could reach her, he would...

"NO! He is innocent. You cannot take him.' Jesse started forward toward her. The big angel next to her stepped in front of him, grabbing his wrist hard and the one with the sword swung it his way, effectively stopping all sound and movement.

"Now. Lancaster, where were we? Oh yes, Hell. You are going. Maybe not today, or tomorrow. But trust me, you will be going and I will be the one to..." Her words trailed off and she stared off. The other male angel looked to Helmut and then back to Nida.

She turned her attention back to Marcus. "Well, just be warned. Sethiel," she looked to the angel who still held Jesse's wrist, "You impart the rules and do the tuning. You are then to report to Mikhail once you're finished." She looked into Jesse's eyes, "Listen well, vampire, and try not to break the rules. I do not want to see you again because if I do, the least thing I will do is mark you." The sarcasm practically dripped from her words. Of course she thought he would do it, and she relished the thought of...

With no further words, the bright light flooded the room and when it dissipated, Marcus and

Jesse were alone with the angel holding Jesse's wrist. With no angelic energy to hold him, Marcus first pitched forward, catching himself, and then pushed himself back to his feet. He took a step toward Jesse.

"Back off, Lancaster. Please don't make this hard. All I am going to do is inform him of the rules and tune him. I'm not here for you at all." Sethiel said.

"Look, I know why you are here and, except for that bitch and her bulldog, I don't have a problem with you angels. But if you ever put your evil, filthy fucking hands on any of my progeny, I will end you. Got it?"

Seth stared at the man, then turned to Jesse. "This isn't going to hurt. It's just mechanics, I will just be changing the frequency of the vibrations of your aura so the angels can find you easily. Every vampire gets this tuning."

Jesse looked at the angel with an expression of complete contempt. "I know you stupid overgrown pigeon. I've been a ghoul for almost 150 years and I know the routine."

Seth calmly continued, "You will also need to memorize what I am going to tell you next. If you forget, or worse, purposely disobey them, you will be visited by the woman and man who just left. Depending on the infraction, she will either mark you," he gestured toward Marcus, "Like your maker, or you can be taken straight to Hell."

"Angel, I will recite the rules to him, you just need to get his tuning done and leave." Marcus was angry that this was happening at all, cooperating would get the stinking angel out of his penthouse faster.

"No, you can't. Even if you weren't marked, I still have to do it to make sure he gets all of it." Seth addressed Jesse. "Ignorance of the rules is not a defense to any infraction, you will be held to account regardless of your remembering or any other excuse. Now, sit down, please, we will go over the rules. Lancaster, you can leave, I will not harm him."

Jesse walked to the couch and sat down and Marcus followed him, sitting as well, "I'm staying here. This is my home and I refuse to leave it."

"That's your prerogative. Do not speak and do not interfere. If you do, in any way, I will get Helmut back to hold you if you do. I'm certain you don't want that one."

"Fine, go ahead and get this done and leave." Marcus hated getting threatened.

"Okay, Mr. Chamberlain, here are the rules for vampires to follow. Listen well. You will not make but one vampire every hundred years. Any more and you will be marked. No vampire you make can be younger than 20, older than 60, infirm, mentally feeble, or criminal. No making a vampire for revenge or to plot against the Church or any of the agents thereof. You will feed from volunteers, never from the unwilling. You will only make a vampire from the willing—never without permission from the person who is being turned. You will abide by the secular laws of the human population you live with and not commit crimes."

"Any violation of these rules will result in swift

attention and you will be hunted and marked for the violation. You are only allowed three violations and then you will be removed from the population and taken directly to Hell for punishment. As you can see on your maker, the marking is done on the top of the right hand, each mark contained in one-third of a circle burned into the flesh. Enforcer angels Nida and Helmut, who you just met, are the ones who will administer this mark. A third Enforcer will be witness like I have been. You cannot hide from them, you will be found and you will be marked. The marks are permanent and done on the hand to be public. Anyone who knows of the vampires will recognize them and as you gain marks, you will become a pariah in your community. You should make it a habit not to associate with those who are marked, lest you be drawn into their crimes and judged for them."

"You are to be tuned after these rules are imparted. Your tuning will interfere with the natural frequency of your aura and personal energy signature. This tuning will change it to a frequency that will be registered and can be easily located by the by the angels. Every angel will know you have been told the rules, you cannot plead ignorance of them as an excuse for the sentence of the mark."

Seth stopped. He had been able to hold the new vampire's attention, even over the various sighs and grumbling Marcus had been making. "Before you are tuned, do you have any questions or requests?"

"No, I am clear on them. Get it over with."

Jesse knew he would remember, he had seen Marcus take the mark and had lived with him long enough to know other vampires who suddenly disappeared, never to return. He just wanted this over so he could finish talking to Marcus.

"Then I will do the tuning." Sethiel reached out and held his hand above Jesse's head. Jessie noticed the temperature dropped, like the air conditioning was on full blast, then almost instantly turned so hot he was sweating through his silk shirt. "Great, another one ruined," he thought, oddly calm about the whole thing. Next came the inability to breath as if his soul was being yanked out of its anchor within him, then slammed back into him, rocking him back into the couch. Once that subsided, he could breathe again.

"You okay?" Sethiel asked, putting a hand on Jesse's shoulder, which the vampire quickly shook off.

"I'm fine. That's it?" Jesse asked.

"That's it. You're done. I will leave you with this caution, do not try to break the rules. While I'm not nearly as strict as my boss and Nida, they are quite strict in their edicts. Be warned. I wouldn't want you to end up in Hell any earlier than you will." With that final comment, the flash once again filled the apartment and the angel was gone.

"You okay, really?" Marcus put his hand over Jesse's. "I hate those angels more than anyone else in the universe."

"I'm fine. Weird feeling, but I'm fine. I do think

I need to go eat and lay down a bit, if you don't mind."

Marcus stood and pulled Jesse to standing. "I think that's a very good idea. I still have some work to do but I can come join you shortly and ..."

"I'll be in my own bed, in my room. There are too many issues that are unresolved and undiscussed that didn't change." Jesse allowed Marcus to hug him, then walked away toward the hallway to his room.

"Jesse, I love you. Sleep well." Marcus said, almost whispered.

"I hope so. I want to love you too."

Chapter Twenty-Two

LILLY WAS SITTING on her bed in her nightgown, Gregory's wrist in her mouth. She periodically had to come off of it when she had to laugh, she was finally getting the hang of not taking her lips off the seal over her puncture wound while giggling at the movie. She looked at the window by her and saw that the sky was just beginning to lighten with the dawn.

A knock on the door sounded over Gregory's laughter and as he hit pause on the VCR, he called "Come in" for her. The door opened with Marcus's hand on the knob.

Am I interrupting something?" the smile on his face surprised Gregory, who had a feeling that something was up.

Lilly took one last pull on the wrist and then closed it off. "No, I am just finishing my breakfast. I'm finding that I must eat right before I go to sleep or I get very nauseous about halfway through the day." She turned to Gregory, "Thank-you, Gregory. There should be a steak or something in the ice box so you can build back up."

He smiled lovingly, "If you need me later, just

let me know. We can finish watching the movie later."

"What movie are you watching?" Marcus asked, "I can come back in you..."

"Nah, that's okay. The movie is *Shaun of the Dead*." Gregory ended the pause and the regular broadcast channel came on.

Lilly laughed, "Zombies are so funny. Yes Gregory, we can finish when I awake. Thank-you, sweetie." The smile she gave her ghoul was genuinely given, Marcus thought.

Gregory bent down and planted a kiss on her cheek and then nodded to Marcus as he walked out the door.

After the door closed, Marcus came to the bed. "Mind if I sit?"

Lilly patted the bed in front of her.

As he lowered himself onto the bed, he reached out and took her hand. "Don't worry, there's not going to be any arguing or surprises. I've just come down to let you know that I'm so sorry for our fights and I want to clear the air and ask if this relationship can start over."

Lilly studied his face, the softened lines and the sparkle in his blue eyes. She could tell he meant what he asked. "Okay, sure."

"Good!" Marcus kissed her fingers, "So we are going to be parents at our age. I'm afraid I have no experience in dealing with babies or children, you're going to have to teach me what I need to know."

"I have no idea either. I had a very different experience growing up and we really didn't have children in Mahogany Hall. The girls that became with child would either leave the house or get a tea from the conjure woman in the Quarter. If she returned, the baby was left in the care of someone else or given to an orphanage. We are both going to have to learn much before the baby gets here."

"You said that you wanted to raise this child in the Church. I am assuming you are referencing the Roman Catholic Church. While I don't object in theory, I know that we will not be able to attend with him, vampires cannot enter sacred ground."

Lilly frowned, "No, we can go to Mass, I've gone on each Sunday morning since moving here. I have made confession and have gone to communion."

"I remember you went once, you're telling me that you've been going regularly and even getting sacraments?"

"You sound surprised. I have had no problem going to Mass. I do have a bit of exhaustion due to the sun being up. Isobel comes to get me so I'm not in the sun. I feel certain our child will be able to be taken to the Church nearby, St. Michael's, once he's here."

"You said 'him', you believe it's a male?"

"I don't know. I don't mind having either gender as long as the baby is healthy."

"I agree. From what I have been able to find out, vampires cannot get pregnant or have babies. I'm not doubting your veracity, but I wonder how this happened and what the baby will be. After all, we are reanimates."

"Reanimates? What's that?" Lilly was confused

by the word, she was a vampire, she thought.

"People who have died and are now living again. Reanimated. Some of the mortals will call us walking corpses."

She shivered. "What do you mean? He will be a baby." She shook her head at his question.

"I know that. What I mean is will the baby be human or will he be a vampire? What do we do if the baby turns out to be a vampire?"

"I honestly have no idea. I had hoped you would have known someone who knew or could find a book somewhere that had the answers."

"No, but I may be able to get an ally in the Vampire Council to check the library. I will have to be quiet when asking, we cannot allow Xun to know what is going on. I have no idea what he would do, but given the baby is my child, I expect Xun will try to abduct him. I do not trust him or many others on the Council not to use our child as a pawn in vampire politics."

"You think he's in danger?" Lilly pulled her hand away and laid it protectively on her stomach.

"I do not know that for a fact but Xun is an opportunistic bastard, he has never not taken advantage of anything I have happening. I don't trust him. We have to be very quiet about your condition." Marcus let that sink in before going on. "I will protect both of you with Xun's life, if he comes for you, either by himself or by proxy, he is as good as dead again, I will destroy him and his house line to the last man."

"Marcus, that's not necess…"

"The hell it's not, you are my progeny, the baby is my blood. I do not allow enemies to interfere with what is mine without consequences. You will be protected at all times, never be alone without a guard."

"But I have my own life and I do not relish being held in a prison, no matter how opulent it is."

"I will have guards with you. Gregory will be trained to protect you, he will be the one closest to you, he has the responsibility to insure you safety. You did a good job picking that boy as your ghoul, by the way. You will be protected just like in San Antonio. If I'm unable to check on you, Jean will be my second and your staff will report to him."

"But I am..." Lilly hated it when Marcus started making decisions for her.

"No, we have to think of your and our baby's safety. Oh, and I will be moving Jesse to another apartment and you will be moving into the penthouse apartment so you will have the advantage of the extra security there." Marcus had stood up sometime during the planning and was pacing as Lilly had come to recognize as his working attitude.

"No Marcus. I will stay here with Isobel and we will add the security here. I will not move. Jesse will not move on my account, he already hates me enough. Please keep him close to you and we will all be able to get along."

"He's not real happy with me either. It seems that saving his life was not something I should have done. He never wanted to be a vampire, even thought it would assure our continued relationship forever...maybe."

"It's still new to him. Even though he has been with you for many years, this is a big adjustment. He's probably in shock, realizing he was going to die and that you loved him enough to turn him. Give him time, he will embrace the changes once he knows that it will not have changed him inside."

"I hope you're right on that, I cannot bear to lose him." Marcus returned to his seat on the bed.

"You won't. By the way, considering all the drastic changes in our lives, do you believe you can be with him and yet be with me as well?"

"I have enough love to go around. You and I will stay to raise the baby, you will always have me around. Jesse has been with me since the Civil War and I love him very much. He will remain my love, now forever."

"So you are going to stay in your homosexual relationship while trying to raise our baby? Do you really think that is good for the morals we try to teach him?"

Marcus stood up again, running a hand through his hair. "There is nothing wrong with loving someone. Maybe you should examine your moral compass. Here you are, a former prostitute who has had sex with two different men recently. You are pregnant without getting married first. You are really not the best arbiter of right and wrong, you know."

She winced, he had a point. "Okay, neither of

us are qualified to raise a child. Maybe we should consider giving him up for adoption. That may be the best thing for him." It was the last thing she wanted to do but she couldn't make Marcus leave Jesse alone so she would have to give the baby to someone who could raise him. The very thought broke her heart.

"I would consider that but what if the child is a vampire? We have no medical example to point to giving the outcome of two supposedly sterile vampires conceiving a baby. For all we know, this baby can be a vampire from the beginning. Can you imagine a couple of human parents trying to raise that child? And if we did end up with human adoption, it will break a big rule of the Vampire Council of not allowing humans around without our glamouring them. And if the Council finds out the baby is born and we are the parents, we could be forced to give him up to them and that would happen only if I and the rest of my line are finally dead."

"*What if Marcus isn't the father?*" Baron whispered. "*It could be Sullivan's kitten. And he wouldn't be making these demands.*"

Lilly stopped talking, her brain fighting the sunrise and trying to work through Baron's suggestion.

Marcus watched her for a couple of minutes as she seemed to zone out. He finally tapped her knee, "Lilly, darling, are you okay?"

She pulled back out of her thoughts, blinking. "Oh, I'm sorry. I'm very tired, can we talk later so I can rest?"

"Certainly. Get some good sleep and we will talk later." He rose and kissed her on the cheek like Gregory had, then left her to sleep.

As THE ELEVATOR doors opened into the penthouse, Lance met Marcus, tail wagging and barking.

"Hello boy. Glad to see me, aren't you. I missed you too." He bent down and rubbed the dog's ears. "I need to go talk to Uncle Jesse. You can come along." The dog started barking as he did the typical Sheltie spins. "I guess that's a yes. Let's get this done and then I'll feed you and we can go sleep."

Marcus walked down the open hallway and grabbed the doorknob to Jesse's apartment, drawing up short when the knob didn't turn. Jesse had, for the first time in decades, locked his door.

Knocking, he called out "Jesse, open this door." Thinking better of his demand, he added, "Please." Lance added a single bark.

"Go away. I don't want to see you or speak with you. Just go away." Jesse's voice sounded tired, he probably was feeling the dawn's pull to sleep.

"Just let me in. I'm concerned about you and I want to check on you."

"You've checked. I'm a vampire. I guess that's good enough for you since you did it to me."

"Listen, I had to do it. You were dying and I

couldn't bear to lose you, especially to that fat bastard Nelson Mishkoph." He put his arm on the door and leaned his forehead on it. This was not going the way he planned it. "You had died, Jesse They had to shock you to bring you back." Damn it, he felt a tear fall from his eye.

The door opened suddenly and Marcus lost his balance, stumbling past Jesse and falling very unceremoniously to the floor, face first. This started Lance barking at Jesse and sitting between him and his master on the floor. The ghoul-turned-vampire laughed.

"I'm glad this makes you happy." Marcus rolled over and stood up. He put his hand to his face. "Wonderful, I've broken my nose." Pulling his hand off of his face, he saw blood and let fly a string of profanity culminating with several inventive uses of the word 'fuck.'

Jesse couldn't help it, he laughed, the royal Marcus Lancaster's fall and resulting discomfort struck him as hilarious. "It's not often that you do something so awkwardly human." He dissolved into another fit of giggles. Taking a breath, he managed to say, "I have to admit your blood smells very nice."

"Are you quite finished with your amusement? Not that I am rushing you but I want to go clean up so we can talk."

Jesse gestured toward the bathroom, doing a little condescending bow as he did. Marcus growled, "I know where it is. Let's meet in your kitchen."

As Marcus stalked off, Jesse watched his ass,

he had a spectac..." Stop it, dumbass. I'm supposed to be angry with him, remember? A little sex won't cure that." He lectured himself.

It was obviously a split personality type of day, his inner voice shot back "Yeah, but it will take the edge off, oh, and we're not a dumbass." He shook his head, marveling at how someone sane could do that sort of self-conversation.

"What are you shaking your head over?" Marcus walked across the room. I thought we were going to meet in the kitchen."

"Nothing important. I would rather talk about whatever you want to discuss here in the parlor."

The older vampire noticed the appearance of antiquated word from Jesse's time of the 1850's. That showed his partner was not comfortable with talking to Marcus as they had for decades. This talk would fix that, Jesse would see reason.

"Okay, the parlor it is." Marcus walked to the couch, sitting where there would be enough room for Jess to join him. Ignoring the offer, Jess pulled up a wing chair across from Marcus, sitting back with his arms crossed.

"So, you called this meeting. Let's get it over with, I need to sleep."

"Just a few minutes. I need to apologize and beg your forgiveness. I know you did not want to be turned but..."

"No buts. You knew that, you knew it for decades, yet you didn't consider my wishes, you wanted your boy toy and what Marcus Lancaster wants, Marcus Lancaster will have, no matter any other consideration."

Marcus took a deep breath even though it was unnecessary. This was not going to be as easy as he had been with Lilly. "I know, I was extremely selfish, I couldn't just watch you die."

"Exactly, you made the choice for me and I just have to live with your choice. That is so selfish, but that's your entire life story. You use people and when it suits you, you take everything you want. Should I be grateful that you didn't let me die?"

"I love you." The words were barely audible, even to a vampire with better hearing that a human.

Jesse laughed. "Love? I don't think you could spell the word, much less define it. I know your definition is not the same as others. You confuse love with ownership. How many times have I disappointed you and was punished for it? Silent treatment, left alone for weeks while you don't check in to see if I'm sick. When you are angry, at me or anyone else, you rape me, beat me and make me the victim of your abuse and anger. This, THIS is your definition of love."

Marcus's mind sought anything he could cite as an act of love and came up short. "Yes, I'm a selfish bastard with a mean streak. I am not really good at the romance game, ask anyone else who has been with me. I suck at it, a joke for a vampire.

"But Jesse, I don't know if you remember anything between our trip to San Antonio and waking up in the plane as a vampire."

"No, I actually don't. We planned to go to San

Antonio for some reason but that's it. You said you couldn't let me die. What did happen, why did you think I was dying?"

Marcus closed his eyes and tried to settle within himself, he had to hold both his temper and anguish. "We took you and the girls to the Menger because a hurricane was headed toward Houston. I had a command appearance before Xun and the damned Council. I had no choice. I could not be there to protect you and I will forever regret that. What I was told by everyone, including Brian Kennedy, you and Duncan Morrison decided to go to a local gay bar. Something happened there and Duncan was shot dead. You were beaten so badly that they had you in ICU. You were listed as a 'John Doe' because you were unconscious and had no ID, or even a room key, to hint who you were. Duncan had no ID either. So they could not identify who you were for several days. Thankfully, Isobel saw the news report and contacted the police immediately. That's how you were found.

"Everyone rushed to the hospital to stay with you. Something bad happened. An assassin, dressed as a nurse, got into your room and injected you with some sort of poison. That's when you crashed, dead. Thankfully, they shocked you back but you were in very, very bad shape. The limo driver Kennedy hired, Ace Abernathy, was killed in the parking garage. Gregory was wounded."

"Who is Gregory? Is that the black kid that was in the room when I was turned?"

"Yes, that's him. He evidently helped the girls and Lilly is needing live blood so she made him a ghoul. Anyway, I got back as soon as I could. I put Castro on investigating who tried to kill you. The information is that Nelson Mishkoph was behind your beating, Morrison's murder, Abernathy's murder, Gregory's shooting, and the murder attempt on you at the hospital."

"Mishkoph? I thought he was a two-bit hustler who was trying to get your company."

"He is. But that human thinks I will just roll over and give up if he does things to hurt me, those close to me. Evidently they took great glee at hurting you. Kennedy did some asking around and one of the walking dead went back into the bar you were in, the Bonham Exchange, and was bragging that he was celebrating someone being put into their place. That man's already dead at my word, he just doesn't know it yet. The others and their boss will be dead soon."

"I didn't know..."

"I know you didn't. The beating did a lot of damage. We were lucky that you still lived for me to get you on the plane headed home. I had hoped you would make it here, I could nurse you and give you enough blood to speed your healing, I was not planning on turning you. But you crashed in the plane and Dr. Young said..."

"Young?" Jesse felt like he needed a list of the new people around him.

"He was the surgeon who originally worked on you in the hospital. I hired him to come with us. He was the one who told us you were dying when you went into cardiac arrest. He watched you being turned..."

"Great, another vampire in the making." The sarcasm dripped in Jesse's words.

"No, he's going to stay on with us be on staff, and learn vampire medicine."

"Why didn't you just glamour him and kick him off of the plane?"

"Because he didn't glamour. He's got a strong will and it didn't work." Marcus rubbed his temples, "I know that all I could think about was having you back with me. I would have asked you if you were able to respond but the need to turn you was because you couldn't respond, you had died again. I had to move fast to be able to bring you back. I did what you had told me never to do but I did it because I couldn't bear to lose you."

Jesse sat silent, watching the vampire fight his own exhaustion and the need for sleep. He was going to need to spend some time processing what he had heard. Morrison was dead? He couldn't remember much of anything after getting to the Bonham. A vague memory came flooding into bright clarity. "That son-of-a-bitch" he let fly.

"What?" Marcus sat forward.

"The guy in the bar. I'm drawing a blank on his name but he purposely targeted me to get me out to where the attack happened. I do remember going toward the dark alley with him to knock off a piece or two. But, that's where the memory goes blank. I have no idea from there."

"Don't strain. You may have memories come back over the next weeks. Having just that much helps, we will be able to go back and find out who it was. I'm sorry you got hurt and those bastards killed Morrison, his wife is pregnant again and I know this has to be hard on her and the kids."

"You are taking care of them?"

"Oh yes. They will want for nothing, it's already set up."

"Good. He disliked me but he was fair and he died trying to help me." Jesse shook his head. "I had no idea that I had caused so much trouble."

"It's okay, none of it was your fault. If anything, it was the Council's fault for taking me away during a crisis."

Resignedly, Jesse loosened up, looking Marcus in the eye. "Okay, give me time to acclimate to this new 'me' and then we can discuss our relationship."

"Thank you. And thanks for telling that bitch angel what you did to keep her from marking me. I know, given your anger at me, you could have just let her do it, but you spoke up for me, fought for me, and you didn't have to. I owe you for that one."

"Yes, you do." Jesse smiled. "And we may yet get past this enough for me to collect on it."

Marcus smiled, then the smile died on his lips. Jesse leaned his head to the left, an affectation that Marcus recognized as questioning. "About this thing with Lilly's pregnancy..."

"Lies. I may not have been a vampire for very long but I have lived with them and even I know that is not possible. She's trying to paint you into a corner, Marcus. Maybe to try to get you to herself."

"I don't know. We have a positive pregnancy test and Dr. Young is getting a sonogram machine so we will know for sure." He reached out for Jesse's hand and to his relief, Jesse took it. "She will not...cannot replace you. You are my number one and always will be," he said reassuringly. "She will always be number two. If she is pregnant, I will keep her around for the child. You will always be with me... that is if you decide we should be together and I hope you do."

While he couldn't say it aloud, Jesse squeezed his lover's hand. He would end up forgiving Marcus, he always did.

What a messed up world he had awakened to.

Chapter Twenty-Three

IN THE GROWING darkness, Isobel stood at a window looking toward downtown Houston, the huge buildings still lit, she always thought they looked like a giant crossword puzzle.

Lilly would be up soon. Gregory would be coming over as dinner. Marcus would be in yet another meeting in the main board room on the 15th floor.

Marcus.

Isobel had never seen him as distracted as he was since coming back from Switzerland. Once the crisis with Jesse was solved and Marcus had assigned Dr. Young, Jack as he insisted, to be Lilly's personal physician, her boss had thrown himself into his work. He spent long hours in that conference room with Jean and with several of the corporations big wigs, including Gunny Castro, who was having to deal with his own job along with whatever assignments Marcus piled on him.

Jack had busied himself setting up the clinic, including ordering the newest 3-D ultrasound equipment to monitor the growth of the baby and check for any abnormalities. Until it came in, he had been doing daily checks the old-fashioned way. Good as far as it went, but definitely inadequate for such a unique case. Isobel had been with her through all of these.

Marcus had put Jack in touch with Dr. Scott Harkness for consults. Harkness was a vampire, turned sometime in the mid-1700s in Wales. He had gone to various medical schools all over the world at different times to learn the latest human medicine techniques, which he documented along with variations for vampire medicine. He had, with assistance by the Vampire Council, created the only vampire medical school in existence. He was the only one with any experience with pregnancy but that was only from his human classes. Evidently he was dubious of the report of a pregnant vampire. Isobel had set up the original call which had not gone well. Harkness had argued with Marcus on the validity of his claim of pregnancy. He had even called Marcus a, what was it? He called him a showboating fraud and then declined the offer.

Marcus had been furious. He got his internal investigative people on it, checking to see what Harkness would do. Come to find out, Harkness had discussed going to work for Lancaster. Some had been urging him to reconsider working for Lancaster, others had said he should run as far away from the man as he could get on the planet, and look for a way off the planet just to be safe. Due to the requirement of the H.I.P.P.A. patient confidentiality, which applied to vampire as well as human medical patients, he had not gone into details, only to say that Lancaster was trying to recruit him to work for him. Which was good for Harkness's health. Marcus didn't like his job offers bandied around in public. But it did highlight the fact that the Vampire community seemed to all know Lancaster with varying opinions.

Marcus was never one to dismiss or forgive any insult or slight. So, when Harkness called to resend his refusal, Marcus refused to speak with him. Instead, Harkness talked with Isobel. He impressed her with his genuine regret and his sincere offer of assistance.

It was a herculean task to convince the intractable Marcus that, by not accepting Dr. Harkness's offer, he was putting Lilly's and the baby's health in danger. But, Isobel was finally successful in convincing him to magnanimously hire the best vampire doctor for his child.

So, Jack and Harkness had been working together for the last couple of weeks while examining Lilly. She was very unhappy with all the attention and she was very protective with the baby.

The entire second floor had been taken over and dedicated to the most elaborate and well equipped clinic and laboratory imaginable. The human staff had been assiduously screened by Brian Kennedy and represented all medical specialties that Jack thought might be needed. No expense had been spared.

Isobel was going over staffing when Security alerted Jack of the arrival of yet more large boxes and crates that contained even more medical equipment. To Jack's delight it was the newest 3-D ultrasound machine. He had a very difficult time resisting ripping into the heavy wooden crates with his bare hands.

The boxes held the sonogram machine. He had been mesmerized watching the technicians assemble his latest toy. Isobel had left him to it and, a day or so later, which was tonight, gleefully had sent word to Isobel that he would like to see Lilly about 9 p.m. for her first sonogram.

She hoped that Dr. Harkness would be there to give advice on anything vampire-specific.

MARCUS SAT IN his chair at the head of the conference table. The white board was filled with names in blue, arrows, and lines in red showing a hierarchy.

"Okay, we have each of the squads defined, how long do you think it's going to take to bring all these employees over? And how are going to stop the Enforcers from coming in and dragging the entire army straight to Hell?" Castro stood by the board after having spent the last six hours going over employee rosters, choosing candidates who might make good vampire soldiers, and redoing it as everyone in the room argued about it. The human support staff had left for the night, leaving the vampires and Castro to work well into the night.

"Nous ne savons pas, mon ami, we will have to take that chance if we are to raise enough of an army to challenge hell." Jean took a sip of his coffee and frowned. "I must find the person responsible for this outrage you are calling coffee, Marcus, and teach them how to do it right."

"I have sent out for chicory coffee for you, it will be here tomorrow, that employee is off tonight. And we don't know how long it's going to take. To stay off the radar, hopefully, we must insure that each soldier is made by someone that has not sired a progeny in the past one hundred years. One every century is the rule."

"When the hell did you pay attention to the rules, boy?" Castro pulled the cigar stub out of his mouth, waved it in Marcus's direction and then shoved it into his mouth again.

"Since I know that if this doesn't go by the rules, we won't get a chance to deal with the angel's bullshit before they all swoop down on us and drag the whole race to Hell." He looked at the board, studying the names again. "We have to keep accurate records as well. Jesse is the only one available who has..."

He stopped in mid-sentence as Jesse walked into the room. He looked at the board, then back at Marcus.

"Jess, we..."

"Were just talking about me, my ears were burning. Why is my name at the top of that list and what the fuck kind of problem are you going to get me into this time?" He walked to the chair at the other end of the table and sat down.

"We are working on the plans for the army that we will be making to take on the angels. Since you're the only one here who has not turned someone in the last hundred years. You are going to have to be the Index Case, you will be starting the new army with the person we bring in to be your progeny."

Jess closed his eyes. "I'm not even turned a quarter of a year and you have me becoming the vampire dad to someone and then I'll have scads and scads of grandchildren. Are you stupid or are you trying to get rid of me? You want me gone so you and Lilly can cozy up together and raise this imaginary vampire child she is trying to blackmail you with."

"Jessie, that's not..." Marcus stared at his lover like he was looking at him for the first time.

"It's not what, Marcus. Not what you want to do? You want me to make someone a vampire, another poor soul who has to figure out how to learn to live, survive, on this new diet? No, Marcus, find another guy, I'm not going to do it. Just not." Jesse started to stand up.

Castro pushed him back down into the chair. "Just sit there, Nancy Boy and..."

Jesse leapt up and hit Castro so hard he flew across the room and hit the wall, sliding down, unconscious.

"What the hell was that?" Marcus was immediately at one side of Castro and Jean was standing with Jesse, a hold on his wrist that could, with just a twist, break it.

Castro woke, rubbing his jaw that was swelling and turning a dark shade of purple. He looked around, trying to get his bearings, then started spitting. Pieces of his cigar was coming out in wet gobs, hitting the floor with a wet squish. As he did, he saw Jesse standing behind Marcus, his fists still clenched.

"Nancy, I'll let you have this ONE, but the next time you pony up and start to hit me, you better make sure you put me down forever. I will not let you skate on it again."

"Don't call me..." Jesse flared, taking a step toward the downed man, pulling at Jean, trying to shake his hold.

Marcus raised his voice, "Enough. Jesse, you have no idea what your body is now capable of now. You could have easily killed Castro." He helped the Gunny up. "Jorge, stop baiting Jesse or he'll hit you so hard your bell will ring far into the future. Now, let's get back to work, Jean, call downstairs and have either Jack or Harkness come up here and take a look at that jaw."

"I'm all right, boy. There's nothing that Nan...Jesse," he corrected himself, "can do that I can't deal with." He walked, wobbling a bit, and sat down in a close chair.

Jesse went back to the chair he had been sitting in and planted his backside as Jean laid down the cell phone.

"Now, if recess is over, I need to figure this out and we need to be very careful about how we make these vampires so that the angels aren't aware until we have pulled their wings." Marcus said, sitting back down.

"I'm not sure that can be done without their knowing, Marcus." Jean said, "They will find them and if we're not discovered as we are turning this army, we will be discovered when we start pulling the wings off these butterflies."

Castro looked at Marcus's hand where the marking was. "I've heard the angels are usually pretty swift to mark a vampire who turned someone without permission of the one who is turned. Why haven't they marked you for Jesse?"

"I won't be marked for him, he gave permission when he became my ghoul, according to them."

Castro looked between Marcus, Jesse, and Jean. "I know consent is important to the angels for some reason. So, won't Jesse be marked for turning his first as well? If they're not consenting?"

Marcus nodded his head, "Marking comes after tuning and if you had consent, it's not going to happen."

"Okay, I think, since I'm going to be putting my people through this, I need to step up and be the first. Might as well do it now so I can get started working through that list." Gunny walked over to Jesse, eying him as the younger man stood. Jorge Castro realized just how much of the vampire life he didn't know, even living and working so close with Marcus. "Does this tuning thing hurt?"

"No, it just feels like you're getting twisted a bit, temperature changes, that sort of thing. Nothing that you haven't dealt with as a Marine.

Gunny, are you sure about this? Of everyone in this company, you would be the only one that I wouldn't ask to do this." Marcus watched both men as he spoke.

"Yes, I'm sure. Never send your men out to do something you wouldn't do and never leave anyone behind, two rules that were beat into me in boot and I did it to many, many recruits over my time. Hell, I would probably still be doing it except for the damned legal stuff that made me retire."

"You didn't retire, Castro, you were decommissioned." Jean laughed.

Castro shot the Frenchman the evil eye, "No, I got sent to pasture. Decommissioned would mean I lost my standing in the Marines, mine's still valid."

"Sorry, Gunny. I didn't mean it like that. But, of course, you do know what they do with the studs they put out to pasture, right?" The old pirate laughed, smirking as he did. Castro had heard the stories of pirates back in Jean's day, he could just imagine what he meant.

"Okay, reign it in, people. We have Castro consenting to being turned by Jesse. Then Castro turns someone on his staff and the turn list goes as we plan. I'm going to put in a call to Eadwina and get her to turn Mitch," he pictured that big Italian ghoul of hers with those dark eyes, hair, and huge fangs, that would be enough to scare anyone, "And then start with the ghouls of the New Orleans vampires who she trusts to be part of our plans. I would hit up several other older vampires but I can't control them and there's no telling who is working for the Council and who would keep it quiet." Marcus didn't look forward to talking with his maker. Eadwina, the regal red-headed Scottish woman who had taken to being a Southern Belle, had refused to turn anyone since she turned Marcus. He wasn't sure that he could get her to turn her beloved ghoul. He did know that Mitch would jump at the chance to be turned, they had discussed it when he had stayed down in New Orleans in the mid-1930s, before Marcus had volunteered to fight the Nazis in World War II. What else did he need to add to this potential cluster-fuck? "It usually takes a day or so to let the new vampire get their system switched over to use the blood. So we have a one-day turn around to make a new vampire."

"That's a long time to even start this project. And what are we calling it?" Jean said, looking at the board, counting the number of vampires to be turned in a week.

"I don't know. We'll be pulling the wings off angels? What do we pull the wings off of, and don't say flies, that's a reference to Dracula's Renfield and I don't want to go anywhere near anything that Vlad might object to."

"Vlad?" Castro asked.

"Dracula, his real name was Vlad III, Prince of Wallachia, from House Drăcule now known as Vlad Dracula, or Vlad Tepes, which means Vlad the Impaler."

"Isn't he just a movie and book character?"

"Oh no, he's very real. Everyone thinks Stoker

used him for his book, Dracula, and in part he did. But the real Vlad was Vivode, which means Duke, or Prince of the country of Wallachia, an area of Transylvania. He ruled three times in 1448, 1456–1462, and 1476. He is known as a vampire in lore but he really was turned after he was deposed at age 17 in 1448. During the other rules he was a vampire, fighting against the Turks and his own brother, Radu. He had a look-alike who did his daylight activities and he, the doppelgänger, was the one who was beheaded by a cousin who was also a Turk, Basarab Laiota. Vlad had made such bitter enemies of the Turks, who he lived with in his youth, and who taught him to impale and to fight viciously, that his double's head, once severed from its body, was sent to Constantinople. Vlad disappeared at that time, living in part in England, where I met him. We are of the same house, Drachenfeur. Our founding sire was a man from Iberia named Aman, we don't know much about him. Aman made Viktor Alexandru, who was my sire's maker and he also made Vlad into a vampire. Aman had met him at the Sultan of Constantinople and wanted him, so he waited until Vlad became ruler and then turned him. So, basically, he's my uncle in the line."

Castro thought a moment and said, "So I am in your line by Jesse?"

"Yes, you will be. I am Jesse's sire and he's going to be yours, so you are going to be part of Drachenfeur. And yes, you will be a great grand-nephew of Vlad."

"So where is he now? Is he going to be involved in this war?"

"He's retired. He is no longer active in the vampire community and wants nothing to do with any of us. So, I'm in charge now." He clapped his hand on Castro's shoulder, "We need to get busy on this. About the name, how about Operation Butterfly, we're pulling the wings off the angels, sounds reasonable to me."

"You're the boss. But, have you considered that the angels could discover your plans before you even start on this?" Castro asked.

Marcus rubbed his eyes. Even with the sun up, he had not been able to sleep to get at least some rest. Dreams and nightmares kept him restless. He hadn't slept enough to know all of the things bothering his dreams but high on that list was Lilly, the pregnancy, and the future.

What the hell was he doing, starting a war with the angels when he had a potential wife and child? And what was he doing to Jesse? What kind of future did he have if he was going to end up being without Jesse? He closed his eyes to get mental control again. What had been started had to be followed through, he had to do this. To not go forward would give those who do have the basic information of the plan the chance to inform Xun and the Council.

He opened his eyes and stared at Jesse. "Jess, I need you to turn Castro."

Jesse started to object but Marcus held up a hand. "Please don't start. There are things going on around this that require us to follow through with it."

He turned to Castro. "Do you have anyone you trust enough to be your first meal after turning? You need a lot of blood after the change."

Castro smiled the smile that made even Marcus wary. "Oh yes, I have someone in mind. She's the one I've been watching after the senior accountants and the outside auditor said that the books have been coming up short about eight times a month, more or less."

"I remember you telling me that someone was skimming and you were going to investigate. I take it you found the culprit?"

"Oh yes, she didn't cover her tracks well enough. It was the tier one secondary auditor in accounts receivable. The name might not mean anything to you, it's Kirsten Skinner." If there was one thing Gunny hated almost more than incompetence was a thief.

"You have her on ice somewhere?" Marcus trusted Castro to be discrete as well as having a plan for the remains.

"No, I have all the evidence," he pointed to a file folder on his stack of books and laptop. "I figured I would talk to you after this meeting about how to handle her. Since you need a ready blood supply, she will do nicely."

"Get her up here. Are Roberts and Massey on duty? Might as well get this started."

"I'll get them to bring her up."

Marcus thought for a moment. "Since she doesn't know what's coming, have Massey get her and have Roberts wait up here by the door. I want them here to deal with the body and also if Ms. Skinner doesn't cooperate."

Castro didn't need to reply, he pulled out his cell and made the arrangements.

"Okay then, Castro, are you sure about this?" Marcus did not want anything to pull the angels in until he was ready.

"Yes, boy. I've wanted this since I hired on with you and discovered your secret."

"Okay then. As soon as our blood supply gets here, we will do it. Any questions about the process?" Marcus was glad Castro was going to be turned, it meant he would have his friend around forever and he wouldn't have to hire and train another Chief of Operations. That was, unless the angels decided to drag him, or Castro, off to Hell. That wasn't going to happen, not as long as Marcus was there to insure it. He snickered.

"What caused that laugh?" Castro saw the slight hint of mischief in his boss's eyes.

"Ah, just thinking about you. A vampire and a Marine, a very deadly combination. With the angels trying to rid the world of us, sooner or later they will get around to you. When they do, I figure there will be a trail of plucked angels littering the road to Hell. You won't go easy."

Castro smiled. "They have no idea."

The door opened and Roberts followed Massey and a curvaceous woman with strawberry blond hair.

The smile she had worn dropped into a frightened frown.

Castro stepped forward. "Ah, Ms. Skinner. Let

me introduce you to our boss. This is Marcus Lancaster."

"Interesting to meet you, Ms. Skinner. Can I call you Kirsten, let's not stand on ceremony, shall we?"

Jean, Castro, and Jesse all stood silent. Marcus was a professional womanizer, even with his relationship with Jesse, and he knew how to work with a woman to get her to do everything he wanted, even without the glamoury. He kissed her hand as he led her to a chair, holding it so she could sit down. The two guards stepped up behind the chair.

Marcus could hear her heartbeat speed up. So could every other vampire in the room as hard as it was beating. She was afraid of something. She had no idea how much she should be afraid.

"I guess you are wondering why I asked for your attendance?" It was a trite saying but so appropriate, her heart sped up even more and the smell of fear floated on the air conditioning.

From behind him, he heard a groan. Jesse had to be feeling the fear and his fangs had probably descended. If they took too long, Jess might eat Castro's dinner.

The accountant stared at the man in front of her then to the boss she answered to.

"Well, you see, Mr. Castro came to me with information about some issues with the assets of Lancaster Industries. He had an outside forensic auditor go through the last six years of the records. And guess what we discovered." Marcus said very calmly as the woman in front of him began to cry.

"There's no need to cry, Ms. Skinner. It will not change the facts. What is the total amount of the missing money, Gunny?"

Castro picked up the folder and opened it. "Seven hundred twenty thousand, six hundred seventy-four dollars, and twenty six cents. That includes the total for the nineteen accounts she tapped."

Jean whistled, "That's quite a treasure, ma belle."

Kirsten had let her head fall until her chin was on her chest when the amount was read. Marcus stepped up, placing two fingers under her chin and lifting her head up.

"Ms. Skinner. Is there a reason you decided to appropriate almost a million dollars from my accounts?"

Her answer was whispered.

"Louder, please. Why did you steal from me?"

"I started to borrow a little to help get my bills paid. I meant to put it back." She wiped her tears and cleared her throat. "I didn't get much. But someone found out. He started keeping records of my I.O.U.'s and he insisted that I borrow three times what I was already doing and give it to him. I did it because he threatened to come to you and tell. Then he asked for more. Soon I wasn't taking any money for myself, it all went to him."

Marcus and Castro exchanged glances. "Did you know about this, Gunny?"

Castro stared at the woman, "No, I didn't. Who is this man, what department does he work in?"

She shook her head, "I cannot tell you, sir. He said he would kill my family if I told on him. He would not kill me, he would give you all of the information and see to it that you put me in jail. I can't risk it." She began to cry again.

"Not sir, I work for a living. You are more afraid of this guy than you are of me?"

Jean walked around the table and knelt down in front of her, looking in her eyes. "Belle, you have nothing to fear from this scoundrel. You should have come to Mr. Castro or Mr. Lancaster when he first started taking money. You could have worked to pay what you took, you might go to jail for a bit. But now you are in a big trouble with both men. The best thing you can do is tell them who did this. It will go a long way toward keeping you safe."

Kirsten's eyes glazed over for a moment, the crying stopping. Marcus noting that his friend had just did a bit of glamoury. "I can't. I am afraid."

"You should fear Mr. Lancaster much more than you fear this rogue. Trust me, you do not want to make him angry, you will be hurt more if you do." He took her hand, "Belle, tell me who is the reprobate you protect."

She stared at him, then said, Taylor Giantti. He is the supervisor in tier three." She withdrew her hand from Jean's and put both hands over her face.

"Gunny, you ..." Marcus started.

"Good as handled, boy, good as handled, and I will take great pleasure in it as well."

Marcus nodded. "Now, what are we going to do about your original sin? What do I do with a thief in my organization?"

"Please sir," she wailed, "I'll do anything..."

Marcus smiled smugly and looked to the other men in the room, bending down and whispered to her, "I will not kill you, you are not going to jail. You have another purpose that I want to take advantage of." He straightened up and stepped back. "You will feed my new grand-progeny."

She stared at him. "What is..."

"It's my progeny, my 'son' you might say, it's his progeny. We are vampires." He knew what her reaction would be, it was a usual reaction from humans that found out about vampires.

She laughed, even though her face was red, puffy, and tear-stained. "You don't talk funny," she looked at Jean, "Except you, of course. And it's not Halloween, you're not wearing a cape and I don't see any fangs." She snickered, glancing around at the group of men surrounding her.

Marcus didn't laugh, no one did. She stifled her snicker with a hiccough. He looked toward Jesse, who came forward, and then at Jean. With a nod of his head, Marcus's fangs dropped down and he smiled at her. So did the other two vampires. "Not kidding, we are vampires. And you, my dear, are going to be the blood donor when we make Mr. Castro into a vampire. You will donate for a few more as well."

She shrank back, looked around to find the door, "I think I will decline. I quit. I'll have someone pick up my things." She stood up and turned around to leave, running into Massey and Roberts who blocked her way to the door.

"No, you are going to do it. You will not leave the building unless I have you taken out."

She started to scream. Jean looked into her eyes again, "Ma chere, please be silent. This is not a bad outcome, do not provoke Mr. Lancaster into doing something much more harmful to you than just donating blood."

She calmed, sitting back down and staring straight ahead.

"Thank-you, Jean." Marcus pulled his fangs up and looked at Jesse. "You can feed for a moment, not more, just enough to take the edge off. Once you're done, you will take Castro's blood and then turn him. She can be fed from twice. Castro, you will need to pull away from her when I tell you, we don't want to deplete her. I have a better idea that killing her. We need sources of blood for our new vampires, so we keep her. We'll have to come up with a few more, but this way, we don't have to think of ways to get rid of dead bodies."

Castro nodded as Jesse walked up to Kirsten. Kneeling down, he slipped an arm around her and tipped her head to the side. Turning his head toward Marcus, he smiled, "I guess I can feed from a girl for now. I would like to find a male donor later, though."

"You won't need one, I'm going to make sure you have all the blood you need, right here." Marcus remarked, tapping his own neck. "Now get on with the feeding so we can tend to the business at hand." Jesse put his mouth to her neck and struck.

As he was feeding, Marcus turned to Massey and Roberts. "Do you want to be turned as well?" He knew they would stay quiet about what they had seen and he knew that they knew about vampires as well. Two strong men would make good vampires.

Massey spoke first, "I would." Robert agreed, nodding his head.

"Good, we will put you in line and get you turned." He turned to Jesse, "Okay, Jess, that's enough." He tapped Jess on the shoulder, pulling on it when Jess didn't disengage immediately. Jess let go and stood up, licking the blood from his lips.

"Castro, are you ready?"

"Yes, let's do this." Castro stepped up to Jesse, pulled his tie off and took off his shirt. The big Marine Corps eagle, globe, and anchor symbol was tattooed on his right upper arm in color, with the symbol of the Second Marine Division under it. It wasn't the first time Marcus had seen the Gunny without a shirt but it always startled him to see not only the tattoo but the scars from things he didn't want to talk about.

Gunny laid his neck onto his right shoulder, offering the left artery for the vampire. Jesse held his upper arms and started to strike.

The door slammed open, startling everyone, and the security, Jean, and Castro pulled weapons from their holsters.

"What? I'm just in time, looks like. We need to talk." The man stood in the doorway.

"Gery" Marcus growled.

Chapter Twenty-Four

I SOBEL AND LILLY walked into the new clinic that Dr. Young had set up. He was talking to Gregory and smiled as the girls walked in.

"Hi ladies. I have everything set up and ready to go for your sonogram." Jack said.

"What about Dr. Harkness, is he here for this?" Isobel really wanted the vampire here when they tried something new.

"No, he called and said he had something else come up and he was headed to an emergency situation. He will be here for the next one."

"I'm not sure about this, is it going to hurt?" Lilly had no idea what sonogram was but if it included anyone in the medical profession or their tests, she was sure it would probably hurt.

"It's going to be fine, Lilly." Gregory spoke up. "Women get these done all the time now."

"He's correct. All this is sound waves, you can't hear them but they paint a picture on the computer screen for the doctor and family to be able to see the baby and also to determine if there are any anomalies, where the placenta is in relationship to the cervix, and we can even see the sex of the fetus if you want that information."

Lilly had caught about half of that. See the baby, check. See if it has anomalies, check. See the sex, check. Whatever a placenta and cervix was, she had no idea. But if the doctor knew, that's all she needed to know.

"Can Isobel and Gregory go with me? I'm a bit afraid of going in alone."

"Of course, if you want them in there, it's fine."

"*And you're going to let me in to see the kittens too.*" Baron said to everyone who could hear him, which was everyone in the room but the doctor. He walked into the clinic and straight toward Lilly, rubbing himself around her legs.

"No cats. Not in my clinic. I'm not a veterinarian, I don't do animals." Jack frowned at the cat. He had seen him board the plane in San Antonio and knew that he lived here with Lilly, but he wasn't going to allow him to just walk into his clinic and get cat hair all over the equipment.

"*I won't shed on his precious equipment. Tell him I'm going in there with you and that's that.*" Baron stared into the eyes of the human, willing him to allow him in.

Lilly came to his aid, "Dr. Young, Baron is not your average cat. He's very clean and he is with me. I want him there."

"I won't risk the sterility of the clinic by having that feline in the clinic. It's safety, for you and for all the other patients."

"He's not going to risk anything. I promise. There's one thing you might want to know, Baron, as I said, is not an average cat. He's a vampire, just like me, just like Marcus, Jean, and Jesse." Lilly knelt down to pet the cat.

"A vampire cat? Really? You can't change a cat into a vampire, I thought that only humans could be changed." Jack knew Lilly had to be lying to him and he wondered why.

"Yes, he's the very first vampiric animal. I turned him years and years ago in New Orleans and he's my friend. I want him with me and if he can't be, I won't go in there." Lilly hated laying down the law to people but when it came to Baron, she would stand on the words she spoke.

Just to make sure that the doctor got the point, Baron yowled and then opened his mouth. His fangs, at their usual cat-like size suddenly dropped another few millimeters. Jack stared at the points a moment and then turned to lead them to the exam room. "Bring the cat." Baron chuffed his approval and Jack looked back at the big tortoise shell cat.

The world, once again, had twisted his reality. He wondered, briefly, what else he was going to find out wasn't just a myth or storybook creature.

As they turned so that Jack could show them to the exam room, a red-headed woman walked into the room wearing blue scrubs. "Excuse me, Dr. Young?"

The group turned and Dr. Young nodded, "That's me."

"Hi, I'm Reba King, I was a nurse over at University hospital in San Antonio. One of the human resources people told me you had come here and had given notice there. I checked with the Lancaster Industries personnel department and they hired me to be your nurse here."

"I generally hire my own people, I don't re-member seeing you around." Jack was suspicious of this.

"I worked nights in geriatrics so I didn't see many people, except our patients anyway. Before that, I was a floater. I've been in all the depart-ments at one time or another. I guess you could call me the Renaissance Night nurse." She laughed nervously. "Anyway, I had heard you were the best surgeon at University so I applied to be on your team. Unfortunately, they informed me you quit and went to work for Lancaster. I applied here in hopes of being able to work with you, learn from you, improve my skills."

She noticed the skeptical look on Jack's face, "Oh! O hope you don't think I'm a creepy stalker or anything, I just wanted to learn from the best and that's you..." She stopped and tried smiling, "I'm not making a good first impression, am I? I'm just so nervous."

Dr. Young reminded himself to talk to Marcus about the hiring process within his organization. "I guess you work here, welcome aboard. You are dressed to work, how are you in obstetrics?"

"Excellent." She said brightly.

"Good, Then you can assist on a sonogram."

"Yes sir." She smiled and followed the group.

Once in the room, Nurse King looked through the cabinets until she found a gown. She handed it to Lilly and told her to put it on, taking all of her clothing off. Isobel went in to help her, showing her how to manipulate the snaps on the shoulders.

"It doesn't close in the back!" Lilly exclaimed. "I think she gave me a smaller one. I need a larger size to..."

Isobel laughed. "No, that's the way these things are made. I know you're uncomfortable and I can shoo Gregory and the doctor out until we get you settled on the table if you would like."

"That might be a good idea. I should get another to cover my legs when I get up there as well."

"No, there's a sheet to cover you. What's going to happen is that you'll lay down and get comfortable on your back. We'll put a sheet on you and then call the guys back in. The doctor will need access to your abdomen so he'll pull the sheet down to just above your pubic hair and the gown up to just under your breasts. He's going to put some jell on you so that the wand will work better, then he'll rub the wand on you and that will let him see what the baby is doing. It's really just simple and quick. Don't worry, I'll be right there with you." Isobel squeezed Lilly's hand and led her over to the table and helped her lay down, looking through the cabinets until she found a sheet to cover her with.

"Okay Dr. Young, we're ready," the nurse called out. The door opened and the guys walked in, Gregory waiting until Baron sauntered in to shut the door. Dr. Young turned the lights off, leaving only a faint glow from a lamp in an opposite corner and the monitor on the sonography machine.

He pulled the sheet down and the gown up, just like Isobel had described. "Okay Lilly. I'm going to put this jell on you and then I'll run this wand over your abdomen. Let's get started. Let's get a look at the first ever vampire baby, shall we?"

Reba King wasn't sure what he meant by vampire baby, vampires didn't have babies. Maybe the baby was taking more of the woman's nutrition than normal somehow. She shrugged the questioning off as she paid attention to the procedure.

Dr. Young sat down on the stool between the machine and the table. "Lilly, this won't hurt at all. You may be a little uncomfortable because I may have to press down on the uterus, your womb, to be able to make sure I get good pictures, but that should be it." He held up a squeeze bottle. "This is a jelly-like material that allows the transducer" he motioned at the gray thing on the end of a cord laying on the machine top, "to slide over your skin easily. It's usually cold but I wanted you to be comfortable with this so I warmed it in the sink."

He squirted the jelly on her lower abdomen. She had expected it to be cold, the room was very cold. But it was warm, which felt good. Isobel was shivering, Lilly noticed, she always seemed to be able to judge how the ambient temperature was by watching Isobel. While temperature didn't affect her, and probably all vampires, the humans felt it.

Jack broke Lilly's thoughts, "Okay, let's begin. I'm going to place the transducer against your skin and we'll start getting the pictures of that baby." Reaching over, he flipped a switch on the machine to begin.

The room exploded in a choir of screams and yowling. Lilly pushed herself away with her legs as she slammed both ears with her hands, falling off the table, the sheet going one way, the gown the other, leaving her almost naked. Nurse King tried to reach her but Isobel and Gregory were between her and her patient.

The cat was screaming a pained yowl and launched himself at the machine, scratching at the picture and the buttons before he passed out, falling to the floor twitching.

"Turn it off, it's hurting them!" Gregory yelled over the screaming as he dropped to the floor to cover Lilly.

Jack Young turned the machine off by grabbing and pulling the plug from the outlet on the wall. His hands shook, something that had not happened more than a couple of times since his residency training. The new nurse seemed frozen in place, unsure what to do next.

Lilly was sobbing, holding her abdomen protectively and leaning in Gregory's arms. Her ghoul was rocking her, running one hand on her hair and talking softly to her. Isobel was holding Baron, stroking his fur and talking to him. Jack wanted to examine her but he also realized she needed to get soothed first.

As she tried to calm, Lilly heard, *"Lilly? What's happening? Why are you screaming? Who is hurting you?"*

Sullivan. She didn't want to tell him. She slammed the link between them closed, disconnecting.

As things quieted, Jack motioned to Gregory to lift her and place her on the table. The moment her leg touched the table, she kicked out, throwing her and Gregory into Isobel and Baron and the entire group hit the wall.

Damn, the woman had a strong kick, Gregory thought. He never dropped her and the moment he could re-calm her, he placed his wrist to her mouth. Out of the corner of his eye he saw Isobel do the same to Baron. Both vampires struck simultaneously, taking the blood offered. Jack looked at the nurse and shrugged, feeling like the odd person out.

Reba King wasn't just the odd one out, she was shocked at the chaos. She wasn't around vampires and the feeding was a shock to watch. Lilly's color had paled as she struggled with the sound and, as she fed, her color came up again.

Vampires. Not the usual thing at a clinic and certainly not a pregnant vampire. And obviously the cat was also a vampire, the other woman had fed it from her wrist. "Interesting." She thought.

Once the feeding ended, Lilly closed the punctures and licked the remaining blood from her lips. She bit her wrist and gave Gregory a small amount of her blood in return. Isobel held her arm out and Lilly closed Baron's punctures as well. Once Gregory had finished, Lilly offered her still-bleeding wrist to the other ghoul, who took a small amount from her as well. Baron then crawled off of Isobel into Lilly's arms, purring and rubbing on her face.

"*You okay?*" He asked.

"*Yeah, you?*"

"*Yeah, but that better not happen again.*" Baron growled.

Isobel asked. "Lilly, do you know what happened?"

The vampire shook her head. "It hurts! He said it wouldn't hurt but it was so loud, it hurt my ears. And my stomach hurt like whatever that noise was hurting my baby too." She reached out for Baron, who was still shaking in Isobel's arms. "It must have hurt Baron too."

"*What was that?*" Baron asked both Lilly and Isobel.

Lilly shifted her attention back to the doctor. She pointed at the button on the machine "that noise happened when you touched that button,"

Gregory was chewing on his lip, deep in thought as he held Lilly's hand.

"Doc? You said this was a sono—gram" he stressed each syllable, "That first part, sono, is like the sonar the ships use, right?"

"It's sound waves, very similar tox...oh." Jack looked at the machine.

Gregory looked first at Isobel and then at the doctor "The sound, while we cannot hear it, some animals, like dogs and cats, do hear high frequency sounds."

"And since vampire hearing is much keener than humans," Isobel filled in, "They could hear the sounds. The high-pitched sound hurt their ears."

Lilly spoke up. "My ears hurt and it felt like my stomach was going to explode."

"Hmmmmm." Jack was trying to get the incident to make sense. "The baby must have been able to hear, or feel, the sound waves as well. And physics tells us that sound waves travel through water as a vibration, just like in air. The amniotic fluid must have struck the baby and hurt as well."

"So, you are saying that we cannot have sonograms as a way to check on Lilly's baby, Doctor Young?" Nurse King asked.

"Looks like it. We won't be able to use the handheld Doppler fetal heart either, it works the same way. I'm going to have to rely on the old methods." He reached into a drawer and pulled out a stethoscope. "Lilly, I want to make sure this hasn't stopped the baby's heart."

Reba reached out to Lilly, who took the offered hand and stood up, handing off the cat to Isobel she stepped up to the table, climbing up. She covered the vampire with the sheet and helped her put the gown back on.

"Everyone in here has seen me naked, I can do without all the cloth." Lilly smiled.

"Yeah, you are comfortable nude but some of us are uncomfortable with your ability to be comfortable. I think the cloth is a good idea." Isobel smiled at her.

"Speak for yourself, woman. She's beautiful." Gregory said.

Dr. Young moved the sheet just enough to put the stethoscope on Lilly's abdomen. He moved it around a bit and then stood up. "Heart sounds okay and the baby is still moving around. I think we've averted danger with this one. I want you to go rest, no serious movement for a day or so, just let yourself get past this a bit." He turned to Isobel, "I think Baron needs to do the same thing, no really big outings until he has rested more. One of you might go over to the Randall's next door and pick up a cat box for him for the moment."

Lilly allowed Reba to help her off the table, "Go ahead and change into your clothes, Lilly, I can take you out to the car when you're ready."

"That's not necessary, nurse. We live upstairs in a large apartment. If she feels well enough to walk, it's not far. But that part is up to her."

Lilly turned to face them, the sheet draped on her like a toga, "I can walk. It quit hurting so I'm fine." She went to change and then returned.

"Thank you, Dr. Young and Nurse King. You tried, it's not your fault we didn't know I could hear the machine noise."

"Call me Reba, all of you, please. And I was just doing my job."

"Let us know when you need to see us again." Isobel said as she took Lilly's arm.

Gregory took the other and they walked out.

As they got to the elevator, Baron twitched his tail as he entered, "*Just so you know, I am NOT going to use a cat box, got it?*"

Chapter Twenty-Five

"I 'M GLAD I got here in time." The thin man with strawberry blond hair and blue eyes smiled as he kicked the door shut behind him. He flipped his left hand and all the non-vampires in the room froze where they stood. Marcus noted that the man was wearing an old fashioned zoot suit, bright neon green, complete with chain and spats. And a big hat with a huge ostrich feather.

"What the hell do you want, demon?" Marcus figured that the demon just appeared in the building outside the conference room's door, bypassing the security guards who carefully guarded the Lancaster Industries headquarters. "And let Gunny and the two guards out of the freeze, they know about vampires."

The intruder made a gesture like shutting off a wall-switch and both guards wobbled on their feet before looking to their boss for explanation and orders. Castro glared at the interloper.

"Okay, there's your guards and the other guy. Of course, if they try to get frisky with me, I'll make it permanent just before I take them with me home. First of all, Lucy sends her regards and her regrets that she couldn't be here herself. I've been sent to help you. Second, I was delivering that little 'package' we wrapped up in Europe. I kept it a little longer than expected but it was so much fun, I didn't want to box it up and bring it to you. Third, There's no way that you're going to be able to accomplish what you are wanting to do without outside help and I figure asking the angels to help you with turning them into vampires is problematic at best."

"Gentlemen, this is Gery. He's a demon. We met in Switzerland after I finished talking with the ghouls. The so-called 'package' is the first angel in our beginning operation. She was listening in on our plans and we took care of it." Marcus turned to the demon, "We have discussed this, Gery, you're going to help us learn how to do what we need to do, it was expected that you would be here sooner than this."

"You weren't here. I tried to make it in for you and I kept getting told you were out of touch and wouldn't be back for a while. Then I got a little busy on a couple of projects and lost track of time. I didn't even try to call again. I hate trying to get through the corporate blocks. It was only because I was monitoring both your airfield and this building that I was able to find out you were back. I had to go pick up that angel to bring here before we talked. She's ensconced in one of the small office rooms, locked in and wearing a copper ankle wrap." He laughed, "That room, I'm afraid, has a blacked-out window in the door, I didn't want her knowing what was going to happen before it happened."

Marcus walked around to the head of the table by the boards and gestured for everyone else to take their seats. Massey and Roberts remained next to Ms. Skinner.

"You might as well have a seat, gentlemen, she's not going anywhere." Gery said, "I put someone into suspended animation and they stay that way until I let them go, lose my strength to maintain it, or…"

"I kill you." Marcus nodded and the two men sat at the end of the table, close enough to grab their charge if she moved.

"Which won't happen if you want to keep your vampiric body this side of the veil. You don't think Lucy wouldn't relish getting you into her hands?"

When Marcus didn't reply, the demon continued, "We have to get some vampires started tracking and capturing some angels. While your cute little progeny did it without help, believe me, the angels will have been briefed and will be on guard. And, quite frankly, they will be able to trace any captured angel right back to this building unless you get some help putting it under some sort of force field that will not allow them to see through it. You need something to scramble energy signatures with the vampires and angels before they get here. Are you prepared to hold the angels we pick up and bring here, have a place to put them while the change takes effect and then somewhere to make them willing to work against Heaven, that's going to take a bit of doing?"

"I have a place to put them. There are two floors in this building that are equipped with isolation cells."

"Not the usual office design, I must say." Gery smirked.

"They were built years ago for a special project. They are now empty. One floor can be for holding the angels until we turn them, the second can be for turned ones that we have to program to do what we need to do." Marcus looked to Castro who was nodding in agreement.

"Okay. What about dinner? You prepared to feed all of these new vampires?" Gery turned and looked at the woman sitting away from the table, "One blood doll is not going to make it if you want to feed everyone. You're going to need a bunch more. That means getting ones that fit into the angel's laws and a place to hold them while you do what needs doing. And a staff for a blood bank so you can pull blood off of some humans without their noticing it, kind of a vampire "Catch & Release" program. Storage facilities for the blood. Transportation, unless you mean to gather all of the angels from Houston, which, once again, will bring the unwanted attention."

He looked at Marcus. After a second or two, he shook his head, "You haven't thought of any of this, have you? 'Let's just make a few vampires out of angels and then kick the door open in heaven,' and you expect the Archangel Mikhail to just roll over and hand you everything you want. I want what you're smokin' because it is surely some good stuff, makes you dream up fiction."

"I've thought about it. I have enough people to deal with the blood issue, just the employees here will do a lot of it, we open up a company blood bank to supply the security people we have in the field..."

"Read: mercenaries." Gery said, unimpressed.

"Yes, mercs. And some of them may be pressed into service as blood dolls, if I find that the blood donations aren't enough. I think Castro can scare up a few employees that need "attitude adjustment.""

"Whatever. You have to have a plan to do it. All of this has to be plotted out and solid before you even go down to turn Alice, which is the name she was using as a human. You have to be very adaptable and be able to change procedures at a moment's notice when you see or even catch a whiff of problems. And, Lucy wants to know what's in it for her?"

"You said Lucy wants to help to get back at Heaven for the fall. Isn't that the reward for her in this?"

"Her?" Jesse and Jean said at the same time, "Lucy is a woman?"

"Lucifer, yes, she's a woman." Gery sat back and sighed dramatically, noting with an eye roll of disgust, that this was the 9,666th time he had explained this. Then there was a spark of amusement at the very irony of the count. He continued, "Former archangel, keeper of the dimension that her brother, Mikhail, sent her to. The one that they call Hell." Gery buffed his fingernails on his shirt and then looked at them.

"No, there's no way. Why are all the Bibles convinced that Lucifer is a male? Wouldn't that have come out before this?" Jesse asked.

"Have you studied history, youngster? The authors of the Bible were living in a male-dominated world. Women, especially powerful women, were antitheses to the norm. Their women had to be subservient to their male society. The Apostle Paul wrote about that in that letter to the Ephesians, chapter five. It was very much something that was done at the time. Another thing, your English language treats all personal pronouns as masculine, unless describing someone specific and in third person, they say 'he' and 'his'. It is only recently that the language started being an attempt to make all third person discussion neutral. The Bible doesn't treat the language with gender neutral, it says 'he' for everything. Not necessarily male." He looked at Jean, "And your French does the same thing. And, on top of it all, the Bible had many translations over the centuries, and not all of them were done without comment, or political persuasion. Besides," he reared back in his chair and plopped his spats on the conference table, "Who here does not think that the female has the guile, intelligence, fortitude...and beauty...to be the ultimate adversary?" The room was silent. "Well, there you have it!" He knitted his fingers behind his head and stared haughtily at the ceiling.

"Thank you so much for that insightful history lesson, Gery, but you didn't answer the question, what's the payout for Lucy?" Marcus could have done without the lesson.

"My thought is, the payout is that you vampires will make enough angels into vampires that heaven has to fight you. Think of the demons as Switzerland, we stand to get rid of enough angels to be able to take Mikhail out of power and put Lucifer back on the left-hand throne of Heaven. We supply you with angels and we deal with the angels like we are friends right up until the war ends, then we assert our might."

"And what do we get from this, exactly?"

"You vampires are free. You can do what you want to do with the humans. Marry them, bury them, make them slaves, even eat them if that's your bend. We just simply don't care. You're our progeny anyway, just a way to get at the angels and keep them busy."

It was not the first time Marcus had heard about the vampires being connected to the demons.

Gery prattled on, "One of the louder television preachers has used the discussion of paranormal beings as a way to keep his flock in line. To him and his followers, vampires, the ghosts, and the werewolves are real."

"Aren't we?" Jesse asked.

"Of course you are. But your average human thinks you're a Halloween story, a myth used to scare children and ignorant adults. Oh, that is until, somehow, you had a couple of authors back in the 1700s decide to write books about the mythological vampires. I still love the Stoker one about Vlad Dracul, it paints him in such a serious villain vein, no pun...well, it's intended, who am I kidding. Now the vampires in high school that sparkle, what's that all about anyway? It's just one of a bunch of vampire books that have been coming out since the late 20th century, seems like everyone wants to ride the coat tails of the big name vampire writers like J.R. Ward, Chelsea Quinn Yarbro, Anne Rice, and Rachel Caine."

"Enough, Jesse, Gery, let's just finish what we need to finish. What is it you are going to do, today, Gery?" Marcus was fast losing his patience. He had too much to do to play audience for a self-absorbed demon that was bent on being a history professor.

Gery looked up at the ceiling. Marcus stifled the urge to say "stop looking to heaven to save you," it would only make the talkative demon find a new subject to pontificate on.

Gery glared at Marcus, "I heard that. You want me to really pontificate? I can..."

"No. I don't want you to do anything more than getting to the point so I can get back to work. I'm working on a deadline here."

"Ba Dum Bum, ching," Gery made motions of drumming. "No need to get punny with me, Marcus."

Marcus called Gery's glare and raised it to lasers.

"Oh all right. You are a real pain in the ass, don't you know. Ok, we are going to do these one at a time. First, turn whomever you want so this mass turning can happen. Line up some blood donors and get that ready. Your mundane shielding, by the way, is woefully inadequate. I'll seal the building from angels once you remove the two you have in residence and I will then..."

"Wait. What? Angels in residence?" Marcus interrupted the demon who had been ticking off points on his fingers, the same time those same points were magically appearing on the white board across the room.

The counting hand made a fist. "Yeah, angels in residence. I didn't stutter. This building practically reeks with angel putrescence. You have angels in the building, not had, but *HAVE*. It's very prominent for those of us who can smell it. As it is, I'm going to have to take three showers and send my suit to the dry cleaners to remove the smell. You know I should charge you for..."

"Where. Are. The. Angels? Can you play bloodhound and show me where they are?" The last thing Marcus wanted was to have an angel in residence who would go running to the damned angel enforcers when he started his plan.

With an indignant huff, he leveled a cold gaze at Marcus. "I will not work for you. It's your problem and you have to figure it out for yourself, vampire. I'm here to seal the building, which I can't do at the moment. I am here to tell you how the demons will be aiding you find and subdue the angels you're going to be plucking and sucking. I am not here to be your dog. Got that?"

Marcus snarled, "Got it. How do I reach you for the seal once I have found the angels in the building?"

"I'll find you." The demon disappeared, which

broke the spell holding the woman, who blinked twice and then stood, trying to leave in her confusion. Two meaty hands pushed her back down into the chair.

"Let's get this over with." Marcus nodded to Jesse, who walked up to Castro, wrapped his arm around him and put one hand over the man's buzz cut hair, holding his head steady. He sunk his fangs into the exposed neck and began the turning.

Chapter Twenty-Six

L ILLY WALKED INTO the living room, her hands rubbing the little bump she was now very aware of in her abdomen. Isobel was busy on her computer with the television going with some drama. Lilly stood looking at what was happening, dramatic music and two people fighting, then ending up in a passionate kiss that moved from one room to one with a bed.

"You want to sit and watch it? It's called a soap opera, or a daytime drama. They are all about the angst and screwing, this one is called 'Days of Our Lives'. Right now, that man on the screen is named Lucas, the woman is Sophie, they're dating. There's also a woman named Sami who has a baby with Lucas named Will, and Austin is her new boss. You'll catch up with the story in a week or so, it's something to fill the hour in the afternoon, I've been watching since it first came on in 1965, I think I've seen more people die and come back from the dead on this show than in the entire vampire community. I tape it so that I can watch it at night, it comes on during the afternoon."

"Sounds....fun?" Lilly kept watching until it turned into another advertisement, again with two people in the bathtub. "What is this about? Why are they showing two people in the bath?"

"It's for erectile dysfunction. I guess they can't show the two people screwing so they have them in separate bathtubs holding hands."

"This is about a pill to have sex? On the television? They talk about that stuff on here?" Lilly tried not to sound shocked but sex wasn't even discussed in polite company in her day, that was left to the brothels like she worked in.

"Oh honey," Isobel stifled the laugh, "You haven't see anything yet. They have whole cable channels dedicated just to sex shows. If you are curious, I can turn the channel..."

"NO!" Lilly surprised herself with the shout, "I, I think I can leave that one alone for a while."

"I can too. You okay? Do you need to feed again?" Isobel started to stand up.

"I'm fine with that. Gregory will be here soon. I was wondering if you had seen Marcus recently."

"He's busy working, he and Jesse have been closed in for the last month or so with Jean and Castro. I've tried to get an audience with him but his personal guards won't even let me inside to talk to him. He keeps sending them out to tell me to leave him alone, he's busy. There has been a steady stream of men and women going in and out again. I've seen Jacob bringing new people in and taking them to one of the conference rooms for something, I have no idea what. He's not talking either."

"I had hoped he would come out at least to go with me to see Jack and listen to the baby's heart. He needs to at least show a bit of concern about this."

"Are you wanting him to be in the delivery room when you have the baby?"

Lilly looked shocked, "No, men don't belong in the birthing room, I'm actually nervous having Dr. Young examine me without you there. I was hoping to talk to him about finding a female midwife to deliver the baby."

Isobel again stifled a laugh, "Men go into the delivery room with their wives all the time now. They watch the baby come out and they usually cut the umbilical cord. They have medicine that will keep the pain down so you're not that uncomfortable. You can even watch the delivery with mirrors and they make birth video all the time so you can show the birth to family and friends."

Lilly was shaking her head even before Izzy finished the sentence, "They said we were disgraceful as prostitutes, how did the society get so decadent? I will not have Marcus in the room, he's certainly not going to watch this, in person, on a mirror, or on a video." She stopped and thought a moment, "Would you go with me when it's time? I want you there to help me, I want you to deliver the baby, Dr. Young can stay out. I bet that the nurse, Reba, can do the delivery with you. She must know how to deliver a baby if she's a nurse, right?"

"I can talk to Jack and Reba for you, but I

really think you need to discuss this with Jack yourself. There is something called the HIPPA rule that says the doctor cannot talk to anyone but you unless you let him know in writing and you can withdraw that permission at any time. Jack hasn't really said anything to you about that law but I'm sure that if I go down there to talk to him, he will say I can't."

"They made a rule that a doctor can't talk to someone? Why do that? Does that mean I have to have the baby's permission to talk to him about the baby? That doesn't make sense."

This time Isobel just let the laugh happen, "No, sweetie, you will have to talk for the baby until he or she is 18, that's when a child becomes an adult and can handle their own medical care. The rule is to allow you to say who can and cannot know about your medical treatments. I'm actually surprised he didn't have you fill out paperwork before your first appointment. I guess he wasn't set up to do that yet, you should ask him this afternoon about them."

"I want you there with me today. You can ask him and I'll sign whatever he needs to have, I want you to be there with me for all of it. If I don't sign for Marcus to be there, they will keep him out, right?"

"True, you can keep him out but why would you want to? He's the father of the baby, he really should be there."

Lilly sighed, "Well, should be and wants to are two very different things. He's not asked me how I'm doing, how the baby is, said hello, nothing. I haven't seen him, really, since we got home from San Antonio and he came to apologize to me for being horrible to me and make a few 'suggestions' on how to handle the pregnancy. I'm not sure if he is really going to be a proper father, he doesn't have time for me, how can he have time for a child?"

"He's a big, busy man with a major corporation and a lot of demands on his time, but I've never seen him not take care of his obligations, and this baby, Lilly, is a giant obligation. Give him a chance to catch the business up good, Castro's been in charge while he was gone and he's probably the best at running the company. However, I know he has boards of charities he is on, he does a lot of fund-raising for many organizations, and those were things that Castro couldn't deal with. So he's trying to get his obligations caught up. You are part of his life and he's going to be back in his regular," she chuckled, "rut soon and you'll be part of it."

"I'm not sure I like being called a 'rut'" Izzy was worried that Lilly was angry with her until the smile hit her eyes, then her mouth.

"Just don't worry, okay? I tell you what, you go take up your side of the couch, I'll grab some ice cream for us, and we can watch the soap opera together."

Lilly wrinkled her nose, "Ice cream doesn't even sound good."

"Trust me, this will hit the spot." Izzy disappeared into the kitchen. Lilly found her way to the couch, sat down and propped some pillows around her to get more comfortable, and let her thoughts stray. Izzy came back in and handed a carton to her.

"I really don't think that I can eat..." She pulled the top off the container and sniffed, then grinned. "How did you make ice cream out of blood?"

"Not really ice cream, more a frozen ice but I figured the cold might be a good thing and you can hang with me and eat as we watch TV. Try it."

Lilly took the spoon and dipped it into the carton. Pulling it out, she sniffed it and then put it into her mouth. She made a wilting movement and then smiled, "Oh that's wonderful! It is great."

"Good, you like it. I was worried about it but I figured I would let you decide whether it was good and if you want more made."

"Keep this in the...freezer...and I can eat some when I want something cold. Thank you so much for thinking of this." Lilly reached across the pillow and touched Izzy's arm, then put another spoonful of the red ice into her mouth, smiling.

"Ok, that's solved and now we can see what Sami is going to do with that baby of hers." She grabbed the remote and worked on starting the show over.

As THE NIGHT was waning and the ice cream eaten, the girls had started talking again. Mostly about the baby but Izzy worried about something else, how would life change for everyone with a baby, possibly vampire, and the need for a relationship between Marcus and Lilly. She knew that Jesse was hopelessly in love with Marcus and the news of a baby that would link Marcus with Lilly, no matter whatever relationship he would have. Would Jesse be able to let her into Marcus's life without being jealous? It was all a big mess, no matter who ended up together.

Her train of thought derailed as Lilly stiffened beside her. Isobel let her mind open and she heard Baron.

"...*I'm telling you, it is not my fault, that damned dog followed me into the elevator and when we got downstairs, he managed to get out of the door when I did and he's taking off.......HEY! Get back here, stupid....don't go...Ah no, jeeze. Lilly, get Isobel and get down here NOW! I've got a huge problem on my paws and this will take humans.*" Baron's voice sounded extremely stressed. And what was Lancelot doing going out the door?

Both girls looked at each other, melted ice cream cartons abandoned on the coffee table and they both ran toward the elevator. Izzy pushed the button about a dozen times, trying to get the car to go faster once they got into it. Something was very, very wrong.

Once the doors opened, the women sprinted out into the lobby and then looked around, trying to find out where Baron was.

"*I'm out in front of the building, next to the place the cars drive to get in the park. Hurry!*"

Lilly pushed on the door and tried to get it to open. Jacob Cronin stepped away from the security desk and approached them. "Is there something I can do, ladies?"

"Jacob, good, we need to get outside now, unlock the door, please!" Isobel said.

"You know you should have your building key with you at all times, don't you?"

"Jacob. Don't you lecture me. I think Lancelot has got out, we must get him before Marcus finds out. Or would you like to be the one who has to tell him..."

Jacob waved his key across the pad and Lilly shoved the door open, "Get him and then knock on the door. I'll be watching for you so I can let you in. Go!"

They sprinted through the door and around the corner of the building, trying to find Baron.

"*Over here, now, before someone else drives by. He's right here.*" Baron was walking circles around a ball of fur on the street.

Lance.

Isobel got there first and gently picked up the dog. He was limp, unconscious, and there was a tire mark across his mid-section. Someone had ran over Marcus's prized canine. "Oh God, no! Baron, what happened?"

"*Stupid ran after me when I came out, then he took off ahead of me and there was a car and he didn't stop and I don't think the car could see him, it went on past and turned the corner. I don't think he's breathing.*" Baron was walking circles around Isobel's legs and loudly mewing.

"He's not breathing. Lilly, he's not breathing! Oh, Marcus is going to be so angry that he got out with Baron. He's going to be so pissed at us, and especially at Baron." Isobel had tears running down her face, cradling the dog and rocking him gently.

"Isobel, let me have him. Let me see him." She took the animal from her friend's arms and checked him over. "He's not been gone long, right Baron?" As he left her arms, Isobel began to sob uncontrollably. Lilly felt her own tears fall down her cheeks and a drop hit the dead Sheltie's fur.

"*Right. I have only been out a couple of minutes, I called you just as soon as it happened.*"

"Good. Then here's what we're going to do. Let's go back away from the windows and then Baron, I'm going to ask you to do something, you need to turn Lance."

"*I am not going to put my paws on that flea bitten mutt, especially when his owner is going to blame me for him being hurt in the first place. If I'm going to get hurt, I'm not going to help.*"

"Baron. Please!" Lilly couldn't believe that the cat wouldn't help her.

"*And I would have to sink my teeth through both layers of his fur. Do you know how awful the taste of undercoat is?*"

"Baron!"

"*I've bit dogs before. Not as tasty as rats, not like those at that river back in San Antonio.*"

"Baron, please. If not for the dog, for me and Isobel. Look how upset she is, she loves Lance."

Between sobs, Isobel managed to say, "Marcus

is going to shit baby farm animals in the living room if we give him a dead dog! And I won't be able to calm him."

"*That I would like to see, goats, cows, and chickens in his precious room. He complains of MY fur but he lets this shedding moron on all the furniture and...*"

Lilly was fuming, "Ok, don't do it. I will go to him and tell him the dog died. I don't think he will harm me, much."

Baron looked at her, gold eyes seeming to swirl as he growled. He looked at the dog, then at Izzy, then back to the dog as Lilly began to walk back toward the front of the building.

Isobel turned to walk away as well. "I guess we can bury him on the grassy area near that big tree. He used to love peeing on that tree, made Marcus crazy because dog pee..."

"*Oh all right! Fuck it! Or rather unfuck it!*" Baron stopped walking, "*I will turn the damned dog. Let's at least go into the drive area, I hate an audience when I eat.*"

Lilly laid Lancelot on the pavement in the darkened loading dock area.

"Thank-you, Baron." Isobel stepped back with Lilly, giving the big cat room.

"*I'm not doing this for Marcus. I'm doing it only to get you two to stop the tears. In Lilly's case, it's a big waste of tasty blood.*" He stood over the body of the dog. As he opened his mouth, Isobel could see his fangs drop. Then he struck, pulling on what blood the dog had, then he bit his own leg and laid it over the dog's mouth.

Lilly wasn't entirely sure that the turning would work. Baron had been alive when she turned him by accident. Lancelot was dead, or almost dead as they began, his back and both back legs broken, probably injuries inside of him as well.

This had to work. Not for Marcus, but for Lancelot's life. The dog was so sweet, loyal to a fault, even with someone like Marcus. She put her own arm up to her mouth.

"Wait, Lilly, let me donate my blood to him, you need all of yours for the baby." Isobel put out her arm to be lacerated for the donation.

"No." Lilly shook her head as she ripped into her own arm, then sat down next to the animals.

Baron backed off, "*This has to be done by a vampire to make a vampire.*" The blood he had put into the dog's mouth had mostly leaked out and down into the white ruff of fur on his chest.

Lilly nodded as she pulled the dog into her lap. "Lancelot. Lance, hear me. Drink so you can live." She stroked the canine's throat to help him swallow. At first it filled his mouth and ran out. But with Lilly's urging, Lancelot began to lick Lily's wrist, drinking the blood. Then he bit her, striking fast and pulling the blood into his mouth. As he did, Lilly could feel the bones moving back to their place and healing. Once they were finished, Lilly pulled her arm away and licked to seal the wound. Lance sat up and looked around, then moved to put his front paws on her shoulders and licked her face. His Sheltie smile revealed longer, sharper fangs.

"It worked!" Isobel exclaimed as she grabbed Baron up and hugged him.

"*Okay, it worked. I know you are thankful, but really, squeezing me is not necessary and it might actually hurt.*"

Lilly and Isobel laughed, "Hurt? Might?" Lilly asked between giggles.

"*Yes, this is totally undignified and one of my feline females may see and that would hurt my chances with them.*"

As Isobel loosened her hold, she felt the cat tense before leaping free.

"Okay, we've averted one disaster, we might as well go back and tell Marcus what happened." Lilly led the way, Baron at her heels. Lancelot walked, almost prancing, next to Isobel.

MARCUS WAS IN his office just off the living room, dealing with some of the business minutia that Castro wasn't able to handle while his boss was off dealing with the Vampire Council. Time with the turnings had taken a toll on his business and he had left the running of the vampire volunteer drive in Jean's capable hands and come back to the peace and quiet of his private office.

He laid the fountain pen down, staring across the room at the monitors, signing contracts, reading through proposals, and making upper management personnel decisions was the worst parts of the job in his opinion.

Something caught his eye and he turned up the sound on the KBQ news channel. A buxom blond wearing a deep-cut red blouse, the color of blood, was talking, "...the existence of private prisons in Thailand, Europe, and Afghanistan run by the CIA and a private security company, Pricor Security, owned by American entrepreneur Nelson Mishkoph. Our own investigative reporter, Scooter Dickson, has uncovered the prisons and the fact that Al Qaeda fighters have been transported and interrogated in the prisons. Scooter will be hosting an hour-long program on the CIA, Pricor, and the so-called 'black sites' that are not under the scrutiny of Congress or any other agency tonight at 9 pm. Tune in..."

Marcus stabbed the mute button. "Stupid fool" he mumbled as he picked up the pen. Just as he started to refocus on the proposal for a new security operation in Bogota Columbia, he heard the elevator chime and the doors open. Just what he needed, visitors when he was trying to work.

Lancelot was barking as he streaked toward the office, he turned the corner at the door and leapt several feet into Marcus's lap and started licking his master's face. "Hello boy, what's gotten into you?" The Sheltie began to cover his face with enthusiastic doggie kisses that he had to close his eyes to keep that wet tongue out.

"Marcus?" Isobel called as she followed the dog toward the office.

"In here, Izzy." His eyes still closed, he put the pen down, nothing was going to get done with the chaos. He opened his eyes and looked to the door.

Isobel and Lilly walked into the office and Marcus noticed that the damned cat followed Lilly. He really hated that cat but he couldn't get rid of it without upsetting Lilly, which would not be wise, especially in her condition.

It was at that point he turned his gaze back to the dog enthusiastically licking his face and noticed the fangs. Not dog-length canine teeth but longer, vampire-looking teeth. He pushed the dog out to the edge of his lap so he could get a better look at him and noticed the dirt, dark marks on the dog's hind quarters, and the blood on the white ruff.

"What the hell is going on?" He growled, stopping Lance from further wet kisses by putting him down to get a better overall look at him. "Sit!" he commanded and Lance immediately obeyed.

"Marcus, we need to talk to you about that." Isobel said, motioning for Lilly to sit down.

"I can see that you do."

"It's about Lance. We..." she hesitated, not sure, in the face of his growing anger, if she wanted to do this in person. Maybe the phone would have been better.

"What happened? He's a mess and he's changed, what the hell happened?"

As she wound up to talk, Lilly let her words rush ahead, as if saying it fast would make it easier. "Lance snuck out behind Baron. He got into the road. Got hit by a car. Baron let us know and we went to try to help."

"Baron let you know," he drawled, his anger beginning to boil. "How?"

Lilly wasn't going to let Marcus know that Baron could talk to her, "He came back up and then went out again. His yowls let us know that something was very wrong. We got to the front of the building and Lance was laying in the road, not moving." She looked to Baron and then to Isobel, "He was dead, Marcus. We were trying to help and we managed to get Baron to turn him to bring him back."

"Baron turned my dog, my champion show dog, into a vampire? Do you have any idea what that does to his value."

"Leave it to the bastard to think of money first." Baron said. Lilly shot him a look to quiet him, "Yes, we do. But his value would be a lot less if he wasn't alive. We wanted to bring him back to you and that was the only way he was going to be alive to be with you."

Marcus looked at the dog. The dirt was road dirt. The dark marks were tire tracks. The blood on his ruff must have been the cat's. "Did you at least get a license plate? Did the driver stop to help?"

"No, we saw no one. We took him to the side of the building and worked in the delivery bay to get him back for you." Isobel took over for Lilly.

Marcus punched some buttons on the keypad next to him and the closed circuit camera feed from the last hour started rolling. There was Lilly and Isobel, holding a very limp Lance, then walking to the delivery bay. The camera from the bay took over and he watched as Baron bit the unconscious dog and then, a few moments later, bite his own leg and put it to the dog's mouth. Lilly stepped up and then bit her own arm, taking over feeding Lance. The dog kicked and then stretched, standing up carefully." He turned off the monitor. "You honestly changed my dog into a vampire."

"Marcus, it was either that or we would be burying him. He was dead. What Baron and Lilly did was save him, bring him back to you."

"As a fucking vampire! I cannot ever show him again, you realize that, right? You have changed his attributes and the judges would find the fangs and questions would be asked."

"Yes, we changed him. If we didn't do it, you wouldn't have a dog at all, much less to show. Lance has worth much greater than just a show dog, remember, you love him and at least you have him here with you." Marcus's attitude had upset Isobel, she had not counted on him being angry over showing the dog.

"*Where are the baby farm animals? I don't see any?*" Baron quipped in what Lilly hoped was a bid to lighten the tension in the room.

"*Hush, Baron*" Lilly answered, "*I don't know that he's going to accept Lance back. Can you handle having him as part of our family if he rejects him?*"

Baron stared at her with his eyes glowing the annoyed gold she recognized. "*I guess so. He's my, what's the word...*"

"*Progeny.*"

"*Progeny and I have to take care of him. Thanks a lot, Lilly. I'm now a father. I have been before, I know I have a few kittens out there, probably, before you turned me into a vampire, but this one isn't a cat."*

Marcus pet the dog, thinking about all the changes in his life since Lilly came back. His life was upended more than he ever thought. His lover hated him and was now a vampire. His dog was a vampire. He had three new mouths to feed with Lilly, Baron, and now Gregory, not that it was a problem, just something new. And, he was going to be a father, something he never wanted, much less thought about seriously. Everything had changed and it was all due to one weak moment in the summer of 1900. He rubbed the bridge of his nose.

"I guess it's going to have to be okay, I won't kill him and I do love him. Thank-you for saving him, even if he is in this condition."

As if the dog understood what he had just said, Lance barked, jumped back into his master's lap, rubbed his nose on Marcus's cheek, and then made a big, wet lick up his face.

Chapter Twenty-Seven

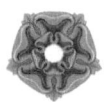

MARCUS STRODE INTO the 10th floor training center, looking for a report from Jean and Jessie about the status of Operation Butterfly. He had opted to come down to the center rather than go back to his office and call them up to the penthouse.

He had just come from the medical clinic and yet another doctor's visit with Lilly for the baby. Jack Young said everything was progressing, she was getting bigger a bit earlier than predicted but still within expected statistics.

Lilly, on the other hand, was having much more emotional changes than either Marcus or Jack expected. One moment she was happy, the next she was crying. Or worse, she went from Happy Zero to Sixty Pissed Off and Yelling. Isobel seemed to be able to handle her and Gregory was very welcome to her and her hormonal tirades. The last time Marcus had asked her to calm down, she threw a lamp at him, shrieking about how he really screwed up her life.

No, he was much safer with the ever-growing Lancaster Vampire Army, at least they were sane and normal.

He wasn't paying attention and walked straight into Jean. Looking up, he touched his friend's shoulder. "Sorry Jean, I didn't see you."

"No problem, mon frere. You look like a man who needs a good stiff drink. I have some 25 year old Chivas in my office, we can speak there while we drink."

"Thanks Jean, I will be happy to drink your scotch. It will make up for all my rum you drank in Campeche."

"Whose rum? I think you forget that I was the pirate, you were the sailor." He laughed heartily, a sound that resonated within Marcus's body. He smiled but didn't laugh.

When was the last time he laughed?

After they reached the office, Jean let his secretary know they were not to be disturbed, unless it was an emergency. Vicki Rose was a pretty little blond, that Jean had taken as his ghoul and then made her his secretary.

Once they shut the door, Jean brought out the scotch and poured a generous amount in two glasses.

"More Lilly drama?" he asked.

Marcus rubbed his temples before picking up the glass. "When isn't it Lilly drama? I swear she wasn't like this a hundred year ago. She was so sweet and submissive. Now..."

Jean nodded his head in agreement and chuckled, "Now she's your progeny and, somehow, pregnant. Certainement, I wouldn't want to be you right now."

Marcus slammed the scotch and grabbed the bottle, pulling it over and pouring him a double, slamming it down as well.

"Oh, mon ami, slow down on the alcohol." Jean said, making a grab for the bottle. Marcus pulled it away and poured yet another while shaking his head, "I tell you, Jean, I'm about ready to turn this whole mess over to you and..."

"No sir. I wouldn't take it."

"I would become inactive and move somewhere nice and quiet. Play tennis, read, and just ignore the rest of the world. Vlad does have it right, it's not worth it to keep up appearances." He drained the glass.

"Marcus, you wouldn't survive the first month of a life like that. You would be looking for the next challenge, the next pay-off. You've been that way since our days at Campeche. You tried to quit the sea, tried to make it as plantation owner, you didn't even last one season before you sold everything and burned the house to the ground. There's no way you could walk away now."

"I know. It's just that whole 'Baby' situation is getting to me. I seem to be busy trying to keep her calm and happy and it's bearing down on my real life.

"She still asking you to reject Jesse and marry her in the Catholic Church?"

"Oh yeah. She wants us to both go see this Father Keller and get counseling so I will change my mind on marriage and being homosexual." Marcus shook his head.

"Joys. Of course, you have explained that

vampires don't go to church, it's part of being a vampire. And you're not homosexual or she wouldn't be pregnant."

"I know. Tell that to her, she is convinced I'm going to give in."

"Ma frere, I wouldn't want to be in your shoes for anything. Why not let her go off with her progeny, that vampire whatever his name is?"

Marcus threw the glass, shattering it against the wall. He picked up the bottle and took a large swig.

"You do realize you can't really get drunk, you remember this, right?" Jean was concerned. Marcus only acted like this when he was stressed.

"I'll have someone clean that up," Marcus said, taking another drink. "If we knew where that angel was, I would have already had him killed because of what he did to her. Even as pissy and bitchy she is, I don't want her to be placed in the position of getting hurt again."

Jean raised an eyebrow. He knew Marcus liked rough sex, he got off on the control, the begging. He had stepped in when it got out of hand when they lived in Campeche, now known as Galveston, to stop Marcus from killing a couple of women. "So, no angel. Maybe throwing yourself into work will help."

Marcus waved the bottle at him, "Probably. Where are we in the process as of today?"

"We've made a total of five angels into vampires. Or tried, three of them died before we could get enough blood into them. We've lost five of our own vampires catching those five to begin with.

One-to-one loss rates are not going to get us an army to fight the angels."

Marcus took another pull on the bottle. "So we have had two successes?"

"Oui, but neither of them have spoken since being turned. Both seem not to care what happens to them. They are still in restraints because two of those who died killed each other simultaneously to escape. The other was in a cell and once no one was near, we were watching the close circuit television as he bit his own wrists multiple times and he bled out before we could get in to stop him."

Marcus shook his head, "So we have been off schedule from the time we started. Great. Have we had any help at all from the demons?"

"Oh oui. They are acting as bait and they jump the angels for us. They take the wings and dispose of them and they take the rings. We get what's left to work with." Jean didn't add that he hated sending his vampires out to work with the demons, their enthusiastic fighting was why the five vampires had died, they simply didn't bother to avoid killing whomever was standing there.

Marcus finished off the bottle and it joined the shattered glass at the base of the wall, bashing a hole in the wall as it blew into a million pieces.

"Feel better?" Jean shook his head at Marcus's temper tantrum.

"No, but I need to figure out how to step this up. Where are we on turning employees?" Marcus stood, stretched, and began to pace.

We're three quarters of the way through those

who have signed on. Eadwina has turned Mitch and he is coordinating the New Orleans unit, they are turning Lancaster employees in Louisiana and Mississippi. We have a London office, an Asia operation, and Ian Campbell O'Malley is flying down to Australia next week to head up their start-up. We have an estimated 12,000 vampires planned in phase one, and then another 12,000 in phase 2. Our target plan is to capture and turn 5,000 angels by February."

Marcus nodded, that's about 1700 a month. I'm not sure that we can make that on our present time table. Let's reevaluate once we get past New Year. That's another three weeks to analyze and get a handle on timing. By then, we should be at your 1700 or we will need to adjust things.

Jean got up, going to the bar, pulled out another bottle of Chivas and waved it at Marcus. "I'm getting another one. Please try not to swallow this so fast or I'll have to move you down to the cheap stuff. Sit down or you're not getting any of it, your pacing is driving me to madness."

As Marcus laughed, sitting down and taking a new glass with the scotch, the door opened and Jorge Castro stepped through, pulling the strong metal door closed behind him.

"Gunny, just the man I was going to come see next." Marcus waved his operations chief over.

"I need to go to my office, I got a call from Benjamin Senai that we have a problem."

"Oh?" Marcus would let Jorge take care of it but he liked to be in the loop, especially when there were problems. It seemed like he had been spending less and less time doing business and more time trying to take over the vampire community. At least he could depend on Gunny to handle stuff.

"Yeah, we have a hacker in the S.O.C. We've been watching the files and could tell they were being copied but it took us awhile to find out who and where. This guy's a pro, he was going outside the company and then coming into the intranet to give the appearance it was coming from Russia."

"But it's someone here, in the building? One of my employees?"

"Unfortunately yes." Marcus noticed that his right hand man's fangs dropped down. "I don't know who, yet. I'm going now to find out just who needs to have a talk and then decide how to handle it. I will keep you informed." Castro worked to get his fangs to retract and then jammed his ever-present cigar into his mouth and walked out, the only real hint of just how pissed the Gunny really was.

Jean stared after the former Marine and quietly remarked, "I wouldn't want to be that guy once he gets pulled aside."

"He won't live long enough to regret his actions."

Jean sought to lighten the mood, the black cloud over Marcus was back at the new situation, "You know who would get a kick out of hunting angels?"

Marcus laughed. "You're thinking about Gregori Rasputin?"

"Yeah, Rasputin would love to have a part in this fight. He always wanted to stop the angels.

Jean looked out the window, "I wonder where that crazy bastard ended up?"

"Well, Xun would be the one to ask. Rasputin was a member of Furstenhaus Drachenmeer. Evidently Xun got the Council's elite guard to go get him. He totally disappeared after the attack on him in Russia. There are rumors of him being in the dungeon of the castle, or buried alive somewhere on the castle's grounds. Maybe once this fight with the angels ends and they are no longer protecting their lackeys on the Council, I can spend a few years persuading Xun to tell me what he did with Gregori, along with some of the other secrets he holds." Marcus had been a friend of Rasputin's, hosting a few parties when the renowned monk was popular with the Czarina.

"Can I watch that one?" Jean smiled a smile that used to frighten even the most hardened pirates in his crew.

"Of course, mon ami. I wouldn't deprive you of a little fun." Marcus stood and stretched again. "Let's go see what you've been doing up here." The men walked through the door, heading to the training and holding rooms.

Chapter Twenty-Eight

A FEW HOURS later, Marcus was at the computer on his desk in his penthouse office, trying to work out schedules for the next social season while at the same time dealing with the Operation Butterfly and also trying to deal with the Mishkoph issues. Usually Isobel did this scheduling of the social things but she was dealing with Lilly and all the baby stuff. The girls had been shopping again, picking up things to build a nursery. Isobel was lobbying Marcus for room for Lilly and the baby in his penthouse but Lilly hadn't acted like he was supposed to be thinking about moving her. She was continuing to insist he come for the seemingly daily doctors checkups and also go to mass with him on Sundays. The doctor wasn't hard, it was just downstairs and didn't take long but he had yet to acquiesce to the trips to church.

His current problem was how to fit in a fundraiser for the children's hospital around the different events leading up to the Houston Rodeo, trying to find a time to make two different social events on one night, and then the events for Galveston's Mardi Gras, including crowning, masquerade balls, and the parade. The Krewe of Sanguineaux, made up of the area's more well-heeled vampires, was going to have several events, as usual. Marcus was on one of the committees for the krewe and he hadn't made a meeting since the hurricane.

How the hell did Isobel do this? Why the hell wasn't she doing it now?

Marcus picked up the phone and dialed Isobel's number.

"Hi, you've reached Isobel Kincade, I'm not available to take your call, please leave a detailed message and I will get back with you soonest."

Beep.

Damn it. "That wasn't helpful," he mumbled to himself.

There was a knock at the door. "Come in." Marcus growled, harder than he should have.

The door opened and Castro walked in, leaving the door ajar. "Son, we've got a problem." He went to the table where Marcus kept the scotch, poured a partial glass, and went to sit in the chair on the other side of the desk.

"Now what?" Marcus stood and went to pour his own glass.

"Well, we've got a small army turned but it doesn't make the kind of numbers we are going to need. We've managed to keep them alive until we can feed them enough to get them to cooperate, with a little cooperation from Gery's troops. But I just don't see this operation being successful in the long-term. Should we cut our losses and be done with it? Oh, and we are going to need a new blood doll for Houston, seems Ms. Skinner is not handling the work too well and is spending more and more time in bed recovering."

"Well, find one for us. And if she keeps lingering, go ahead and kill her. We are not going to quit working on this." Marcus tried not to bite the head off of his COO but it was hard. "We have to make this work, to get them off of the vampire community. We keep going."

Jorge Castro shook his head, "Okay but right now I'm seeing this as a potential liability and huge problem eventually. Isn't there another way to go about this? Maybe get our hands on this, what was her name, the one who puts burns on your hands like that one," he pointed to Marcus's right hand, "and hold her until they agree to stop?"

"Not that I wouldn't love to get my hands on that bitch, whose name is Nida by the way, but I can't see us being able to do that, especially with the big guards she brings with her. That blond with the flaming sword in particular. But I'll give it some thought and try to figure out if it might work." Marcus sorted through papers on his desk, "Do I have a report from the German efforts yet?"

"We have tried to get some idea as to how large the effort is going to be there but right now there's no real information coming out. We have better numbers, however, from Buenos Aries, we were getting no information until last night. We now have a count, they've had 40 attempts, 15 captures, and after doing the procedure, we have eight new people.

"What happened to the others?"

Castro smiled, "They died, there was no consistent reason for it, some suicides, a few bled out, and the others tried to escape. But only seven deaths in a week, not bad."

"Seven died? Who is dying, Marcus, and why are you concerned about it?" Lilly stood in the door with Isobel behind her.

Marcus stood and walked toward her, "Hello Lilly, dear. Unfortunate things that you shouldn't worry about. Did you and Izzy have a good time shopping?"

"We got a few things. Who is dying?" Lilly wasn't giving it up with a bit of patronization.

"It's our group in Brazil, they've had an attack on an installation, we're guarding oil platforms, and we had seven deaths in the attack. I'm arraigning for the bodies to be flown back and for notification of next of kin. We're also setting up survivor's funds for each family involved and paying for the funerals. I have also sent reinforcements to track down and capture the attackers, we will make sure to find out who ordered this attack, no matter how we have to do it."

Jorge Castro raised an eyebrow, it never ceased to amaze him just how easily Marcus seemed to be able to lie to others. "I'll go check on the arrangements, I will let you know when we have them set." He slipped out around the ladies, beating a hasty retreat to the elevators.

"Are you discussing torture? Now you're killing people?" Lilly ignored Castro's exit.

"I'm not talking this with you, it's my business and you will stay out of it. I will handle it the way I see fit."

"Marcus! You don't have to be so gruff." Isobel scolded him. "Apologize to Lilly."

"I'm not apologizing, she's interfering in things she has no business in."

Lilly tried ignore his boorishness and bring down the level of tension. "Well, we're here to get you to come down to the apartment to see what we picked up for the baby and then go to the doctor's appointment." Lilly caught sight of Baron coming out of the elevator and heading toward her.

"I'm so busy right now, Lilly. I will have to beg off this one and let you handle it. I do need Isobel to go to her office and check the arrangements for the social calendar for the next couple of months. I've been trying to set them up and I'm woefully inadequate for that job."

"I'll get right on it. Lilly, let me know if you need help with organizing things in the nursery. I'll be back to the apartment in a couple of hours to help you." Isobel left for the elevators as well. She turned around a couple of steps out of the door, "Oh, and Marcus, try to calm down and be nice to Lilly."

Marcus scowled, "Yes Mommy." Changing his gaze to Lilly, he said, "Please let me know what the doctor says and we can go next time to see him. I'll try to get free to have dinner with you later," Marcus walked around to the chair behind the desk and started shuffling papers, an obvious sign of Lilly's dismissal.

"Marcus, we still need to get some things planned out and I need your attention." Lilly walked further into the room and sat down in the chair Castro had vacated. Baron followed her, sitting beside her on the floor and started bathing himself.

"I'm busy, Lilly. We will have to do this later. I have a lot to do right now." As he was speaking, Lancelot stepped out from under his feet, stretched, and walked toward the door.

"Marcus, you've been busy for the last couple of weeks. I need to have your attention on this baby stuff, I need you to want to be involved with this process since this baby is yours." Baron was ignoring the people, his gaze fixed on Lance.

"Look," Marcus slapped the desk with both hands and shot up out of the chair, "I am busy! I don't have time for this shit, I need to work on my business and your constant nagging and moaning isn't making it any easier."

Lilly's eyes filled with blood tears, much to her consternation. "I see, I will just take myself out of here since I'm interfering with your business. Don't bother coming to the doctor from now on, I will handle it."

Marcus blew up. "I'm tired of your passive-aggressive shit, your unrelenting demands on me, and your whining. I am a very busy man, I have a very heavy schedule with your demands, the council's demands, and this crap with the angels. I can't spread myself any thin...."

The sound of dog barking and cat snarling

stopped his rant. As both humans turned, they saw Lance jump on top of Baron and try to bite his neck. And the fight was on.

Baron rolled, throwing the dog off of him, then jumping him with claws and fangs extended, tearing the skin of the Sheltie, fur flying in every direction as the dog spun to try to throw the attacking cat off. The noise grew to a loud cacophony of snarling, biting, hissing, and growling as the animals ended up rolling across the floor.

"Baron!" Lilly cried as Marcus shouted his dog's name. Both walked over to try to pull the animals apart but Marcus stepped in front of Lilly.

Lilly reached for Lance who mistook her grab for the cat and sunk his fangs and teeth into her hand. With a yelp, she pulled back, dragging the teeth through the skin. Baron slapped the dog across the nose and he let go.

"Damned cat," he roared. He pushed Lilly roughly aside and reached down to grab Baron and pull him off the dog.

Baron was done with the antics of both the dog and his owner, he twisted in Marcus's hand and raked his claws down the side of the vampire's face, digging deep trenches into the skin.

"Fuck!" Marcus threw the cat behind him as he grabbed his face, the cat flying into the wall.

"Marcus! NO!" Lilly stepped toward him.

He grabbed her arm roughly. "Bitch, I'm going to kill that cat," he managed to get out about the time that Baron made the huge leap and landed on Marcus's back, digging in with all claws and biting the back of Marcus's neck.

The vampire roared in pain, reaching back toward the cat, who managed to move away from the hand as he continued to hold the back of Marcus's neck. Finally, he seized the cat, pulling him out of his skin roughly, the blood flowing from all the injuries and ruining the Desmond Merrion suit he wore. He put both hands around the cat's neck, squeezing as he continued to growl like a dog.

Lilly grabbed his hands, trying to pry them off of the cat, "Marcus, stop! Please! Stop! Lance started it, not Baron!"

"I don't care! I will not put up with this." All of his controlled fury and frustration flowed into his hands. "He will not allow this demon to hurt my dog, or me. He's done it for the last fucking time." He managed to snarl as he squeezed harder, the cat's eyes widening as he swung his legs in the air trying to grab something to make the man stop and let him breathe. Marcus shrugged Lilly off and began to twist the cat's head around with one hand.

A sharp pop and Baron went limp. Lilly screamed in horror. Marcus laughed maniacally and threw the body back against the wall. Baron slid down and then was still.

"You bastard!" Lilly whirled on Marcus, beating him with every ounce of energy she had, aiming for the scratches on his face.

His head twisted with the force and he laughed at her. "Now I can get back to work, without that damned demon cat, and without you. Get out."

She walked to Baron's body, lifting it carefully, holding his head. Her blood tears flowed, tears of rage and abject sorrow. At that moment she no longer saw Marcus for what she wanted him to be but for who and what he truly was ... A deranged monster!

Tears still flowing, she cradled Baron's limp body in her arms and left the penthouse in hostile silence.

She reached her apartment, sobbing. She retreated into her room and carefully, gently laid Baron's dead body on the bed.

"Oh, Baron. I am so sorry! I should have never trusted that bastard. I've kept trying to make him see that we should love each other, if nothing else for the sake of the baby. But I was wrong and now you're dead and I'm alone, so very alone."

As she pet the cat, she wished him alive again.

"*Lilly*?" She heard in her head.

Sullivan.

"I thought I told you to go away and never contact me again." She spit back at him, taking her anger and sadness out on him.

"*I'm sorry, I felt your anger, and sorrow. What's wrong?*"

She contemplated not telling him, just shutting him out without comment.

"*I just need to know...*" Sullivan sounded sad and angry at the same time.

"Marcus killed Baron, Sullivan. I am so very," she struggled for words without feelings, failing as miserably as she felt. "I'm so tired of everything and everyone. I wish I had never left the crypt. Go away, Sullivan. I need to try to figure out where to bury my best friend and then where I can get enough money to go back to New Orleans. Please go and leave me, Sullivan. I don't want to hear from you, ever again. Don't be like Marcus and continue to bother me."

She mumbled to Baron, like he could hear her, "I'm so sorry, we should have gone home when you wanted to, you were right all along."

"*I will always be here for you, all you have to do is reach out and...*"

"Goodbye Sullivan." She mentally slammed the door on the link, descending into silence.

She cried for a while, then began to try to make plans. She didn't want to bury Baron on the building's grounds, she didn't want him to be that close to his killer. She wanted to take him back to New Orleans and bury him where she could visit him daily. But she wasn't sure if she could get there before his body began to rot.

The whole thing started her crying again.

She stopped, gasping to try to stop the hiccups that had resulted. Something had caught her attention but it wasn't there. She hung her head down and began to fight the tears again.

Then she heard it and stopped, focusing on trying to hear it.

Finally, she caught it, faint but there, she hoped she did, anyway.

"*I'm not dead yet.*"

Baron.

Chapter Twenty-Nine

ONE OF THE apertures in the ceiling opened and three Shadow angels floated down to the operations area where Uriel stood checking over the daily rosters and reports. They stood silently, wings folded, until their boss looked up.

"Report?" Uriel asked.

One of them addressed him. "Sir, we've been following Kozeil. He has been leaving here and meeting with a demon, Rosalin."

"Do you know why?"

The angel in front, Athriel, shook his head. "Not entirely. He was very circumspect and there was a demonic force around them that didn't allow us to hear much of what was said. But the name 'Lilly' came up. While we couldn't hear much more, the mention of that name made the demon smile."

Uriel considered the information.

"That's not all, sir." Another angel, Dalquiel as he recalled, spoke up, "There is also movement with the demons in connection with both the Vampire Council and a vampire, Marcus Lancaster. The demons have visited Lancaster both after a visit to the castle in Switzerland and also in Houston, in the vampire's business building. The demon in both cases is one named Gery. He said," the angel stopped, then spoke again, this time in the voice of Gery, *"I'm Gery, personal procurement of Tartero, which you know as Hell. I work for the Queen of Hell, Lucy. Humans always believe the word Lucifer is a male name. Anyway, as I was saying, you're planning a little rebellion and Lucy offers you assistance.'"* His voice went back to normal, "He and Lancaster cut the wings off of Nelchiel, the demon has her ring. The demon took her to the vampire's business building in Houston."

The third angel spoke up. "The demon entered that building with Nelchiel. We did get in and saw them chain her to the floor in a room. There were two other angels on premises. One is Rebangiel, a Guardian who has managed to get herself hired on Lancaster's staff as a nurse named Reba King. She is connected to a ghoul named Gregory Freeman, we checked the connection ourselves."

The angel, named Jerigiel, meant that he had checked the silvery blue energy connection that is formed between Guardians and their charges.

Jerigiel continued, "There is also an Enforcer there, without his wings, going under the name of Robert Essex."

Athriel nodded, "There's also a very strange signature, sometimes reading as vampire, but other times shifting to angel, then back to vampire again quickly. We could not get a very good read on it.

Uriel didn't comment, he sent a ping to Ranguel that they needed to speak.

"Is that everything?"

Jerigiel ruffled his wings, "There will be a demonic shield over the Houston building. I'm sure that the demon who showed up with Nelchiel told Lancaster that he would place it once the vampire found the two angels in the building, he couldn't do that before they were found."

"I see. Thank you for the report. Continue to follow Lancaster and Essex, as well as Koziel and the demon. We need to know what they are doing." Uriel turned his back and started floating toward the Enforcer's stations and the Shadows left the area.

He reached the Enforcer's station and Ranguel didn't say a word, he just motioned to Uriel and headed toward Mikhail's Office.

The door opened and closed behind them. Mikhail was sitting behind his desk, going through a book, writing in the margins. "Yes?"

"Mikhail, we've had a report from the Shadows." Ranguel began.

"I know, we have demons, there's another angel who is missing, presumed turned to a vampire by Marcus Lancaster, and Essex is in the building, along with Rebangiel. I need to know how they are all doing, not just where they are. We need to have the same information that Lucy is getting from her demons if we're going to stop her."

"Sir, we also have a very odd signature there, we're not sure what it is." Ranguel said.

Mikhail looked at his archangels, "I'm aware and investigating, let me handle that one. I also know we're beginning to miss several angels out of all departments. Several of them are dead. We're now at war, gentlemen, and we're behind the curve as Lucy works to build her army to bring it here to take over. I need intelligence gathered from all sectors, much more than we have now.

"What I need is a total report, daily, on who is missing, who is dead, we need to keep working to get that information. I want Koz pulled out of the rotation and imprisoned. One of the high security cells that we used for Lucy's rebels."

He pushed the book aside and stood up. "I need a meeting with all the Archangels and department seconds this afternoon. Put your best replacements in charge while it happens, we will be quite busy for a while and I don't want any problems in the ranks. Come prepared with lists and plans on how to deal with the effects of the demon's kidnappings and deaths. After the meeting, I will have some errands to do and I will be leaving here for a bit. Gabriel will be briefed and in charge while I am away. See you in the main conference room."

The door behind the archangels opened. They turned, without comment and exited.

"Okay, ours is the next move, Lucy. I hope you are ready." Mikhail left his office, shutting the door behind him.

Chapter Thirty

ESSEX PULLED THE last of the flash drives, put it in an envelope, and quickly hid it inside his backpack. The information on it was the minor stuff he found, he had already mailed three of the drives, with the information he deemed most important, to a post office drop box in Lebanon, Kansas. The angels had established it as the main post office to allow for the movement of more human information without raising suspicion. It was managed in the name of a woman who resided in nearby Blaine, Kansas. An angel would come and collect the mail and take it back to H.H.A.D. He hoped that it would be enough for whatever purpose Mikhail needed.

He had scrutinized the previous flash drives before he mailed them. The files painted an entirely different picture of the Marcus Lancaster that most people knew. He had details of illegal arms sales, mercenary operations that had killed women and children, the torturing of various people he had targeted, and even the seizure and killing of vampires he had a grudge against. While the killings of the vampires wasn't against the rules the angels set down, many others were not only illegal, but sinful things. It was a wonder he hadn't been killed by someone before this newest project.

Essex could only hope that the angels would take action once this was all examined. Someone up there had to know about this before the files confirmed it, but it wasn't taken care of yet.

Lilly was in the hands of this monster.

Essex started to close out all the folders he had opened in the course of this last transfer when four of the building security came in. Behind them one of his co-workers, Ben Senai and the big boss, Jorge Castro. They looked around the SOC and then walked straight toward him.

His heart began to beat harder, they had figured out who had been in the files, that was the only answer.

"Mr. Essex?" One of the officers asked. He was Jacob Cronin, the head of the security desk in the lobby.

"Yes, that's me." Cronin knew who he was, by name and by sight. Essex guessed this was protocol.

"You need to come with us. Bring your pack and do not touch the computer."

Essex played out the part. "Why? What's this about?"

The Gunny spoke up, "You will find out soon enough, get your ass out of that chair and come with us. I'm not going to ask again."

Okay, that was how it was going to play out.

Essex slowly stood and picked up his pack. Ben reached out and grabbed the pack away from him and Cronin took his arm to guide him out of the room.

"I can walk, let me go." Essex jerked his arm out of the security guard's hand.

"Don't even think of getting frisky on us, just come along so we can get this over with." Gunny said, causing his prisoner to turn to look at him. "Get going."

The group walked to the elevator and took it to the 18th floor. He walked through the security department, a maze of rooms and computers with duty boards on the walls, the hum of many monitors and computers hitting his ears. One whole wall was full of closed circuit televisions and at least five of them had his face. Each showed a different view, they had been watching him and had him on tape. One had the flash drive in his hand.

He was busted. Red handed.

They took him back to a room with a solid door. Cronin put his ID card into the slot on the lock and punched a code, then put his thumb on the lighted pad. This had to be a special room for this floor, the other employee floors just needed the ID to open the doors.

Not really reassuring for an easy and quick getaway. No one would know he was here outside of the company people.

When he looked around, there was nothing in the room. "What is this place?" he asked. Four white walls, all made of concrete, was the entire interior decoration.

"A high security isolation cell," responded Cronin stoically.

"Yea, you can yell all you want to, no one can hear ya'" snarled Castro.

Jonah Cronin's dark expression expressed his anger and disappointment. He thought he was pretty astute but obviously not because he had been so easily deceived by this affable computer nerd....An industrial spy working for Nelson Mishkoph no doubt.

Essex listened to Cronin's internal ramblings, trying to evaluate his present situation. He felt sorry that his deceit had so disillusioned the man because Essex really did like him. Jonah always had a welcoming smile and friendly wave for him.

He sat down on the floor and reclined against the wall. They had even taken his pack with them. Nothing else to do until someone came down to question him.

LILLY WAS FEEDING Baron in the living room when the doorbell rang. She licked her wrist and walked to answer it, wondering who it could be.

"Maybe if it is Marcus, I can get at least a bit of satisfaction out of slamming it." She thought as she opened the door.

No Marcus, but who was behind the door was just as bad.

"Jesse, I don't want to talk, go away." She

tried to close the door but he put his hand out and stopped it, then muscled his way inside.

"I heard about the damned cat." He smiled, gloating. "Awwww, too bad!" his contempt was accentuated by a little giggle.

"What do you want?" She wasn't about to let him go into the parlor with Baron still recuperating.

"Nothing. I just came to tell you that you won't be seeing your boyfriend again. Marcus has taken Robert Essex and is going to kill him for stealing information from the company. I just wonder if he shouldn't kill you too, seeing that you were probably involved in the thefts as well."

"I don't know what you are talking about. Mr. Essex is just my friend. I need to go talk to him." Lilly knew there would be trouble if Marcus killed the angel.

"No, you're not going to talk to him. I just wanted to tell you that he's gone, so you won't worry that pretty little head of yours." Jesse turned around to leave. He grasped the handle of the door, paused, and turned back, a malicious grin on his face.

"On second thought, you should go talk to him, let him know you love him before he dies. Maybe Marcus will be merciful."

Lilly looked back toward the parlor, wishing Isobel was there. She wanted to go try to rescue Essex but she needed Isobel to tell her if it was an exercise in futility. But she was still in her office somewhere in the building. Lilly had to make a choice now.

"Okay, I will go with you, take me to Mr. Essex so I can get any messages to his family."

"*Don't go with him.*" Baron sounded stronger but she knew he was still healing. "*Don't trust him! He is not going to let you go once you're where he's taking you.*"

"*I need to try, Baron. I promise, as soon as I know where I'm going, I'll tell you and you can tell Gregory and Isobel. I have to try to help Essex.*" She whispered back to him.

"Lilly, let's go." Jesse took her arm to pull her along.

"Do NOT touch me!" Lilly jerked away from Jesse's grip and walked out the door, Jesse following.

They entered the elevator and Jesse pushed 18. He didn't speak to her as they dropped the few floors. When the doors opened, he pointed the way and walked with her toward the room that Marcus had designated for Essex's cell. "He's in here, allow me." He went through the security lock procedure and then pushed the door open and Lilly walked in.

The door slammed behind her and she heard the locks trip.

"Lilly!" Essex stood up, "What are you doing here? You need to go, I'm in trouble and Lancaster is coming."

"Why are you here? Jesse said that you have stolen something, and Marcus is going to kill you for it. What do they think that you did? You couldn't have …"

"Yes, I did take something. Information. They

believe me to be an industrial spy for one of the Lancaster's rivals...a Nelson Mishkoph. You need to get out of here. I don't want you in the outcome."

"I'm not leaving. Marcus is going to have to see reason. I need to try to make him at least see that taking some notes isn't grounds for a death sentence."

"This man is evil, Lilly, more evil than any of us suspected. That information I took..."

"Give the information back to him. Apologize. He will have to see reason and let you go. Probably fire you but that should be it."

Essex smiled, despite his apprehensions. Lilly was so trusting. "No, there's more to it than that. Most is gone, the tiny bit I have on me is stuff I did today. I can apologize forever and Marcus Lancaster won't let me live through this, his ego will not allow me to survive. I'm a dead man."

"Tell them that you're..."

Essex cut her off. "I can't. I took on this mission knowing that this was a possibility. Don't let Lancaster know I'm an angel, especially not an Enforcer. He has a special kind of hatred for us."

"Essex, I can't let him kill you. I'll tell him that you're the baby's father. That we slept together and the baby isn't his. Let him think me a whore and that I was out only for his money when I said it was him. I don't care."

"Wait, what? Baby? You're a vampire, you can't... Don't complicate this with a lie." He looked at her. There was a bulge under her clothing that he hadn't noticed.

"Everyone says that but I am. I've had a doctor checking on me almost every day and he said he can even hear the heartbeat of the baby with a stethoscope. I've heard it too. No one seems to know how it could happen but it did. I'm with child."

Essex began to panic. He knew he could keep Lancaster from harming her if he needed to but if she told him that he wasn't the father, he might kill her. Hell, he might do it anyway, just to get rid of both of them, it was totally within his character. "Lilly, you have to promise me that once that bastard comes through that door, you'll yell at me and tell me you never want to see me again. I've hurt you, I've laughed at you, and I've told you that you are going to Hell because you're a vampire. You must convince him that you hate me, it's the only way you might be safe. You cannot tell him I'm the father of the baby, he will kill you."

"No he won't. I don't think... Yes, he killed Baron but that was because..."

"Wait, he killed your cat? And you're still defending him?" Essex couldn't believe what he was hearing.

"He tried. Because Baron is a vampire, he's not easily killed. He's mending and should be better within a week or so. Lancelot, that's Marcus's dog, attacked Baron, who merely defended himself. Marcus got mad and grabbed him. Baron struck his face, drawing blood and Marcus strangled him and broke his neck. But he's going to be okay, somehow being a vampire has kept him from dying like he did when you tuned him."

Essex couldn't help but smile, that damned cat was using up his nine lives just trying to be a vampire. "I'm glad he's going to be okay. I like that cat." He smiled, but became serious immediately. "But that should tell you that Lancaster is psychotic and he will kill you. Please Lilly, promise me you'll repudiate me when he comes in and let him kill me so he won't kill you."

The door opened, hitting the wall as it swung.

"You need to tell me what, Lilly?" Marcus demanded as he entered the room.

MARCUS WAS SITTING in his office talking with Jesse when Jorge walked in.

"We found the asshole. We have him in one of the isolation cells on 18, cooling his heels until you can get down to talk with him. We took his backpack and found this," he held up the flash drive.

Jesse reached out and took the drive, handing it across the desk to Marcus, who inserted it into the computer and called it up on the wall monitor. There were files, his files, from his private drives. Lists of items he had in storage. Lists of contacts in various countries. Lists of enemies, some of whom were long dead.

If the thief had these files, he must have taken the entire drive.

"Where's the rest of it?"

Jorge shook his head, "Not found. We even tossed his apartment over in the towers and nothing. He didn't even have much in the way of personal effects, a few books, a few CDs were it. He didn't plan on being here long, looks like."

"Anyone else we suspect of working with him?"

"No. He's stayed pretty much to himself during the time he's been working here. Gone to a few movies, played a couple of video games with some of the guys in the SOC but that's it." Most people describe him as a loner.

Jesse looked at the files. He knew this jerk, it was the one who was talking to Lilly in the cafeteria that night, the night that Marcus assaulted him for lying to him about it. He owed her a little payback. "I need to do a few things. I'll be back in a few."

Marcus waved Jorge to the chair. He kicked the computer feed over to the closed circuit system and punched in the coding for the cell on the 18th floor. They watched the man sitting on the floor, doing absolutely nothing, his eyes closed, his arms around his knees. Then something happened that he didn't expect. He saw the door open, the security code coming up on the screen as Jesse's. But he didn't see his lover enter, Lilly did. As she entered, the man stood up.

Marcus turned up the volume on the feed. He heard her greeting and his confession about having been in the private files. Then he heard something that, at first, he wasn't sure he heard over the growl that Gunny let off behind him at the sentence. Marcus ran the feed back to check.

"Tell them that you're..."

Marcus ran it back again, repeating that last line, then listened as the man said, "I can't. I took on this mission knowing that this was a possibility. Don't let Lancaster know I'm an angel, especially not an Enforcer. He has a special kind of hatred for us."

Marcus paused the feed, the recording continuing.

"He's a fucking ANGEL?" Marcus yelled.

"Sounds like it. I guess he's not a Mishkoph spy after all."

"I remember Gery telling me there were two. I wonder who the other is." Marcus searched his mind for another new face, someone who could be the other spy. He had already cleared the new medical staff with his trips to the clinic, "It's got to be someone in the computer department, that's the only ones we have permanently on staff besides the security detail and I know none of them are angels."

"I'll try to track it down, son. Meantime, you probably need to go down and confront your progeny about the fact that she's friendly with an angel.

"Oh, this is very illuminating. I want to listen to the rest of it. No telling what revelations they will have in store for us. Besides, they're not going anywhere." Marcus pushed play again. At the information that his prisoner wasn't just an angel but one of the hated Enforcers, he balled up both fists and punched one of the other plasma-screen monitors, the front glass shattered in spider webs as his hand went through the layers and out the back and into the wall. "I've seen enough. I need to get a couple of guards, pick up Jesse, and we need to go handle this one. I will enjoy turning this one into a pile of goo, we may not get to the point of turning him."

Marcus turned and stormed into the elevator, punching the panel button for 18 so hard that Gunny grabbed his wrist to keep him from breaking that as well. "Son, don't break the elevator, I don't relish climbing the cables to get out of here."

Marcus punched his fist into his hand a couple of times, trying to release the tension and energy that was climbing with every moment. The doors opened and Marcus stepped out of the elevator. Jesse was still in the hallway, leaning on the wall waiting for what promised to be great fun for him.

"You know what's going on in there?" Marcus barked.

"Don't tell me they're having sex." Jesse looked at the ceiling in disgust.

"No, he's talking to her and she's talking to him. He's a fucking angel, did you know that?" Marcus fumbled in his pocket to find his key card.

"He is? Well, damn, that's a good thing, right?" Jesse pulled the card out of his pocket, "Here, let me help." Jesse repeated the security procedure and swung the door open. Marcus punched the door open so hard it hit the wall behind it. Jorge entered next with Jesse following but not shutting the door behind him.

"I'm glad he's going to be okay. But that should tell you that he's psychotic and he will kill you. Please Lilly, promise me you'll repudiate me when he comes in and let him kill me so he won't kill you." Essex said.

The door opened, hitting the wall as it swung.

"You need to tell me what, Lilly?" Marcus demanded as he entered the room.

Lilly spun around at the door crash and cried out in surprise.

"What do you need to tell me, Lilly?" Marcus repeated, his voice hardening as he said each word.

"Well, I..." She started.

"Lancaster, I'm the one you are here to talk to, Ms. Marchantel had nothing to do with anything I did." Essex pulled her behind him as he stepped forward closer to Marcus.

"Oh really? You're defending her, ANGEL?" He snarled.

Lilly gasped and grabbed onto the upper part of Essex's left arm. He shrugged her off.

"Yes, I'm defending her, VAMPIRE." Essex matched his snarl, "Deal with me." Essex balled up his hand, hoping the vampires would back off.

"Well, we do have something to settle but tell me, how did an Enforcer angel come to work for me and what were you doing with the information you were stealing from my systems?"

"Well, you got me! But you are too late. Heaven has enough information on you and your dealings, for your final judgment and send you to

Hell. Where you belong.

"It wasn't hard to get hired on here. Your 'security' and 'background checks' are pathetic." At the insult, Castro growled and almost bit through his cigar.

"Hired with false creds? Well, if I wasn't going to kill you, I'd fire you."

Lilly tried to step around Essex, he put his arm out to stop her, "Please, Marcus, don't kill him. He's an angel and he's the father of the..."

"Lilly, stop talking." Essex snapped.

"No, go on, tell me how you want me to accept him as the father so I won't kill him. Tell me that I'm not the father of that baby you carry. You're willing to lie to me to save his miserable skin?"

Lilly began to get angry, "No, I hoped you would back off before you get into trouble with the archangels. They will take you to Hell, Marcus. Even if I hated you for what you did to Baron, I don't want to see you go to Hell. I want you to repent and get whatever you have done stopped so that you can stay here."

Marcus laughed, "Repent, ask for forgiveness? You think it's that easy? No, you stupid bitch, you have no fucking idea what you are saying. There is no repentance for us vampires, the angels, and God himself, don't give a flying crap what we say or do, they will eventually get us and drag us all to Hell, even you, you naïve little bitch. I'm better off killing this asswipe and telling God he died rather than trying to repent. So spare me the anger, it bores me."

Lilly tried again to get around Essex but once

again he stopped her. "Whatever you're planning, Lancaster, get it over with so that Lilly can rest. She's distraught...."

"I am not. Stop telling him..."

"Shut up, Lilly," Both Marcus and Essex said simultaneously.

"Do it, Lancaster. Send her out of the room so we can get on with this."

"No, she stays. It guarantees you will behave until I get tired of playing with you and end the fun." Marcus grinned, his fangs dropping.

Jorge watched this, then leaned over to his boss and whispered conspiratorially, "Boss? There's another possibility..."

"What do you have in mind, Gunny?"

"We're busting our hump trapping, stripping the wings, and trying to turn angels into vampires..."

"Wha...NO!." Lilly cried out, trying once again to step around the angel in front of her.

He whirled to face her. "Lilly, just stop. He's going to do what he's going to do. Don't think he won't hurt you if you piss him off enough. You need to think of that baby. Back OFF! Whatever happens, it's what I signed up for."

"No, Essex. I won't let you surrender to him to be killed, or worse. I saw what it did to Sullivan to be turned, I don't want you to go through that."

Essex reached out and stroked her cheek, "Sweet Lilly. This is not my choice but it is my decision. Can't you understand that? Let it go... Just let ME go."

Lilly stared into his eyes. She could see his

determination, but she also saw love. It hurt her heart to think that he would be killed, but it hurt more to think that he would be turned and end up crazy. But she would back off. "Ok, let your will be done."

"Thank-you dear one." He kissed her cheek softly and then turned back to face the vampires in front of him.

"Awww, wasn't that sickeningly." Jesse taunted. He mimed throwing up in the corner.

"Jess..." Marcus turned to Jorge. "Gunny, here's what I'm going to do. I'm going to drain him part way, then I'm going to give him to you to finish off. Then you'll turn him and we'll take him to the training area to see if he wakes up."

"Sounds like a plan, son. Let's get this done."

Lilly rushed forward, dashing around Essex before he could grab her. "No, Marcus. Please, you can't do this!" She raised her hands in a vain attempt to stop him.

Marcus grabbed both of her wrists and squeezed until she screamed, breaking the delicate bones in her wrists. They would heal, it would be painful, but they would heal very quickly. He handed her off to Jesse, "Don't hurt her further, but hold her, I don't want her interfering again."

"Gladly." Jesse took her and held her arms as she strained to get away, trying to kick him and Marcus both.

She started to cry as Marcus rushed Essex before she could blink and sunk his teeth into his neck. Essex moaned but didn't fight as the blood began to leave him. He could feel the world begin to spin and his eyesight dimmed. He was light headed when Marcus pulled out and Castro grabbed him, repeating the strike in the other side of his neck.

As Essex watched the light grow even dimmer around him, he sent a mental prayer to Mikhail to take care of Lilly, then thought of Sullivan and Seth one last time. The three musketeers would be down to two, he didn't want to live as a vampire, he had seen too much. Then he gave himself over to the darkness, hearing his heartbeat slow, then stop.

Lilly was sobbing by the time that Jorge Castro dropped the dead angel to the floor.

Castro himself was drunk on the strong blood of the angel, something that the reports hadn't passed along. It was no wonder they were losing vampires in the attempt to turn them, they could barely stand, much less think for a few minutes. He staggered to his feet, the energy beginning to surge through him.

Castro stood. New insight just dawned. Jesse, still holding Lilly, spoke up, "Marcus, I have an idea. Why don't we let Lilly turn him? She has one turning this year and a second would earn her a mark and she would be closer to being damned. We let her turn him, we let the angels come and mark her, and then she'll know why we are fighting this."

Marcus considered the proposal. "You have an idea there. Lilly, you will turn Essex. You may even have privacy to do it." He nodded and Jesse not only let her go, he pushed her forward so she tripped over the body of the angel and fell.

She caught herself with her hands, the healing wrists breaking again. She screamed and crumpled to her floor. The three vampires started toward the door.

Marcus paused. "You have the choice. You can turn him and make him one of us, or you can let him die. His life or death is entirely in your hands."

Marcus wheeled around and marched out. Castro followed and Jesse brought up the rear. He paused with the door knob in his hand. "Have fun kiddies!" with a final malicious laugh, he closed and locked the door.

Lilly awash in tears and pain, cradled Essex's head in her lap. "I am so sorry! Please forgive me." Her wail of agony could not be heard ...

Acknowledgements

No author does this type of thing without LOTS of help, support, encouragement, and just plain love. I've been blessed with some of the best.

First, my beloved husband, Bruce. He's the one who began to talk me into doing this and he's heard every word of it, multiple times. He's talked to me about each character like they're real, put up with my temper when I've been upset at how it's going, held me when I cried over something the characters have done that made me sad, and generally became cook, dishwasher, housekeeper, and chauffer while I worked on the books. No one has ever had the kind of support and love that I have with him. Thank-you so very much, my love.

The only way a book becomes a great book is with a fabulous editor. Cat McNulty is my editor and she's very, very fabulous. It's a lot of work to read someone else's stuff and do the suggestions, along with all the spelling and such. She does it, on time always, and never resents it when I say "No, I said it that way for a reason, it's going to be apparent in books in the future." She's also got great graphics training (and a great eye) and I can't seem to do anything without her. Love you Cat!

People have been awesome with help on questions, the little research things I can't find in books or want some more good information on.

- Melody Groeker – San Antonio info including Bonham Exchange
- Bill Singleton – Large Aircraft
- Arthur Burnet – Flight Information and Small Planes
- Lou Mancel – Memories of Marcus's Building (we used to work there)
- Various other information:
  - Lea-Ellen Borg and her cousin
  - The Nanoerotica Facebook Group
  - Paranormal Romance Guild

And then there's all the friends who became characters here. Yes, you got in, it's been fun, hope I did you well enough.

- Lia Rees—the ghoul at the Vampire Council
- Kristen Skinner—the accountant who got caught (and no, you're not dead yet, be patient!)
- Reba King—the angel known as Rebangiel, surprise, this one's from Glenn!
- Heith Spencer—the Lancaster guard from San Antonio at the hospital
- Keith Blackketter—Officer from San Antonio Police Department at the hospital
- Valna Asterman—Chief Nurse, ICU, San Antonio hospital
- Jorge Olivares—the namesake for Jorge Castro (not in personality, though, the real Jorge is much sweeter and much happier!)
- Vicki Rose—Jean's Ghoul/Secretary

Copyright Acknowledgements

There are a few copyright items put into the books for authenticity. Each are held by the copyright owners and no infringement is intended.

Boeing Aircraft

Movies—

- Air Force One – Columbia Pictures
- The Matrix – Warner Brothers
- Mr. & Mrs. Smith – Regency Films
- Lord of the Rings – New Line Cinema
- Star Wars – LucasFilm and Twentieth Century Fox
- Mrs. Doubtfire – Blue Wolf Productions

Altoids – Jacob Suchard

Walgreens

Propolol—Fresenius S.E. &Co.

Dr. Pepper

Chivas Regal – Chivas Brothers, part of Pernod Ricard

Menger Hotel—San Antonio

Bonham Exchange—San Antonio

Desmond Merrion Tailors – Marcus's Suit

Television:

- Days of Our Lives – Sony Pictures and Corday Productions
- Sylvester & Tweety – Warner Brothers

Actors:

- Robin Williams
- Hugo Weaving

Coming Soon

Archangel's Gambit

Chapter One

THE BIG, BLACK bulletproof Cadillac Escalade streaked through the stifling humidity of the Florida night. The dark, almost squat, surly man scowled as he stared blankly out the window. The potentially lucrative business trip to Russia and Eastern Europe had not gone as planned. Nelson Mishkoph had hoped that the meetings with his potential clients would result in orders for security services and arms. Damn Marcus Lancaster!

Damn him to Hell.

He had somehow gotten ahead of him and circumvented the attempt to negotiate a contract with the Serbian arms company that Nelson had wanted to add to the portfolio. Not only did Lancaster stop the negotiation, he managed to keep Pricor from even getting into the neighborhood where the door was.

He had a mind to kick the back of the seat in front of him, except that it would ruin the leather and startle his driver.

A roll-over wreck was never a good way to get rid of the anger he was carrying.

He let his head fall back on the headrest. Lancaster's face and smart-assed grin haunted him even when he tried to relax.

That man would have to be taken down by force. The message he had sent through Marcus's gay lover should have provoked a reaction. Nelson had heard nothing. Not even a threatening phone call. This non-response was curious and somewhat disturbing, he should have heard, if nothing else, a threat for having the little fag beaten to a pulp.

Nothing. Not one damned word. The whole beat down and the shooting of the chauffeur and poisoning of the fag in the hospital came to a grand total of $295,000. The poultry sum would never be missed from petty cash, he wouldn't have to take it out of his own pocket, or the Pricor budget.

Money he would delight in taking out of Lancaster's hide once he took his company from him.

Then the curdled visage of his harridan wife, Lauren, loomed to the front of his thoughts.

He was not joyously anticipating the incessant haranguing he was sure to encounter as soon as he walked in the front door. She was going to be a bitch once he walked in from this trip. He had been in an important meeting with the Serbian Deputy Minister of Industry and Privatization, Dragan Popovic. It had taken him almost a year, and almost a million dollars in 'incentive money' to get an audience with the guy to discuss the possible purchase of Radulovic Arms. In the middle of the critical negotiations, Lauren called.

She bitched about a florist messing up a delivery of flowers to her mother. What the fuck? She wanted him to call, from the other side of the fucking world, to straighten out the florist. She had ordered daisies and the florist had delivered roses...her mother hated roses. Yes, the world, no, the universe, revolved around Lauren Rabinowitz. He ground his teeth so hard his jaw ached.

All the way to Serbia. Like he could do anything about it, even if he would. Was she...worth it? He would love to divorce the bitch, if it wouldn't cost him all of his money and his company, but he would walk away with nothing...maybe even less than nothing. Her parents not only had bank-rolled his company start-up, but they also, to guarantee his slavish loyalty, had all the paperwork and proof of every questionable and illegal thing he had ever done. Even though his father-in-law was dead, and gratefully it was a long, painful one, his wife was just as evil. She was helping Lauren suck him dry.

He would love to give her to Lancaster, make her his problem so the ass would not pay attention to his job for once. Even better, he would love to make Lancaster the killer when she was found dead.

Which, if she kept up the shrew personality, would be happening sooner than later.

When the hell did life get so damned complicated? All he wanted to do was build the world's finest mercenary company, grease a few palms, and find a nice, leggy blond with no brains to hang on his every word.

Instead he gets Lauren Rabinowitz, her mafia parents, and Marcus Fucking Lancaster. Who the hell did he screw in his past life?

The Escalade slowed, the ornate iron gates opening automatically to allow entrance into the ostentatious Aventura estate. He let loose an audible groan, the light was on in her room as well as downstairs in the formal. She was waiting to pounce on him and launch the latest tirade about how miserable her life was and what a petty disappointment he was. Just what he wasn't looking forward to.

He made a mental note: next trip back from the airport, take the limo. It had a bar and was equipped with several bottles of Grey Goose vodka. Then he could get nicely toasted, to properly prepare him for what awaited.

The big SUV slid to a stop and the chauffeur opened his door. Mishkoph exited and looked up at the white stucco facade and wished he could be back in Europe. Anywhere but where Lauren was.

The car pulled away and out the gates. The luggage left on the curb by the driver would be carted up by the security staff, after they were checked out. He took a deep breath to brace himself for the invariable onslaught. He entered the house to the blaring caterwauling opera shit that she supposedly loved. Nelson knew it was pure affectation. Pretentious fucking shit. He peeked into the formal, great luck was with him, Lauren was nowhere to be seen.

He hastened to the bar and grabbed a chilled bottle of Goose. He lovingly glanced at the blessed clear liquid, with this he could drink himself into oblivion. He grabbed a second bottle, just to make sure. Now, if he could just make it to his room, he would be safe in his sanctum until morning. He quietly and quickly bolted up the stairs, two at a time.

This was the dangerous part. He had to get past Lauren's suite undetected. He crept past her door. Out of the corner of his eye he noticed something quite odd. A white linen napkin, folded into the shape of a cone, was sitting on the floor in front of Lauren's door on the polished marble floor. Curiosity overwhelmed his desire for stealth, he put one bottle of Goose on the floor and lifted the cloth, recoiling in horror.

It was a finger, adorned with an obscenely huge diamond wedding ring and impeccably manicured scarlet lacquered fingernail, severed at the main knuckle.

Lauren's finger.

He roared her name and grabbed the doorknob to her room, trying to open the door.

Locked.

He beat on the wood, screaming her name. The door stayed solid. He looked up at the camera that was supposed to be monitoring the hall, searching for the lens.

Gone. A couple of screw holes where the thing should have been.

His shrieks of alarm echoed into silence. Suddenly the solitude he had reveled in only a moment before was now uncomfortably eerie.

Where was everybody? He paid his guards

good money to be there and to guard his stuff and the bitc....his wife.

"Joseph! Grant! Someone, get in here now!" He yelled out, trying to summon the guards. "Adelaide!" He called the maid's name.

Nothing.

He hurried to his room, to the safe where he kept his gun collection. He grabbed the first one he could and ran back down the hall, still carrying the open bottle of Goose. He ran from room to room, nothing seemed out of place but the cameras were all... gone. No alarms blaring, nothing.

He ran down the stairs, shouting the entire way, hoping for any response. He reached the French doors that lead to the pool.

Suddenly, it was if someone had dropped an ice cube down his back. A chilly shiver shook his entire body and a cold sweat erupted across his forehead.

He ripped open the left French door and rushed out into the humid night. Rounding the shrubs that protected the pool from prying eyes, he slid to an abrupt stop.

The now blood red pool contained the bloated bodies of his wife, her maid, his mother-in-law, the cook, and three of his best men, the guards of the estate. All floating in the bloody water.

He dropped the Gray Goose, the bottle shattering on the concrete.

Attached to the broken umbrella over one of the poolside tables, was a note. Once he could move again, Nelson walked to the paper and looked at it.

You're Next. M.

In one respect, Marcus Lancaster had done him a great service. However, what irritated Nelson most was now he was going to have to hire a whole new household staff.

He calmly removed his cell phone from his pocket and punched in 9-1-1. As he waited for the answer, he thought...

"Game On..."

Books In the Fangs & Halos Series

Book One: Lilly's Angel
Book Two: Marcus's Vampire
Book Three: Vampire rEvolution
Book Four: Archangel's Gambit